CROWN OF CONSPIRACY

THE ILVANNIAN CHRONICLES BOOK 1

KARA S. WEAVER

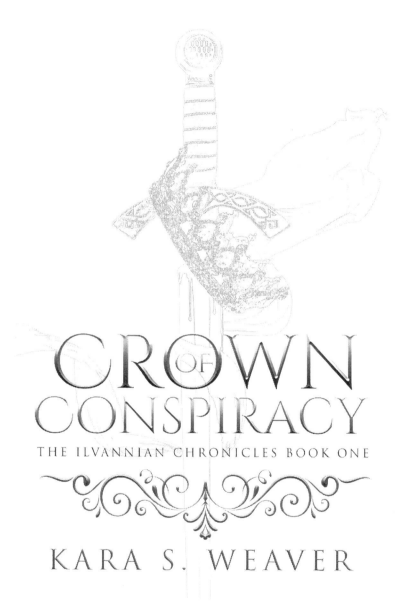

CROWN OF CONSPIRACY

THE ILVANNIAN CHRONICLES BOOK ONE

KARA S. WEAVER

To Caite and Owynn
Always follow your dreams

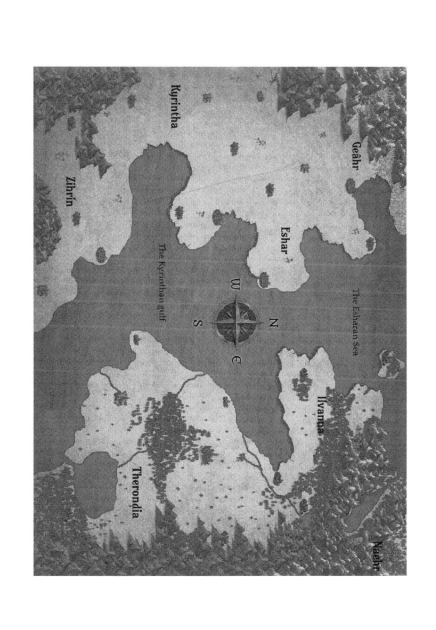

PROLOGUE

ARAYDA

With my heart racing in my chest, I felt my way through the dimly lit tunnel, my mind firmly on the task ahead. One offer. One wish. The rough stone underneath my fingers reminded me of the times ahead if I didn't do this—the dry air I inhaled a promise of what it would feel like every day if I didn't succeed. Even though she was next in line, Azra could not ascend the throne, no matter the cost. If she did, we would lose everything us Ilvannians treasured to her totalitarian regime.

The royal healer had been clear—one more child, or I wouldn't live long enough to raise the next. One child, and she had to be a girl, for the sake of Ilvanna. I love my sons, and I love my husband, but on their behalf and everyone else's, I had to do this, if only because the Council rejected a law enabling a male to inherit the throne.

No man would ever rule Ilvanna.

Breathing in deeply—inhaling the scent of chamomile, lavender, and rosemary on the air—I stepped through a set of heavy curtains into a circular cavern room lit by hundreds upon hundreds of candles.

1

I did not envy the *haniya* in charge of this sacred duty.

A giant slab of stone stood in the middle of the room, and up close I could see it was engraved with intricate lines and the marks of the Gods. I trailed my fingers delicately over the lines, following every curve, groove, and mark, until I found the one I was looking for—two crescent moons drawn within a full moon depicting the beginning and ending of life. According to our scholars, a second concept was of it being a mother's womb at the start, middle, and end of a pregnancy.

It made perfect sense since it was Xiomara's mark after all.

I traced my fingers over the other symbols reverently, knowing them all by heart. If anything, Mother had instilled a healthy dose of respect for the Pantheon into me, even if she had done it through veiled threats. Little did I know they would be the ones I would turn to in my hour of need. My hand traced along the lines of the dagger, and the snake coiling around the cup which were the marks of Esahbyen and Aeson, respectively. The coiled snake was a strange mark, but then, Aeson was a strange God—paragon for artists, musicians, and healers. The dagger on the other hand was plain and simple, apt for the God of War.

Stepping back, I regarded the altar with mixed feelings. Mahrleyah, leader of *Hanyarah*, hadn't been very specific in her instructions for this part of the ritual. All she had been clear about was to bring an offer for the Gods if I wanted my wish granted. It had been hard finding one. The tight feeling in my throat did nothing to alleviate my nerves as I placed my Mother's sapphire necklace on the altar before I went down on my knees. From this angle, I could see candlelight play over its multi-faceted surface, sending its reflection dancing on the cavern walls. A smile tugged at my lips as a stone settled itself in my stomach. It had been a gift from Mother before she died, and the last tangible item of hers that I owned. I breathed in deeply, and willed my pounding heart to calm down.

It was now or never.

Sweat trickled down my back, my chest, and stomach.

Had it been so hot all this time?

I closed my eyes and breathed in deeply, rubbing my hands over my thighs before settling them in my lap.

"Xiomara, lady of life, mother of women, guardian of the womb, I beseech you. Troubled times are ahead for my people. Please, hear the prayer of a faithful daughter."

As expected, it remained eerily quiet and for a moment, I felt like a complete and utter idiot.

I tried again.

"Please," I continued, "I need your help for the sake of my people. For the sake of Ilvanna. I don't know who else to turn to."

Tears stung my eyes, and as they fell down my cheeks, my hands lay shaking in my lap. If this failed, the consequences would be dire, even if they were hundreds of years away. If anything happened to me, and I had no heir to the throne, everyone would be at *her* mercy.

I had only one chance.

"I like it when they beg," a deep, smoky, masculine voice came from behind me.

"You just like them on their knees," a second, more melodious, and feminine voice answered, "begging or not."

A deep, rumbling laugh echoed through the cavern, sending my heart into a wild frenzy. "You know me well, Sister."

The woman snorted. I didn't recognise either of the voices, but as it was a slow and painful death for a man to enter the sacred valley of *Hanyarah*, it left only one conclusion for me to come to. Surely they couldn't be a God and Goddess, could they? It was too outrageous to even consider them as actual living and breathing beings, let alone answer the call of someone like me.

"Arayda, is it?" the woman asked.

I nodded demurely, not sure if I should move or stay where I was. It made me acutely aware of what I was wearing, or rather, what I wasn't wearing.

"Please, get up," she said, her voice gentle. "I don't much enjoy talking to someone's back."

Rising to my feet, I wrapped the robe tighter around me, keeping my eyes downcast as I turned towards them.

"No need to cover up," the man purred, a playful grin ghosting around his lips.

"Esah!"

The man called Esah harrumphed. "What? It's true."

Glancing up from under my lashes, I observed the two who couldn't be anything but Gods. They were tall, even for Ilvannian standards, both beyond handsome with hair the colour of pearls and eyes the colour of the ever-changing skies. Both were clad in traditional clothing—tight floor-length robes with long sleeves and a wide sash around the waist. Hers was the colour of ice on a clear winter's day, while his was the colour of smouldering embers at the bottom, blending into the russet-gold colour of dancing flames.

He had to be Esahbyen, judging from the way she called him. I guessed her to be Xiomara.

"My apologies for letting you wait," she said. "I had a hard time convincing my stubborn mule of a brother to come."

My head snapped up, and I stared at her slack-jawed. Had she really just apologised to me? I shook my head and bowed deeply.

"It is your time, *Irà*. I am the one who should be patient."

"Well-mannered too," Esahbyen commented. "This is getting better and better."

"Ignore him," Xiomara said as she glared at him, only to let her gaze settle back on me, "for now..."

My eyes drifted over to Esahbyen, and I caught him

smirking at me while cleaning his nails with a knife. A shiver ran down my back.

"What you ask is quite something." Xiomara fixed me with a hard stare. "Are you willing to pay the price?"

I swallowed hard and nodded. "Anything to keep my people safe."

"Are you willing to pay *any* price?" Esahbyen asked. "Any we ask of you?"

"Yes."

Xiomara looked somewhat troubled at my answer, her lips a thin line, her eyes hard.

Esahbyen grinned at her. "I like her spirit."

"I'm sure you do," she said with a sigh before turning to me. "You're asking for a life, Arayda. You are aware of that?"

I nodded again. Annoyance at their amount of questions began building up inside of me, but I needed their help, so I gritted my teeth and dampened my anger. Esahbyen stalked closer, much like a predator would its prey. He moved behind me and stopped, his body a mere inch from mine. Strong hands ran down my shoulders and arms, warm breath tickling my skin as he leaned forward, sending my heart into a frantic beat.

"I can give you exactly what you want," he whispered, tucking a lock of hair behind my ear, his voice like a lover's caress. "No questions asked, but you will not like what I ask in return."

I looked at him confused. "But you're the God of War. How—?"

The moment I opened my mouth to ask this question, I realised what he meant. I glanced at Xiomara, whose expression was unreadable.

"It is he who shall grant you your wish," she said, "and so it shall be he who claims the price. Are you willing to accept that?"

"What will you ask?" My voice was barely a whisper as I stood shaking in his arms.

I felt the deep rumble in his chest as he laughed. "You will not know until such a time as I claim it. Are you still willing to move forward?"

Apprehension filled me at having to make a commitment to something I didn't know the terms of. I had been trained to negotiate with people—not with Gods. There was no compromise in this. There was nothing to settle.

But what if his request would be to send my sons off to a war they might not get back from? What if he wants one of them in exchange for a daughter? What if he—?

I broke off the thought as a sickening feeling threatened to overwhelm me. It didn't do to dwell on the what ifs. I either accepted his terms and receive what I desired, or I did not and would be left with a fifty-fifty chance of conceiving a girl.

I'm sorry Gaervin.

"I accept," I said, straightening my shoulders, refusing to look at him.

A lazy grin spread across his immaculate features, which up close were even more exquisite than I had initially thought.

"I think it's time for you to leave, *Sister*."

He didn't even so much as glance at her as he said this, his arms snaking around me to undo the knot of my robe. Xiomara disappeared in front of my eyes, a faint echo of her voice in my head wishing me good luck. I tensed when he dropped the robe from my shoulders and slowly turned me around.

Esahbyen looked solemn.

"You understand that by accepting, you agree to all my terms?"

I nodded, but remained silent.

"As you wish, *Tarien*."

IT WAS A BEAUTIFUL SUMMER NIGHT, the scent of lavender and

marigold heavy on the air when my daughter arrived safely into the world. It had been nine months since I'd bonded with a God to have her, and while it filled me with complete joy, a sense of dread overshadowed the event. Gaervin looked happy and extremely proud at the little bundle in my arms, tears brimming his eyes.

I couldn't tell him he wasn't her biological father—to do so would be to admit adultery—and even though Ilvannians were known to have someone on the side, we were mostly monogamous after we'd chosen a partner. Gaervin was mine, and the father of our sons Evanyan and Haerlyon, who came bounding up to my bed in happy ecstasy at that moment.

It would be best if none of them knew.

"She's so tiny." Evanyan breathed.

"She's so pretty," Haerlyon murmured, placing a small hand on her cheek.

Having all of them here in my room, on my bed, made me the happiest woman in the world. For the last nine months, a single thought had been foremost on my mind, and now with Shalitha born, it returned.

A life for a life, Tarien. That is what I desire.

Esahbyen had told me his terms just before he left me in the cavern room, a dark, solemn look in those ever-changing eyes. I had cried for a very long time after, realising what I had condemned someone to. I had cursed myself, wished even he had not gotten me pregnant, but as time wore on and my mooncycles didn't come, I knew he had done exactly as he had promised.

He'd kept his end of the deal.

I feared it was mine now.

THAT NIGHT, when everyone aside from myself was subject to

deep, blissful sleep, the God Esahbyen appeared. His ember-and-russet-gold robe was replaced by a jet-black version, his pearlescent hair shimmering in the candlelight as he walked over, ephemeral eyes fixed on the little bundle asleep in my arms.

"Can I... hold her?"

The question took me by surprise, leaving me slack-jawed. For a moment, insecurity passed those graceful features, before he composed himself. Carefully I lifted our daughter into his arms, endeared by how gently he held her, cooing and murmuring to her in the old language.

"You'll be a feisty one, *shareye*," he whispered, "and you'll turn many heads, but I'm afraid there's more in store for you. For when past and future come together, and love and hatred silently gather, when darkness your only companion at night, only then shall be your return to the light."

My heart stopped when I heard his words.

"What have you done?" I stared at him wide-eyed.

He looked at me solemnly. "Our daughter is meant to be more than just the average *Tari*, Arayda. She's the one who will bring change to Ilvanna the likes of which have never been seen before. Her path shall not be easy, and there is no guarantee she will live through it, but it has been set."

"You said it would be a life for a life." I barely caught the sob in my throat. "I never imagined it would be hers! That's cruel!"

He smirked at me. "Is that what you think?"

"I'm not sure what to think anymore," I replied with a scowl. "You just damned her to... to... whatever that was!"

Esahbyen watched me gravely. "Who says it's damning her? Now, as for our agreement, it's why I'm here."

He handed me back our daughter, and I couldn't help but hold her tight against me—perhaps a little too tight, because she started to fuss and cry.

"I've chosen that life."

I swallowed hard, closing my eyes. "Who?"

"Your husband."

My eyes flew open, and tears started rolling down my cheeks of their own accord as I watched him. Shalitha started to cry too, and while shushing her and inhaling her new scent—trying to regain a sense of serenity—I bargained with the God of War one more time.

"Please, not yet," I said. "Let her grow up with a father who can be here. Let him teach her the things she needs in life. Let my children grow up with him until they are old enough."

Esahbyen looked from me at the bundle in my arms, ever-changing eyes guarded. "For her sake, I shall agree, but on one condition."

"Name it." I whispered.

"On the day of her one hundred and twentieth birthday, the day she will be regarded a child no longer, it is by your hand he shall die."

A sob caught in my throat. "But I am no fighter."

"By your hand or mine," Esahbyen said. "Mercy or torture. Your choice."

And so I struck another bargain with a God to prolong a life I wasn't ready to take. The thought of it being my hands which would eventually kill Gaervin nearly drove me insane over the course of the next weeks, giving the healers reason to believe it was a malady of the womb. As time wore on, however, and the children grew up, I put the fear aside. One hundred and twenty years wasn't anywhere close, giving me enough time to come up with a humane way to kill my husband.

Until then, I would enjoy every single moment with them.

CHAPTER 1

*P*erched high on the city-walls, one foot dangling over the edge, I savoured the apple I had filched from the kitchens, watching people go about their usual business. Merchants and farmers from all over the country came to sell their wares, or to trade. People left the city to go on business elsewhere, while others came here looking for jobs. The main gate was always a bustle of people, and it never ceased to impress me.

Just as it never ceased my desire to get out.

I envied the people who came and went as they pleased, having no one to answer to but themselves. If I'd ever go outside the walls on my own, I'd sail the seas, journey to different lands and meet new people. I'd learn new languages, and new cultures, and come back home more educated. I'd bring gifts for my brothers, and maybe for my nieces and nephews if Evan ever got serious with a woman. As it was though, my every step was watched, my every decision questioned, and there was always somebody I had to answer to.

I was a prisoner in my own home.

If I ever did go out of the gates without permission, it would only be a matter of time before my guards found me and hauled me back to the palace, where I'd be subjected to one of the many lectures I could recite by heart. Even without going out of the city, they'd find me within no time. It never stopped me from running away though, if only because the exercise it gave me— while my guards were giving chase—was a good one.

A sudden disturbance at the gate caught my attention. I sat up and swung my other leg over the side to have a better view of what was going on down below. Two guards halted a young man not much older than myself, asking him something. I was too far away to understand what it was or what he answered, but from the squared shoulders and set jaw of the young man I figured it wasn't anything positive.

One guard placed a hand on his hip, gesticulating heavily, most likely to get his point across.

"State your name and business," the guard said loud enough for the city to hear.

"Grayden Verithrien," the young man said, "and I'm looking for a job."

"There aren't any jobs here," the guard all but yelled. "Why don't you go back where you came from, *mahnèh?*"

Even from this distance I could hear the venom in the guard's voice on the last word.

"I've been told there's always a job in Ilvanna." Grayden folded his arms in front of him, not impressed by what the guard had told him. "Why don't you just let me through, before this gets ugly?"

The guard took a threatening step closer, but Grayden wasn't perturbed—he didn't even flinch. His unimpressed demeanour made me chuckle, and I was about to go down to mingle in the conversation when they both drew their sword. The second guard stepped forward, arguing with his companion before stepping away, throwing up his hands and shaking his head. He obviously didn't want to partake in this. I could hardly blame him.

Neither the guard nor Grayden backed down.

With a sudden lurch forward, the guard attacked him with a wide swing, leaving so much room, Grayden side-stepped easily. It surprised me the guard didn't get knocked down to his ass straight away. The next attack from the guard came from above, intent on plunging the sword into his shoulder, but Grayden fended off the blow with relative ease, looking positively bored.

"Is that all?" he asked. "I'm sure they'll have a job opening soon if you keep this up."

His words angered the guard enough for him to drop his sword and charge Grayden instead.

"There she is!"

My thoughts were interrupted by voices I knew only too well. I cursed when I looked down at the gate where two of the *Arathrien*—also known as my personal guard—had appeared. One of them pointed in my direction.

"Come down *Tarien!*" Elara yelled. "Don't make us come and get you."

I flashed them a grin, and dropped myself from the wall on the other side as quickly as possible, hopping down the ledge, dashing into a crowd of people while pulling my hood over my face. Grinning madly, I weaved my way through the city streets into the third circle.

Catch me if you can.

I passed dirty, white bricked houses in my headlong flight through narrow, windy streets, startling people as I passed. The scent of bruised fruit mingled with unwashed bodies, and mouldy wood with rotting flowers, hung in the air like a heavy blanket. People sat inside their front door on rickety stools, chatting to their neighbours, while dust-covered children were playing games in the streets, some of which ran along the moment I sped by. Others hailed me with waves and shouts.

"*Tarien!* Stop!" Xaresh bellowed.

I stopped, turned, and placed my hands defiantly on my hips, waiting for them to catch up. As soon as I felt they were getting too close, I bolted with a triumphant laugh escaping my lips, disappearing into the crowd or around a corner.

Where was the fun if they'd lost me altogether?

I glanced over my shoulder quickly, and after I turned a corner, ran into someone so hard, I fell back on my ass. Disoriented, my eyes zeroed in on a pair of stormy ones, set in a handsome face haloed by pristine white hair. Elongated ears were the most prominent feature, aside from perhaps the deep scowl on his face. I grinned impishly at Talnovar—*Anahràn* or Captain —of my guards, and scrunched my nose.

"Up."

"Yes, Sir."

He hauled me to my feet without a by-your-leave. Folding my arms in front of me, I scowled at him. Behind us, my others guards had finally caught up, and doubled over, gasping for air.

"By *Vehda*, you're slow." I flashed them a wicked grin.

"I'd hold that tongue if you wish to keep it, *Tarien*."

The tone in Talnovar's voice warned me not to mess with him, so I quickly snapped my mouth shut, biting back the retort on the tip of my tongue. He stepped behind me, placed his hand on my shoulder, and propelled me forward through the crowd we'd gathered. The look on his face made them part so quickly they stepped on each other's toes.

I tried not to chuckle.

ONCE BACK IN the first circle of the city the crowd had thinned to only a few people, and Talnovar stopped and turned to me, covering his eyes with his hand. I bit my lip, and glanced apologetically at Xaresh and Elara, my other two guards.

"On a day like this," Tal said with a sigh, "you really had to run away?"

"I didn't run away," I replied, straightening my back. "You knew exactly where I was."

He raised an eyebrow, glancing over at the others.

"Oh, you mean them…"

Xaresh gave me a deadpan stare as I shrugged. Elara barely kept her face in check, and I realised she didn't mind this as much as the others did.

"You owe them an apology."

I grinned. "I owe them a drink."

Talnovar stared at me so profoundly, I quickly offered my apologies to the both of them, signalling I'd get them a drink once we were back.

"I swear," Talnovar muttered, "you'll be my death one day."

"I doubt that."

We walked back to the palace in relative silence—Talnovar up front with Xaresh, conversing in low voices, Elara next to me, motioning Tal had a stick up his behind. It sent me into a laughing fit in no time. Both men looked over their shoulders at us, and I could have sworn Talnovar even looked somewhat amused.

"How much trouble am I in?" I asked Elara in a whisper.

She shrugged. "Depends on who gets to you first I suppose."

I groaned loud enough for Talnovar to hear, and this time it was he who chuckled. When we arrived at the palace gate I stopped, captivated by the sight of Grayden talking to Evanyan. Two surly guards stood off to the side, one of them glaring at the young man.

"Wait up, please," I said, and jogged over to my brother.

Talnovar started to protest, but I was out of his reach faster than he could stop me. When Evanyan saw me, he waved me over, the look on his face promising no good. I regretted walking up to him, and considered turning tail, having no mind to listen to my brother's lecture, but I had to speak on the stranger's behalf. He could fight, and we could use everyone able to hold the proper end of a weapon.

"I wish I could say I'm surprised to see you here, sis," Evan said, his lip curling into a half-smile. "Gave them a good hunt?"

I shrugged. "Just Xaresh and Elara. You know Talnovar doesn't do the chasing part."

Evan shook his head slowly.

"I'm glad I'm not an *Arathrien*," he said, looking thoughtful. "Is there anything I can do for you?"

I grinned impishly, looking at the young man from the gate who was trying his hardest not to stare at me. His appearance up close was a bit of a surprise. Although his complexion was as light as my own, his hair was as black as the night, highlighted with snow white streaks, a trait uncommon in Ilvannians. It was his eyes which caught me off guard the most—a grey so light it looked almost translucent.

With a shake of my head, I turned to Evan.

"As a matter of fact," I replied, "you can, and it concerns him."

I nodded in Grayden's direction.

Evan's brows shot up in surprise. "Oh?"

"I saw him fight at the gates," I said. "You should let him try out."

"I know he did." Evan sighed. "It's why he's here, as well as *them*."

He pointed at the two sullen guards standing off to the side, kept in check by one of the men-at-arms on horseback. From the *araith* on his arm, I could tell he was a *Sveràn*—lieutenant in the common tongue—although his division eluded me. That was Evan's department.

"About that," I said. "The left one didn't fight. The other made a very poor attempt."

Grayden broke out coughing when I said that and turned away with a mumbled apology. The guard in question glowered at me, fists balled at his sides.

"Anyway," I continued unfazed, "I'm probably expected for a lecture somewhere. See you around Ev."

Pecking my brother on the cheek, I left them and walked back to Elara and the others.

"What was that about?" Talnovar asked, guiding us inside.

"I told Evan to let that young man try out," I replied with a shrug. "He's got fighting skills."

He stared at me flatly.

"What?" I asked. "I was watching them when *they* found me."

I jerked my thumb behind us, indicating Xaresh—whose brows shot up in surprise—and Elara, who flipped me off unladylike.

"All right, sorry," I murmured.

Talnovar looked amused. *Arathrien* weren't just hired, nor were they just any man or woman capable of fighting—they were men and women who'd stood out in one way or another, and all of them could fight exceptionally well. They'd been handpicked either by Talnovar or by his father Cerindil, my *Anahràn* before him.

I think Xaresh had been chosen because of his everlasting patience. The Gods knew I'd try it before the new *Arathrien* even got a foot into the door. Elara was especially skilled in the use of several weapons—most of which were small and hidden.

"You," Talnovar began, waiting for me to catch up, "need to freshen up and change into a dress."

I scowled at him.

"Your mother is expecting you."

17

ILVANNIAN DRESSES WERE RENOWNED for their glamorous looks, and torturous dressing time. Fortunately, the dress they'd helped me in today only had two layers instead of four, which was reserved for formal attire. The underdress was a smooth silk—which I always thought felt sensuous on bare skin—and the overdress was a sheer affair, cinched at the waist with a wide sash.

I kept adjusting it with a sneer on my face, afraid it would come undone and reveal more than I cared for as I followed Talnovar to Mother's reception chamber. During our walk there, he quickly updated me on what I could expect—mostly formal stuff Mother wanted me to learn so I would get an idea of what it would be like as *Tari*.

"It might still be two-hundred years from now," I said with a deep sigh, "before I have to take over."

"Or just two," Talnovar replied, a gentle smile on his lips. "It's part of the job, so put on your game face and suffer through it. I'll see you on the fields after for training."

I nodded and squared my shoulders. "Deal."

Training always made me feel better.

He escorted me into the room with a soft chuckle, bowed respectfully to Mother and took his leave. I envied him for making that decision with no one batting an eyelash. With the politest of smiles, which I didn't feel, I turned to Mother and walked over, placing a soft kiss on her cheek as they expected me to do.

"Daughter."

Although it was the way for her to acknowledge me in a formal situation, it always felt strange and distant. Most of the time it felt as if she poured a bucket of ice-cold water over me— it stung that much. I inclined my head as I sat down at the table, folding my hands in my lap to keep from fidgeting. Whatever this was about, having most of the council members present meant it was serious.

"As you are all well aware," Mother began, "there have been sightings of Therondian forces at the border, and there have been skirmishes resulting in casualties amongst our people."

People murmured and nodded. I remained quiet, staring at my hands in my lap with a slight frown.

"On top of that," she continued, "we need to find new ways to generate income, or it will become a problem in a few years."

"We can increase taxes?" someone offered.

"Or create more money," another one said.

"Neither will work," I said quietly without looking up. "Creating more money will devalue our coin, whereas an increase in taxes will ensure people will spend less. If anything, you should decrease taxes based on income."

The council members stared at me as if I'd gone utterly mad. Mother looked impressed.

"And how do you propose we do that?" Yllinar spoke up.

Yllinar Arolvyen was one of the local noblemen living in the city, well-known for his wealth and general bad temper, not to mention his dislike for women in a position of power.

I imagined it was hard for him living in a matriarchy.

"People who have little money won't be able to pay the same amount as those with money do," I said watching him calmly. "It would only be fair if those with more money paid a little more taxes than those with less. People without money can't even pay it and should therefore be exempted, up to a certain extent."

Yllinar huffed, rising to his feet in defence. "You're telling me you want to take more of *my* money, money I worked hard for, than from some dirt-poor *lyadrin*?"

I was about to reply when Mother held up her hand.

"That's enough," she said. "My daughter has a valid idea, but we need to look into it before we make any decisions. Sit down Yllinar."

Throughout the meeting, he kept staring at me with such a brooding expression on his face it sent shivers down my spine.

After Mother adjourned the meeting, I excused myself quickly and made my way out of the council chamber, hoping to be fast enough.

I wasn't.

In the chaos of leaving the room with everyone else, Yllinar grabbed hold of my wrist, pulling me closer to him.

"I don't like your ideas, *Tarien*," he hissed as he walked me outside. "You'd be wise to think before you speak."

I stared at him. "I don't care for threats to my face. Let me go, or I'll call for the guards."

The moment I did, the guards would respond, and Yllinar would be in more trouble than he bargained for. He took a menacing step closer before letting go of my wrist, looking at me as if I were filthier than the dirt under his shoes. I watched him walk off in a brisk pace.

I released my breath, unaware I'd been holding it.

"Is everything all right?" Elara asked as she stepped up to my side.

I smiled at her and nodded, not entirely sure I was.

"Yeah, I'm fine," I lied. "I need to redress. Again. Talnovar's expecting me on the fields."

TALNOVAR WAS ALREADY training with the other *Arathrien*. Surrounded by the four of them, the many rookies watching him were proof of how impressive he looked while fighting them off. On the field, with a fiendish grin on his face and not a care in the world, he looked young, free of the burden of being in control all the time.

He looked happy.

As *Anahràn*, he usually behaved much older than he was, pretending to be an uptight bastard and a stickler for rules. I disliked him when he was in such a mood. Watching them train awakened my eagerness to participate.

I grinned at Elara. "Shall we join them?"

Amongst my *Arathrien*, Elara was the only woman, but she fought as well—if not better—than any of the men. Without warning, we stepped into the fight, eliciting gasps and whispers from the rookie crowd. While it wasn't unusual for women to take up arms, it usually wasn't the noble ones who did, and both Elara and I were exactly that.

My focus was on Talnovar, and him alone, while I circled him, sword positioned to strike. The moment he parried a blow from Xaresh, I stepped in for an attack, which he bypassed easily. He twirled around fast and whacked me on my ass with the flat of his sword.

I yelped.

"Focus!"

I unlocked my knees, bending them slightly as I watched him and circled him, biding my time while the others attacked him or parried his blows. It was during one of his attacks I stepped in low, dodged his swing and tapped him on the ass. He turned on me with a growl, dropped his sword, and charged me. People around us squealed and yelped in pure shock. I discarded my sword and ran away from him at high speed, knowing full well he was the fastest of us two. He suddenly grabbed me around my waist, yanked me back and dropped me to the ground, drawing out a loud grunt.

He held a small knife at my throat.

"Yield?"

I flashed him a playful grin. "Never."

Turning away from the knife, I twisted his arm and hit him on the wrist hard, so he had no choice but to drop it. I grabbed the knife, got to my feet and launched myself at him, all in a matter of seconds. Surprised by this move, he could not stop me, and we went down in a tangle of limbs. Triumphantly, I sat down on his chest, holding the knife in both hands at the hollow of his throat.

"Yield?"

He laughed, dropped his head and arms to the ground, and tapped out. "I yield."

Grinning madly, I rose to my feet and helped Talnovar up.

"Well done," he said, his breath hitching.

I beamed. He didn't compliment often.

We walked back to the others quietly, both stretching and slowing down our breathing. Halfway there, Talnovar suddenly stopped and looked at me impressed.

"Where did you learn that?"

"Elara."

He shook his head with a chuckle. "I should have known. She's got some mean tricks up her sleeve."

"She does." I grinned. "And they're very helpful."

He rolled his eyes.

Elara beamed at me proudly when we returned, giving me a high-five as I took up position next to her to listen to Talnovar as he went over the next part of the training session. This time I would stand in the middle and had to defend myself while the rest attacked. I assumed a guarding stance, my legs wide apart, steadily planted into the ground, and my arms up to shield my face, weapon at the ready. I focused my eyes, trying to notice every movement around me. No matter how remarkable they were as fighters, they were bound to project their intentions in some way. All I had to do was catch this hardly visible motion in my peripheral vision.

Xaresh stepped forward first, moved into a frontal attack, and pulled his arm back, aiming to strike me in my sternum. I caught his movement and stepped back quickly, applying a middle block to deflect his punch, easily. But while I was preoccupied with Xaresh, I failed to notice Elara. She moved in from my side stealthily—her attack a complete surprise. I had to take a few quick steps to close the distance between us and as I did, she pushed off the ground, turned her hip, and extended her leg forward into a forceful jump. Her instep collided with my unprotected side, crashing into my ribs.

I grunted. The force of the impact pushed me back, but I kept my balance. Anger and frustration boiled up within me as adrenaline spiked through my system. Suppressing the pain, I breathed out deeply, regrouped and assumed a guarding stance, ready for the next attack.

While recovering from Elara's kick, I circled in place, trying to catch their next move. I caught Xaresh's attack on time and parried his blow, but in the time it took me to fend it off, Talnovar blindsided me, placing his sword at my throat, stormy emerald eyes watching me unamused.

"Focus, *Tarien*," Talnovar said, stepping back.

"I am!" I growled in response.

The next series of attacks came in rapid succession, and side-stepping, parrying and counter-attacking became increasingly more difficult as they continued relentlessly. I knew Talnovar wouldn't just give up because I was tired—he'd make me push through, because the enemy would too. There would be no rest in a real fight until you were the last man standing. His reasoning was sound, but it was hard to keep going if the ones opposite you weren't your enemy, knowing they'd stop before they hurt you.

When Xaresh accidentally cut my arm and drew blood during one of his attacks, Tal called it quits.

"Apologies *Tarien*," Xaresh said, looking guilt-stricken.

I smiled. "It's fine. A cut won't kill me."

"I'll bring her to see a healer," Talnovar said. "Xaresh, Elara, make sure you're guarding her room when we come back."

With a nod and a slight bow, they walked off, leaving Talnovar and me behind. The cut was still bleeding, so he ripped a piece of his shirt and wound it around my arm.

"You put up a good fight," he said, "but you have to remember to keep your arms up."

I rubbed my face. "I know, but they tire easily."

Talnovar nodded, the look on his face a dead giveaway he'd already thought of a solution to that problem. I rolled my eyes, not looking forward to whatever he'd come up with.

TRUE TO HIS WORDS, he brought me to the infirmary where one of the more ancient of our kind met us as he shuffled out of the antechamber, looking more than a little annoyed. Then again, Master Dahryen always looked like that.

"*Tarien. Anahràn,*" he said gruffly. "What can I help you with?"

Talnovar inclined his head. "Just a cut Master Dahryen, but one I'd like to be looked at."

"All right, show me where."

He gathered his equipment and sat Talnovar down on a stool. Biting my lip, I tried to keep a straight face, watching him amused.

"It's not me," he interjected. "It's the *Tarien.*"

Master Dahryen's brows rose in utter confusion. "Why her?"

"She's the one with the injury."

Talnovar looked somewhat bemused at the old healer, displaying the graceful patience he had with almost everyone but me.

"Oh," the healer murmured, "right, *Tarien*, if you please."

We switched places, and after removing the bandage, took my arm out of my shirt, wrapping the good one around myself. Talnovar had the decency to look away. Master Dahryen inspected my arm from up close, murmuring more to himself than to us. He cleaned it first, and followed up by prodding the surrounding skin with long, bony fingers.

"How did you say you got this injury?"

I smirked. "Training. With swords."

The shocked look on his face was priceless—the warning look on Talnovar's wasn't.

"A *Tarien* shouldn't be playing with swords," Master Dahryen muttered. "It's unheard of."

"It may one day save her life," Talnovar said.

The old healer huffed, his head shaking all the time he was administering his care upon me. It had to be stitched, which hurt so much I took to cursing in the old tongue. Master Dahryen looked smug when he finished it, and I had to admit it didn't look half bad with a bandage around it.

"Don't soak it within the next three days," he said. "And if it gets dirty, clean it. I'll see you at the end of the week to take the stitches out."

"Yes, Sir," I muttered, putting my arm back in my shirt.

Talnovar had somewhat of a mischievous look in his eyes as we left, but it was gone the moment we stepped out of the infirmary.

"He really doesn't like me."

"I don't think he likes anyone," Tal said.

I snorted. "Fair point."

Silently, we walked to my bedroom so I could get presentable for dinner. Mother had made it very clear during breakfast she expected all of us there, no exceptions. It also meant she expected us to look our very best.

"We'll be outside," Talnovar said, opening the door to my bedroom. "Yell if you need anything."

"What about some freedom?"

His lip quirked up in a half-smile. "Get yourself ready."

DINNER, as it turned out, was just with Mother and my brothers. She dismissed all guards and servants after we had received our plates. Evanyan, stoic as ever, waited quietly for whatever was to come—Haerlyon was lounging in his chair, not a care in the world. Neither of them seemed worried. I, on the other hand, was wringing my hands, regarding Mother apprehensively.

"You impressed me with your idea daughter," Mother said in between bites, watching me. "It even impressed some council members."

I huffed. "Not everyone seemed happy with the idea. Besides, it's not even mine."

Mother raised an eyebrow. Evan and Haerlyon both sat on the edge of their seats now, paying attention while shovelling their food in. It wasn't often Mother praised me for doing something right.

"Your grandmother came with the idea many centuries ago," I said. "Ilvanna has never been more prosperous."

"I didn't know you paid attention in history class," Haerlyon looked smug. "Did it hurt?"

I glared at him. "Not as much as a spoon to the face will."

He snorted, deigning me unworthy of a proper reply. Evan looked quietly amused, giving me a slight nod of encouragement when he noticed I was watching him.

"Did you know our grandmother's grandmother was the best strategist Ilvanna has ever seen?" I said at length, looking at Haerlyon. "Not a single man alive or dead has ever defeated her, and she lived during the time wars happened every other week."

Evan whistled in appreciation—Haerlyon stared at me as if I'd gone daft.

"And," I continued, "she was the first woman who made her sons *Zheràn*, breaking with tradition only women could hold positions of power."

In my peripheral vision, I saw Mother smile, a look of appreciation in her eyes.

"Regardless of who came up with it," Mother said. "It's an interesting concept, and the council would like to hear more. Are you up for it?"

I stared at Mother, food forgotten. "Seriously?"

"Why not? You pitched it the first time."

Biting my lip, I stared at the broth in front of me, not sure of what I should do. The fact Mother approved of my idea was an achievement on its own, but to be allowed to speak to the council members all by myself was a real victory.

"I'll see what I can do."

Mother smiled, but it was gone within the blink of an eye. "There's something else we need to talk about."

Here it was—the real reason she had summoned us all for dinner. Evan perked up interestedly. Of course he would. Haerlyon looked plain and simply bored, regarding Mother with a lazy smile on his face. I wasn't sure what to make of it.

"There have been offers for your hands," Mother said. "Well, one for either Evanyan or Haerlyon, the other for Shalitha."

The three of us frowned. Evan looked no longer interested, but the boredom was straight out of Haerlyon's face.

"By whom?" Evan asked, eyes narrowing slightly.

Mother looked momentarily uncomfortable. "Nathaïr and Eamryel Arolvyen."

"Over my dead body," Haerlyon and I announced simultaneously.

Evan looked thoughtful. "Where did that suddenly come from?"

Mother told us the offer had come in slightly over a week ago when it became apparent our resources were dwindling faster than expected. Additional to the offer came a large sum of money.

"So he's buying his way in," Evan observed.

Mother nodded. "That is one way to put it."

"And you are seriously considering this?" Haerlyon asked.

"That man is no good," I added, "and his children clearly follow in his footsteps."

Mother raised her chin, brushing her palms together. "Yllinar is too important a figure to have against us. I have to throw him a bone."

"By marrying us off to his hell spawn?" I muttered. "That's quite a bone if you ask me."

She glared at me. "I will not marry you off to his son. That would give him too much power. Nathaïr however…"

She left the words unspoken, looking at both my brothers. Haerlyon turned a deadly shade of pale, which was quite a feat considering our complexion was nearly white to begin with. Evan regarded our brother for a moment, drumming his fingers on the table, the tell-tale look of him coming to a decision on his fine features.

I knew what was coming next.

"I'll do it," Evan said. "I'll marry her."

Haerlyon sighed in deep relief, slumping back into his chair. Even though Evan had just agreed, I saw a momentary flicker of pain cross his eyes when he looked at me. I smiled faintly, lost for words.

"Very well," Mother said. "I'll see to the arrangements."

From the tone of her voice, I could tell she wasn't happy with them either, but she had more to worry about than just the three of us.

"Please excuse me," Evan said, rising to his feet.

Without waiting for approval, he left the room, Haerlyon quick on his heels. Mother rubbed her temples, eyes closed.

"I hope you have a superb reason to do this Mother," I said, getting up. "Otherwise you might just have alienated your son."

I placed a kiss on her cheek and left the room, wrapping my arms tight around me. A disquieting feeling had settled in my stomach, leaving me cold and shivering.

"Are you all right?" Talnovar asked, falling in step beside me.

I nodded. "Just tired."

The bland look on his face told me he didn't believe me, but for once he didn't pursue the issue. I was grateful for it. Although happy Mother wouldn't marry me off just like that, the fact she had to do so with Evan didn't sit right with me. The thought of Nathaïr becoming family was one I refused to entertain until I absolutely had no other choice.

She and I had never been the best of friends.

CHAPTER 2

"Talnovar will be livid if he finds out you disappeared, again," Elara said. I observed her from under my lashes as she ran a hand through her jaw-length hair. All noble-and-royal-born Ilvannians had been blessed with white hair, but both Elara and I liked to add colour to it. Today hers was green—mine had blue streaks throughout.

With her long legs swinging over the wall she looked every bit the truant I did, except she wouldn't get into trouble.

"I brought you along," I offered. "It should count for something."

Elara snorted. "He will have my hide if he finds out I allowed you to miss lessons with your tutor to sit here."

"I am forever in your debt."

Her clear, hearty laugh rang out over the walls, lifting my spirits. Of all my *Arathrien*, she was probably the most like me, although perhaps less inclined to rebel and break rules. With a deep sigh I turned my head to the city.

"Care to share what's on your mind?" she asked at length.

"Not particularly," I replied with a shrug, "but that won't stop you from badgering me until you know."

"You know me too well." She laughed. "Besides, it's better to talk about it. Knowing you, you'll end up throwing stuff around or running off, anyway."

"Maybe."

Pushing my hair out of my face, I watched the people down below scurry around like ants, contemplating how to tell Elara what had happened the night before. My serious dislike for Nathaïr was known far and wide due to our quarrels and the unparalleled abilities of courtiers and their less than altruistic gossip. Maybe that was all it was making me hate her marrying my brother. Regardless, I couldn't shake the feeling her father had an ulterior motive.

He always did, and it made little sense he'd spend money on it, frugal as he was.

"Mother's marrying Evan off to Nathaïr," I said after a while, tucking my hands under my legs. "It was either him or Haerlyon."

"Why her?"

"No idea. To get a foot in the door, perhaps?"

Elara furrowed her brow. "That makes no sense."

"It happens all the time," I pointed out. "Evan sacrificed himself."

"Why would he do that?"

I shrugged. "No idea. Maybe because Evan likes her more than we gave him credit for?"

Elara shook her head. "No, that can't be it. Knowing Evanyan, there's more behind this than liking her. We all know he likes her about as much as a sack of sand."

"She's as useful as one."

"Speaking of which," Elara said with a nod of her head, "there he is."

Evanyan came riding up to the gate looking rather splendid in his formal attire, and his long, white hair loosely over his shoulders. I frowned. He never wore it loose.

"I didn't even know he had left."

Getting to my feet, I watched as his horse entered the city, walking up the main street to the palace. People moved aside as he passed, inclining their head as he did. As my gaze zeroed in on the petite figure behind him, I felt a wide grin spread across my face.

I turned to Elara. "We need to go."

Dropping off the ledge, I waited for her to follow suit before hurtling myself through the crowd without checking if she was following me. I ran through the fourth circle gate on main street, and the third and second. It was the only road connecting the palace to the main gate and the circles to each other. The gates served as safety in case an enemy army came knocking at our door.

Close to the first circle, I slowed down to a jog, and while waving to a guard as I went through the gate, ran into someone. Next I knew, he grabbed my arm, and I was staring into Yllinar's face.

His nostrils flared and his lips tugged down at the corners, and when I tried to yank my arm loose, he wouldn't budge. We were just out of sight for the guards, and Elara wasn't there yet.

Why was she so slow?

"You again," he growled. "Are you deliberately out to get me, *Tarien?*"

I scoffed. "If I were out to get you, you'd know."

He tightened his grip around my arm, pulling me closer.

"Had you been my daughter," he hissed, "I'd have shown you some discipline right here, right now."

I smirked. "That explains a lot."

Just as he brought up his hand to strike me, Elara rounded the corner, so he let go of me quickly, stepping back.

"Stop being in my way," he hissed.

I snapped my mouth shut before it would get me into more

trouble, and watched him walk away briskly, passing Elara with a muttered good morning.

"There you are," she panted, looking nowhere near amused. "I won't cover for you next time if you pull off a stunt like this again."

"Sorry," I murmured, rubbing my arm. "I was just excited."

Elara sighed and shook her head. "Fine, come on. Let's see why you were in such a hurry."

WE'D BARELY PASSED through the gate and into a corridor when a petite figure came barrelling my way. Her violet hair streamed behind her like a banner, her dress rustling while her slippers *flip-flopped* on the marble tiles.

I was barely in time to catch her as she launched herself at me.

Twirling around, we both laughed, and when I placed her on her feet, Mehrean kissed me on the cheek. With her five-foot-two figure, she was probably one of the smallest women I'd ever seen, but she made up with a demanding personality you couldn't ignore.

Evanyan came strolling up with a lazy smile on his lips, fingers hooked in the collar of his chainmail.

"You're back!" I grinned at Mehrean.

She chuckled. "I am."

I tilted my head. "For how long?"

"For as long as you'll have me," she said. "The Sisterhood has agreed to my terms to serve the *Tari* and *Tarien* of Ilvanna indefinitely."

Grinning madly, I hugged her again. "You must be exhausted."

"It's all right." She smiled. "Evan was kind enough to come pick me up halfway."

I raised an eyebrow and was about to ask how he would have known when I realised she'd have contacted him. Glancing at Evan, he shrugged nonchalantly, a catlike smile on his lips.

"Come on, let's get you settled."

We made our way into the palace together, excitement coursing through my veins as if they'd just told me I could go out of the city on my own. We were about to enter my room when Talnovar's voice boomed through the corridors, alerting everyone there. I cursed softly, closing my eyes.

Mehrean chuckled. "What did you do this time?"

"I may or may not have failed to see my tutor," I murmured, "but I didn't go out alone!"

Mehr snorted. "Good luck. He doesn't look happy."

After resting a gentle hand on my arm, she stepped inside her bedroom. For a moment I considered slipping in after her, but Talnovar was already there.

"A word please, *Tarien*," he said in a strained voice.

My bedroom was closest, so I invited him inside, closing the door quietly behind him. I glanced around my chambers, realising I'd made a mess of it that morning trying to find my shoes. For some reason—and I blamed the size of my room for it—I always lost something or other.

My eyes zeroed back in on Talnovar.

Leaning back against the door, I watched him warily. He turned to me quickly, an angry expression on his face. Whatever he saw on mine, however, stopped him, his lips frozen at the start of a sentence.

"I don't want to talk about it," I said with a sigh, pushing myself away from the door. "I know it was wrong, but I needed to get out."

I laced my fingers together, pacing up and down my bedroom.

"What's going on?" he asked, following my movements with his eyes.

I glanced up at him, biting my lip. "Last night, Mother told us there have been offers for our hands."

He stiffened ever so slightly at the news. With a nod of his head, he sat down in a chair, hands clasped between his knees as he leaned forward.

His knuckles were whiter than usual.

"Go on."

"The offers have come from Yllinar," I continued, "for Eamryel to marry me, and Nathaïr to marry one of my brothers."

Talnovar looked confused for a moment. "Why ever would he do that?"

I shrugged. "Power?"

He cast me a dark look.

I smiled faintly. "Anyway, she won't marry me off to his son for exactly that reason, but she will have to marry Evan off to his daughter."

Talnovar pinched the bridge of his nose, a soft groan escaping his lips.

"No wonder Evan stormed out last night," he said, "looking like he was about to commit murder."

"He wouldn't let Haerlyon make the choice. You know what he's like."

Talnovar nodded slowly. "Well, interesting times will be ahead."

"That's quite the understatement," I said.

His mouth curved into a smile, but it didn't quite reach his eyes, and I realised despite my confession, I was still in trouble.

"Come on," he said. "Let's do something else."

I raised an eyebrow. "Do what?"

I'D EXPECTED to get a scolding. Whenever I did something

wrong, he had the tendency to give me a good talking to and point out the rules rather than choose my side. I had expected him to do anything but this. Instead of getting mad at me for running off, he steered me to the training fields with a smile on his face, his hand lingering gingerly between my shoulder blades.

Àn were sparring with the rookies. Haerlyon was standing off to the side yelling orders. One trainee looked at me with a smile, and I realised it was Grayden. Nodding in acknowledgement, I turned my attention back to Tal, knowing how displeased he would be if I didn't focus.

"We will start training your arms," he said. "Today."

I scowled. "You're joking?"

"Do I look like I am?" he watched me with steely eyes.

"You never do," I replied, giving him a flat stare, "but how is this punishment?"

"So you'd rather have me yell at you?" Tal smirked.

"Right now? Maybe?"

"I can still do that." He flashed me a roguish smile.

I awarded him a deadpan stare.

"And do the training," he added.

I stared at him. "You're mad."

He grinned. "Love you too. Now, down to the ground and give me fifty push-ups."

"Fifty!"

"Want me to make it a hundred?"

Glaring daggers his way, I went down to my knees slowly, not taking my eyes off of him. Placing two hands under my shoulders, my toes in the grass, I pushed myself up, and lowered myself again. Tal placed his foot on my backside.

"Keep everything straight."

The sutures in my arm didn't agree with the pressure put on them, but I wasn't about to give in, knowing Tal would expect me to do my best and more. In all truth, this was one of the few things worth doing my best for as far as I was concerned.

"How's your arm?"

"Painful."

He just nodded. "Fifteen more."

The last ten push-ups were pure, debilitating agony because my arms simply refused their task. I managed, but by the time I got to fifty, I wasn't able to push myself to my knees anymore. Instead, I just flopped down on the ground spread-eagled, enjoying the cool grass against my face.

"Get up."

"No."

"Get up," Tal hissed, prodding me in the side with his boot, "now."

I groaned. "Why?"

"Your mother's here."

I jumped to my feet, surprised my body did me this one favour after the torture I just put it through. I was barely in time to dust myself off and pull my shirt straight before she was upon us. Everyone around us bowed or inclined their head, even Talnovar. I just watched her approach with apprehension, annoyance rising within me.

"I'm in so much trouble," I muttered.

Talnovar smirked. "You think?"

Sarcastic *grissin*.

"Mother," I said, placing a kiss on her cheek when she was close. "What can I do for you?"

"Someone has told me you did not find your way to your tutor this morning," she said, looking at me.

A snort from behind me made me want to hit Talnovar with something. Hard. Mother merely raised an eyebrow, and he coughed an apology.

"Not at all Mother," I said. "I just had other plans."

"I'm glad you've got your priorities straightened out," Mother said, "and I might just let it slide, if you do me a favour."

I looked at her in suspicion of what was to come next. Mother didn't do favours, and she let nothing slide. She could order me to go to my tutor if I ever wanted to see the training fields again—babysit the smaller children of the palace—deal with people she didn't want to deal with. The possibilities were endless, and I shuddered at the thought.

I wrapped my arms around myself, furrowing my brows. "What kind of favour?"

"A week from now, we will be celebrating Evan's and Nathaïr's engagement," Mother said. "She will arrive at the palace two days from now. Make sure she feels welcome."

"But Mother…"

"This is the favour," she interjected, brooking no arguments. "You can turn it down, but I promise the punishment for your disobedience will be more severe."

Before I could answer, she had turned on her heel and walked away, followed by two of her *Arathri*. I just stood there staring after her, arms dropped to my sides, unsure if what had just happened was real. Behind me, Tal was howling like a wolf, slapping his thighs.

"This is why you didn't lecture me!" I yelled, turning on him. "You knew!"

He smirked. "You never listen to reason. This time, you had to feel it."

I gave him a firm shove against the shoulders, and stomped away, considering briefly to leave the palace altogether. Instead I went to the palace gate, sitting down with my back against the wall and my knees drawn up. I wasn't breaking any rules this way.

Rubbing my temples, I stared out into the distance, watching the main street snake lazily to the main gate as if it didn't have a care in the world. The circle gates on its way were but a minor nuisance, nothing more.

"Judging by the look on your face, I can only assume you and Arayda are still at war?" a sensuous, feminine voice said.

My gaze shot up, and I felt a wide grin spread across my face as my eyes settled on the one person who'd never judged me.

"Aunt Azra!"

I jumped to my feet into her open arms, hugging her tight. She didn't visit the palace often, but when she did, she always came back with incredible stories of her adventures, and more often than not, trinkets she'd gathered. It had been at least five years since last we'd seen her, and although it wasn't much in Ilvannian terms, it was still long.

She put me at arm's length, looking me over admiringly.

"You've grown into a beautiful young woman, little niece," she said. "You must have men lining up for you."

I looked over her shoulder and shook my head. "Not by the looks of it."

"I see there's still nothing wrong with that tongue of yours either."

"You're the only one who seems to think so," I replied, giving her a one over. "Can I help you carry anything?"

She nodded. "Please, I've got some gifts here for you and your brothers, if you could bring those, I'd be much obliged."

I took the bag from her and swung it over my shoulder, hissing at the movement pulling at the stitches.

It drew Azra's attention.

"What happened?" she asked.

"I had a run in with a sword," I replied with a shrug. "Nothing serious."

"Arayda's finally allowed you to train?"

I shook my head. "I think condone is a better word for it. She still doesn't like it, but she can see its value by now."

Azra just smiled.

A guard heralded our arrival at the palace, looking slightly confused as he couldn't just announce *Tarien* and be done with it. Technically, we both were, but Azra refrained from using the title for reasons unknown to me. It gave her an independent flair I loved so much it made me wish I was more like her. She was a second daughter though, whereas I was first, and so I was destined to inherit the throne should Mother die.

For all I cared, Evan could rule the country.

"Mother might be in reception," I said, looking thoughtful. "Let me bring you to your room."

Azra nodded while I called for some servants, issuing orders to prepare my aunt's room as quickly as possible. She chuckled softly as they scooted out of our way, off to do what I'd just asked them to do.

"You'll make a fine *Tari* one day."

I snorted. "I highly doubt that."

"You shouldn't," she smiled at me, eyes warm and caring.

As we walked down the corridors to the royal quarters, Haerlyon waylaid us, bouncing down the hallway, looking as happy to see Aunt Azra as I was.

"Auntie!"

She hated when he called her that and he knew it, which was exactly why he kept doing it. He embraced her hard, lifted her from her feet and twirled her around. She might have hated that even more. Haerlyon laughed and put her back on the ground, placing a kiss on her cheek.

"Good to see you," he said. "You look well."

"You haven't changed a bit," she said, looking him all over. "Still as dashing as before, but twice the nuisance I bet."

He looked perturbed. I laughed.

"You know you missed me Auntie," he grinned.

She stared at him, her head tilted slightly, a glint of amusement in her eyes. Haerlyon was rocking back and forth on his heels, an impish grin on his face, looking for all the world like a child waiting for presents.

"The room is ready, *Tarien*." A young servant had come up so quietly, I nearly jumped out of my skin.

I smiled and nodded. "Thank you."

With a light blush on her cheeks, the girl left us, and Haerlyon and I escorted Aunt Azra to her room.

"I see you haven't changed a thing," she said with a smile, placing her bags inside. "Thank you."

"If you need anything, just ask a servant. I'll let Mother know you've arrived."

Azra smiled. "Do not worry, *shareye*, I know my way around the palace. I'll see Arayda at dinner tonight, and you."

Excited, we left her room, almost skipping through the corridors like two happy children. Haerlyon laughed for a moment longer, and turned to me, a mischievous grin on his lips.

"I'm sorry for what Mother's making you do."

I pulled a face at him. "You've heard then?"

Haer smiled wryly. "Everyone has."

I groaned while passing a hand over my eyes. "Thank you, I'd almost forgotten."

"Good thing I didn't."

While I loved Haerlyon with all my heart, sometimes he could be a pain in the ass, especially at such moments where he was so incredibly thoughtful.

"You're incorrigible," I muttered.

He grinned. "You love me."

"Only on even days."

He kissed me on the cheek and left me to my own devices, whistling as he strutted through the corridors. If anyone was turning heads, it was him. There was something about him that made everyone love him, and as a sharp pain of jealousy went right through me upon that realisation, it dawned on me how much I envied him.

When I turned to make my way to my bedroom, voices caught my attention, and I was just in time to see Evan leave Mehrean's bedroom, holding her hand. I snuck closer to catch what they were saying, feeling horrible for doing so. He turned to face her, running a hand through her hair reverently.

"I'm sorry it has to be this way," Evan said.

Mehrean cupped his cheek, almost standing on tiptoe to do so. "We knew this could happen, *shareye*. Don't be sorry for this ending—be happy for the times we spent together."

The ghost of a smile played on his lips, but by the way he hung his head, I knew he wasn't remembering those happy times right now. This was why he'd been so sad the night he agreed to marry Nathaïr.

He'd been in love with Mehrean.

My heart went out to him, and as quietly as I could, I slipped away, not wanting to impose on the little time they had left together. Nathaïr had better be kind to him, or she'd be in trouble.

THAT EVENING, we assembled in Mother's chambers to welcome Azra home and listen to her stories. Mother hadn't been happy with her return, yet it didn't seem to bother Azra at all. I knew there was some history between them—I just didn't know what it was. It made me wonder what it was Mother couldn't forgive her for. No matter what Azra said or did, Mother always disapproved in some form or other, the scowl on her face as she watched her sister testimony to that idea.

"I've brought you something," Azra said, putting her traveller's bag on her lap.

Haerlyon received a beautiful ornate dagger Azra told us

came from far away Kyrintha. It wouldn't be practical, but it would sure look beautiful in his bedroom. Evan received a long sword inlaid with rubies and sapphires fit for a king, according to Azra. Ironically, Ilvanna had never had a king and would likely never see one either. Nevertheless, it impressed Evan, which didn't happen often.

For me she had two silver bracelets crafted as delicately as a spider's web, and a tiny knife I could hide in several places.

"The bracelets will look marvellous on you," Azra cooed as she locked them around my wrist. "They're made of the finest Kyrinthan silver."

"This is amazing!" I exclaimed, turning from the bracelets to flipping the knife over and over in my hand.

It was the size of my smallest finger, and much thinner than that, but no doubt deadly when applied in the right region. Elara would appreciate it. Haerlyon whistled when he looked at it from all angles, almost reluctant to give it back. Mother appeared less pleased with the gift, but she said nothing. Evan shared Mother's feelings on it, scrunching his nose when I offered him to have a look. I was over the moon with the presents, grinning at Azra stupidly.

"Where did your journeys take you this time?" I asked, folding myself in a chair in front of the fire. "You've been gone so long!"

Azra chuckled softly. "Oh, I've been overseas little niece, and seen the most marvellous places, people, and even creatures! Did you know there are animals with one lump on their back which can be used as horses? They're called *camelles.*"

"That sounds odd," Haerlyon said.

From the corner of my eyes, I saw Mother shake her head softly as if she didn't believe one word of it. I scowled at her, wondering why for once she couldn't just enjoy the time together and be happy. Turning back to Azra, I focused on her instead as she told of faraway countries with miles and miles of sand, no water, and beautiful, colourful clothing the likes of which we couldn't even begin to imagine.

"When I was there," Azra said, turning to Haerlyon and myself, "a young son tried to overthrow his father. In secret, he'd gathered many followers, and then one day, he attacked out of nowhere! His father, a smart and rather cunning man, had seen the betrayal coming from miles away, and was prepared. Instead of killing his father, the young son killed a servant instead. It was too late when he found out his mistake, and come dawn, his father had him beheaded. It was rather gruesome if you ask me. Barbaric even!"

"Did this happen overnight?" Haerlyon asked curiously, leaning forward in his chair.

"Of course not," Azra said. "The young son had been planning this for years. He was just waiting for the right time."

I listened with rapt attention as she weaved a story of wondrous events. It all sounded like a fairy-tale, and although a part of me doubted the validity of her story, it was a great one nonetheless.

As the night wore on, Azra excused herself on account of having travelled for weeks with little rest, and left us with well-wishes and hand-kisses. All but Mother, who watched her with a guarded expression as she left, wished her a good night.

"Don't believe everything she tells you," Mother said while rising to her feet. "Doubtless less than half is the truth, and the remaining part is twisted in such a way it benefits her."

"Why do you hate Aunt Azra so much?" I asked. "What has she ever done to you?"

Anger flashed in Mother's eyes in a way I'd never seen before, her lips set in a thin line.

"Out," she hissed. "Now!"

The tone in her voice was enough frighten me, so I grabbed my gifts and bolted out of her room, not stopping until I was back in my own. My headlong flight startled Xaresh, who was on guard duty, so much, he stuck his head inside to check everything was all right.

"Fine," I murmured.

"You sure say fine a lot when you aren't," he commented drily.

Xaresh stepped into my room uninvited. I glared at him. He returned my look unimpressed, leaning back against the door with folded arms.

"What happened?"

"Mother got angry," I said, throwing the bracelets to the side. Xaresh picked them up, and placed them gingerly on my dressing table, looking at me via the mirror.

"So?" he asked. "Your mother gets angry at you a lot."

Biting my lip, I stared right back at him, and away, insecurity taking hold of me. I rubbed my arm, then folded them in front of me. In the end, I did look back at him, fingers nervously fumbling with the small knife.

"It wasn't like that," I whispered. "She was *furious*—you know? The kind of fury where she goes all quiet, and you can feel it in the air, but she will not yell at you?"

He just nodded.

"It wasn't pretty."

Rubbing the back of his neck, Xaresh regarded me quietly. With a deep sigh, I placed the small knife on my bedside cabinet, staring at it for a bit longer, wondering if I'd ever need it.

"What did you do?" he said.

I turned to him, insecurity coursing through me. "I asked her why she hated Azra so much."

Xaresh gave me one of those dazzling smiles lighting up his entire face and walked over to me. Gently, he took my hands in his.

"*Tarien*," he began, "you're a remarkable woman in general, but would you heed some advice?"

I wrinkled my nose. "Depends on what it is."

"Think before you speak, *Tarien*," he said. "It'll get you into trouble less, and people will like you better for it."

"Am I that unlikeable?"

He chuckled softly. "No, not at all, but your words can be harsh."

"The truth's seldom anything else."

"It's just not always yours to give."

Regarding him in silence, I sighed and nodded. "All right, I'll try."

"Maybe…"

"Don't push your luck." I glowered at him. "Goodnight Xaresh."

Xaresh looked amused. "Sweet dreams, *Tarien*."

CHAPTER 3

*O*n the morning of Nathaïr's arrival, I woke up before the crack of dawn, too restless to fall back asleep. I'd been dreaming of the faraway country Azra had told us about the night before, but instead of it being her story, it was mine. With a shake of my head while rubbing my face, I dispelled the last remnants of my dream and slipped out of bed.

I put on some trousers and a blouse, slipped my feet into my boots, and grabbed a cloak from a chair. At this time of day, the garden could be chilly, and I had no desire to freeze to death. I went out the backdoor, knowing an *Arathrien* would be posted at the other one. It surprised me nobody ever bothered with this side though, but then nothing ever happened around here, so it wasn't necessary.

As I stepped outside, I heard the early birds sing their songs of joy, greeting the morning with pure bliss and happiness. The air was crisp, the kind I expected just before a snowstorm which was quite likely to happen in these regions at this time of year— courtesy of the Ilvan Mountains. I pulled my cloak tighter about me, breathed in deeply, and crept past the other bedrooms, not wanting to wake anyone.

Once in the garden, I eased up, ambling past the colourful array of flowerbeds, silently enjoying the sweet scents they emitted as I ran my hands over them. The sound of the birds, the fresh air, and the flowery scent calmed my mind and the built up tension from the past two days.

Mother couldn't have chosen a better way to punish me. Nathaïr and I had never gotten along, if only because she was a sheep in wolf's clothes. I still remember the day when she pushed me into the water so long ago, knowing I couldn't swim properly—or the day I turned one hundred and twenty and was no longer considered a child, and she'd coated the inside of my under robe with poison ivy a few days before. Rash and blisters had covered me head to toe. Mother had been furious with me, not believing I had nothing to do with it, at least not until one of my ladies-in-waiting found out about the undergarment.

Throughout the years, Nathaïr pulled more such pranks, deliberately drawing me out to see my temper flare. Last time we'd had an altercation it was because she'd stolen a dagger from Evan and made sure they found it in my bedroom. I had been so mad I had punched her in the face and broken her nose. Mother had forbidden me training for two moons after.

If she tried anything today, I shouldn't give in to it. I wouldn't give in to it. Today, I'd be impeccable in every possible way, meaning I'd keep my sharp tongue on a leash like Xaresh had suggested. The first day after I had promised change, I failed miserably. I hadn't even been awake for long when my mouth was faster than my brain.

My eyes settled on the white marble palace walls, glittering in the sun's pale yellow rays before I descended the stairs to the training fields, careful not to slip and go down on my ass the rest of the way. Finding a spot out of the wind, I closed my eyes, breathed in deeply, and went through the forms slowly, concentrating on every single step. My thoughts cleared like clouds on a sunny day, allowing me to calm down, relax, and to focus. If Tal wanted me more focused, I would be.

Not once did Nathaïr, or her antics, cross my mind.

"Good to see another lark," a vaguely familiar voice sounded up.

I spun on my heel, my heart beating frantically in my chest, eyes wide. At this hour of day, I expected no one, so it surprised me to find Grayden standing there, hands stuffed in his pockets.

"Oh, it's you." I breathed in deeply to calm myself.

"You sound sorely disappointed."

I shook my head, plastering a smile on my face. "Not at all. Just startled. Nobody's usually out around this time of day."

He flashed me a smile, rubbing his cheek. "Apologies. I didn't mean to scare you."

"It's fi—, all right."

Ever since Xaresh told me I said fine a lot, I'd started paying attention to it. I used it a lot indeed.

"What are you doing here this time of day, anyway?" I asked, narrowing my eyes slightly.

"I was taking a stroll," he replied with a shrug, "when I saw you out here."

I nodded, pulling my cloak tighter around me as the wind picked up.

"I wanted to thank you," he began.

"For what?"

He flashed me a genuine smile this time. "For speaking to Master Evanyan on my behalf."

"Well," I said. "You knew how to hold the proper end of a sword. Couldn't say the same for our guard."

Grayden chuckled. "He gave it a fair try. I almost felt sorry for him when you said what you did."

"I say the truth," I said with a shrug. "I'm not known for being nice."

He smirked. "Somehow, I doubt that."

Tilting my head, I looked at him. "What makes you say that?"

"If you were truly so unfriendly, I doubt people would admire you so much."

I huffed. "You're clearly not from around here."

"Do you always counter every compliment you receive? What is it you fear?" he asked, tilting his head a little.

I narrowed my eyes. "You sure have guts to speak to me like that."

He shrugged. "I don't see the point in tiptoeing around the issue either."

I laughed, shaking my head. His frankness was refreshing—charming even—but it could get him into more trouble than he bargained for.

"It's Grayden, isn't it?" I asked out of curiosity.

He blanched and inclined his head. "It is, milady."

I chuckled. "Now you call me milady."

"Would you prefer *Tarien*?" he asked. "Or Your Majesty perhaps?"

"Milady is fine."

I don't mind if you just call me by name, but my Mother, brothers, and the rest of the palace dwellers might have something to say about that.

Grayden inclined his head, a soft smile playing on his lips. By now, people were gathering on the fields for training, some of whom were eyeing us with sleepy eyes. My gaze locked with a pair of piercing, emerald eyes, belonging to the only person who annoyed me and made me happy at the same time.

"Make yourself scarce," I said, "if you value your life."

He was about to ask why when he followed my gaze and saw Talnovar skip down the stairs. With a bow of his head, Grayden took his leave. I placed my hands on my hips, stance wide, waiting for Talnovar to catch up with me. When he did, the happy, easy look on his face puzzled me.

"Are you going to yell at me?" I asked, narrowing my eyes.

He looked surprised. "What for?"

"Sneaking out of my bedroom?"

"You were where I expected you to be," he said with a shrug. "I'm glad to find you started already."

I shook my head, rubbing my temples. "You're so confusing."

"You're rubbing off on me," he grinned.

"Why are you so eerily happy today?" I muttered. "The worst day of my life has arrived. You're not supposed to be this happy."

It was his turn to look puzzled. "What are you talk—, oh! You mean Nathaïr?"

I scowled, rolled my eyes, and dropped my arms alongside my body.

"I promise to go to every lesson if I don't have to do this." I begged. "Please don't let me do this. I'm afraid I'll commit a heinous crime within an hour of her arrival."

Talnovar looked amused, placing both hands on my shoulders. "It won't be as bad as you think. Besides, I doubt she'll stick around you for very long. She's bringing her own entourage as far as ladies-in-waiting are concerned, and I'm sure she's got more than a few friends here at court."

"I don't see the point in showing her around. She knows where everything is already."

"Maybe so," Tal said, "but this isn't about you showing her around, it's about you determining your power over her."

"I still don't like it."

He smirked. "You don't have to like it. You just have to do it."

"You're an ass."

Within a second of my saying that, Tal flipped me over his hip, and onto the ground, fixing my arm at an awkward angle while applying pressure on my shoulder joint. I yelped in surprise.

"What are you doing!" I shrieked.

He applied a little more pressure. Enough to hurt, but not enough to maim.

"Getting you in the proper mindset," he said.

With a loud growl, I pulled free when he loosened his grip, and got back to my feet. I unclasped my cloak, threw it to the side, and mirrored his stance. He grabbed my shirt at the shoulders, just as I did his, and grinning tried to throw each other off balance. Obviously, with Tal being the stronger of us two, he had me on the ground three times within a matter of minutes.

"Focus," he muttered. "You know how to do this."

Hand-to-hand combat was as much a part of training as armed combat was, and although my height was in my favour, my weight wasn't. So far, I'd only managed to get Elara, who was lithe and strong—much like myself—to the ground a couple of times. The men were all taller, definitely more muscular, and a good deal heavier, except for maybe Queran, the youngest of all.

He looked wiry, but none of us would ever mistake him for being weak. Queran was much stronger than he looked, and deadly with ranged weapons of any kind. It's why he was the only one allowed to carry a bow and arrows inside the palace.

"It's not about the weight," Tal whispered in my ear. "It's about chance and properly executed technique at the right moment."

He pushed and shoved me none too gently, trying to either kick my feet from under me or throw me over his hip again. During a moment where he pushed me, I surprised him by stepping back and pulling him out of balance. I hooked my foot behind his and gave him a firm shove. He fell forward and pulled me with him as he kept hold of my shirt, turning as we fell.

I landed on top, drawing out a loud grunt from him.

"Nice one," he grimaced, rubbing the back of his head. "Sneaky too."

I looked pleased. "You told me to be creative."

"I did, didn't I?"

The impish grin was back on his face, and I couldn't help but stare into those mysteriously vibrant eyes scouring my face. Emerald wasn't a colour often seen in our kind, but on him they looked exquisite. He was about to bring his hand to my face when a loud cough startled us. Looking over my shoulder, I found Evan glaring down at me, arms crossed behind his back. I scooted off of Tal as quickly as I could and jumped to my feet.

Tal got to his feet much slower, clearly less impressed with Evan. Straightening his shirt, I noticed the impassive look sweep across his features, taking away the twinkle from his eyes. I looked anywhere but at my brother.

"I shouldn't have to remind you such a thing is inappropriate?" Evan said.

I sighed, refraining from awarding him with a massive eye roll. "There's nothing inappropriate about someone catching my fall."

Evan opened his mouth to retort something, thought the better of it, and closed it with a shake of his head.

"Nathaïr arrives around noon," he said, looking anything but pleased. "Mother told me you'd be her welcoming committee."

I scowled at my brother. "Unfortunately."

"Get freshened up and properly dressed," he said, looking me up and down with a disdainful look in his eyes.

Someone had woken up on the wrong side of the bed this morning.

I rolled my eyes and muttered something incomprehensible before stalking off with my arms wrapped around me. I had no desire to dress up as a doll to please Nathaïr, but if I wanted to get out from under this task, I had to go all the way, and beyond.

Better get my best dress with the most layers out, and show them I can be the perfect hostess, even to a snake.

"Shal, hold up!"

Evan came running up to me, holding my cloak in his hands. I slowed down, but didn't stop, still annoyed with his earlier response, and the whole situation. He caught up quickly though, and halted me by stepping in front of me, a slight frown on his face.

"Hey," he said. "What's wrong?"

"You really have to ask?" I asked with a sigh, rubbing my brow. "You know what Ev, we'll talk about this later, all right? I don't want to say things I might come to regret."

A momentary flicker of hurt crossed his features, but saying nothing he placed a kiss on my forehead as a response. As I passed, he handed me my cloak, and stepped out of the way. Because I was sure an entire parade would be waiting to prepare me for this official affair, the stillness of my bedroom when I entered surprised me. Queran merely inclined his head when I stepped inside, while I stared around slack-jawed. Under any other circumstances, at least a dozen people would have been present—there was nobody inside now. I inhaled deeply, and exhaled slowly, enjoying the momentary peace.

Mehrean poked her head around the corner to the adjacent room.

"I figured you'd like it better this way," she said, watching me with a mischievous glint in her eyes.

I laughed, shaking my head. "You know me too well."

As HANIYA, she was well-trained in the care of others, both mentally, and physically, and she concocted the most amazing oils and creams with delicious scents. My favourite was one smelling of vanilla, oranges and wood—a comfortable scent which always brought me to the present. It reminded me of warm summer nights spent with loved ones, lying in the grass, star-gazing in silence, with bowls of fruit as midnight snacks, and vanilla tinged *ithri* cooled down with ice and flavoured by oranges as refreshing drinks.

It had been a while since we'd had one of those nights.

"Everything all right?" Mehr asked, pouring water over my head.

"Just reminiscing."

I sighed in pure bliss while she was washing my hair, her fingers massaging my scalp until I nearly fell asleep. My thoughts drifted off to practise with Tal that morning, and how he had felt beneath me after I'd landed on top of him. His strong hand would have felt marvellous on my face, and I could almost imagine it, until that feeling was rudely torn from me when Mehr tossed a pitcher of water over my head.

"Gods!" I gasped, my heart racing. "You could have warned me!"

"I did."

Glaring at her, I pushed the mop of wet hair from my face, my scowl deepening when I saw the smirk on her lips. With a deep sigh, I slumped back in the tub, ready to go under and not come up, but Mehrean had other plans.

"Come on," she said. "Time for the rest."

"I could do this on my own, you know." I said, arching a brow.

She looked amused. "You could, but you won't."

"Today I would. Not that Nathaïr deserves it, but I'll show everyone I can be a proper *Tarien*." I replied. "Any other day, however, I just don't see the point in dressing up. What with training two to three times a day, I keep redressing."

"Your mother would be happy with training just once a day," Mehrean said.

I snorted. "When all the stars align and the heavens come crashing down."

"It's just today," she commented, "and it doesn't matter whether or not Nathaïr deserves it, it's what needs to be done. Once she has been properly installed, she will not be a bother to you any longer."

"I highly doubt that," I huffed, glaring at her.

Mehrean smiled, handing me a robe. "Even if that's the case, there's no point in worrying over it now."

"I'll worry over whatever I want to worry," I said, taking the robe from her. "Why do I need to bow down to her? She's nowhere near my status, and will never be, even if she marries my brother. Why do *I* have to be the one agreeing, and not her? It makes little sense."

"I assume because this is what your Mother has been trying to teach you all along," Mehrean said, placing me in a chair. "Restraint and serenity. No matter how you feel about someone, you cannot let your emotions overrule your head. Not as *Tarien* —never as *Tari*. Don't you think your Mother would have loved to give in to her emotions at times? What do you think would happen if she does?"

I gritted my teeth. "Probably nothing good, but I'm not like Mother, and she's definitely not like me."

Mehrean chuckled softly. "I think you have a very warped image of your mother, *Tarien*. Be at your best behaviour while you're around Nathaïr so she cannot set you up to fail. Talnovar and Xaresh will be with you. Can you do that, without your tongue getting the better of you?"

I swallowed hard and nodded, still not happy with this agreement. "I'll try."

With a smile on her face, she towelled down my hair before rubbing one of her oils in it, reminding me of the air just after it rained, and the cold, chilly mornings on the fields. It took Mehr forever to sort my hair, but when she finished, it was dry, and shiny, and complicated, and girly, and delicate, and everything I was not. It was completely impractical in a fight.

Looking into the mirror, I grimaced at my reflection. My mop of white, unruly hair was curlier than usual, and was left hanging loosely over my shoulders. I blew a strand of hair out of my face with a loud puff, watching wide, cautious eyes staring back at me. The moment this was all done, it would go in a braid, no excuses.

"This"—I sighed, encompassing all of myself with a wave of my hand— "is ridiculous."

Mehrean didn't reply as she helped me into the sheer underdress, wrapping it tight with a small sash. She added a second underdress of a midnight blue colour, sporting a set of floor-length sleeves, over the first. Mehr tightened it properly, and I couldn't help but wonder who had invented these murderous contraptions. The more layers she added, the more cumbersome it became, giving me a hard time breathing. It was as if she had placed something heavy on my chest, slowly squeezing all the air out of my lungs, constricting me in my breathing, my moving, even my thinking.

The last piece of garment to follow was an overdress in the same midnight blue colour as the previous one, except it was lavishly decorated with white and silver beads, running from hemline to hemline, and top to bottom. The worst part of the dressing ritual came when she placed a wide silver sash around my waist, binding it so tight I wasn't sure I could ever breathe again.

It felt as if somebody had locked the door and was about to throw away the key.

Mehrean took a step back to admire her handiwork, both hands on her hips. "Perfect."

I grunted. "If you don't care about breathing."

Mehrean rolled her eyes.

I slid into a pair of easy slippers, and glanced at myself in the mirror one more time, turning this way and that to view every angle.

"This doesn't look half bad though," I murmured.

Would he like it?

In all honesty, I had every bit the appearance of a *Tarien* as I should.

"You look fine," Mehr said. "Now go out and be the perfect hostess."

Rolling my eyes, I quickly snatched Azra's gift from my bedside cabinet, and tucked it between my breasts while stepping out of my bedroom. An indrawn gasp startled me and I caught Xaresh staring at me slack-jawed.

"Xaresh. You're catching flies."

Tal snorted and quickly turned away. Xaresh snapped his mouth shut, still unable to look anywhere else.

"Wow," he breathed, recovering himself. "This is the best you've ever looked, *Tarien.*"

I cuffed him on the arm. Hard. He yelped in surprise, and while rubbing the sore spot, Xaresh muttered under his breath. Talnovar looked as if he was about to choke on something any second now and did his best to avoid my gaze. Heat rose to my cheeks, and I quickly stepped away from them, shaking my head.

Professionals as they were, they stepped in line behind me, their faces composed, and shoulders straight. People stared and murmured as we passed them. Some whispered behind their hands and pointed at me, followed by a giggle or an outright gasp. Balling my hands in my sleeves and closing my eyes, I was seconds away from turning around and going back to my room.

"Lift your chin. Don't listen," Talnovar murmured, his hand brushing mine. "Let them whisper."

It wasn't as if I never wore dresses—I just never made a fuss out of looking spectacular in them. Nobody was vying for my hand, and I was outdoors more than I was indoors, so they were entirely impractical. People just weren't used to seeing me like this, which could explain their reactions.

It did nothing to ease my fear of their opinions though.

We arrived at the courtyard moments before the clatter of hooves echoed through the gate, and a large party of men and women rode in, Yllinar and Nathaïr up front. I snorted at the display of power simply because they lived a stone's throw from the palace. This charade was unnecessary, and it just went to show Yllinar enjoyed flaunting his wealth for the world to see.

It sickened me to know people were starving in the outer layers, while people like him spent their money as if it was nothing. Rumour had it he came by his money dishonestly— over the back of others—but no amount of investigation into it had yielded any merit to these allegations. People who'd spoken about it suddenly disappeared, and while that was unsettling on its own, it couldn't be tied back to him.

As his penetrating gaze settled on me, it felt as if he was peeling every layer from my body right down to my soul. A deep-seated loathing coiled trough my gut like a snake as I watched the trademark sneer play on his lips. I tore my gaze away from him, and over to Nathaïr looking splendid in her silver dress—her hair tied back in a perfect half-braid, and everything else just as immaculate. It didn't matter what she wore, it could have been a plain sack for all it was worth—she always looked stunning.

It was such a shame her personality didn't match the outside. I felt certain the saying 'gaudy mirrors hold ugly truths' applied to her in every way. She wasn't known for being nice to those she deemed beneath her, and sucked up to those she needed— except me, obviously. You should see her around Mother and my brothers though. By *Vehda*, she'd even try Talnovar if she knew it would work. Fortunately, he cared about her as little as I did, and probably even less, so she never got very far with him.

59

Xaresh was a different story altogether and remembering how she had tried to seduce him in the past made me feel sorry for him all over again.

Her gaze swept over me so fast I doubted she even paid attention, but as it did, I noticed the insecurity in her eyes, despite the holier-than-thou smile on her lips. Involuntarily, I balled my fists at my side, swallowing hard, resisting the urge to wipe the smug look off her face. Someone stepped closer, and then Tal murmured in my ear to let it go.

"Don't do anything you'll regret, *Tarien*," Xaresh said under his breath.

Inhaling deeply, I calmed myself, plastered a smile on my face, and walked up to our guests.

"*Irìn* Yllinar," I said, inclining my head. "*Irà* Nathaïr, be welcome to your new home."

My voice didn't sound as steady as I'd wanted it to, and I cursed myself for letting them get under my skin. I noticed the secretive smile they shared before they dismounted, and I quickly glanced around for any support.

From the corner of my eyes, I noticed Haerlyon lounging against the palace walls, regarding our little party with a scowl on his face. He took a bite of his apple, tossed it and pushed himself off the wall, sauntering away with his hands in his pockets. When I turned back, Nathaïr's gaze swept me up and down, and an identical look to her father's appeared on her face.

Were they born with that sneer?

"I'm surprised you came to welcome me," she said, "but it's good to see they polished you up."

I bit my cheek so hard I could taste blood, but I kept the smile on my face, and inclined my head lightly.

"The rest is too busy with more important tasks," I said. It earned me a reproachful look from both Xaresh and Talnovar.

Nathaïr pretended not to have heard it, and looked across

the courtyard, chin up daintily. Yllinar watched me through narrowed eyes, but soon was the subject of a staring contest between himself and Talnovar, who'd stepped between us.

"Let me show you to your chambers," I said. "I'm sure you'd like to freshen up before the *Tari* wishes to see you."

It looked as if an entire family was being moved what with the amount of stuff Nathaïr had brought to the palace. I counted at least eighteen heavy chests, half a dozen bags, and at least two dozen small boxes. Her own men weren't enough to carry all of it, so I had to call in help from several guards to get everything to her room. I couldn't help but stare wide-eyed at the amount of… stuff being carried into it.

"*Nohro ahrae,*" I murmured for my guards' ears only. "How much clothing does a woman need?"

"You've got clothing," Xaresh remarked drily.

"Not *that* much!"

Tal looked amused. "Are you saying you're not a woman, *Tarien?*"

I stared at him flatly, but couldn't help but smile. "You are—"

He grinned. "An ass?"

"I was going to say incorrigible," I replied, doing my best not to stare at him longer, "but ass works."

He laughed wholeheartedly first—a sound reverberating in my core—but stopped quickly, the trademark scowl back on his face instantly when Nathaïr and Yllinar stepped out of the room. I swear he changed expressions faster than Ilvanna's weather did. How I still plastered these fake smiles on my face was beyond me, but I did, listening to insult upon insult heaped on my person.

"How could you possibly let me stay in a filthy room like this?" Nathaïr screeched.

"Shouldn't she be closer to her fiancé's room?" Yllinar interjected.

"You really cannot do *anything* right, can you?" she was close to fuming right now.

I opened my mouth to reply when Xaresh stepped in, towering over the three of us.

"You'd do well to remember who you are speaking to, *Irà Arolvyen*," he said, "or your words might be considered treason."

My brows shot up in surprise. I'd expected this from Talnovar more than from him. Nathaïr opened her mouth to retort something and looked at her father, who stepped back in a light bow to admit defeat, for help.

So he did know which lines they'd already crossed.

I clasped my hands gingerly, lifting my chin ever so slightly as I stared at her father, only to let my gaze settle on the smaller woman in front of me. A part of me wanted to yell at her, but I had promised to keep my dignity and not let my emotions reign supreme.

Nathaïr wouldn't get to me this time.

"Rest." I smiled. "Someone will pick you up for your meeting with the *Tari*."

"Can't we go wander the palace instead," she purred, looking not at me, but at Talnovar behind me. "I'd love to see *all* of it."

I glanced at him, feeling the heat rise to my cheeks, my insides coiling as she all but draped herself around him. By Esahbyen I wanted to hit her. Tal closed his eyes briefly, his jaw tensed as he remained eerily quiet. The look on his face was enough for me to know his answer. With a fake smile, I opened my arm and guided her away from her bedroom, away from Tal.

"Shall we?"

She'd spent time at court long enough to know where everything was, but I could understand why she didn't want to be penned up in her bedroom. It was just the worst change of faith I was the one who had to put up with her while we made our way through the palace. Xaresh stayed with us as Talnovar excused himself for other business, as did Yllinar. I wasn't sad to see him go.

In the garden, Nathaïr suddenly halted in front of the fountain and turned to me, her expression calm and collected. I motioned Xaresh to stay right where he was with a flick of my hand—out of sight, but within earshot.

"Let's get this straight," she said, all pretence forgotten. "I don't like you, you don't like me, but trust me when I tell you I hate these arrangements as much as you do."

It surprised me she did, but I didn't care to ask why.

"Regardless," she continued, "I will not waste an opportunity like this, so you can be absolutely sure I'll do everything in my power to keep it."

I smirked. "Don't worry. I'll stay out of your way if you stay out of mine."

As she took a step closer to me, I was glad I was taller than most of the Ilvannian women. Nathaïr was a good half a head smaller than I was, and daintier too. If she tried something, I would have her flat on her back before she could finish her sentence. I folded my arms in front of me, looking positively bored.

"You might be the *Tarien*," she hissed, "but don't think for one minute I'm impressed or scared by you."

I shrugged. "I honestly don't care if you are, as long as you are courteous to my brother and don't break his heart. I'll break yours if you do."

The threatening tone in my voice didn't leave up to the imagination, and from the look on her face I could tell my message had come across loud and clear. Puffing herself up, she stomped her foot once, pivoted on her heel, and stormed off into the palace. I exhaled slowly and sat down on the side of the fountain, rubbing my shaking hands over my thighs.

Xaresh was with me instantly.

"She's a nasty piece of work," he murmured. "Are you all right?"

I swallowed hard and nodded. "She'll be more trouble than we bargained for."

THE EXACT AMOUNT of trouble became clear during dinner that night. It had surprised me to find Nathaïr sitting on Evan's right side, even though she was technically his betrothed, and I couldn't help but feel sorry for the miserable look on his face. Azra had joined us as well, and the light shake of her head when she looked at me told me I was in trouble. Mehrean was there too, probably as a courtesy to her position, and I was glad to find she sat next to me. Haerlyon was on my other side, lounging in his chair as usual.

"I've heard some disturbing news today, daughter," Mother began the moment I took my seat.

Here we go.

"Nathaïr tells me you've been rather unfriendly," she continued, "and even threatened her."

I stared at Mother—who returned the look unperturbed— then at Nathaïr, who had a smug smile playing on her lips.

"If anyone was being unfriendly, Mother," I replied, trying to keep my voice steady, "it was her. And I've no idea what threat she could possibly be talking about."

"Something about you breaking her heart if she breaks Evanyan's?"

"That was hardly a threat," I scoffed. "That was a warning."

"You have a strange sense of justice, daughter."

"Considering the fact she's defied my authority on more than one occasion today, I've been nice."

"Regardless." She looked at me. "You behaved inappropriately, and for that, I shall punish you."

"Excuse me?" I whispered, feeling all heat drawing from my face.

Haerlyon sat up next to me, frowning. "What happened to innocent until proven otherwise, Mother? Are you that angry at Shal that you believe a perfect stranger—no offense—over your own daughter?"

I sat trembling in my chair, but not from cold. Fury coursed through me, and it took me all effort of will not to give in to it. Closing my eyes, I felt Mehrean's hand on mine, squeezing lightly. At least she was on my side, together with Haer.

"There were witnesses, Haerlyon," Mother said.

He huffed. "Really? Because I cannot recall being asked my side of the story."

Mother watched him with newly kindled interest. "I didn't know you were there?"

He shrugged, a light grin on his face. "I wanted to see the madhouse as it arrived."

Mother stared at him incredulously.

"Fine," she said, rubbing her temples. "Speak."

"Nathaïr insulted Shal the moment she rode in," he said. "Never acknowledging her, never greeting her by title. In fact, I believe Nathaïr insulted her, in the presence of two of her *Arathrien*, and those present in the courtyard. I can ask around if you want Mother, I'm sure there are some who'd love to speak up for her."

Nathaïr glared daggers his way.

"After Shal showed the lady to her room," Haer went on, "Nathaïr continued insulting our *Tarien* to where Xaresh stepped in and warned her not to go any further unless she wanted to be arrested for treason."

Evanyan looked at me, eyes empty and sad. He shook his head from side to side like a man in denial, before resting it in his arms. My chest constricted painfully at the sight of him. He'd be caught in this fight for as long as either of us was around. Haer was about to say more when I rose to my feet, placing a hand on his arm to stop him from talking.

"All of what he says is true Mother," I said, "but I did say those words to Nathaïr. I shall await your punishment, but would ask you to allow me to step away from the table. I no longer desire any food."

I didn't even wait to be excused. As soon as I stepped away from my chair, I walked out of the dining room, doing my best not to run. When the door closed behind me, I picked up the hem of my dress and dashed out of the palace, down the stairs and onto the fields, over to a group of *àn* still training.

Taking the sword of one of them, I twirled around, eyesight blurry from unshed tears. My chest was heaving as if I'd run ten laps around the field, and I was practically breezing like a horse. Just because I'd accepted the punishment, didn't mean I agreed with it.

I'd done it for Ev. Not to appease Mother.

"Fight me!" I ordered.

The *àn* stared at me either blankly or wide-eyed, but none of them stepped up.

"Are you deaf?" I yelled. "Fight me!"

Some shuffled away, others stared at each other. I kept yelling for one of them to fight me. None of them did.

"I'll fight you," Grayden said.

Without even acknowledging his presence, I turned to him and attacked, but I was unfocused, and charged wildly with no rhyme or reason to it. I just wanted to hit something as hard as possible. Grayden parried my strike with ease, enraging me even further. I lashed out at him from a crouch, but he fended me off, barely stepping back. I didn't even cause him to break a sweat.

I kept attacking him until there was no fight in me left. Until then, he kept a defensive position, carefully parrying or avoiding my attacks entirely. Sobbing, I sunk to my knees, dropping the sword to my side. My throat tightened while my chest constricted, and my head was one dull, throbbing mess.

Grayden sat down beside me, but didn't say a word. Instead, he let me have my meltdown in peace, for which I was more than grateful, and by the time I finished, he offered me a kerchief.

"Thank you," I said, wiping my nose. "You're too kind."

"Not a problem," he replied, wrapping his arms around his knees. "Do I want to know what happened?"

I shrugged. "It's nothing."

"Like your fighting?"

I scowled at him, tossing the kerchief his way. He caught it elegantly, a lazy grin on his lips. Out of nowhere, I started shivering uncontrollably. Wrapping my arms tight around me, I tried to fight it off, but realised it was getting cold and I'd just spent some time crying.

"*Tarien*," Tal's voice cut through the fog in my mind. "Are you all right?"

I looked up. "Not particularly."

Between the two of them, Grayden and Talnovar helped me to my feet, of which the latter escorted me back to the palace.

"Thanks for obliging me," I said, looking over my shoulder at Grayden.

"Anytime, milady."

Once we were well out of earshot, Talnovar broke the silence.

"That was quite a fight you put up," he said. "It's a good thing Grayden knows how to parry."

"I wouldn't have hit a tree had it been right in front of my face," I said, keeping my teeth from chattering. "You've been watching?"

He flashed me a charming smile. "I may have."

I frowned. "The entire time?"

"Almost."

I stared at him. "Why didn't you stop me?"

"Would it have helped?" he asked, looking down at me.

"Probably not."

Tal chuckled as he opened the door to my bedroom. "There's your answer."

Candles had been lit all around the room where it was blissfully warm, and comfortably toasty with the fire roaring. Not until then did I realise how cold I really was despite three layers of clothing. I knelt in front of the fireplace, glancing up from under my lashes to find Talnovar leaning against the door, the look on his face troubled.

"What's wrong?" I asked.

His gaze settled on me, and with a light shake of his head, he pushed himself away from the door, a gentle smile playing on his lips.

"Nothing, just thinking," he said.

I raised an eyebrow, a smirk on my lips. "Of course you are."

His lip quirked up in a faint smile. Whatever was troubling him wasn't something he'd share just like that, so I dropped it.

"Could you do me a favour?" I asked.

"Which is?"

"Untie this *nohro* sash," I said. "Please?"

He hesitated, but did walk up to me as I got to my feet. Without saying a word, he deftly untied the sash and I could feel his hands tremble. A strange sensation manifested in my stomach, and the moment he stepped away, I released my breath.

"Anything else you need me for?" he asked, looking anywhere but at me.

I shook my head. "No, I'm good."

"I'll be outside if you need anything."

"Oh," I said, feeling somewhat disappointed. "All right. Goodnight."

"Sleep well, *Tarien*."

He left without even looking back, which was so unlike him

68

I wondered what had gotten into him. After struggling out of the three layers of doom, I slipped into a nightgown and made myself comfortable in bed, curling up into the corner with my back against the wall.

I always felt safest that way.

CHAPTER 4

A gentle hand on my shoulder woke me up to darkness. Barely visible in the candlelight, Evan stood next to me, his finger in front of his lips motioning me to be silent. With his other hand, he beckoned me to get up. Rubbing my eyes, I swung my legs over the bed, peering at him.

"What are you doing here?" I whispered.

"Getting you out."

I rubbed my face sleepily. "Out of what?"

"Just get dressed. Sturdy clothes, nothing fancy," Evan said in a hushed voice.

I got out of bed, and as quietly as I could, I got dressed in leather trousers, a sturdy cotton shirt and soft leather boots. I placed the small knife from Azra in one of them before swinging my cloak over my shoulders. Evan took my hand and guided me out of my bedroom, and into the garden. He must have come in that way.

"Where are we going?"

I looked at him with curiousity, because this was something I'd have expected from Haerlyon, not from him. Evan flashed me one of the rare grins that lit up his entire face, highlighting the mischievous sparkle in his eyes which he usually hid behind a stern mask. I couldn't quite make out what he was up to, but knowing Evan, there was more behind this than him making up for the previous night with Nathaïr. It wasn't until we arrived at the stables, where Haerlyon was waiting with Orion and Hadiyah, that I understood my brother's need for secrecy.

"We're going for a ride? You and I?"

Evan rubbed the back of his neck, smiling. "It's the least I could do after yesterday."

"You're actually taking me for a ride?" I repeated the question in disbelief. "The day after I angered Mother?"

"Unless you don't want to?"

I grinned. "Are you joking?" Tilting my head slightly, I regarded my brother. "Mother will be livid though."

"And Talnovar will most likely kill you," Haerlyon added, sparing his brother a look with a wicked grin on his face. "Just thought I'd let you know."

"I left Tal a message," Evan replied with a shrug, mounting Hadiyah. "He can have a go at me when we get back."

Haerlyon chuckled softly, holding on to Orion's reins while I mounted him. It had been a while since I'd gone riding, and when I had, it had been with a full escort. They never allowed me to get too far ahead.

We set off slowly, walking the horses through the gate where for some reason the guards looked in the other direction as we passed. How odd. The same happened at the other gates—whenever we arrived, the guards looked anywhere but at us. My brows furrowed thoughtfully, and I realised with some jealousy it was this easy for Evan. What I didn't understand was why the guards weren't stopping me. I noticed the smug smile on Evan's face, and when he looked at me, there was a challenge in his eyes.

I smirked, knowing full well what he meant. In the past, whenever we'd gone out riding, he had challenged me to a race as soon as we passed the gates. Looking up, I saw the main gate was up ahead, and as soon as we passed underneath it, we spurred our horses into a gallop. I whooped in sheer delight, hovering just above the saddle, my knees pressed firmly against the saddle flap. The wind whistled passed my face, its icy tendrils small knives against my skin, cutting and biting.

Cooped up at the palace as I was, forced into political conversations and philosophical debates I didn't much care to have, I felt numb. The only time things felt right, was when I was training out on the fields, but although I loved doing it, most of the times I was going through the motions because I had to.

Now, for the first time in a while, I felt alive.

Evan's hair, usually braided down his back, now trailed behind him like a snow white banner, and the worry which had been etched on his face for the past few days was momentarily erased. He was grinning like a madman, guiding Hadiyah expertly down the path with his knees, until he pulled in her reins to slow her down. I did the same with Orion and had him trot up to her side.

"Are you going to tell me the reason for this surprise?" I asked at length, my eyes taking in the ocean's view ahead.

As much as I loved this surprise, I knew Evan well enough to know he did nothing without reason, and him apologising for what his fiancée did wasn't a good one. We both knew what Nathaïr was like, and we both knew my brother hadn't been at fault. So if that wasn't the issue, what was?

Evan regarded me with his head slightly tilted, his words startling me from my reverie. "Why do you think there is one?"

"Oh, I don't know." I rolled my eyes. "Because it will annoy at least five people in a matter of seconds when they find out I'm gone, and your spontaneity usually ends the moment you step out of bed. Plus, you're not one to go against the rules, so there has to be a really good reason for you to do this."

Evan smirked, threading his hand through his dishevelled hair. "What if I told you *I* had to get out of the palace for a change?"

"I'd say I can't blame you."

The miserable look on his face wrenched my heart, yet it evaporated as quickly as it had appeared when he composed his features to perfection.

"About last night," he began, shaking his head, "I'm sorry for what happened."

"You're not the one who's supposed to apologise," I said with a shrug. "We know what she's like."

The hand on the reins tightened into a fist and he closed his eyes, swallowing hard. I could see the muscles in his jaw work as if he was fighting off some unwanted emotions. When he looked back at me, the pain in his eyes was paramount.

"I'm afraid, sis," he said. "Of all the things I've done in my life, this is the one that scares me the most."

"Why?"

"Because she's unpredictable. Marrying her will be the most stupid mistake I'll make in my entire life."

I shrugged. "Then don't. Call it off."

"And then what, *shareye?*" He rubbed his face. "Have Eamryel marry you?"

"If that's what it takes."

Evan shook his head slowly. "No, I couldn't do that to you. It's my duty to—"

"Duty be damned Ev! Not everything has to be done because someone tells you to do it. You're allowed your own life and happiness."

He snorted. "You keep forgetting a tiny detail in that train of thought."

I watched him unimpressed, folding my arms. "Which is?"

"We're royalty," he said. "We don't get to choose."

"Nonsense."

Evan flashed me a humourless smile. If we'd ever get to agree on that topic, the stars would fall out of the sky permanently.

"Did you bribe the guards?" I asked at length, looking at him.

"I may have asked them to look the other way,"

I laughed. "There now, don't go all crazy."

As he smirked at me all mirth gradually left his expression as it turned into one of misery instead. All colour, as much as he had any, drained from his face, and his eyes drooped and looked unfocused. I couldn't be entirely sure, but he appeared to be shivering, as if he was spiking a fever.

"Ev? Are you all right?" I asked, catching the worried tone in my voice. What was happening?

"Not sure." He looked back at me just before his eyes rolled away and he slumped forward over Hadiyah's neck, falling to the ground unconsciously.

"Ev!"

I jumped off of Orion and skidded over to him, dropping to my knees at his side. With difficulty I turned him on his back, brushing his hair off his face. My hand came up bloodied. Upon closer inspection, I found a clean cut on his forehead, caused by something sharp from the looks of it. It hadn't been there before, so I assumed he'd hit something on the way down.

I rose to my feet and rummaged through his saddlebags, but as I feared, he hadn't brought any bandages. Taking Azra's small knife with trembling hands, I tore a piece off my sleeve, dabbing the blood away as best as I could while contemplating our precarious situation.

While Orion or Hadiyah could carry the both of us easily, getting his deadweight body on top of either of them would be a challenge. I knew I wasn't strong enough to lift him. We were stranded, unless one of the horses lay down so I could place my brother onto its back.

Resting my hand on his forehead, he was so hot it felt as if I'd stuck my hand in a fire and was deliberately keeping it there. His chest rose and fell with rapid breaths, soft moans escaping his lips as if he was in pain, and I realised I couldn't move him. I tucked a lock of hair behind my ear, shocked at how much I was shaking. My heart began racing as it occurred to me I had no idea what to do.

We were at least half a morning's ride away from the city, so even if I got him on horseback, it would be an uncomfortable ride, not to mention dangerous. The best thing I could do now was to get us all to safety and try to get his fever down somehow, in the hope someone would start missing us.

"Hang in there," I murmured, placing a kiss on his brow. "I need you here."

By Aeson, lord of medicine, keep him safe.

I rose to my feet, and placed my hands on my hips, looking around to survey our surroundings. We had arrived at the edge of the *Hahran Woods*, which was both a blessing and a curse as it was renowned for its dangerous wildlife. Although it would provide us with a safe cover from the elements, it also made us vulnerable to whatever was lurking in its depths. Regardless, I had to find a place which would keep us safe and dry without going too deep into the forest.

I stared at Evan lying half-conscious on the ground, my chest constricting as the ramifications of our plight came crashing down on me. Although the army would lose one of their *Zheràn* if Evan died, it wouldn't be detrimental to Ilvanna. If I died, it was another matter entirely, which is why Mother rather kept me in the palace.

"By *Vehda*, lady of the hunt," I muttered, "you couldn't have complicated things more had you tried, brother."

I took off my cloak, immediately regretting my decision as the cold wind bit my skin, and tucked it around my brother's shoulders and hips. He might not be heir to a throne, but I'd be damned if I let my brother die. Swallowing hard, I took another look at him and steeled my resolve. I had to find us a safe place, so against my better judgment, I started walking away from him, deeper into the forest, trying to keep the horses in sight. After what felt like hour, my eye fell on a small cave up ahead. Looking back, I realised I had no clear sight on Evan or the horses anymore, and I could feel my chest tighten in response, my breathing picking up speed. My eyes darted back to the small cave. From this distance, I couldn't see how deep it was, or if it would provide any cover at all, but that was where we had to be safe.

I made my way back to Evan and the horses, ducking under branches, trying not to get caught on any of them. I was glad to find both the horses and Evan were still where I had left them. Kneeling down, I hooked my arms under his armpits, and pulled him towards the hideout I'd seen, grunting and cursing him in the old- and new tongue.

"Gods Ev," I muttered. "The least you could've done was skip a few breakfasts."

I half expected him to reply, so when he didn't, a sharp pain knifed its way through my chest, settling in the pit of my stomach.

"Come on brother," I pleaded, breathing heavily from exertion. "Say something. Anything. I'll even go into the discussion of duty and honour with you. Just... wake up."

Still, he didn't reply.

By the Gods, Ev, don't do this to me, whatever's wrong, snap out of it. I need you. I will always need you.

I didn't know what to do. If it had been a matter of outrunning my guards, I'd have come up with a dozen ways out already, but this—this was something else entirely.

I DON'T KNOW how long it took me to get Evan to our hideout, but by the time I did, I was exhausted, and my shirt, soaked with sweat, clung uncomfortably to my back. After having made my brother as comfortable as possible, I went back to get the horses. They didn't like having to go off the trail, pulling at their reins while whinnying and snorting, but I didn't want to leave them at the edge of the forest either. If Evan started feeling better throughout the night, we could leave first thing in the morning, provided we survived and didn't become a wolf's meal.

I tethered the horses close to our hideout, which had turned out to be nothing more than an overhanging rock, before I went looking for firewood. Despite it still being light out, and nobody anywhere around, I stuck close to Ev and the horses, gathering as much wood as I could carry.

It had been a long time since I'd built a fire. Father had still been alive and at my side, telling me patiently how to get it started, even after I screwed up for the umpteenth time. I could hear his voice in my memory, but his words were jumbled and incoherent. Why couldn't I remember?

The first few tries failed, and every time it did, my chest constricted. I could swear the rustling in the undergrowth became louder each time, and I could just feel eyes boring into my back. It would only be a matter of seconds now before a wolf launched itself at me and tore out my throat. I tried again, and again, but no matter how fast I spun the twig between my hands, nothing happened. I glanced over at Evan, trembling heavily underneath my cloak. If I didn't get this fire going fast… The alternative didn't bear thinking about, so I set to kindling the fire with new-found strength and determination. I rubbed the twig between my hands, remembering to move them up and down rather than keep them in the same position.

"Please," I murmured, my heart racing in my chest, "catch fire. Come on."

By now, my hands were sore and there was no doubt in my

mind I'd have several blisters come nightfall, but I didn't care. I had to get this fire going to get Evan warm and hopefully keep the night critters at bay. I didn't relish the thought of becoming wolf bait. Or worse.

I'd heard there had been sightings of bears too.

The moment the kindling caught fire, I whooped with delight, quickly moving to add wood. The fire roared to life in a matter of moments. Sitting back on my heels, I admired my handiwork, feeling my frayed nerves settle somewhat.

Turning to Evan, I found he was looking at me, glassy eyes shifting and unfocused.

"Hey there handsome," I murmured, untangling him from my cloak.

Placing my hand against his cheek, I realised he was still burning up. I had to get his fever down somehow.

"All right big guy," I said, looking him over. "Time to strip."

He murmured something, but I couldn't catch what it was. I undid his leather jerkin, my fingers stiff and unwilling to cooperate due to the growing cold and blisters from starting a fire. I knew this was the easiest part. Getting his arms out would be more difficult. As I turned him on his side and got his left arm out, I noticed how shallow his breathing was.

Please Xiomara, lady of life, please let him live. I'll do anything if you'll just keep him alive.

With trembling hands, I got his other arm out. So far, so good.

His shirt was another matter entirely.

After trying several ways to get him out of it, I opted for the easiest one and cut it open at the front. His shirt was soaked through already, so I tore it where I could to get it away from him. Once he was stripped, I sat down next to him, my back against the wall protecting us from the worst of the cold. I picked up a stick to stoke the fire, unease settling in my bones as my mind wandered off to the night ahead. I rested my other hand on Evan's shoulder so he knew I was there.

BEAUTIFUL HUES of purple and pink showed through the canopy, heralding nightfall, and with it the awakening of the night creatures. I smiled at the thought something as beautiful as the night sky could hold dangers beyond our wildest dreams. Neither howling wolves and scurrying rodents, nor the horses' nervous moving, did anything to improve my fear. It was what it was though, and I'd just have to find a way for us to survive till morning.

I placed my hand on my brother's neck to check his temperature, and although he was still hot to the touch, it wasn't as bad as before. If only I knew what had caused this, I could do more to help him. Not that I was a healer, but I remembered Master Dahryen telling Mother to have us wear as little as possible whenever we had a fever. I didn't want my brother to freeze to death either. He still hadn't woken up—just spoken to me in his fever dreams, and even then I wasn't sure he'd been talking to me.

He kept murmuring apologies.

Evan never apologised.

I leaned forward carefully, placing extra wood on the fire to keep it going. By then it was getting rather cold, so I wrapped Evan firmly in my cloak while I pulled on his leather jerkin. It would stave off the worst of the cold at least, even though it was way too big for me. Crawling a little closer to the fire, I rubbed my hands on my thighs, and held them up. My stomach was growling in protest, but there was only half a loaf of bread left, and I'd rather have something in case we'd be out here longer than I hoped.

Vehda keep us safe.

My gaze returned to the night sky, my thoughts wandering off to Tal's dismissal the night before, and how disappointed I'd felt when he'd left. I could have used some company.

Orion's sudden whinny startled me back from my reverie. As I rose to my feet, a low growl sounded up from the darkness, setting my heart to a right frenzy. *Gods no.* I slowly turned toward the origin of the sound, and next thing I knew things were happening all at once. Orion and Hadiyah both screamed as the growls of wolves echoed around us, their eyes reflecting the firelight. Grabbing a stick from the fire, I swung it in front of myself and Evan to keep the wolves at bay. Although they didn't dare come closer to the fire, they did stalk closer to the horses, who were gearing up into a right frenzy. They'd be wolf meat if I did nothing now, but I didn't want to leave Evan either.

My eyes darted from my brother to the horses, my breathing coming hard and fast. If I'd choose him, the horses would be a meal—if I went for the horses, I risked Evan's life. Torn between keeping him safe, or free the horses, my eyes swept across our hideout, settling on the fire. It wouldn't be the best solution, but it might keep him safe. I kicked several logs off of the fire and around my brother, glad the ground was just dirt, while praying to the Gods it was enough for the wolves to leave him alone until I returned to his side. With a battle cry tearing from my lips, brandishing a burning stick like a sword, I lunged at the wolves closest to the horses. The sudden action in combination with the fire scared them off.

All except one.

I went down to the ground face first when he jumped on my back. The burning stick dropped from my hand because of the sudden impact and fell down on the ground close to the horses. It spooked them so badly, they reared, pulled their reins free, and fled. The thuds of their hooves disappeared into the dark night.

We were alone.

My only hope was them finding their way home, alarming Haerlyon, or maybe Tal. At this point they could warn Nathaïr for all I cared, as long as someone would come for us.

What if I can't win? What if the wolves get Evan, or me? What if they're too late?

I quickly turned on my back as a low growl in my ear set my heart racing in my chest, and I was barely in time to pull up my arms and legs to keep the wolf from tearing out my throat. *By the Gods, that smell.* Its breath was so nauseating, my sides clenched tight, ready to throw out the contents of my stomach, but all thoughts of that ceased when it grabbed my arm. A scream loud enough to awaken the dead tore from my lips, and in pure survival instinct, I kicked the wolf off of me.

The first time.

It attacked again.

Although I scrambled out of the way, the wolf was faster, and it clamped its jaw around my leg. A hot, fiery pain shot through my body as teeth sunk into my flesh. I kicked its snout repeatedly with my other foot, as hard as I could, until it finally let go with a growl so low, I could feel it rumble in my chest. Getting up would be pointless—the wolf would be faster no matter what I tried.

I had to kill it.

It crouched low to prepare for an attack, and I resisted the urge to curl up in a ball so it couldn't grab me again. Slowly, I pulled up my knee, and slipped the little knife into my hand. It was all I had, and I had to make it count. The moment I moved again, it attacked.

I threw up my arm.

If there were words to describe the sensation going through me as its jaw clamped shut around my arm, I would have used them. Time slowed down, stars danced in my vision, and a sickening feeling took up residence in my stomach. If I hadn't already been lying on the ground, I was sure it would have risen to meet me. I jabbed the small knife into the wolf's neck at the same time as it bit into my arm, driving it home as deep as I could.

Several times.

A warm, sticky substance gushed over my hand. The scent of blood combined with its foul breath permeated my senses as the wolf dropped on top of me. I heard it wheeze and felt it spasm as it lay dying. A disgusted feeling crept up on me, until the full scope of the situation hit me, and I freaked out. Screaming and kicking, I tossed the carcass off of me, and scooted away from it until I felt something solid in my back, all the while ignoring the fiery pain in my leg.

The other wolves had retreated, but I could still hear them howling in the distance. My body was growing heavier by the minute, my heart was racing in my chest, and my arm and leg were on fire. I wanted nothing more than to sleep. I hopped over to Evan, threw the stick back onto the fire, along with some extra wood, and sat down next to him, grunting as my leg gave way and I hit my back against the wall.

This was going to be a long night.

Noticing I was trembling, I lay a hand on Evan's shoulder seeking comfort. Drawing air into my lungs was the hardest task I'd had to do in a while, and my ribs and back felt bruised to the point it had me wonder if they were broken.

Evan suddenly lay his hand on mine, slowly but firmly, sending my heart into a new frenzy.

"Oh thank the Gods," I breathed out. "You're alive."

He was shivering as much as I was, so I crawled against him and pulled the cloak around both of us. If the wolves wanted us, they could have us— we weren't in any shape to fight again. I'd rather die in the arms of my brother near a warm fire than on my own in a cold bed, anyway.

THE SOUND of baying dogs triggered the flight response in me. I wanted to run, to get away from here as fast as possible, until I remembered my brother. Fighting the urge to flee, I sat up in a crouch ready to protect Evan with my life. My leg immediately gave way, and I fell forward on my knees. Only then did I notice my surroundings, even though they were still rather blurry. The remnants of the fire were within reach, I could feel the ashes under my hands, and Evan was behind me, I could feel him there, but why did I feel so weak?

I remembered the fight with the wolves, and how the wolf had grabbed me, but I had sustained no other injuries. It couldn't be that, could it?

"*Tarien!*"

"Evan!" a familiar voice shouted.

A second voice added. "Shal!"

Several people were shouting our names, so I got up, to show them we were here. The dogs were getting closer—their baying caused a painful ringing in my ear which in turn resonated in my head.

"Gods, be quiet," I muttered. "Fleabags."

Someone yelled my name again, closer this time, and moments later, knelt in front of me, gathering me in a pair of strong arms. More voices came closer—most of them sounded worried. Focusing on the one holding me, I realised it was Talnovar, and the lines etched into his features told me he was more than worried. I brought up a hand to trace them, surprised at the amount of blood on my fingers.

I frowned, looking cross-eyed.

"I don't think I feel too well," I murmured, "but I'm glad you found us."

Talnovar half-laughed, half-choked. "Gods Sh— *Tarien*. You gave us a proper fright."

"Master Evan's burning up too," Xaresh said from somewhere behind me.

83

I was wondering why he said too. I didn't have a fever, did I?

I turned my head to look at Xaresh and suddenly burst out in a fit of giggles. "You both look so weird today."

Talnovar lifted me in his arms with a grunt and rose to his feet. They were conversing, but I couldn't quite make out the words, and the longer they spoke, the further away they were. I shrugged, or thought I did, and drifted off. With them here, we'd be safe. I could let go.

Don't leave me.

THE SOUND OF VOICES, or rather the urgency in them, brought me back to my senses. Something was hammering away on the inside of my head, and my throat felt like I'd been eating sand for the past week. I coughed, wincing at the sharp pain lancing through my chest. When I tried to sit up, I found out the hard way my arm was unwilling to hold my weight.

It felt numb.

I shut my eyes tight, and opened them again, hoping my vision would stop swaying and the sick feeling would subside. Someone, I think it was Tal, was pacing up and down at the end of my bed taking large, firm strides. Xaresh sat on the bed next to me, his hands deftly working on something I couldn't quite make out, but he was completely focused on it.

Evan lay in the bed on my other side, still asleep, still extremely pale, but the sickly sheen he'd had before was gone. Beyond his bed, several council members were arguing in hushed voices with a healer I didn't recognise. He was young, but the look on his face was a clear sign he wasn't impressed with what they were telling him. My gaze returned to my brother and continued to Tal and Xaresh.

"You'd better not be mourning me," I murmured.

Xaresh's head shot up in surprise. His eyes were bloodshot,

and the light tremor in his body showed he hadn't had a proper rest in a while. Tal stopped mid-pace, turning to face me.

"You two look worse than I'm feeling," I said, trying to prop myself up against the pillow, determined to do it myself.

Xaresh moved quickly to help me, treating me as if I were a fragile doll. Although I rolled my eyes, I was grateful for his help when I noticed I couldn't properly use my leg to push myself up. Talnovar stood at the end of my bed, watching me with a colourful array of expressions crossing his usually impassive features. He looked haggard and worn, the dark circles under his eyes testimony he had slept little. He opened his mouth to say something, but closed it again, raking his fingers through his hair while shuffling from one foot to the other. It was so unlike him I stared, my head slightly tilted. Xaresh propped up the pillows behind me, fussing over me like a mother hen.

"Xaresh, stop it. You're making me nervous," I said.

He gave me an impish smile and sat down again, picking up what he'd been working on. It appeared to be a wooden animal.

Talnovar looked as if he was in pure agony, but the moment I wanted to ask what was wrong, the young healer was at my bed, half the council in tow.

"How are you feeling, *Tarien?*" he asked.

"As if I got attacked by wolves."

Xaresh snorted beside me, but said nothing. The young healer raised an eyebrow, but again, looked rather impervious.

"Any pain?"

I gave him a deadpan stare. "No, not at all, aside from the fiery sting in my leg and arm, and the persistent throb in my head, I'm peachy."

"She sounds fine," Xaresh offered.

"Yes, her wit knows no bounds," the young healer said, sarcasm dripping from his voice. "On a scale of one to ten, how much pain are you in?"

I shrugged. "I don't know. Eleven?"

A smile tugged at his lips, and there was an amused look in his eyes. It was gone the moment he turned to the council members.

"I'm afraid *I* will not allow the *Tarien* out of bed for the next few days," he said. "You must find another solution."

"We can't," Chazelle, one of the elderly council members, said. "She's needed."

Talnovar stepped forward. "She's also recovering like everyone else."

Everyone else?

"At least she's awake," Nya added.

Talnovar crossed his arms in front of his chest as if he needed to physically keep them from me. Xaresh had quietly walked up to Tal, placing a hand on his shoulder, but he shrugged it off. Was this why he was angry?

"She's not going anywhere," he insisted. "End of story."

Chazelle pulled herself up to her full height, barely reaching his shoulders. "This country needs to be run."

"Isn't that what you are for?" he asked.

"We don't have the power to make certain decisions," Chazelle huffed. "She does."

I cleared my throat. "*She* is also right here and very much capable of hearing you. So, who will tell me what in all the Gods' names is going on?"

Everyone turned to me. Talnovar pinched the bridge of his nose, eyes closed, the look on his face nigh to pleading. Both Chazelle and Nya looked uncomfortable, and the other council members had lost their voices. It was Xaresh who offered an explanation.

"Everyone has fallen ill, *Tarien*," he said. "Your mother, your brothers. Even your aunt, Nathaïr and Mehrean. Everyone."

So not just Evan fell ill. This can't be a coincidence.

"Clearly not everyone," I commented drily, "or you wouldn't be standing here arguing about me."

"With the threats at the border, *Tarien*," Chazelle spoke up, "we cannot afford having no one on the throne. We need someone who can make decisions."

I snorted. "And you're looking at me for that?"

Talnovar made a strangled noise in the back of his throat and turned away, fists balled at his sides, body shaking. From the familiar tic in his jaw I could tell he was ready to punch something, or someone. The young healer murmured something in his ear, and he nodded. The torn expression on his face when he looked at me went through me like a knife, and when he turned on his heel and walked away, an uncomfortable feeling settled in my stomach.

"If there was another way," Chazelle said, "we'd do it, but as it is, you're the only one we can turn to."

I closed my eyes and rubbed my forehead, grimacing a little at the pain it caused in my arm, cursing the wolf in my mind for grabbing the predominant one. Breathing in, I looked at the young healer, realising I didn't even know his name.

"How much do you reckon I can take?"

He shrugged. "Based on your stamina, if you rest enough and don't walk too much, I'd say you'd be able to manage for a few days. Beyond that, it's anyone's guess."

"What are our odds if I do not step up?" I asked, looking at Chazelle.

She shrugged. It was Leyahl, one of our *Zheràn*, or general, who stepped forward, bowing slightly.

"If I were our enemy, *Tarien*," he said, "I'd attack when we're weakest, which I would say is right about now."

"I was afraid you would say that." I sighed.

My eyes darted over to Evan who still hadn't woken up despite everything going on around him. I hadn't saved his life to possibly lose it in a war I might prevent as long as I did what I had to do. It reminded me of our discussion about duty before he collapsed. The irony wasn't lost on me.

"Give me some time to get ready," I said, and frowned. "How long have I been out for?"

"Less than a day," the young healer said. "It's mid-afternoon."

I nodded. "Have everyone assembled in the throne room come nightfall. I'll be there."

The council members bowed, and took their leave one by one, until only Chazelle was left, her hands clasped demurely in front of her. Xaresh had taken up position on the bed next to me, straight-backed and solemn faced. The frown on Chazelle's face showed more than she was letting on to.

"*Tarien*," she said. "There is more."

"What do you mean?"

"The reason all fell ill is poison," she continued, looking at me. "Some are whispering how it is odd that you didn't."

I frowned. "What are they whispering *exactly*?"

She avoided my gaze. "That you poisoned them."

I stared at Chazelle, only to burst out laughing a moment later. It probably wasn't the best response considering the gravity of the situation, but it was so outrageous I couldn't help it.

"This is the best thing I've heard in a while." I hiccoughed with laughter. "Whoever in their right mind would accuse me of that?"

Chazelle looked away, fumbling with her hands. She knew who it was.

"Out with it Chazelle," I said. "Unless you want me to report this to Mother once she is well again.

"*Tarien*, really," she began, looking at me, "it doesn't matter who did, most people do not believe the lie."

I sat up, straightening my back, biting back the pain. "But it *does* matter, Chazelle. Whoever is spreading the lies is on the brink of committing treason. They'd be well reminded of that fact."

Chazelle paled at my words, bowed deeply and made a hasty retreat. Xaresh shook his head slowly, a frown on his face.

"You've got an opinion too?" I asked somewhat annoyed, slumping back against the pillows.

"Many in fact, *Tarien*, but none of them matter right now."

Rubbing my temples, I looked at him, resisting the urge to laugh, only because I had no idea what to do with this situation.

"What's wrong with Talnovar?"

Xaresh shrugged. "I think it upset him the Council pushed through. They've been at it from the moment you returned."

"This should be fun," I muttered, running a hand through my hair.

The young healer cleared his throat, catching our attention. The stern look on his face made me roll my eyes.

"I'm not a willing participant in this decision, *Tarien*," he began, "but I understand that at times, duty comes first. I'd rather have you in bed for the next week, resting and healing, but as it is, I strongly advise you to take as much rest as you can. Let people come to you."

"I like your way of thinking," I said, "but who are you again?"

He smirked. "Soren's the name. I've taken up Master Dahryen's position. He couldn't continue."

I wasn't sad to see the old man with his prodding and poking go, but I wasn't sure what to make of Soren either.

"So," I began, biting my lip, "how bad is it?"

"In all truth? It surprised me to find you still alive and in one piece."

I winced. "That bad?"

"You'll be scarred for life," he replied. "But at least the wolf didn't tear off your flesh. You've been very lucky."

"Luck had nothing to do with it," I muttered, rubbing my arm in memory. "How's Evan?"

"Your unconventional way of cooling him down probably

saved his life," Soren said, "but I don't know what damage the poison has done to his body."

I nodded slowly. "How about the others?"

Soren glanced at Xaresh.

"She deserves to know the truth," he said with a shrug.

Soren breathed in deeply and nodded. "Some are worse off than others."

"That's not an answer," I said. "What aren't you telling me?"

"Only your mother and brothers haven't woken up yet," he said, shuffling from one foot to the other. "The others have. They're already doing better."

I pursed my lips in thought. "When did everyone fall ill?"

"Your mother fell ill during the night," he said. "The others throughout the day, I think."

"So whoever is behind this targeted Mother and my brothers. Whatever for?"

Neither men had an answer for me. Running a hand through my hair, I regarded my surroundings for a brief moment.

"Well then," I said with a deep sigh. "Best get ready to run a country."

CHAPTER 5

A cacophony of sound thundered from the throne room. I could hear it from the antechamber where I was waiting to address the people of my realm. Biting my lip, I sat rocking back and forth, nervously twisting the webbed bracelet around my healthy arm. My heart was racing, and I noticed the room was spinning a bit. At least the pain in both my arm and leg were manageable after the concoction Soren had given me.

I exhaled slowly to calm my nerves.

"You don't have to do this," Talnovar murmured from my side.

I smiled faintly. "Yes. I do."

For the first time, I understood exactly what Evan always meant with us having no choice in certain matters. If I made the one easiest for me, it would be detrimental to many people. I could make it, but it wouldn't be fair.

Talnovar squeezed my shoulder gently, which sent a tingling sensation down my spine. It felt… strange. Good… but strange. I knew he would be there. Xaresh and the others were spread out across the throne room together with some of Leyahl's men, easing my nerves at least somewhat.

If anything happens, they'll be there. If anyone tries to dispose of me now, whether by ranged attack or up close, I'm sure they'll be ahead of things. They have to be.

This meeting was the perfect opportunity to assault me and take down every single member of the Royal House.

The thought alone made me nervous.

"Are you ready, *Tarien?*" Chazelle asked.

"Not even close," I murmured.

It felt like slipping from a branch and falling down at breakneck speed, my heart in my throat knowing the ground is coming closer. That feeling was nothing compared to how I felt now.

She smiled gently. "They're waiting for you."

The branch snapped under my weight, dropping me to my death.

Carefully I rose to my feet, and with support from Talnovar, hobbled into the throne room, doing my best to keep my head up high, greeting people with a smile as I passed them. Whispers rose around us, but they sounded curious rather than spiteful like they usually did. Some murmured it was good to see me, and others wished me a quick recovery. It surprised me until I realised I was now the one they had to please to get what they wanted.

Once we got to the dais, Talnovar and Xaresh helped me by lifting me up. Stairs had proven to be an issue with my leg. With careful, deliberate steps I walked over to the throne, and swallowed hard. I wasn't supposed to sit there, not yet. My throat tightened as my mind envisioned Mother sitting there in her official regalia. Sitting down on the throne made me feel like an impostor—she wasn't gone yet. A gentle hand on my arm made me turn around, my eyes quickly meeting Talnovar's.

He gave me a curt nod—the pain I'd seen in his eyes earlier still present.

"I'm fine," I said in a voice audible for him alone.

I wasn't sure I was, and I wasn't sure he believed me. He inclined his head and stepped behind me, clasping his arms behind his back. People fell silent and looked at me when I turned in their direction, their penetrating stares making me feel as if I was naked. The thought did nothing to help against the nerves. When I opened my mouth to speak, and nothing came out, my throat tightened and my palms became clammy. I refrained from rubbing them down my thighs by keeping them alongside my body. I swallowed away the lump in my throat. I could feel the tension in my shoulders and the hair in the back of my neck stood on end.

What would Mother do?

Give them the illusion of looking at them, but instead look over their heads. They will never notice, and it will make speaking easier. Stand here, shareye.

She had placed me right where I was now, pulled my shoulders back, and lifted my chin.

Now speak.

"*Irà* and *Irìn*." My voice rang out surprisingly clearly. "Thank you for coming here on such short notice."

People murmured amongst themselves, so I waited for their silence like Mother would.

"As some of you may have heard, *Tari* Arayda has succumbed to an illness," I continued. "During such time as she needs to recover, I will oversee all her tasks and obligations. If you have any concerns, you are welcome to discuss them with me during the appointed time. I will, however, have to ask for your patience and your willingness to come and see me."

The murmurs became louder now, and I had to raise my hand for silence.

"Every and all business will go through me. If it doesn't, be prepared to defend your choices."

At this, voices rose to a tumultuous, raucous sound. People spoke loudly or even yelled, the noise rising in a crescendo of garbled communication. It was funny to see how they didn't seem to realise this had the opposite effect.

"What about appointments?" someone yelled.

"They will be kept," I replied.

Another one spoke up. "And what if I have a problem with somebody?"

I smiled. "Then we'll settle it."

"Do you even know how to, *Tarien?*" someone else asked.

People started murmuring again, discussing the question amongst themselves. I breathed in deeply, looking for the person who had spoken. It was a young lord, Evan's age maybe, surrounded by a few other young lords, all differing in age. The smug look on his face told me he was showing off. Looking him over, I noticed the *araîth* snaking around his wrist, marking him of the Lahryen household. I knew his father was an *Anahràn* in the army, and a loyal man to the throne, which made his remark all the more surprising.

"Are you questioning my authority, Amaris?" I asked calmly.

He clasped his hands behind his back, his chin lifted ever so slightly. "Not your authority, merely your ability."

Talnovar tensed beside me—Xaresh made to step forward. I held both back with a slight gesture of my hand. If they fought my battle now, nobody would ever take me seriously.

"I see," I replied thoughtfully. "Would you care to elaborate?"

"You've never ruled a country before." He waved his hand dismissively. "What makes you think you can do it?"

I rubbed my chin, looking thoughtful. "Ah, I see."

Around him, people looked amused and here and there I could hear a chuckle. While his bravado might have impressed his friends, it did nothing for others.

"Just a quick question. When was the last time you ruled a country?"

Amaris crossed his arms in front of him, eyes blazing with arrogance. "That's not the point."

"Isn't it?" I mused. "All right. You are absolutely right in saying I have never ruled a country before, and between you and me, I'd be more than happy to leave that to our *Tari* for at least two hundred more years and more, but you know, she had to get ill."

I shrugged with a half-smile on my face, pacing up and down the dais with carefully placed baby-steps, putting as little weight on the injured leg as possible. Clasping my hands behind my back, I turned to the crowd, my eyes zeroing in on Amaris.

"I think she did it on purpose," I continued, "getting ill I mean, just so I could take over. I mean, all I've done for the past hundred years or so is getting ready for this moment. But... what's a hundred plus years of extensive training and education?"

Amaris' cheeks turned red as a beet, and the longer I stared at him, the more he bowed his head.

"I'm not mad at you," I said. 'It's a fair question all-in-all. I just think, considering the circumstances, you'd have been wise to rephrase your question and show me the proper courtesy, instead of showing off to your petty little friends."

He mumbled something, but he was too far away for me to hear. People around him snorted, and voices resounded throughout the hall. It was now or never.

"For your lack of respect," I said, "and your poor attempt at treason, I think a night in prison will do. Guards?"

The throne room fell silent when the guards made their way through the crowd and escorted Amaris out. His father might not be happy with my decision, although I guessed upon hearing what had happened, his son would be better off in jail for the night. Before the crowd could burst out into anything, I turned back to them and spoke loudly and clearly.

"I realise you have no reason to trust an untried *Tarien*," I said, "but no *Tari* in our history ever descended the throne knowing fully what was awaiting her. I will do the best I can, considering the circumstances, and that's all I can do. If you think you cannot deal with this, you are more than welcome to leave the palace. Permanently."

The throne room remained silent for a moment longer, then someone shouted 'to our *Tarien*', and the rest followed suit.

I inclined my head and indicated to Tal and Xaresh it was time to go. The pain in my leg became more excruciating by the second, and my head was about to explode. Once back in the antechamber, I flopped down in a chair, clenching and unclenching my fist as I tried not to scream while writhing in pain.

A sudden dizziness overpowered me, and I would have slumped over had hands against my shoulders not kept me upright.

"Easy there," Tal muttered, looking none too pleased.

He was kneeling in front of me, holding me back in my chair. I tried to focus on him, but it was hard—the room just wouldn't stop spinning.

"There's two of you." I chuckled. "And you look so—"

Tal smirked. "Let's not embarrass yourself *Tarien*."

Strong hands around my leg sent shivers down my spine in a not altogether unpleasant way. Next thing I knew, Tal picked me up.

"Let's get you to Soren," he murmured.

I pouted. "I don't want to."

He smiled at me, his eyes sparkling, but as soon as we were out of the antechamber, his lips pressed together in a thin line, and his body tensed up underneath me.

What was going on with him?

THE INFIRMARY WAS quiet this time around. Talnovar placed me back on the bed I had previously occupied, looking drained and annoyed, deep lines on his face testimony to that fact. He promptly sat down on the bed next to mine, running both hands through his hair, letting out a deep breath. His shoulders were hunched, and he looked anywhere but at me.

It was so strange seeing him like this.

"Tal?"

He looked up surprised, an attempt of a smile on his lips, a weary look on his face. I realised I'd never called him Tal to his face before.

"Yeah?"

I furrowed my brow. "Are you all right?"

"Just tired," he said.

"Liar."

"Pot and kettle." He smirked. "Nothing to worry your pretty little head about."

"As if seeing my *Anahràn* on the brink of a nervous breakdown doesn't worry me," I said with a derisive snort.

He stared at me flatly. I sighed, closing my eyes.

"I wish you'd just yell at me," I said at length.

Tal looked at me in surprise. "Why?"

I shrugged. "Because it's better than whatever brooding mood you're in now. I can deal with you yelling at me."

"You're not the one I want to yell at," he murmured, balling his fist.

His eyes returned to mine as he leaned forward, tucking a wayward strand of hair behind my ear. His hand lingered a second longer than was appropriate, before he pulled back, looking away. I released my breath in a low puff, not realising I'd been holding it.

"You need some rest." He rose to his feet. "You'll need all your strength tomorrow."

He turned away from me while rubbing the back of his neck, sighed and made for the door. It was clear he was hiding something, evading my questions the way he did, but I would not press him. The last person I wanted to lose was him.

A sudden commotion at the door drew my attention, stopping Tal short. Several council members were trying to get passed Xaresh who had literally parked himself in the door opening, arms crossed.

"We have to see the *Tarien*," Chazelle demanded.

"She needs to rest," Xaresh said. "You can come back tomorrow."

"It's urgent," she added.

Xaresh grunted and let only one person through. Tal stepped aside but stayed close, a calculated look back in his eyes. That look eased me. Chazelle walked up to me, shoulders squared, but her eyes were moving skittishly.

"That was an excellent speech, *Tarien*," she said, fidgeting with a ring.

"But?" I asked, refraining from rolling my eyes.

She frowned. "Was the show with the Lahryen lord necessary?"

Tal shifted his weight behind her, narrowing his eyes. I propped myself up on my elbows, grimacing at the pressure on my arm.

"If I hadn't," I explained, "nobody would have taken me seriously ever again."

"But a night in jail? It's humiliating," she protested.

I arched a brow. "As if calling me out like he did wasn't? He should have thought of that before he opened his mouth. What do you think would have happened if people had found merit in his words? He could have riled up the entire throne room and ended my reign before it even started. He was disrespectful, and his words bordered on the line of treason. I needed to make an example of him." Carefully I lay down again, gritting my teeth. "Besides, one night won't kill him. If anything, it'll teach him some manners."

"What about his father?" Chazelle asked, a light frown on her face.

Tal snorted. "The kid will be safer behind bars."

"Very well," she sighed, shaking her head.

I knew she didn't approve of my decision, but she wouldn't question me again.

"What was the urgency?" Tal asked, leaning back against the wall.

Chazelle glared at him before turning back to me. "There has been news from *Ohzheràn* Imradien. More forces are gathering at the borders, although they appear to be making no move to attack."

Tal stiffened at the mention of his father's name, eyes narrowing to slits.

"How many?" Evan asked softly.

We all stared at him.

"His message didn't say, *Irìn*," Chazelle replied calmly. "Shall I send a messenger?"

"No, Cerindil will keep us informed," he murmured.

"Thank you Lady Chazelle," I said. "I'll see you tomorrow."

As soon as she was out, I pushed myself up with whatever strength I had left, swinging my legs over the bed. Tal was on Evan's other side, helping him sit up.

"I had the weirdest dream." Evan yawned.

"Oh?" I said.

He stretched himself and winced, a confused look on his face as if he didn't know what made him do that. When he looked at me though, he smiled.

"You were fighting wolves." He chuckled. "Quite ferociously. I think you even killed one."

Tal and I exchanged glances, and I smiled, stroking some hair out of his face. His skin was still warm to touch, but not as ridiculously hot as the night before.

"Ev," I began, "what's the last thing you remember?"

He tilted his head, looking at me. "I think we went out riding?"

I just nodded.

The look on his face as he tried to remember what had happened after was painful to watch. He just didn't seem to be able to come up with anything.

"What did you dream?" Tal asked.

"I fell off my horse and hit my head," Evan replied quickly. "I dreamt we were in a forest—Shal found us a place to stay and built a fire. She fought wolves, and she fell asleep next to me. I don't really remember much after that."

Both of us kept smiling at him. I didn't have the guts to tell him that was exactly what had happened. Knowing Ev, he wouldn't forgive himself for bringing me in danger.

"I'm glad I killed that wolf," I said, placing a kiss on his cheek. "How are you feeling otherwise?"

"Weak," he muttered. "Sick, really."

"You just rest, all right? You'll be up and about in no time," I murmured.

Evan nodded, stifling another yawn. He made himself comfortable on his side and was out again within seconds. I pulled the blankets up to his shoulders and sat back on my bed, hissing at the pain, doing my best not to curse.

"You should heed your own advice," Tal muttered as he helped me lie down. "Rest. We'll be outside."

"You could use some sleep too."

He smiled. "We'll sleep in turns."

"Liar."

Tal smiled again, and for a moment there was an amused look in his eyes.

He left the infirmary in long strides.

I SPENT most of next morning visiting those who had fallen ill. Soren had been adamant, almost refusing to let me go because I was in so much pain, but after enough cajoling and a proper drink of whatever concoction he gave me, he allowed me to leave. The drink had been a medicine of sorts numbing the pain for a while, and while it tasted awful, it did its job.

"Where do you want to go first, *Tarien?*" Xaresh asked.

"The training fields, knowing her," Tal snorted, looking entertained.

I rolled my eyes at him. "I want to visit Haer first, see how he's doing."

Both men nodded, following my slow progress through the corridors, offering support when needed. Although Tal was in a better mood, which was to say the brooding look had made way for the impassive one, I'd rather hear him laugh, but in the current situation, it might be too much to ask.

When I entered my brother's room, I found he was awake, propped up against a pile of pillows which made me envious. He grinned so widely upon seeing me, I could have sworn it'd split his face in half. The moment I hobbled forward though, favouring my good leg, the grin made way for a frown.

"What in all the Gods' names happened to you?" he exclaimed, eyes widening.

I shrugged. "Long story. How are you feeling?"

"As if someone hit me over the head repeatedly," he muttered, "and continued with the rest of my body."

The clattering of cups alerted me, and looking up, I saw a young guard I recognised step into the room, carrying a tray. His eyes widened upon seeing me, and his jaw went slack. Haerlyon looked as if he was about to die on the spot. I burst out laughing, motioning the young guard to come closer.

"Don't stop whatever you're doing on my account."

Both of them stared at me. I shrugged.

"What? Everyone with half a brain knows about your preferences, Haer."

"Good thing half the court has less than that then," he muttered, pulling up the blankets.

The young guard kept staring, tray all but forgotten in his hands. I rose to my feet, hopped over, and took it from him, shuffling back to the bed where I sat down, pouring both my brother and the young guard a cup.

"Drink. You look like you need it," I told both of them.

"How long have you known about my… preferences?" Haer asked, taking the cup.

The young guard took it with trembling hands, mumbling a thank you.

"Years," I said.

Haerlyon blanched and buried his face in his cup. I looked at his love-interest, who was doing his best to appear inconspicuous.

"Tiroy, right?"

He nodded in surprise. "It is, *Tarien*."

"I had not expected you to know his name." Haerlyon arched a brow.

"He's one of the guards who usually throws me an apple when I'm at the gate." I grinned. "Keeps me fed."

Tiroy turned a deadly shade of white and looked as if he'd rather be anywhere but here. I laughed again and turned to my brother.

"Don't be mad at him," I continued. "He's also the one who always tells Tal where I am."

Haerlyon grunted, staring at Tiroy.

"I'd best go see Mother." I sighed, rising to my feet.

My leg gave way, dropping me to my knees in an instant. Tiroy was at my side a second later, helping me up, while Haerlyon watched me with a wary expression in his eyes.

"Before you leave," he said, "tell me what happened?"

I stared at him, running my hand through my hair. "No time. I have to visit Mother and run this damned country."

"Shal." The tone in his voice was one of warning. "I'll come out of bed and terrorise you until you tell me."

"I'll tie you to that bed if I have to," I muttered.

He snorted. "I'm surprised you haven't been."

Rolling my eyes, I relented with a sigh. "Tal would have preferred it."

Hopping over to him, I kissed him on the cheek before limping out of his bedroom as fast as I could. Xaresh and Tal both gave me a questioning look.

"Remind me to apologise to him when we're both better," I murmured.

"What did you do?" Xaresh asked.

I smiled faintly. "I refused to tell him what happened."

"Harsh," Tal remarked drily. "Haerlyon might not forgive you for it."

"He wouldn't forgive himself if I told him the entire story either."

Tal looked at me as Xaresh took it upon himself to support me. "How so?"

"Because he knew where we were," I said. "Or at least he knew that we'd gone."

The thin lipped look on Tal's face didn't bode well, so I looked away, rubbing my neck. He sighed loudly and shook his head.

"You'll be the death of me one day, *Tarien*," he murmured, a wry smile on his lips.

Xaresh chuckled softly but refrained from saying anything.

As soon as I stepped inside Mother's bedroom, the heat hit me full in the face, nearly sending me back. The persistent smell of vomit and urine was the second slap to the face, and gagging, I made my way inside, quickly covering my nose and mouth with my sleeve. Xaresh looked like he would throw up—Talnovar had conveniently excused himself just before entering. An uneasy feeling washed over me, although I wasn't exactly sure why.

Walking over to Mother's side, one of the healers halted me. Unsurprisingly, he was wearing a mask.

"I wouldn't come too close if I were you, *Tarien*," he said. "Your mother is very ill."

I stared at him flatly. "Really? I had no idea."

Without waiting for an answer, I pushed passed him, hopping over to Mother's bed. She had the same sickly sheen on her skin as Evan had had, and when I placed my hand on her cheek, she was burning up.

"She needs to cool down," I muttered.

I remembered what Soren had said—how my unconventional way had possibly saved my brother's life.

"Douse the fire. Open the windows," I ordered. "She needs to cool down."

"*Tarien!*" the healer shrieked. "Your mother needs warmth. The sudden cold may kill her."

I drew myself up to my full height, enunciating each word as I glared at him. "Open the windows. Douse the fire."

He folded his arms in front of him. "No. With all due respect, you do not know what you're talking about. If we do that, your mother might die."

"And she *will* die if you don't follow my orders *now!*" I growled.

The healer didn't move, so I yelled for the guards, and ordered Xaresh to get Soren. Two of Mother's *Arathri* stepped inside the room, frowning.

"*Tarien?*" Rurin asked.

Rurin was Mother's *Anahràn*, and although gruff, I knew he would do anything to save her life.

"Take this man to prison," I said coldly, "for disobeying orders and the attempted murder on the *Tari*."

Maybe he just doesn't know what he's doing, like me, but I cannot have him walk around and be disobedient. Let him dwell on the consequences of his actions down there.

Rurin stared at me a second longer than was necessary, but he nodded, took the healer by his arm and hauled him out of the bedroom. The remaining healer looked at me wide-eyed and quickly set to doing as I'd ordered. I turned back to Mother and pulled the blankets away from her. Her nightgown was soaked through.

"What's going on here?" Elara asked.

"Elara, thank the Gods. I need your help."

She sidestepped the frantic healer, a frown on her face as she saw me struggle Mother out of her nightgown.

"Xaresh sent me," she mumbled. "*Tarien,* what *are* you doing?"

"What does it look like?" I muttered. "Undressing her of course."

Elara set to helping me. It was good to have someone who did what I asked without defying me, although I was sure the questions would come later. Just after we'd gotten her out of the dress, Soren and Xaresh rushed in, the latter still looking rather sick.

"Xaresh, stand guard outside," I ordered.

He nodded, looking at me in relief. "As you wish, *Tarien.*"

"Why is it so stuffing warm in here?" Soren asked, looking at the other healer. "Were you trying to boil her?"

I snorted, quickly composing myself as both men looked my way. Elara looked at me amused, mouthing an *I like him* to me. I smirked. The remaining healer murmured an explanation too low for me to hear, after which Soren sent him away. He walked over, his brow furrowed deeply.

"How is she?"

"Burning up," I said. "The same as with Evan."

Soren nodded. "Except that he's out of danger… *Khirr*."

"I ordered the windows opened and fire doused," I said, stepping back. "Her nightgown was soaked with sweat. I figured that couldn't be good either."

He gave me a wry smile. "You should've studied for a healer."

"She didn't give me much of a choice," I replied, stealing a look at Mother.

He tilted his head slightly, his eyes sparkling. "I'm curious to know where you've got your knowledge from."

I shrugged. "I wasn't exactly the girliest girl at the palace and they often found me doing the same things as my brothers. I learned a thing or two along the way about cuts and bruises."

"What about fevers?" he asked while checking Mother's pulse. "Although your method is unusual, it is working."

"Common sense," I said, my eyes shifting to my Mother's face. "If you add more fire to the fire, it'll get worse and out of control, but if you add water, it will die down. I figured the same applied to fever."

Soren glanced up from under his lashes, an amused expression on his face. "Interesting analogy."

Without saying more, he turned back to Mother, a thoughtful look returning to his face. He checked her forehead the same as I had, nodded to himself, and murmured things I didn't understand.

"She needs to be washed," Soren said eventually, "and her bed could do with clean sheets."

Elara and I nodded.

After servants brought in water, we washed and dressed Mother, and cleaned the sheets on her bed. With the windows open and cool air coming in, the room was soon much more comfortable.

Once we had taken care of Mother, I slumped down in a chair and pushed against the bandages in the hopes it would lessen the pain. Soren knelt in front of me, lifting my dress over my knees without as much as a by-your-leave.

"You're an incredibly stubborn woman," he said.

Elara snorted loudly, her shoulders shaking with silent laughter. I glared at her, but she didn't stop. In fact, it had quite the opposite effect as she started laughing out loud.

Soren unwrapped the bloodied bandage from my leg carefully, drawing out hisses whenever it got a little stuck. My knuckles were white from clutching the armrest.

"*Nohro*," I breathed.

With a grimace, Soren tossed the bandage to the side and prodded the skin around the injury. I kicked him in the ribs involuntarily. He grunted.

"Sorry."

He smirked. "Don't say it if you don't mean it."

He looked up at me, a wicked look in his eyes. I liked him.

"Elara?" he asked. "Mind holding her down?"

What followed were probably the worst couple of minutes of my life where Elara held and Soren kept pushing against the wound. A pillow to the face muffled my screams, and by the time he finished, sweat covered me head to toe, and I sat gasping for air.

"What were you doing?"

"Pushing fluid out of the wound," he said clinically. "It's probably what caused the worst of the pain."

I stared at him. "You're a sadist."

"At your service, *Tarien*."

I flopped back in the chair, catching my breath while rubbing my face, as he set to bandaging my leg.

"How's the arm?" he asked at length.

"Still attached."

"Come and see me after you're done for today. I'll stay here for a while, see if your mother's fever goes down."

I nodded.

Elara helped me to my feet, and although my leg still hurt, it wasn't as bad as before. A visit to Nathaïr and Azra was still on the agenda, but the moment we stepped out Xaresh informed me the Council was expecting me.

"How does Mother do this?" I murmured, more than a little annoyed.

CHAPTER 6

The moment we stepped into the council chamber, angry voices barraged us. Members were yelling at each other, and fists landed on the tables so hard, cups rattled on their plates. I stared in shock, having expected everything but this.

"As if monkeys have taken over," I muttered to Elara.

She snorted. "And you get the pleasure of training them."

I rolled my eyes as I limped over to Mother's chair, which was placed ever so conveniently on the other side of the room. Saying nothing, I sat down, placed my hands flat on the table and rested my chin on them, watching the monkeys on display.

"Glad you could finally join us, *Tarien*," Yllinar sneered. "I was afraid you'd run off again."

All monkeys fell silent rapidly, curiosity mixed with apprehension prominent on their faces. It was almost as if they expected a fight of sorts. Elara inhaled sharply, and I knew she'd punch him if he said anything untoward.

"Were you? I'm touched by your emotional capabilities," I replied, my gaze fixed on his.

His lips squeezed into a thin line and his eyes narrowed. Had he been allowed to carry a sword, I'm sure his hand would've gone towards it.

Yllinar curled his lips into a cold smile. "I'm always concerned about your welfare, *Tarien.*"

I hated my title on his lips.

"I am sure you are," I said, sarcasm dripping from my voice. "Before everyone else decides to care for my wellbeing, let's get this meeting started. I have more important matters to attend to today."

"Since when is play pretend at sword fighting more important than ruling your country?" Yllinar asked with a dismissive wave of his hand.

"Since men like you have taken place in the council rather than their position in the army." I rose to my feet, squaring my shoulders. "Is there something you wish to address, Yllinar? Anything you need to get off your chest?"

The sneer on his face made it clear he didn't care to be addressed as such, but the look on mine must have had the same effect, for he didn't reply. Instead, he settled down, lips pressed tight together.

"Wise decision," I said, my eyes still trained on Yllinar as I sat down. "Now why did it sound like all of you were tearing down the council chamber?

As my eyes swept over the assembled party, Nya rose to her feet, wringing her hands. "We were arguing how to best deal with the threat at our borders. Not everyone's on the same page."

She took several gulps between her words, as if I made her nervous.

Let them be nervous.

"It sounded as if you weren't even in the same book," I said, waving my hand in dismissal, "but go on."

"Some think it's best to strike now, while we still have the upper hand," Nya continued, "while others think it's best to wait and see what happens, afraid the Therondians might retaliate."

I stared at her. "I see…"

Both sides have a valid point.

"If we do nothing, *Tarien*, we may look weak," one of the male council members, whose name I'd already forgotten, chimed in. "Attacking will show them we're the strongest."

Evan would say it's a sign of weakness, yet Cerindil might agree with them. It's all a matter of perspective.

"Will it though?" I asked, turning to him. "Pray tell, what will happen when we attack? Ilvanna is at least two times smaller than Therondia, and their men outnumber ours five to one."

"If I may, *Tarien*? Yllinar interjected, glancing at his fellow council member with a smirk on his face.

What are you up to?

My gaze settled back on him. "Go ahead."

"What *Irìn* Ashyer is saying," he began, "is that we can have the upper hand if we move fast. Being outnumbered, the Therondians will never expect such a bold move, and they won't be on time to rally their full forces. It will be over before it has even started."

"And what will happen if they *do* come back with their entire army?" I cocked my head slightly, my eyes settling on Yllinar.

"We can have our borders bolstered by then," Yllinar offered. "With your permission, *Tarien*, we can place fortifications."

"And who will place those fortifications?" I asked, looking around.

"There are enough unemployed Ilvannians down in the third circle we can put to work, *Tarien*," a female council member added.

"And have them work as slaves?" I asked, tilting my head slightly. "Or will you pay them?"

She watched me with wide, lambent doe eyes. "P… pay them of course."

"With what?" I gave her a pointed stare. "Last time we spoke of money, it was clear there wasn't enough, and I told you before, we cannot just create it."

The woman looked away, fumbling her hands. It was Yllinar who spoke up.

"I will have my men bring the supplies to the border," he said. "And I'll pay the ones building the fortifications as part of my... enterprise."

Does he really think I'm this stupid?

I slowly rose to my feet, tapping my pursed lips in thought. My eyes settled on each one of them individually, one after the other. Most squirmed beneath my gaze and looked away—Yllinar was the only one who stared back. Someone needed to teach this man some manners. They were watching me with bated breath as I pretended to consider their answers.

In all truth, I'd already figured out my next move, but I'd wanted to know their thoughts so I could better predict the future.

"How extensive is your knowledge of Therondia, Yllinar?" I asked at length.

He looked momentarily puzzled, but quickly composed his features. "Quite extensive, *Tarien*. Why?"

My lips turned up into a roguish smile, and I had to keep myself from looking entirely too happy. "You will go to Therondia on my behalf as a diplomat and negotiate a peace treaty instead. You will leave the morning after your daughter's engagement ceremony and not return until such time as the negotiations are complete."

He stared at me. The council members stared at me. Only Chazelle looked at me with a new look of appreciation on her face.

This way, he would be out of my hair for a while.

"*Tarien*," Nya began, a note of desperation in her voice. "Do you not remember the last time we sent a diplomat to Therondia?"

I arched a brow. "I do, but I do not see how it has anything to do with this."

In my peripheral vision, I noticed Yllinar staring at me, eyes flashing furiously.

"You're sending me off to my death?" He almost spat, glaring at me. "Is that how you treat your Council?"

"If it gets you killed," I replied. "You're doing something wrong. Besides, the diplomat Nya referred to wasn't killed during the negotiations—they killed him because he insulted a lord, and practically raped his daughter. So unless you plan on doing something similar, I am certain you will do excellently."

Yllinar inclined his head, looking everything but pleased. "As you wish, *Tarien*."

He may have been smiling, but his stormy eyes told me a different story altogether. Ruling a country was much like playing *sihnmihràn*, a strategy based game focused on outmanoeuvring your opponent.

I was good at that game.

Although getting him to do what I wanted felt like a small victory, the way he made a steeple of his fingers while he watched me, tapping the index fingers against his lips, made every hair on my body stand on end. He was up to something, the look in his eyes was a clear indication, but I could hardly base anything on the look in someone's eyes.

Rubbing my temples to massage the headache away, I looked around the table.

"Do we have anything else to discuss?"

Chazelle rose to her feet this time. "There's the matter of the poisoning, *Tarien*."

I perked up in my chair, hands resting on the sides.

"Do tell."

She was wringing her hands. "There's been a vote of

mistrust."

I didn't look impressed.

"It came out in your favour," she said, but didn't elaborate.

I rose to my feet, planted my hands on the table, and leaned to the side a little to favour my bad leg.

"You're telling me you don't trust me?" I asked, tilting my head slightly.

Chazelle blanched. "Not me, *Tarien*. I trust your judgement completely."

"Interesting," I replied, turning to the other council members. "Why did you feel you needed a vote of mistrust?"

Nobody spoke. Shifty eyes refused to meet my gaze. I half-expected Yllinar to reply, but it was Chazelle.

"It's protocol, *Tarien*," she replied, "to discuss matters like these in the council."

I merely nodded and sat down, drumming my fingers on my thigh to distract from the pain in my leg while considering her words. Although I could get behind protocol, I didn't much care for its execution.

"I'm just curious," I said, looking around, "why you think I'd poison my entire family? What would I gain, aside from ascending the throne earlier? It makes no sense for me to poison my brothers in the process—they're no threat. Please, enlighten me."

As expected, nobody had an explanation. Not that I minded —I was completely over this conversation and wanted nothing more than to get out of here.

"Just to get this out of the way once and for all," I continued. "If you think I poisoned my family, you're out of your *Nohro* mind. Let me tell you this and let me be clear. I would *die* before ever hurting my family or those I love. Ask the wolf who tried."

Chazelle and Nya hid their faces behind their hands, but the amusement was clear in their eyes.

One of the members scoffed. "And you want us to believe

you killed a wolf?"

"Are you questioning my integrity?"

He scowled. "Merely your validity, *Tarien*. Killing a wolf—most grown men can't do that."

A smirk crossed my face. "A good thing I'm not a man then. It's a shame you doubt my abilities, and I'm afraid I cannot tolerate that."

After I gave a curt nod to Elara, she stepped over to the council member and hauled him bodily out of his seat, holding him by the scruff of his neck.

"Escort him out of here, please."

Not amused she guided him out, the man protested heavily, trying to take hold of Elara's wrist. Half-way through the council chamber she just grabbed his arm, turned it on his back and propelled him out of the room.

"If there's nothing else we need to discuss," I said. "I adjourn this meeting."

People rose to their feet in soft murmurs. I watched them leave the room in silence, hoping this headache would go away. Slumping back in the chair, I rubbed my forehead, closing my eyes for a brief moment, which was enough time for someone to grab my wrist. My hands clenched into fists when I saw it was Yllinar. He looked anything but pleased.

"You're treading on dangerous grounds, *Tarien*," he muttered. "You shouldn't wake sleeping dogs."

I smirked. "But that's the best part."

He twisted my wrist in such a way he forced me to lean forward. It gave the illusion of a bow I wasn't willing to award him, but it was the injured arm, and Soren would kill me should I injure it again.

"Don't mistake me for a fool."

I looked up at him with a grimace. "Then don't act like one."

As he twisted my arm further, my shoulder started to burn. If he wanted to be nasty, he'd pop it out of its socket.

"I don't play games, *Tarien*," he muttered. "You'd do well to remember that."

I raised my head, looking at him with a playful smile on my face. "But I love playing games."

Disgusted, he let go of my arm and stalked out of the council chamber. Breathing in deeply, I sat back, trembling all over. It made me wonder if Mother had to deal with these kinds of threats daily too.

When Elara stepped back inside, she raised an eyebrow.

"Are you all right?"

I nodded. "Just tired."

I realised I was as much a liar as I had accused Tal of being. With a deep sigh, I pushed my hair out of my face, and shook my head.

"I'm not all right." I admitted with a heavy sigh, rubbing my face. "My head is one aching mess, my leg and arm are on fire, and I hate being *Tari*."

She smiled softly. "You're doing remarkably well for someone who hates it so much."

"I doubt they'll ever trust me after today."

"Oh, they will," she said, looking amused. "I overheard them discussing what happened. It impressed most."

I snorted. "Yllinar's still an issue though."

"Don't let him get to you," she said. "It's exactly what he wants."

"If he stops hurting me."

Even though I said it softly, Elara heard me. I could tell from the way she set her jaw and placed her hands on her hips.

"He did *what?*"

I waved my hand dismissively. "It's nothing."

She didn't believe me—I could tell it from the look on her face—but she swallowed and nodded.

I pushed myself to my feet with a deep sigh, grimacing at the pain in my arm and shoulder. All I wanted was to lie down and get some sleep, but I realised those were treats for the more fortunate. There was no rest for the wicked.

"Let's go see Nathaïr and Azra," I said, steadying myself against the chair.

"And then you're off to bed," Elara said.

"Yes, mom."

LOUD SHOUTING GREETED us when we entered the corridor to Nathaïr's chambers, and with one look at each other, we quickened our pace. I already loathed having to visit her, but if she was in one of her moods, it would be even worse than I'd imagined. Elara opened the door, and when we stepped inside, we were just in time to dodge crockery flying in our general direction. In the corner across from the door huddled a girl, protecting her head with her arms.

"Stupid goose! I asked for the oil! Not the cream! Look at what you've done to my hair!"

Nathaïr was standing in the middle of the room wearing absolutely nothing, her hair sticking out in every direction. It was a disaster, and I had to do my best to keep my face in check.

"Glad to see you're feeling better," I said, folding my arms in front of me. "I wish I could say the same for your girl."

She spun around, glaring at both of us. Elara walked around me, grabbed a sheet from the bed and handed it to her, not saying a word. With her jaw set, she wrapped it around herself.

"Can't your delicate eyes handle such splendour?" she sneered.

I smirked. "I can. Elara can't."

Elara snorted, rolling her eyes at me. Nathaïr gave me her famous half-smile.

"What are you doing here, anyway?"

"Checking in on you," I replied. "To see how you were doing, which from the looks of it, is just fine."

Nathaïr jutted out her hip, folding her arms in front of her. "It's really none of your business."

"About that," I said. "It is. You're hurting one of my servants."

"She's *my* girl. I brought her."

I looked unimpressed. "And you live in Mother's palace now, betrothed to one of the *Tari's* own sons. This isn't good for your reputation."

"What would you know about having a reputation?"

"It precedes you."

She snorted, dropping her arms to her sides. "You really are an insufferable pain, do you know that?"

"So I've been told. Good to see you up and about again," I said, turning around carefully. "Hope you're well soon."

"Shalitha?"

I gritted my teeth, composed my features and turned back to face her.

"How's Evanyan?" she asked, biting her lip.

My gaze fixed on her for longer than necessary as surprise rolled over me. It was the last question I'd expected from her. With a quick shake of my head I dispelled the stupor.

"He's all right I think. Have gotten no bad news, so I assume he's recuperating."

She nodded, and when she looked at me again, the sneer was back. Who would've thought the serpent actually had some feelings hidden deep within?

"I assume the engagement ceremony has been rescheduled?" she asked, hands on her hips.

I rolled my eyes. "Yes."

"Good. I'm glad," she said, looking me over. "Oh, and *Tarien?*"

"Hm?"

"You look terrible."

I looked at her straight-faced, not deeming it worthy of a reply. With a shake of my head at her fickle mood, I left her room, Elara in tow, a permanent smirk stuck to her face. I still had to visit Azra and Evan, and see Soren, though I could thankfully combine the last two.

"I'll wait outside," Elara murmured when we arrived at Azra's door.

AZRA WAS AWAKE TOO. Although she had bags under her watery eyes, she appeared in better health than I'd envisioned. I guess I had expected to find something similar to Mother. Unlike Nathaïr though, she was still in bed, and the moment I stepped inside, she looked up from what she was reading, a smile on her face.

She patted the bed next to her where I sat down carefully, a gasp of pain escaping my lips.

"Whatever happened to you?" Azra asked, eyes wide.

I shrugged. "Disagreed with a wolf."

"A wolf?"

"It's a long story I don't feel like telling," I muttered. "How are you feeling?"

She smiled softly. "Better. I finally managed to keep water inside."

"Sounds good."

"How's Arayda?" She sat up, leaning forward a little.

My mood dropped several degrees at the memory of the foolish healers and their ancient beliefs. Hugging myself, I turned to Azra, shaking my head softly as I spoke.

"I swear they were trying to cook her. The room was insanely hot. Fires were blazing, the windows were closed, and she was lying dressed under two thick blankets. I think, had I not come in when I did,"—I swallowed hard, shaking my head—"they'd have killed her."

Azra wrapped her arms around me, pulling me into her

embrace. She placed a soft kiss on my hair.

"A good thing you came around when you did," she murmured. "She's lucky to have you."

I snorted. "Mind telling her that?"

Letting go, Azra rested her hand against my cheek, stroking it with her thumb.

"She knows, little niece. She knows."

"She just tends to forget." I murmured, a faint smile on my lips. "Anyway, I have little time. I still have to visit Evan, and go see Soren, and by the time that's done, I'm sure everyone needs me."

Azra chuckled softly. "So you're overseeing your Mother's duties now?"

"Yes, there was no other idiot available."

She laughed, shaking her head. Leaning over, she placed a gentle kiss on my cheek.

"Has anyone told you how horrible you look?"

I snorted. "Nathaïr tried."

"You'll always have a nemesis," she said, eyes sparkling.

"Shame mine will be family."

Azra looked at me with her head slightly tilted, biting her lip. Leaning forward, she tucked some hair behind my ear much in the same way as my brothers and Tal would. I swallowed hard, wishing silently Mother would do that for a change.

"Sometimes the hardest road is the easiest to take." She said. "As long as you don't let it lead you."

"That made no sense."

She smiled. "It will. Someday."

Rubbing my face, I looked at her through my fingers, a faint smile playing on my lips.

"I hope you're right."

"Get some rest, *shareye*," Azra murmured. "You're dead on your feet."

As I got up, I placed a proper kiss on my aunt's cheek and

left her room in an unsteady hobble. I got to the infirmary with help from Elara, never having been so happy to be tucked into a bed. She propped up the pillows behind me so I could sit up. Not until then did I realise how sore I really felt.

Evan was still asleep, albeit somewhat restless, and I hadn't seen Soren when we came in either. I assumed, or rather hoped, he was still with Mother, instead of those foolhardy idiots.

"Where are Tal and Xaresh?" I asked. "I haven't seen them since this morning."

"Overseeing rookie training I believe, since Haerlyon isn't able to."

I laughed softly. "I feel sorry for the rookies."

"Just a bit," Elara said, looking amused. "Don't worry about them. They're fine. You, however, are not. Get some sleep, I'll be right outside."

"*Nohro ahrae*, sis," Evan murmured after Elara left. "You look terrible."

I rolled onto my side with a grimace, tucking my hand under my head. "You've seen better days too."

"No doubt." he chuckled and coughed.

It was so bad, he doubled over. I pushed myself up and scooted out of bed. While patting his back, I swayed a little at the sudden pain coursing through my leg.

"You all right?" I asked softly.

He nodded while gasping for air, unable to speak at the moment. When it had subsided, he grabbed a cup from the bedside cabinet and drank a few sips of water.

"I'm fine," he wheezed. "Just coughing a lot."

I could see he'd been coughing up blood and made a mental note to tell Soren when I'd see him. As Evan looked at me, his eyes suddenly narrowed. He took my arm in his hand and pushed up the sleeve in the same move to uncover the bandages.

"You're not fine," he muttered.

I pulled my arm back and sat down, hugging myself. He was

staring at me so intently, I looked away, unable to meet his eyes.

"It wasn't a dream, was it?" he asked at length.

Biting my lip, I shook my head. "It wasn't."

"You *actually* fought a wolf?"

"I was defending us," I murmured.

Evan swung his legs over the bed and leaned forward, carefully peeling my arm away from me. He pushed up my sleeve and took off the bandage. I swallowed hard at the sight of the bite marks, and I saw him pale from under my lashes.

"*Nohro ahrae,*" he whispered, looking up wide-eyed. "And you're walking around with this!"

I shrugged. "My arm isn't too bad."

"What do you mean? There's more?" His voice was barely a whisper.

Exhaling, I pulled the skirt up over my knees, showing a heavily bandaged leg. They were already stained with blood, just like the inside of my skirt from the looks of it. Evan swallowed hard as he took off the bandages slowly. His hands were trembling, and I could see sweat beading his brow.

He continued anyway.

"Ev, lie down."

He shook his head. "Not until I see what saving my life has cost you."

"Not that much," I replied. "Go lie down. I order you."

He merely glared at me, refusing to listen. If he toppled over, I'd yell at him for the rest of his life. Once the bandages were gone, he stared at my leg in horror. It was a myriad of small stitches all around, set off by dark purple and blue splotches. The skin around some stitches was an angry red, and the smell coming off of it wasn't too pleasant either.

"You need a healer," he muttered.

"Yeah, you might be right." My voice sounded faint even to me.

He called for Elara, who came in rapidly, looking at the both of us with a frown. Evan ordered her to go get Soren straight away.

"But you'll be unguarded," she said, biting her lip.

"You'll have nothing to guard if you don't get him now," Evan growled.

She left the infirmary at a dead run. I started laughing out of nowhere, earning a dark look from my brother.

"What's so funny?"

"Everything."

He snorted. "There's nothing funny about this. Shal, this doesn't look good."

"I know," I replied. "But if I don't laugh now, I'm afraid I'll break down crying. I cannot cry Ev."

"Why not?"

"Because I'm not sure I'll be able to stop."

Leaning forward, he placed a kiss on my forehead. "You're a strong woman. You can do this."

"I wouldn't place any bets on it," I murmured. "Everything is."

Soren interrupted our conversation by marching in, followed by Elara and Xaresh. Not Tal. My stomach twisted itself in a knot, but I had no time to linger on those thoughts. The moment Soren saw my leg, he muttered something foul under his breath and told my men to get me up on the table.

I frowned.

"What's wrong?"

Soren quirked his lips. "Can't tell yet, but I have to open a few of those stitches, and you'll most likely hate me for it."

Hate was the understatement of the century. Xaresh held down my legs while Elara made herself comfortable on my chest, watching me. Soren placed a piece of leather between my teeth, so I wouldn't crack them or bite my tongue. Evan propped himself up against the pillows in his bed, watching us with the deepest frown on his face.

I knew exactly when Soren started and understood full well why he had the others keep me down. The cutting of the stitches wasn't too bad, but when he started pulling them out, it was the weirdest sensation ever. My attempt at stifling a scream came undone the moment Soren pulled out another stitch.

"I'm trying to be as nice about it as I can," Soren murmured, looking at me apologetically.

I dropped my head back, chomping down on the leather like a horse would on its bit, staring up at the ceiling while counting to a hundred in the old language. Tears rolled down my cheeks unbidden, but no matter how I tried, I couldn't block out the pain as much as I wanted.

A growl escaped my lips when Soren took out another stitch at the count of twenty-seven. Getting bitten by the wolf had been a tickling sensation compared to what Soren was putting me through now. I bit down on the leather strip again, cursing and screaming in both languages, as I trashed underneath Elara.

Perhaps it was good I couldn't see what he was doing, because if it came remotely close to how it felt, I'd have killed him. A pain beyond anything I could ever have imagined lanced through my entire body. I tried to focus on Elara, but her face swam in and out of my vision.

"Is he taking my leg off?" I murmured.

Elara chuckled softly. "You and your wild imagination."

I remembered nothing beyond that point.

COMING to my senses felt like breaking the surface of water after having gone under to the point of running out of air, or being pulled out of the deepest, most exhilarating dream, leaving me winded and confused. I wasn't sure how long I'd been gone, but upon opening my eyes, I saw I wasn't in the infirmary anymore—they had brought me to my bedroom. My leg was a throbbing, aching mess, but felt better than before.

Carefully I sat up, alerting the person slumped in a chair next to my bed. He sat up quickly, a groan escaping his lips.

"Tal?"

"Here," he murmured, rubbing his face.

He lit a candle and placed it on the bedside cabinet before sitting down in the chair again, leaning forward, elbows resting on his knees. I noticed the bags under his eyes were worse than the last time I saw him.

"You've seen better days."

He smiled wryly. "Can't argue with that logic."

As he pushed his hair back from his face, I saw his movements were jerky and uncontrolled, which was so unlike him it had me worried.

"You should sleep too," I said.

"I just did."

I rolled my eyes. "In a bed."

"Must have misplaced it."

"*Khirr.*"

His lips turned up in a smile, and he sat down on the bed next to me. The movement was stiff, as if it hurt him, and I could tell he was tense.

"How are you feeling?" he asked.

"Not too bad, I think. How long have I been out?"

He looked away. "A couple of days."

I stared at him, trying to make sense of what he'd just said. If I'd been out for a few days, it meant there had been no one to turn to.

"What?"

"You couldn't go on like that," he said, still refusing to look at me. "Soren was clear that if you would take another step on that leg before it had gotten time to heal, you'd lose it. Your brothers made the call."

I swallowed hard, fumbling with the sheets. "What about the city? The threats at the border? The council?"

He smirked. "Oh, they weren't pleased at all, let me tell you that, but none of them seemed willing to cross Soren for some reason. Besides, Haerlyon was well enough to move about again and monitor things."

"That must have been interesting," I said and slumped back into the pillows. "How much is a couple of days exactly?"

"Five."

I gaped at him. "How did you keep me out for five days?!"

"We didn't, mostly." He shrugged. "You woke up in between, but Soren kept you drugged."

"I'll kill him."

Tal stared at me. "That man most likely saved your life. Stop being such a stubborn, arrogant brat."

I stared at him flatly. "He did it without consent."

"But not without permission."

"And who gave him that?" I asked vehemently. "Because I can't recall having done so!"

"I did."

While it was an answer I should have expected, I hadn't. I just stared at him, a heavy feeling settling in my stomach. Even though he'd done what he thought was best, it felt like a betrayal. Shaking my head slowly, I turned on my side, my back to him.

"I want you to leave."

"Shal, please…"

My voice was soft when I spoke. "I want you to leave. Now."

From the corner of my eyes I noticed he brought up his hand to touch me, but seemed to think better of it. With a strangled sound, he got off the bed, and the opening of the door told me he'd left. Someone else entered, but I didn't bother turning around.

I didn't want them to see me cry.

CHAPTER 7

*I*t had been more than a week since my fight with Tal, and I'd barely seen him since, let alone had time to talk to him. I wanted to apologise for that night, but whenever I got close, he had an excuse to be elsewhere. His dismissal hurt worse than the bite of the wolf had, but this time I only had myself to blame. He'd done what he had thought was right to save my life—he'd done his job, and I had held it against him.

At least I could walk again now the wound had healed sufficiently, but my progress was slow and unsteady, and there were still moments I needed someone to support me. I hated it. Fortunately, neither Elara nor Xaresh seemed to mind my presence all that much, though both had given me their opinion on the whole situation—they'd been right, mostly. I really needed to talk to Tal.

Tonight was Evan's engagement ceremony, and I needed to know if he would be there in his official capacity as my *Anahràn*, considering he had shirked his responsibilities as one this past week.

Standing at the top of the stairs, I allowed my gaze to wander over the rolling landscape below and the mountains in the distance. The valley was gorgeous this time of year with the trees in early bloom, changing their pale winter coat for the soft, pale pink leaves of Spring. In the distance, the lake sparkled like a thousand diamonds in the sun.

My eyes zeroed in on Tal, surrounded by a gang of rookies. Even from this distance, he stood out amongst them. He had tied his white hair in a lazy knot, showing off his wide shoulders, his muscles working hard with every move he made. An intense flutter of butterflies inhabited my belly, so I quickly dispelled the thoughts.

They weren't fit for a *Tarien*.

Carefully, I made my way down the stairs to where he was teaching the rookies. To my surprise, Grayden was amongst them.

Tal was so focused on them he didn't realise I was there until our swords crossed. There was hurt in his eyes as he regarded me, possibly resentment and maybe even some anger. I couldn't blame him.

"What are you doing here?" Tal growled.

"We need to talk."

He grimaced. "I don't have time."

"That's why I'm here," I said. "You can talk and fight."

"You're in no shape to fight."

I looked amused, placing a hand on my hip. "I'll make you a deal."

"All right," he said, raising an eyebrow. "What's that?"

"If I win, we'll talk," I said. "If you win, we don't."

Tal smirked. "Deal."

Raising my sword, I settled myself in a guarding stance, noticing straight away my leg wouldn't be able to hold my weight for long, so I had to be quick. Tal rolled his eyes at me and mirrored my stance. The rookies made room for us, whispering excitedly while forming a circle. Most of them looked awed, except for Grayden, who was watching us with deep interest.

We started circling, neither of us making a move. I knew Tal wouldn't start, so I had to, but when I did, I was clumsy and attacked so sloppily he barely had to step aside.

He snorted, looking positively offended. "That's not how I taught you."

"Maybe you have to refresh my memory. It's been a while."

There was a sparkle in his eyes I hadn't seen in some time—the mischievous kind he usually reserved for when he was up to no good. He stepped forward and attacked me with an upward swing. Although I parried, he covered the distance between us in a heartbeat and had me flat on my back just as fast. I looked up the length of his sword into a pair of twinkling emerald eyes.

I lay my hands flat on the grass.

He grinned down at me. "Told you."

To my surprise, he held out his hand to help me to my feet. It was all I needed to catch him off balance and pull him down. He caught himself with his hands on either side of my face. He was close enough I could feel a tremor run through his body—close enough to inhale the scent of wood and air. I swallowed hard, grinned at him, and in one swift move pulled his hand from under him, rolling him on his back and straddling him, a triumphant look on my face.

"You cheated!"

I laughed. "Did not."

"You surrendered."

"I lay my hands flat on the grass." I grinned. "I never tapped out."

He stared at me and harrumphed. I half-expected him to throw me off of him, but he didn't, which surprised me considering the fact we'd gathered quite an audience.

"This isn't appropriate," he murmured.

"Since when do you care?"

He rolled his eyes. "You're incorrigible."

"Will you come see me later?" I asked, a slight pout on my lips. "Please? It's not a conversation for here."

For a moment longer, Tal looked at me. "If you promise to take it easy now. I'm sure Soren hasn't released you for training yet."

So he does keep an eye on me.

"Yes, dad." I grinned and pushed myself off of his chest.

He grunted and glared at me, but the twitch of his lips told me he didn't mind as much as he led everyone to believe. Picking up my sword, I took a few steps back. Tal got to his feet and placed his hands on his hips.

"What are you looking at?" he roared, looking at the assembled crowd. "I don't think I told you to stop!"

The rookies scrambled around for their weapons and got into a semblance of order. I laughed when I heard him bark out orders and seeing their terror-filled faces. As I turned away, I caught him looking at me, a smile on his face. Something between us had changed.

Elara met me halfway the training fields, arms folded in front of her.

"Was that really necessary?" she muttered.

"Was what necessary?"

She snorted. "Fighting? Your leg has barely healed."

"You called that fighting?"

Elara rolled her eyes, throwing her hands up in defeat. Laughing, I made my way back up the stairs, where one of Mother's guards greeted me. She wished to speak with me.

ALTHOUGH STILL LOOKING A LITTLE HAGGARD, Mother had returned to her duties and was awaiting me in the council chamber. The only other council members present were

Chazelle and Nya. I greeted both of them with a smile, and inclined my head to Mother, trying for a curtsy.

"Never mind that," she said. "Let's not stress out that leg too much."

I could have sworn she glared at Chazelle and Nya, but since it was gone so quickly, it had to have been a figment of my imagination. I sat down in a chair opposite the women, resting my arms on the table.

"You needed me?"

Mother nodded in acknowledgement, an amused expression on her delicate features. "Chazelle and Nya here informed me you have done an excellent job during my absence."

"I hardly did anything," I replied. "I barely had time to."

"You upset the Council."

I ran my hand through my hair, smiling wryly. "Sorry about that."

"Don't be. It's good someone put them back in place," Mother said, definitely glaring at the two women this time. "They were getting out of hand."

Chazelle looked anywhere but at Mother, trembling slightly under her scrutiny. Nya was a little bolder and still had her chin up.

"Thank you? I guess."

Mother made a steeple of her fingers much like Yllinar had, but there was no malice in her eyes when she looked at me.

"I'm also informed you threw *Irìn* Ashyer from the council?"

"If that was his name, then yes."

Chazelle snorted. Nya looked at me amused. I shrugged, looking apologetic.

"I didn't really have the time to learn their names."

"What about Yllinar?"

I sucked my teeth in thought, wrinkling my nose. "Well, I didn't like us going to war without there being a clear reason, nor was staying passive an option, so I figured we could send someone. He's always boasting how much he knows about our enemy, so I sent him as our diplomat. He was annoying me."

Mother looked at me, only to burst out laughing moments later, surprising both the women and me. She never laughed like that.

"Oh, daughter." She hiccoughed with laughter. "I like your style."

I watched her in sheer surprise. That was a compliment if ever I heard one. She wiped the tears from her cheeks and composed her features.

"I will let your decisions stand," she said. "They need to know you are to be taken just as seriously as me."

"Thank you."

I was already rising to my feet when she stopped me, calling me by name.

"There's one more thing I'd like to ask of you," Mother said, her tone serious and formal again.

I shrugged. "Sure."

"Will you be Nathaïr's second tonight?"

"Is that even a question, Mother?"

She merely smiled at me.

"Guess not," I rolled my eyes. "Sure, I'll sign that cursed paper."

I LEFT the council chamber feeling more than a little annoyed and stalked passed Elara without even telling her where I was going. In all honesty, I wasn't even sure myself, until I found myself outside in the garden, breathing in deeply as not to give in to the anger rising within me.

"Looks like it went well," Elara remarked drily.

I snorted. "It went brilliantly up to the moment she asked me to be Nathaïr's second tonight."

"Interesting."

"Every time I think she's found a new form of respect for me," I said with a scowl, "she finds a way to completely destroy that notion."

Elara looked thoughtful, leaning back against the wall. "Ever considered her motive might not be to destroy that feeling. Maybe she feels like you can handle these things."

I stared at her icily. "Even then! Why does she have to throw me in with Nathaïr all the time? It's bad enough she's marrying Evan as it is, I don't need her to be a part of *my* life."

She smirked. "Sorry to burst your bubble, *Tarien*, but she already is."

I huffed, folding my arms in front of my chest, but Elara didn't look impressed. If anything, she was amused.

"Maybe it's time you gave that leg some rest," she said, pushing herself off the wall. "You've got an entire night to stand on it."

"Sometimes I swear you and Tal team up just to annoy me."

Elara snorted. "Only when you behave like a petulant child."

I scowled at her.

MEHREAN WAS IN MY ROOM, sitting cross-legged on my bed reading a book, looking for all the world like a dainty little fairy. She looked up when I entered, a soft smile on her lips. Elara excused herself, staying outside.

"What are you doing here?" I asked in surprise.

I sat down on the bed with her and pulled up my knees, resting my head on them. It wasn't the most comfortable position, but this way I could massage my leg somewhat.

"Came to see how you were doing," she said. "They told me you'd been in some kind of accident?"

I snorted. "That's one way to put it. Who told you?"

"Evan."

"What did he tell you?"

Mehrean tilted her head slightly. "It was more what he didn't tell me."

"That sounds like him all right." I shook my head. "And all the rumours are true too."

"Oh, no doubt."

She regarded me with those inquisitive, ephemeral eyes, boring a hole deep into my soul. Sometimes it felt as if it was impossible to keep a secret from her.

"How are you feeling?" I asked. "I'm sorry I didn't get to visit you."

She smiled and waved her hand dismissively. "Quite alright. I figured you were busy with your mother being ill."

"If you call that busy," I murmured, looking cross-eyed. "Remind me never to be *Tari* again."

She laughed. "I'm afraid you have no choice."

"Shame."

A second later a whirlwind stormed into my room in the form of Nathaïr, attended by three ladies all looking positively terrified. Elara strolled in after them, glancing at me apologetically. I refused to get off the bed for my sister-in-law.

"*Why* are you making my life so miserable!" Nathaïr bellowed, hip jutted out, arms folded in front of her chest.

My brows shot up in surprise. "Excuse me?"

"Why did you have to be my second?"

"I didn't have to be anything," I retorted. "I'd have been perfectly happy sitting tonight out."

She took a threatening step closer, towering over me. I wasn't impressed.

"Don't do it."

I looked amused. "Can't."

"Don't do it," she hissed.

"Or what?"

Nathaïr nearly pushed her face into mine and it took me every ounce of will not to push her back. Mother would be furious if I'd get into trouble again.

"Or I'll make you regret the day you were born."

I snorted. "Good luck. Tell the *Tari* you do not accept her decision though."

She gawked at me and pushed herself from the bed, puffing out her chest, lifting her chin. There was a mischievous glint in her eyes as she regarded me.

"Well then," she purred, "as a second it also means you must help me get ready for tonight."

I stared at her this time and slowly turned my head to look at Mehr with wide eyes. She shrugged and nodded.

"You've *got* to be kidding me," I groaned, flopping down on the bed.

What in all the Gods' names was Mother up to, putting me through things like this?

It wasn't as if Nathaïr and I would ever become best friends, certainly not if we were pushed in that direction. Rising to my feet with a sigh so deep, it had to have come out of my toes, I reluctantly followed Nathaïr and her entourage. Mehrean signalled she'd be here when I was done, and I assumed it was to help me get ready for tonight.

Kill.Me.Now, I mouthed to Elara, who looked at me with a mix of amusement and pity. She shook her head, a sly sparkle in her eyes. I had the decency not to flip her off this time.

NATHAÏR'S ROOM was an explosion of colourful clothing. The same whirlwind which had entered my room had gone through here. Her ladies stayed back, eyes like frightened deer as they regarded us from a distance. Elara's brows shot up in surprise. Apparently, Nathaïr wasn't as tidy as I thought her to be.

"If you're looking for a dress," I said. "I found them."

Nathaïr glared daggers my way. I shrugged. She started picking them up one by one and tossed them on the bed in one big pile when they weren't to her liking. Wrapping one arm around herself, with an elbow resting on her hand, she started chewing a cuticle. She toyed with a lock of hair, shuffling from one foot to the other.

Would you look at that? She is nervous.

I breathed in deeply, bit my lip and took a step closer, deciding to give it a chance.

"What's wrong?" I asked.

She placed her hands on her hips in defiance. "Nothing's wrong. I just need to pick a dress."

"All right," I said, not believing her for a moment. "What dress?"

"Well, that's the problem, isn't it!"

Her voice rose in pitch, so I threw my hands up, taking a step back. She sighed and dropped her arms to her side.

"None of these are good enough."

Her words startled me. "Good enough for what?"

"Evan, of course!"

That blindsided me for a moment. With a shake of my head, I focused on her, but I couldn't help staring a bit longer.

"Why would none of them be good enough for him?"

With an exasperated sigh, her eyes nearly rolling out of her head, she picked up a dress from the bed and pointed out everything wrong with it. The neckline was too high, the sleeves were too tight, the model was just wrong for her shape, and the colour was slightly off. Everything she could come up with, was wrong. She picked up a second dress and did the same thing, except that this neckline was way too low, the sleeves were too long, and the model was too tight. The colour was fine enough.

I rubbed my temples as she went through all of her dresses,

explaining in minute detail all their flaws, making sure she skipped none, until no more dresses were left.

"Well," I said, rubbing the back of my head, "you have a problem."

She glared at me. "You think?"

I pursed my lips in thought, turned to Elara and murmured something in her ear. She frowned at me and agreed with a roll of her eyes and left the room.

"How about we get you bathed first," I suggested, turning to her. "You'll feel better after."

"It makes no sense to bathe if I have no dress!"

Folding my arms in front of me, I stared at her. "For once in your life, will you trust me?"

She harrumphed. "And why would you do something for me?"

"I'm not doing it for you. I'm doing it for Ev."

Nathaïr's eyes turned into slits as she regarded me for a while longer, then threw her hands up and spun on her heels.

"Fine. I've got nothing left to lose, anyway."

Ordering her ladies into gear, they drew up a bath in no time. I sent one of them off to get Mehrean, who looked none too pleased when she walked into the room.

Please? I mouthed to her.

You owe me. She responded in kind.

Together we set to helping Nathaïr relax to the best of our abilities, which was to say Mehrean worked her magic upon her, and I sat back, staying out of the way. Throughout Mehr's administrations, Nathaïr held an entire monologue on how she'd change things around here once she was married to my brother. I only half-listened to it, my thoughts drifting off to the conversation I was still supposed to have with Talnovar today.

"*Tarien?*" Elara's voice sounded up from the bedroom. "I got what you asked for."

Rising to my feet, I walked over to her, Nathaïr's eyes trailed on my back. The dress was for my *Araîthin*, due in a few weeks, but her need was greater than mine at the moment. I could always commission a new one. Although Mother might not be too happy with these arrangements, she couldn't fault me for trying—I was doing the woman a favour.

I hung the dress on her wardrobe and took a step back. Nathaïr stepped into the bedroom seconds later, dressed in nothing but a sheet. Her gaze zeroed in on me, a wary look in her eyes, until the dress behind me drew her attention. While its base was the same as any other Ilvannian dress, it differed in the neckline, sleeves and sash.

I watched as she ran her fingers over the gauze sleeves. They came together just above the elbow, leaving the arms bare as the rest of the fabric ran down to the floor. The neckline was demure because of the sheer underdress, while the overdress was a wide V-shape. Everything was tied together with two different coloured sashes, giving the dress a playful look.

The most startling feature was the way the fabric changed from grey bordering on silver to a topaz blue. The colours were definitely more up my alley, but Nathaïr could pull off about anything.

"This is gorgeous," Nath murmured, letting the soft fabric slide through her fingers.

She turned to me, eyes watery. "Where did you get it?"

With my hands clasped behind my back, I gave her a half-shrug, rocking back and forth on my heels. "I had it lying around."

Nathaïr frowned and quickly dashed away the tears. "You're lying."

"It's yours if you want it."

She rubbed her hands over her sides, looking from the dress to me, and back again. "Are you sure?"

I waved my hand dismissively. "Really sure."

She almost squeaked in pure delight, her earlier tirade

forgotten. I could swear there was a collective sigh of relief when she decided to wear my dress. It felt bittersweet to part from it, because I'd loved that dress from the moment I set eyes on it—and that coming from someone who hated dresses was quite something—but she deserved to feel beautiful too. If my dress was what it took, so be it.

"I will have to get ready too," I murmured. "And I want to check in on your fiancé."

Nathaïr just nodded. "Sure. Fine. Whatever. Do whatever pleases you."

And the monster had returned. Gathering Mehrean and Elara, we left her room in companionable silence.

"Why didn't you tell her it was the dress for your *Araîthin*?" Elara asked at length.

I shrugged. "Because it doesn't really matter."

"Look at you being all noble and selfless," Mehr said with a whistle. "Your mother will be proud of you."

"Or she'll go completely nuts," I said. It's anyone's guess."

WHEN I ENTERED Evan's room, he was sitting at his desk, while Haerlyon was lounging on his bed, that ever-present grin on his face. I flopped down next to him with a deep sigh, staring up at the ceiling while rubbing my face.

"Who are you about to murder?" Haer asked.

I pointed at Evan. "His fiancée."

"That bad?"

"Not as much as I thought it'd be," I said, pushing myself up to my elbows. "She was being quite decent, even though she did go through several mental breakdowns in a matter of minutes."

Evan looked up. "How so?"

"Believe it or not, brother dear," I said, chuckling, "she's actually making an effort for you."

139

He harrumphed, turning back to his desk. "Have to see it before I believe it."

"What are you writing?"

Haerlyon sniggered. "Vows."

"Whatever fo—, oh, of course," I said, doing my best to keep a straight face.

Evan sat back with a heavy sigh, and covered his eyes with one hand, a look of pure desperation crossing his face. He grabbed the piece of parchment and threw it behind him onto an existing pile.

"What am I going to promise her I can stand behind?"

"Tell her you'll protect her." I shrugged. "That you'll be there for her in times of need, and times of laughter, stuff like that. Women love to hear that."

Haerlyon smirked. "You don't."

"That's because I don't need a man to save me," I replied. "I know which end of a sword to hold."

Haer burst out laughing. Evan just shook his head at me, turning back to his parchment.

"I think she'll like that," I murmured, pushing myself to my feet. "Now if you'll excuse me, I should get ready too. Mother won't allow me inside looking like this."

I embraced Evan from behind, kissed him on the cheek, and blew one to Haerlyon as I made my way out. Once out of the bedroom, I leaned back against the wall, closed my eyes and bit back the pain.

"*Tarien?* Is everything all right?"

I looked up to find Grayden standing in the hallway, a concerned look on his face. Flashing him a smile, I nodded.

"I'm fine."

"You don't look fine."

I watched him with my head slightly tilted, feeling amused. "Ever perceptive."

"Need some help?"

For a moment I considered turning it down because of propriety, then relented with a deep sigh and nodded. I wasn't sure I could walk the distance without support, and I didn't know where Elara had gone.

"If you could lend me a hand," I said, a faint smile on my lips.

Grayden walked over and lay an arm around my waist just as I lay mine over his shoulders. With me hopping awkwardly on one leg, and him bowed ever so slightly, we made for a funny sight. When I was at my door, he let me go, bowing lightly before leaving.

I hopped inside, closed the door, and sank down against it the moment it was closed, squirming in pain. Laying down, I banged my fists on the floor, gulping the scream at the back of my throat, by now more than a little frustrated at the handicap. Tears rolled down my cheeks unbidden.

"Let's get you ready," Mehr mumbled, helping me to my feet.

Her administrations went past me in a daze. I did what she asked me to do, but my focus was on the pain, my thoughts going back to the night in the woods. A shiver ran down my spine the moment I vividly remembered teeth sinking into my flesh and nearly gagged when the sudden smell of blood came to mind.

"Easy," Mehr murmured, her voice pulling me back. "You're safe."

Gasping for air, I tried to calm my beating heart, looking at her somewhat bewildered.

"Will I ever get over it?"

She looked at me. "Over what?"

"The memories and the nightmares."

"Of course," she said, pulling a comb through my hair. "But it will take time."

We finished everything in silence, and after she helped me into one of my formal dresses, she adjusted some locks of hair. For a change, she'd created an intricate updo. A knock on the door perked me up, and when Mehr opened it and I heard Tal's voice, my heart skipped a beat.

Why did it do that?

The door closed and when I turned around, Tal was standing there, eyes wide, mouth open.

I smirked. "You're drooling."

With a shake of his head, he turned and left the room, closed the door, and stepped back inside again, still looking confused.

"What are you doing?"

"I'm looking for the *Tarien*," he said. "Have you seen her?"

I snorted, grabbed a pillow, and threw it at him. He caught it with an impish grin on his face.

"You are such an—"

"Ass?" he finished. "Yes, you keep telling me."

He moved closer, his eyes fixed on me the entire time, but the pained expression had returned and when he was close, he looked everywhere but at me. I could tell from his rapid breathing, and the way he aggressively ran his hand through his hair, something was up.

We looked at each other for what felt like forever, tension building up between us.

"I'm sorry," we said simultaneously.

He snorted. I laughed nervously. Tal opened his mouth to speak, but I silenced him by placing my finger against his lips. I could feel him stiffen, and his pupils dilated ever so slightly. Swallowing hard, he looked away, hands clasped firmly behind his back.

"I'm sorry for telling you to go," I said. "I understand why you did it. I would have done the same had I been in your position. It wasn't fair of me."

"It wasn't," he murmured, looking up at me again, "but I should apologise for avoiding you for the rest of the time after. I'm your *Anahràn*, I should have been there."

I smirked. "I've had fun with Elara and Xaresh. I think they're happy I can't run so well right now."

"Oh, no doubt," he replied, an amused look in his eyes.

I tucked my hair behind my ear. "Anyway. I hope you'll accept my apologies and take up your duties again tonight."

"You thought I would let you walk around unguarded?" he asked in surprise. "Looking like that?"

"You're not allowed to hit people when they look at me."

He flashed me a cavalier grin. "I can stare them to death."

My eyes nearly rolled back in my head. "*Khirr.*"

With a deep bow and a grin on his face, he left my room with the excuse of him having to get dressed too. It was a formal affair after all.

CHAPTER 8

The ballroom was lavishly adorned with a variety of blue and white flowers, coordinated with the rest of the decorations, ranging from the napkins to the curtains draped along the walls, to give the ballroom a regal and welcoming atmosphere. The salty air of seafood mingled with the rich scent of venison, topped by a variety of herbs I couldn't place. People crowded the room front to back, craning to see who was entering when the trumpets blew and my name and title echoed through the room.

I hated when they did that.

All six of my *Arathrien* were present today, decked out in their formal attire—an armour beautiful to see, but utterly useless in battle. Although made of metal, Cerindil had once explained it was too thin to deflect any kind of weapon. Instead, a sword could run through it like a knife through butter. It had to be light, however, or none of the guards could get through the lengths of ceremonial affairs without succumbing to its weight. Tal, and his father before him, often remarked they were sitting ducks wearing it, but tradition dictated they'd don it to formal occasions like these. Nevertheless, the *Arathrien* looked marvellous in their dark, form-fitted armour, their cloaks billowing behind them as they walked by.

I imagined it being anything but comfortable, much like my dresses.

People bowed deeply as we passed, conforming to even more traditions and silly rules designed to make our lives uncomfortable. Some would call it a privilege being a *Tarien*. To me it was a curse. I had earned none of these entitlements—I'd just been lucky at birth. What got to me most were the murmurs rising as I walked by, if only because I believed they couldn't be any good.

Everyone had an ulterior motive—especially if they stood to gain something.

I took my place between Mother and Haerlyon quietly as the *Arathrien* spread out to pre-assigned posts throughout the ballroom. From my vantage point on the dais, I could see Mother's *Arathri* had done the same. As our *Anahràn*, Tal and Rurin were the only ones close by.

Yllinar stood to the side, accompanied by his son whose sharp, roving eyes were all over me. A shiver ran down my spine, but I couldn't help glancing at him from under my lashes. His long hair was tied back in a sleek ponytail, setting off elongated ears and an uncannily handsome face. The azure eyes would have completed the picture had it not been for the menacing look they held. His lips turned up in a wolfish smile when he noticed me watching him.

I quickly averted my gaze.

To my surprise, Aunt Azra was standing on Mother's other side, and when she caught my eyes, she smiled and winked at me.

"Nath will hate you," Haerlyon murmured. "You look stunning."

I smirked. "I doubt that."

"Why?"

"You'll see," I said, beaming at him.

A moment later, the double doors opened, trumpets blared and Evan and Nathaïr stood in the doorway side by side. Evan looked like he wanted to bolt, while Nathaïr had composed herself quite well. They weren't holding hands or looked anything remotely like a happy couple, but tradition dictated they'd not touch or speak until they had concluded the official ceremony.

I doubted they were particularly looking forward to that.

"Daughter," Mother murmured. "Isn't that the dress for your *Araîthin?*"

I nodded. "It is."

Haerlyon whistled low under his breath. Mother glanced at me, an inquisitive look in her eyes, so I quickly told her in a low voice what had happened earlier that afternoon.

"I'm not sure I should be proud of you," she whispered, "or mad at you."

"You can decide after the party, Mother."

By then, Evan and Nathaïr had made their way up to where we stood, both looking uncomfortable and out of sorts. I gave them an encouraging nod before I took up my position next to Nathaïr. Haerlyon did the same on Evan's side. From under my lashes, I glanced at Tal, and found his gaze zeroed in on me, a smile tugging at his lips. Every time he did, butterflies took up residency in my stomach, so I quickly looked away, focusing on Mother instead.

The first words of the ceremony had passed me by completely, although it most likely had been a welcome to everyone, and an explanation why they were here. As if they didn't already know.

"For the first part," Mother told the couple, "place your hands on top of each other."

Evan offered his hand, and Nathaïr laid hers delicately on

his. Both were trembling, and I couldn't help but smile just a little.

"Shalitha, if you please?"

Someone handed me a veil, and I adjusted it to drape perfectly over their joined hands. Mother asked Haerlyon to tie the rope around it. The rope was an intricately woven pattern of fabrics in the colours chosen for today—the colours representing the couple. It was a slow, particular job, because the rope had to be tied specifically, but knowing my brother, he'd spent hours practising before today.

The following step was their vows, and after having seen Evan struggle that afternoon, I was curious. Haerlyon was rocking back and forth just a little, doing his best to keep his face composed. Evan's face had turned a few shades paler as he looked at his future partner. Even though she'd shown me a different side of her, I still felt somewhat sorry for him. I could only hope it would work out between them.

"I've spent an entire day trying to figure out what I would promise you," Evan said, looking at her. "But I can't promise you more than I have promised any other of the ones I love, but I pledge to you my loyalty and my protection, the safety of my hearth and home, and my company and my love. That's all I can offer."

I swallowed hard at his words and glanced at Talnovar during Evan's first line. The words were Evan to a tee—a perfect summary of a man who'd die before he let harm befall others. It was exactly the reason he was standing there, instead of Haer.

Nathaïr cleared her throat daintily. "I have to admit I had trouble writing mine too. What can I promise a man who has it all already? I promise you my love and loyalty, every day starting today. I'll be by your side when you need me the most, and even when you least want me. I promise you a family of your own, should you so desire. More I cannot give, for it is not mine to do so."

Mother stepped forward, her hands hovering just above their heads. Before we could conclude the ceremony, Chazelle walked up with a large parchment roll and first had Evan and Nathaïr sign it, followed by Mother, Haerlyon and myself. Chazelle rolled it back up and handed it to Mother, who handed it to Ev.

"I bless your words, and with it your betrothal. As of today, you're engaged for one year and one day. It will be on that last day you shall be wed."

With those words, Mother completed the ceremony. People clapped and cheered the newly engaged couple, and it was up to them now to navigate the floor still tied together, to start the first dance. I took up position next to Mother, holding my breath the moment I felt Tal brushing my back.

"Isn't that *your* dress she's wearing?"

"What if it is?"

"Not your kind of dress, anyway."

Surprised, I turned to look at him, but he'd already stepped back. His gaze was on me though, a roguish smile on his lips. He winked, composed his features, and returned to his statuesque demeanour. Looking back, my eyes locking on Evan and Nathaïr—a picture perfect couple out on the dance floor—it appeared as if they'd rehearsed the steps together before today.

Once their dance had finished, the feast began in earnest and people started to mingle. They expected me to do the same, but I was much more comfortable where I was. Haerlyon was lounging against a wall, talking to someone obscured from view by columns, but from the way he leaned forward and how his hand moved, told me it was someone he liked.

A lot.

My guess was Tiroy, who undoubtedly had been given guard duty just so they could spend some time together.

Mother was engaged in an animated conversation with several *Irìn* and *Irà*, leaving me pretty much to my own devices.

Tal was close, but in this official capacity, we couldn't be seen joking together. It would be anything but appropriate.

"Can I just say, *Tarien*, you look dashing tonight."

My gaze settled on Eamryel, Yllinar's son, bowing deeply in front of me. I inclined my head, faking a smile.

"Thank you kindly, Irìn Arolvyen."

"Call me Eamryel."

I inclined my head again, keeping my hands demurely in front of me. What in every God's name did he want? Behind me I heard Talnovar shift weight, but he didn't come closer.

"I was hoping you'd do me the courtesy of a dance?"

I smiled softly. "My apologies, Eamryel, I'm afraid dancing isn't a possibility just yet."

His brows shot up in surprise. "Are you injured?"

"I was."

"Someone should have been there to protect you!"

I could have sworn his gaze settled on Talnovar for the briefest of moments, yet it was gone so quickly I thought I'd imagined it.

"I'm perfectly capable of protecting myself," I replied. "This was a freak accident."

He grunted at that. "A freak accident?"

"Yes," I replied, annoyance building up inside of me. "The wolf drew the short end of the stick."

His frown deepened. "You got injured? By a wolf? It didn't kill you?"

"Obviously not."

He huffed. "You shouldn't have been out on your own."

"Good thing I wasn't," I said. "As said, a freak accident."

"Had you been mine, it wouldn't have ever happened," he said, inspecting his fingernails.

He was baiting me. I took it.

"A good thing I'm not yours then," I hissed. "Excuse me."

I pushed passed him, looking where I could go to avoid him.

This conversation was going in a direction which made me feel highly volatile. Up ahead were Evan and Nathaïr, so I quickly walked over to them.

"Shal!" Evan smiled brightly. "Has anyone told you you look amazing tonight? In a dress no less."

"Not as beautiful as your betrothed though."

"About that," he began. "Isn't that yo—"

I kicked him in the shin.

"I wanted to congratulate you on your engagement. You look like a diamond, Nath."

She blushed becomingly. "Thank you."

With an apology, I left them and snaked my way through the crowd of people around the dancefloor, trying to be as inconspicuous as possible. I was undoubtedly getting on Talnovar's nerves for trying to stay out of sight. Once I found a somewhat more unobtrusive corner, I leaned back against the wall, taking the weight off of my leg, watching people from this vantage point.

Talnovar went to stand close by, as did Xaresh and Elara, none of them looking too happy with my choice. I shrugged.

"I'd have believed you weren't avoiding me had you not snuck through an entire crowd of people just to get *here*," Eamryel said in a low voice from my side.

He stood close all of a sudden—too close. With his hand placed against the wall next to my head, his face just inches from mine, I could smell the alcohol on his breath. Taking a step away from him proved futile as he just moved along.

"It should've been us up there," he said, a slight slur in his voice. "We'd have made the perfect couple."

"You're drunk."

He sneered. "We could have ruled the world, you and I."

"Do you really want to do this at your sister's engagement?" I muttered, looking at him. "I doubt she'll forgive you for it."

"Nath?" He chuckled. "She won't do a thing if she knows what's good for her."

I narrowed my eyes at him, head slightly tilted. "What's that supposed to mean?"

He brought his face even closer, running his knuckles down my cheek as he let his eyes roam freely. "It means whatever I want it to mean. You will be mine, *Tarien*. One day."

"Never."

I placed my hands against his chest and gave him a firm shove, but he was steadier on his feet than I'd expected. In an instant, he was in my face again, but this time had his hand around my throat.

"Feisty." He grinned. "I'll get that out of you yet."

"Over my dead body," Tal growled from behind him.

Eamryel turned at his voice and received a punch to the face hard enough to break his nose and send him into the wall. He screamed bloody murder, drawing all attention to us. Elara positioned herself in front of me, stance wide, arms alongside her body, one hand hovering close to her sword. Xaresh kept Tal from beating Eamryel again.

"What's going on here?" Evan thundered.

Nathaïr's face peeked from behind his shoulder, paling at the sight of her brother. She didn't run to him as I'd expected, and something he'd said tugged at my memory, as if it was trying to make something clear.

Tal's face was flushed, the veins in his neck standing out in a way I'd never seen before. A tic in his jaw had started, and he balled his fists at his sides while his breath was coming in loud puffs. Xaresh muttered something to him, but Tal's gaze was zeroed in on Eamryel cowering on the floor, hands against his nose.

"He hit me!" he howled. "The *nohro* idiot hit me!"

"And you damn well deserved it," Tal spat back. "Touch her again, and I'll break more than your nose."

151

I grabbed Elara's arms, digging my fingers into them as I watched the scene unfold from behind her back.

Evan stared from one to the other, anger blazing in his otherwise bright eyes. "Bring them both to a prison cell. Let them overthink their actions there during the night."

Guards came up to grab Talnovar, but Xaresh held them off. He twisted Tal's arm behind his back and propelled him out of the ballroom. The guards picked up a snivelling and cursing Eamryel instead.

"Have a healer see to him," Evan said in disgust.

When everyone had returned to the frivolities, I slumped back against the wall, trembling all over. Evan knelt in front of me, a concerned look in his eyes.

"Are you all right?"

I nodded. "Yeah. Fine. Nothing bad happened."

Nathaïr stood behind him, a sorrowful look in her eyes. I smiled faintly up at her, before turning to look at Evan again.

"Go enjoy your party," I murmured. "I'll have Elara escort me to my chambers."

He placed a soft kiss on my cheek and made to step away again.

"Ev?"

He turned back to face me. "Yes?"

"Go easy on Tal?" I said. "He was only doing his job."

Evan just nodded, placed a hand between Nathaïr's shoulder blades and guided her back to the festivities. In the meantime, Elara helped me back to my feet. I was in no shape to go anywhere really, but I didn't want to stay either. Using the wall and Elara for support, we made our way to the doors.

Someone bumped into Elara, causing her to let go of me so we wouldn't both stumble. While her attention was momentarily diverted, someone called my title, and as I turned around, something painfully sharp passed my cheek. Stunned at what had just happened, I stared at Amaris holding a bloodied dagger in his hand while watching me with a smirk on his face.

"Payback, *hehzèh*," he hissed, and disappeared into the crowd.

Too stunned to respond, I brought my hand to my cheek, my fingers coming back red and sticky.

"Elara?" I murmured. "Let's go see Soren first."

"Are you kidding me, *Tarien?*" she muttered. "What did you do this time?"

I shrugged. "Upset people."

"You're a walking disaster," she grumbled, pinching the bridge of her nose. "Come on."

SOREN LOOKED ALMOST AMUSED when we entered the infirmary, shaking his head. He sat me down on a chair and tilted my head so he could have a proper look at my cheek.

"If this wasn't so serious I'd think you were starting to miss me," he said, dabbing away the blood. "What happened?"

"Someone didn't agree with my methods."

He raised an eyebrow. I shrugged.

"I have good news," he said, "and bad news."

"Start with the bad news. It can only get better from there."

Soren chuckled. "Your positivity knows no bounds."

"You should try my wrath."

"Either way," he continued as if I had said nothing. "The bad news is that it will leave a scar."

I just looked at him. "And the good news?"

"It's not as big or deep as I feared it was, but I have to stitch it."

"Lucky me…"

Soren placed a cool cloth against my face and told me to keep it there. He moved around gathering the equipment he needed. Once he had it all sorted, he tilted my head again.

"What are the chances of you hitting or kicking me?"

I snorted. "High with a chance of likely."

"I was afraid of that."

He took the cloth away and before I knew, he stuck a needle into my cheek. This time, I managed not to hit him, but only because Elara grabbed my hands in time.

"Squeeze when it hurts."

"I'll break your hands."

She huffed. "I doubt that."

I had expected the stitching to hurt as much as it had done with my leg, but it was over and done with before he'd even started. He applied a cream strongly reminding me of one of Mehr's and sent me on my way with the instruction to come back the next day.

"What really happened?"

I looked at Elara, pushing some hair out of my face. "Not sure. The moment you let go of me, Amaris called me and when I turned around, he nicked me."

"But why?"

"For having sent him to prison?"

Elara snorted. "He's got issues. Should we tell his father?"

"I might let Evan or Haerlyon do that."

She nodded, and we continued our way in brooding silence, until I stopped halfway, turning towards where the cells were.

"I'd like to visit Tal."

"I don't think that's a good idea," Elara replied, pursing her lips.

I turned to her with a frown. "Why not?"

"Let's go to your room first."

Elara was adamant about not seeing Tal, and try though I might, she wouldn't budge. In fact, I was sure if I pushed the issue any further, she'd grab me by the scruff of my neck and carry me to my room. Limping there was more dignified.

She closed the door behind us as I flopped down on my bed,

folding my hands under my head.

"Why shouldn't I go to Tal?" I furrowed my brows. "He's there because of me."

"He's there because he made a choice," Elara said, sitting down in a chair. "He knew full well what the consequences could be. A night in jail is the best of outcomes."

"I'm not entirely sure I follow."

"He didn't have to hit Eamryel. He chose to do it."

I leaned up on my elbows, watching her. "I'm glad he did though. The man's a creep."

"Agreed, but Tal could have just arrested him and escorted him out."

"Then why did he hit him?"

Elara laughed softly, shaking her head. "If you haven't figured that out yet, I won't tell you."

"Fine," I muttered. "But it still doesn't explain why I can't go see him."

She jerked her chin at my cheek as she sat back, muttering about the armour being in the way.

While struggling herself out of it, she continued, "Have you had a look at your face yet?"

"Of course not."

She smiled. "How do you think he would react if he saw your face less than an hour after he got sent to jail?"

"He wouldn't be happy."

"That, *Tarien*," she said, "is more than just an understatement. Do you have any idea how he felt when your horses showed up, without you?

"Orion came back?"

"Not the point." Elara sighed, dumping the armour on the floor. "Tal was beside himself, but he couldn't go until dawn had come. Have you ever seen a caged tiger?"

"No."

She smiled faintly. "Well, let's just say he looked like one. As soon as the first sliver of dawn appeared, he rode out with the hounds and a handful of men. He was fearing the worst."

"Worst?"

"Your death," she replied. "He was afraid you had died somewhere during the night, and when he found you all covered in blood, he thought you wouldn't survive the journey."

I nodded. "But not all of it was mine—I think."

"True, but they hadn't seen the wolf yet." Elara smiled softly. "Anyway, ever since, he has been beating himself up over the fact he wasn't there to protect you. How do you think he'd feel now if he sees you with a new injury?"

"He'd go mad."

"And that is if we're lucky."

I bit my lip while lying down, staring at the ceiling as I contemplated her words. Swallowing hard, I turned on my side, resting my head on my arm.

"But he'll still go mad when he sees me tomorrow."

Elara chuckled and shook her head. "We'll just tell him you had a training accident that morning."

"You're evil, you know that?"

She laughed—a bright, clear laugh reverberating deep within me. No matter how I felt, her laugh always made me feel easier.

"What about Eamryel?" I asked. "What'll happen to him?"

She shrugged. "No idea. I think you'll have to ask your mother."

"First thing in the morning." I stifled a yawn and rose to my feet. "Can you help me get this dress off? I'd like to breathe again.

Once I was tucked in and Elara had taken up position outside my door, I stared at the light of the candle, watching it dance unaware of any problems, wishing I could be it. Something Eamryel had said kept nagging me—something about Nathaïr not doing something if she knew what was best for her. I tried to make sense of it, but my brain shut down for the night.

CHAPTER 9

*T*rue to her word, Elara woke me up for training before the crack of dawn next morning. At her first attempt, I hid my head under my pillow, muttering for her to go away. At her second attempt, I threw said pillow in her general direction, still refusing to get up. Her third attempt was more successful. Grabbing me by the ankles, she literally started hauling me out of bed.

"All right! Fine! I'm getting out!"

She let go, my knees hitting the floor with a loud thud, and with a mumbled curse in her direction, I got to my feet. Next moment, a blouse hit me in the face, followed by a pair of trousers, and my deerskin boots.

"Get dressed."

"I thought you were joking last night," I grumbled.

Elara smirked. "You know I don't joke when it comes to training."

"Does he handpick you for your level of sadism?"

She snorted, throwing the pillow back in my direction. With my second leg caught in my trousers, I couldn't dodge it and caught it full in the chest, dropping back on the bed with a grunt. I dressed as fast as I could and slipped into my boots.

"Let's get this over with then," I said, tying my hair back.

I grabbed my sword and dagger and followed Elara outside. The air was crisp, but there was also a gentle warmth on the breeze hinting at Spring's arrival. I breathed in the cool morning air as I skipped down the steps, seeing the others had already gathered and were warming up.

"You're late," Xaresh called out over the field.

Elara jerked her thumb at me. "Your majesty didn't want to come."

Xaresh watched me from a distance with arms folded. He was a formidable man to behold, standing a few inches taller than both Talnovar and Evan. He was wider in the hips and shoulders though, giving him a stocky look, and it didn't help his upper-arms were the size of tree trunks.

When I came closer, the scowl on his face deepened.

"What happened to your cheek?"

I shrugged. "It has a cut."

"Care to explain?"

"Not really."

I flashed him a grin and quickly set to my warming-up before he'd ask more questions. Although my leg was stiff, it wasn't as painful as I'd expected it to be. I still didn't relish the thought of running though. When Xaresh announced it was the first thing we were doing, I wanted to strangle him with my bare hands.

The first few yards were difficult. Although my leg wasn't used to the impact of running anymore, it held better than I thought it would, but my progress around the field was slow, and my stamina wasn't even close to what it had been. Even so, I was getting around, running. Xaresh stayed close, pushing me beyond my limit in such a gentle way I didn't even realise he had until we were back at our starting point.

I doubled over, hands on my knees, gasping for air.

"Get up," he said, tapping my ass with the flat of his sword. "You know this won't work."

Glaring at him, I pushed myself up, stretching instead. Annoyed at the fact my stamina had gone down so rapidly, I resolved I'd go running several times a day. I hated feeling this vulnerable.

Fight training was more intense than I remembered it to be. Xaresh pushed us to our limits, and over. I had thought Tal was a harsh taskmaster, but Xaresh was giving him a fair run for his money. I concentrated on the slow, calculated steps combined with the parries and strikes as each *Arathrien* attacked me. They were moves I knew by heart, so despite not having trained for almost three weeks, they came to me easily. It made me feel comfortable. It made me feel in control.

For the first time since I went out riding with Evan and fate dealt me a hand full of bad cards, I started to relax. By the end of training, my legs were burning and my entire body was an aching mess. It felt good though. In due time, I'd have my strength and agility back. I was sure of it.

"Are you coming?" Elara asked.

"Coming where?"

She snorted. "You really have to ask?"

"Oh!"

TAL WAS SITTING with his back against the far wall of his cell with his knees drawn up, elbows resting on them, hands in his hair. His head hung low, and even from this distance I could see his knuckles were bloodied. I could only hope it wasn't his, but knew that hope was in vain. At the sound of my footsteps on the stones, he looked up. His eyes were red and the dark circles underneath were a testimony of his night.

He looked terrible.

"*Tarien*," he croaked. "What are you doing here?"

"Visiting the biggest *khirr* in the realm."

His lips quirked up at one corner. He rose to his feet, his movements stiff and uncontrolled. I glanced down, steadying my breathing as the sight of him was more than I could handle. This was so unlike him. Looking back, I saw he was only inches away from me now, and his eyes narrowed immediately upon seeing the stitches. He cupped my cheek in his hand, running his thumb gently over the cut.

He was trembling.

"Don't tell me this happened last night," he whispered, a tic starting in his jaw.

I placed my hand against his, swallowing hard. "It did, but you cannot beat yourself up over it."

"What happened?"

For a moment I considered telling him a lie, but seeing him like this, I decided against it.

"Remember when I sent Amaris to jail?" I began, dropping my hand.

He nodded slowly, wrapping his hands tight around the bars.

"Last night, he cut me," I said. "He called me by title, I turned around, and here we are. It's not too bad according to Soren. It'll leave a scar, but that's it."

Tal gripped the bars so tight his knuckles turned whiter than normal. Swallowing hard, I laid my hands on his. He looked up, a multitude of emotions rapidly crossing his wan features.

"I'm sorry," he murmured. "If I hadn't... he wouldn't have."

"He would have," I replied. "Elara was right beside me, and he still did it by creating a diversion."

He frowned. "He'd planned this?"

"I think so."

Tal growled low under his breath and let go of the bars,

pacing up and down his cell like the caged tiger in Elara's metaphor.

"If I ever run into him" he began, jerking a hand through his dishevelled hair.

"You will let him go."

Tal stared at me as if I'd gone stupid.

"I'll tell Evan or Haer what happened," I said, watching him. "They might be able to deal with it since his father's in the army."

"All right." He didn't look happy. "All right. Fine."

I smiled. "Not everything needs to be sorted with a punch to the face."

"Eamryel had it coming," Tal snapped.

"I know."

He stared at me, but this time in confusion rather than looking as if I'd become an idiot overnight. He rubbed the back of his neck, smiling wryly.

"He deserved that punch," I said. "You were just quicker than I was."

He snorted. "I should've let you."

"Maybe."

Tal sighed deeply, shaking his head. "I messed up though. Evan was livid."

"Can't exactly blame him. You disrupted his engagement party. I'm sure he'll forgive you once he hears what happened."

"You've got a lot of faith in him."

"Ev isn't one to hold grudges." I shrugged. "No matter how serious things are."

Tal came back to the bars, leaning against them with his hands tucked into his armpits, a frown on his face.

"He's dangerous."

"Ev?"

He snorted. "Eamryel."

I shuddered at the thought of him, wrapping my arms around myself. Tal put his hand through the bars and tucked a wayward strand of hair behind my ear.

"Promise me something."

I looked at him warily.

"Don't go out alone," he said, biting his lip. "Not with him walking around freely. If you feel the desperate need to go out, take Xaresh or Elara, or any of the others. Take your brothers for all I care, just don't leave the palace unsupervised."

The hair on my neck stood on edge at the mention of the word unsupervised, and I breathed in deeply, considering his plea. Although it made sense, it also added to everything I already hated, and while Eamryel had scared me the night before, I refused to be afraid of him. Looking at Tal, seeing the scared look in his wide, mysterious eyes, I sighed.

"All right, fine," I said. "I promise."

He looked relieved at my promise, but I felt as if a stone had settled inside my stomach. After what Elara had told me, I didn't want to burden him anymore than was necessary, and he was right about one thing—Eamryel was dangerous.

Something told me we hadn't seen the last of him.

"Let's see if I can talk you out of here," I said.

EVAN WAS out on the fields by now too, back to training the *àn* under his command. I made myself comfortable at the foot of the stairs, pulling my shawl around my shoulders for comfort. Xaresh stood off to the side, but I noticed he was watching me, a light frown on his face.

"Out with it Xaresh," I said.

He flashed me one of his bright smiles. "It's nothing, *Tarien*. Just glad to see you up and about again."

"That makes two of us."

"Sorry if I pushed you too far this morning," he said after a while, plucking at the cuff of his shirt.

I chuckled softly. "I'm not made of glass."

"Some seem to believe you are."

With a snort I looked at him, feeling amused he would say something like that. I cocked my head to the side, regarding him quietly.

"You don't?"

"I believe accidents happen," he said with a shrug, "and I can't protect you from all of them."

I looked amused. "Yeah, well, I seem to attract said accidents like a flame does moths."

"Those weren't accidents."

"And do you beat yourself up over them too?" I asked without looking at him.

He fell silent.

"Not exactly," he said at length. "Though I was rather annoyed Evan hadn't informed us, not personally, that he was taking you for a ride."

I nodded slowly, wrapping my arms around myself. "I can imagine."

The subject of our conversation came walking up right at that moment, and I could tell from the look on his face he was close enough to see my cheek.

"I'll tell you," I began before he could speak, "if you get Tal out of jail."

He harrumphed, folding his arms in front of his chest. "And why would I?"

"Because he was protecting me."

"Figured as much." Evan sighed. "But he can't just hit people."

I smirked. "If he hadn't, I would have."

Xaresh snorted and turned away for a moment.

Evan just frowned as he sat down next to me. "Do I even want to know why?"

"Probably not." I shrugged. "But Tal regrets what he did, and honestly, if Eamryel is already out, allow him to go too."

Evan frowned. "I never released Eamryel."

"Maybe Mother did."

"I'll ask when I see her." He pinched the bridge of his nose. "I'll get Tal out. What happened to your cheek?"

I wrung my hands, looking anywhere but at my brother. To my side, Xaresh perked up. I hadn't gotten around to telling him what had happened either. With a deep sigh I told both of them what Amaris had done the night before, explaining the reason behind it. I rubbed my forehead when I was done, glancing at Evan from under my arm.

His jaw was set, but other than that, all seemed fine.

"I thought you could have a chat with his father," I said. "I don't think he'd be thrilled upon hearing this."

Evan frowned. "Amaris might retaliate though. If he does this after you put him in jail for the night, I don't like to think of what he would do if we turn his father against him."

"Fair enough."

He rubbed his temples, leaning back against the stairs. I followed his example, looking up at the fluffy clouds floating through the sky.

"That dress," Evan said after a while. "Nathaïr was ecstatic about it. She didn't want to take it off."

I chuckled softly. "Good. I'm glad she liked it."

"She did look beautiful," Evan murmured, and I grinned.

"Glad you liked it too."

He rolled his eyes at me and I laughed, placing a kiss on his cheek.

"All right," I said. "I'm going to make myself scarce. Please, let Tal out? Before he does himself any harm."

Evan snorted. "You think he would?"

"He already did," I replied with a soft smile. "I'll see you later."

AFTER HAVING SAID EVAN GOODBYE, we made our way down to the stables. Elara had said Orion and Hadiyah returned on their own, but I hadn't seen either since the attack. Once we arrived at the stables, however, it appeared half the palace was assembled. A dozen horses and more were saddled, and all around, people were saying their goodbyes. Mother was talking to Yllinar, and I could see Nathaïr standing off to the side, arms wrapped around herself. I'd almost expected her to be sad, but she looked rather relieved instead. I wondered why. Grayden was amongst the crowd too, checking stirrups and bridles.

Haerlyon sauntered over to us, a big grin on his face.

"Come to see the party off?"

"I didn't even know they were going."

He chuckled. "It's your mission they're leaving on now."

I looked at my brother with a frown, and it suddenly dawned on me—Yllinar was going on the diplomatic mission.

"Well," I said. "Good."

My gaze settled on someone else amongst the crowd and my heart stopped beating when I saw Eamryel standing alongside one of the horses, his expression thunderous. His nose was crooked, and even from this distance I could tell half his face looked properly bruised.

As if on cue, he looked straight at me.

My breath caught in my throat, and my heart started beating fast in my chest. When he strode my way, all I wanted to do was spin on my heel and leave, but I was sure it would only encourage him. Besides, it showed fear, and I refused to award him that emotion. My thoughts wandered off to Tal in his cell, and I felt anger overwhelm the fear. Squaring my shoulders, and lifting my chin, I waited for him to arrive.

"*Tarien*," he said. "It's good to see you."

I merely inclined my head. "I wish I could say the same."

His lips curled up in a sneer, his eyes taking on a predatory gaze.

"Your mother and my father think it's a good idea if I join him on this mission." He clenched and unclenched his fists at his side. "I can't say I agree."

"It might be educational."

The news of him leaving the city was the best I had heard in a while, but I couldn't let him know this.

Eamryel harrumphed, twisting his lips. "I doubt it."

"I wish you a safe journey, Eamryel," I said, nodding quickly. "May you return in one piece."

If he had an accident along the way, I couldn't be happier, but it would be considered bad form to tell him that. He raised his chin and puffed out his chest. Before I knew, he'd stepped too close for comfort.

"Don't go anywhere," he whispered for my ears alone. "You're mine to own, understand?"

He stepped back as quickly as he'd advanced and bowed deeply. My lips thinned as I pretended not to have heard him. I clenched my fists at my side, locking my elbows and shoulders so I couldn't punch him.

"Be well, *Tarien*."

Without waiting for a reply, he turned on his heel and walked over to his horse. Xaresh laid a hand on my shoulder.

"Is everything all right?"

I just nodded, not trusting my voice.

"What did he want?" Haerlyon pursed his lips.

I shook my head. "It's nothing."

"Is that why you look like you're about to strangle him?" He gave me a lopsided grin.

166

"He's a creep, is all."

Xaresh snorted. Haerlyon laughed softly.

"You have a penchant for understatements, sis," he said for our ears alone. "Stay out of his line of sight, please? I don't trust him."

I rolled my eyes. "You're not the only one who's asked me that, but he's going away now. I should be fine until he comes back."

Haerlyon merely raised an eyebrow.

"What's going on here?" Azra asked from behind us.

Surprised, I turned around, looking at her.

"They're off on a diplomatic mission," I replied. "To Therondia."

Azra looked genuinely surprised. "Why is that?"

"To find out what they want."

She folded her arms in front of her, her mouth set in a hard line as she watched the scene in the courtyard unfold.

"That's a dangerous mission," she said.

I frowned. "How so?"

"The Therondians aren't known for their hospitality." She shrugged. "Their party might very well not survive it."

"It's a risk worth taking."

Azra looked at me with contempt. "Do you think of their lives that lightly?"

"No, not at all. I have faith in them, they can do this."

She forced a smile on her face and refused to look at me. I glanced at Haer, who just shrugged.

"I hope your faith will save them."

She pivoted on her heel and was gone, leaving the three of us staring after her with mouths open and confused looks on our faces.

"What in all the Gods' names was that about?" Haerlyon muttered.

I shrugged. "Beats me."

167

I tucked my hands under my arms, watching the party mount their horses. Grayden looked at me, flashing me a wide smile while waving. I inclined my head, sending up a prayer to whoever would listen to keep them safe.

The clip-clop of hooves on cobblestones indicated the party was leaving. I raised my hand in greeting, my stomach tying itself in knots in memory of Azra's words. If they died, it would be because of me. A shiver ran up and down my spine, so I pulled my shawl tighter about me, feeling rather out of place.

"Want to go for a walk?" Haerlyon asked, looking at me.

I nodded. "Sounds good."

Although it wasn't that cold, I huddled in on myself as we walked back towards the training fields in companionable silence. The clattering of hooves should have been fading in the distance—instead it was coming our way. I turned around slowly, watching a rider less horse pelt down the road towards us, eyes wide in a panicked frenzy, foam at the mouth as if it had been running for miles already. My brain knew I had to get out of the way, but my body wouldn't cooperate. I just stood there, watching its headlong flight in my direction as if in slow-motion. I heard someone yell my name somewhere in the background.

As the horse reached me, something barrelled into me, pushing me out of the horse's path. I landed with my shoulder on a cobblestone jutting out, and a sharp pain flared through my arm and back as if a knife had been stuck into it. Gasping for air, I focused and found Haerlyon lying on top of me. The horse passed us, chased by two stable boys. Haer pushed himself up and sat back on his heels, watching me curiously while pushing his hair out of his face.

"Why didn't you move?"

"I don't know. I couldn't."

When I rolled my shoulder, it still worked, but it was painful.

My fingers were tingling, on the edge of numb even, but I could move them. I blamed the impact for it.

"Are you all right?" Haerlyon asked, helping me to my feet.

"Sore from the fall," I said. "It's not every day dead weight lands on top of you."

He snorted. "You're welcome."

I chuckled softly and threw an arm around his waist, resting my head against his shoulder.

"Thank you."

We continued our way to the gardens and found ourselves a spot between the wide array of roses. It was well-loved by many people. With its cute, white gazebo decorated with ivy and roses it made for a romantic spot where couples could often be found for various reasons. It was empty now, giving us the opportunity to talk more freely.

"What happened last night?" Haer asked, stretching his legs out in front of him.

I closed my eyes, running a hand through my hair. "Eamryel has this bizarre illusion we belong together. I don't know where he got that from. Until yesterday, I've barely spoken to him."

Haerlyon leaned forward, arms resting on his knees.

"He said something which Tal overheard," I continued. "Guess Tal didn't like that."

He flashed me his winning half-smile. "You think?"

"I suppose the words 'over my dead body' were clear enough."

"Eamryel did look rather colourful this morning." Haerlyon grinned. "What did he want just now?"

"More of his perpetual delusions."

"You looked like you were going to punch him," he remarked.

"I was doing my best not to."

Haerlyon stared at me, only to shake his head, laughing softly. Being with him eased my mind.

169

"You can't resolve everything with punching," he said. "Although I'll admit his creep-level is alarmingly high."

I snorted. "You think?"

He nodded sagely. "He'll be trouble. And a man as delusional as him will stop at nothing to get what he wants."

Goosebumps ran all over my skin at his words, and I shuddered, wrapping my arms around myself. I winced at the strain it put on my shoulder.

"Tal's made me promise not to go out on my own with him around." I rubbed my hands on my thighs, shaking my head. "Which makes me feel even more like a prisoner than I already did."

Haerlyon frowned at me. "Why would you feel like a prisoner?"

I gave him a deadpan stare.

"Because I can't do *anything* unsupervised?" I muttered. "Everyone's afraid of whatever that prophecy means."

"I think you being the only heir might have more to do with it."

I scowled. "Well, whatever it is, this palace is as much my home as it is my prison."

"Is that why you run away all the time?"

"What gave that away?" I asked, rolling my eyes. "It just gives me a sense of freedom, even if it's just for a little while."

His eyes suddenly glinted mischievously. I narrowed mine.

"What?"

"I'll take you out tomorrow," he said, "to the gates."

My brows shot up at his words. "You think Tal will let you go? Last time I went out with one of you I got mauled by a wolf."

"We won't be leaving the city." He grinned. "And Sir Creepalot isn't around either."

With a shake of my head and an eye roll worthy of Nathaïr, I looked at him, my mouth curving into a smile.

"I suppose."

He practically jumped to his feet, whooping with delight.

"You're such a beast!" I laughed.

His smile was infectious. "You love me."

I snorted and rose to my feet. As promised, he walked me back to Xaresh, and said goodbye with such a wide grin on his face I was sure it would split his head.

"What's he so happy about?"

I shrugged. "It's Haer. Does he ever need a reason to be?"

Xaresh shook his head, a smile on his face as we made our way back inside. Absently, I rubbed my shoulder, an indrawn hiss escaping my lips as even the softest touch hurt.

"There aren't any plans for the rest of the day, are there?"

"Not that I know of."

Rubbing the back of my neck, I just nodded, my thoughts drifting back to what Azra had said.

"I'll just go have a bath," I murmured. "Will you ask some servants to draw it up?"

Xaresh nodded, a slight frown creasing his brows. I entered my room, glad to find it was empty for a change, and walked over to the mirror. I pulled up my shirt, and turned my back towards it, so I could see my shoulder. A galaxy of colours covered most of my shoulder blade, an explanation on its own why the pain was so incredible. I turned at a sound at the door, and quickly dropped my shirt, moving over to my desk.

It was a mess.

Servants bustled in, carrying whatever was needed to draw up the bath. I stood back, arms folded in front of me, watching them move through my room like ants. Once they were done and had left my room, I started to undress, biting my lip as I tried to pull my blouse over my head a second time.

"*Nohro ahrae.*"

I froze halfway the movement, closing my eyes before I'd

start yelling at Tal for coming in uninvited. He came closer—his footfalls careful and deliberate.

"You could've knocked," I murmured.

"I did."

As I lifted the shirt over my head I grimaced, then lowered my arms in front of me, hiding all the essential parts before turning to him. I was getting sick and tired of his hisses and growls whenever there was something wrong—it added to feeling like a prisoner.

"I'm fine, all right?" I said, before he could even start. "Haer pushed me out of the way of a runaway horse and I fell. It's just a bruise."

His mouth snapped shut, a sceptic look stealing over his features. "You seem to get injured a lot when I'm not around."

"They're freak accidents."

"Yeah well," he growled, jerking his hand through his hair. "Excuse me if they're making me suspicious."

I clenched my jaw, and squeezed my eyes shut, not wanting to fight him. Again.

"I'm not made of glass," I said. "And you can't protect me from everything."

He glared at me, arms folded in front of him. "It's my job to at least try."

"Then maybe you shouldn't hit people in the face and get sent to jail," I yelled, fed up with his overprotectiveness. "Maybe you should just lock me in my bedroom until it's time for me to ascend the throne."

"Don't tempt me."

His lips set in a thin line, his chest puffed out, and his stance was wide, menacing even. I gritted my teeth, staring at him, fists clenched. This could turn ugly.

"I think it's better if you leave," I said, trying to sound calm. "Whatever you were here for, it's better for all involved if we don't get into it now."

He closed his eyes briefly, drew in a deep breath and with a curt nod, spun on his heel and left the room. I sunk to my knees shaking all over, a sob caught in my throat. I all but crawled over to my bed and lay down on it, legs pulled up, silent sobs racking my body.

This wasn't how I'd imagined his return to be.

CHAPTER 10

When Haerlyon picked me up to go into the city the next morning, I told Xaresh where I was going, but refused to let Tal know. Yet again, he'd made himself scarce, neglecting his duties as *Anahràn*. He was acting like a possessive jerk, much like Eamryel did, although Tal was perhaps less creepy. This time, however, I would not apologise, and if he wanted to get mad at me again, he could do so when I returned.

We passed the guards at the palace gates with no trouble. In fact, the guards even greeted Haerlyon and me normally, and it occurred to me—not without a pang of jealousy—it probably was *this* normal for my brother. I jerked the shawl I'd brought over my head.

"That was easy," I said with a frown.

He flashed me his impish grin. "Not everything has to be difficult."

"In your life maybe."

I realised what happened between Tal and myself yesterday still upset me and I was now lashing out at him. Haerlyon wasn't bothered though. In fact, he was already sauntering down the main street as if nothing had happened, chatting up merchants on one side, and greeting locals by name on the other. People knew him, and people clearly loved him, flocking around him like birds awaiting to be fed. It wasn't as if people hated me, but they were definitely warier around me.

As my gaze settled back on him, Haerlyon sat down cross-legged in front of a bawling boy whom I guessed to be no more than fifty years old—young still. He coaxed the boy gently into looking up. Big blue eyes stared at him, blubbering subsiding to sniffles as Haerlyon spoke to him in his ever patient voice. I stood off to the side, arms wrapped around myself as I watched the scene unfold.

"Have you ever met my sister?"

The child shook his head, so Haerlyon waved me over. Reluctantly, I walked over to the pair of them.

"Sit down," Haer murmured.

I stared at him until he grabbed my dress and yanked me down. I sat back on my heels, an awkward feeling creeping over me as I realised people around us had stopped to watch. Some looked at us with curiousity, others downright amused. Most of them were talking and whispering, pointing in our general direction, yet unlike court, it didn't feel menacing at all.

I began to relax and turned my attention back to my brother and the little boy.

"This is my sister," Haerlyon said with a smile. "Do you know who she is?"

The child shook his head.

"She's the *Tarien* of Ilvanna," he continued, "and even she can be a little clumsy. See her cheek?"

I refrained from snorting, my brow furrowing in a slight V-shape while I waited where this conversation was headed. The child looked at me with his head tilted, a curious twinkle in his eyes.

"What happened to your cheek?"

175

My lips curved into a smile of their own accord. "I tripped and fell."

"I did too," he said with a pout, lower lip trembling. "I was playing, and suddenly I tripped, and fell on my face."

"Oh no! Is that why you were crying?"

He nodded. I shuffled a little closer and lifted his chin gently. There was a little blood on it, but I could tell it was mostly just chafed.

"Well now, you're the bravest boy I've ever seen!"

I pulled the shawl from my head, bunched it up and dabbed away the blood with the tip. Within no time, there was nothing to be seen, although I assumed it would sting for a while longer.

"See, you're just as strong as our *Tarien*." Haerlyon leaned in to whisper something to him, loud enough for me to hear. "I daresay even stronger."

The boy beamed happily at his words, pushing out his chest.

"Thank you!"

He skipped off happily to a woman standing in the crowd. She knelt in front of him, a smile on her lips while he talked animatedly, pointing in our direction several times. When our eyes met, she looked away, bowing her head deeply. It made me feel more than a little uncomfortable so I just inclined my head and turned to Haerlyon.

"Your shawl's ruined now," he said, looking at it.

I shrugged. "It's fine. It's only a small corner."

I wrapped it around my shoulders, running my hand over the soft fabric. It had been a gift from Tal a few years ago, but I'd never worn it until the day before. Swallowing hard, I tried not to think about him and resumed my way to the main gate, Haerlyon on my heels.

We clambered up the slope to my hideout. Haerlyon had to help me up the wall this time, my shoulder not allowing me to pull myself up, and once there, we made our way over to my spot. Sitting down with my back against the wall, I slung one leg over the side, and breathed in deeply, looking out over the city.

"This is where you spend time when you run away?"

I gave him a lopsided grin. "Most days, yes."

"Why?"

"I enjoy watching people." I shrugged. "Imagine what they are doing here, or on what adventures they might be going, not to mention the view."

I pointed at the glittering sea in the distance, a deep longing settling in my bones. One day, I'd cross it.

He frowned, his head tilted, legs dangling over the edge, and his hands tucked underneath. "Some people go out for the most boring reasons."

"Doesn't matter. It's the idea that counts."

Haerlyon smiled at me, his eyes flickering with something I couldn't quite place. Closing my eyes, I rested my head against the wall, enjoying the sun on my face.

"It's not a bad place at all," Haerlyon said at length. "I can see why you go here."

"They always know where to find me," I said with a wry smile. "And then I run."

Haerlyon tilted his head. "Aren't you afraid?"

"Of what?"

"Getting caught by someone?"

I shook my head. "No, not really. I always make sure they can see me, so if anyone was out to get me, they'd know."

Haerlyon nodded, but I could see something distracted him and following his gaze, I noticed it was someone rather than something. The longing in his eyes when he glanced at me unmanned me.

"Go see him."

Haerlyon looked torn. "Will you be all right?"

"Of course."

Scampering to his feet, he pecked me on the cheek and clambered down the wall and the slope. Mere minutes later he was practically skipping to Tiroy, who was surprised to see him there. When Tiroy looked up, his eyes settled on me, so I waved, smiling. He inclined his head before turning back to my brother, his face lighting up. To anyone not knowing them they'd look like two men conversing—to me they looked like lovers doing their best not to be found out.

Haer's hand would brush past Tiroy's ever so slightly when he turned, or Tiroy would laugh at something Haer said. It were the small things, but they were there. It reminded me of the moment Tal had cupped my cheek in his trembling hand, stroking his thumb over the injury. It had felt good, safe even, but he had pulled away as if it had hurt him. With a deep sigh and a shake of my head, I dispelled the thoughts of Tal and focused on the people at the main gate instead.

A hooded figure conversing with a Therondian merchant caught my attention almost immediately. The skittish way they looked around, combined with the underhanded dealings clear from up here, made them stand out like a bonfire on a dark night. I drew up my leg, sat down on my heel, and leaned forward a little to see what was going on. It was a shame the hooded figure had his back towards me, but there was something about him which struck me as familiar. I just couldn't put my finger on what it was.

Glancing at my brother and Tiroy made clear they weren't paying any attention to their surroundings, and the second guard present was dealing with a group of travellers causing mayhem at the gates. I could yell, but that would surely alert the merchant and whoever he was dealing with, risking the chance of both bolting. My gaze shifted back to them just in time to watch them conclude their business. Money passed quick enough to go by unseen, and as the merchant turned to other customers, the hooded figure made his way back into the city.

I frowned.

If he'd come from the city, it could mean trouble. Quickly I made my way down the wall, ignoring the tight pull on my shoulder as I hung myself from the ledge. I had to be fast if I wanted to catch up.

I was down just in time to see the hooded figure turn a corner into the third circle and I felt my heart sink. I'd never gone there on purpose—without being chased and in sight— knowing Tal would skin me alive if I did, but now it looked like I had no choice. He tolerated me running off, but he'd never tolerate me risking my life.

I'm sorry, Tal.

Pulling the shawl over my head, I wrapped it around my eye- catching white hair, while making my way through the crowd, dodging as many people as possible.

The hooded figure guided me through several streets, and the farther we went, the more the surroundings seemed to change. Buildings were rundown, shutters hung by a thread and doors were either hanging on their hinges or missing completely. Here were no pristine marble houses displaying wealth, or domestic stone buildings emanating a warm welcome. Here, hopelessness oozed from every nook and cranny. Few people lived here, and I realised a little too late this had to be the criminal's quarters.

Why does Mother let them live here?

The hooded figure halted in front of a shop, its sign adver- tising it as an herbal shop, but in this part of the city, I didn't quite buy it. Once he was inside, I moved over to stand just outside the door, plastering myself against the wall so I could overhear the conversation without being seen.

"Afternoon mistress."

That had to be the shopkeeper.

"Hello Uryal."

My heart stopped, and my stomach sank upon hearing the voice. All lilt, melody, and seductiveness, it was a voice I'd recognise anywhere. Aunt Azra. A loud buzzing in my ears made me focus on what they were saying, but it was hard until I realised it was the rush of blood being pumped into my ears by a hammering heart. I breathed in deeply and tried to calm myself the way Tal had taught me.

I wish you were here.

"Do you have any Fair Lady?" Azra purred. "And perhaps some Narcissus?"

I frowned, wondering what Fair Lady was, or Narcissus for that matter.

"Of course, *Irà*," the shopkeeper said. "Anything else?"

I couldn't quite catch Aunt Azra's reply—I was too stunned by the hooded figure being her. Her business in this shop, or with the Therondian merchant, could not amount to anything good.

Their conversation sounded as if they were rounding things up. It was time I made myself scarce, and fast. By now, the few people living here were eyeing me suspiciously, so I turned away and walked off briskly, seeking shelter in my shawl from prying eyes.

I'd just rounded the corner out of the criminal's den into a better part of the slums when two men stepped in front of me, impeding my progress. I spun on my heel just to see two more men step in front of me, blocking the exit.

None of them looked friendly.

Assuming a defensive position, I pulled the small knife Azra had given me into my hand. The irony wasn't lost on me. I turned around slowly, assessing the situation, monitoring all of them as best I could. The men looked amused.

"Would ye look at that," one of them sneered. "The little doll thinks she can fight."

The other men laughed while drawing daggers from behind their backs. This wasn't a training session. This was real. It was everything Tal had trained me for. As all of them adopted a fighting stance, I noticed one charging me from the corner of my eye. The moment he got close, I sidestepped, and grabbed his arm in the same motion with one hand on his wrist and the other on his elbow, pulling his arm back. A loud snap echoed through the alley, followed by an unearthly howl. The dagger clattered to the ground harmlessly.

A second one stormed me in anger. All I needed to do was pull his comrade towards me so he would catch the blade instead of me. He went down with a grunt and as I let go off him, I charged the second attacker. Too surprised at what I had done, he stood gaping at me as I drove the little dagger home in that sweet spot between the collarbones. My eyes darted around rapidly, settling on the two remaining men as they charged me. Just as I was about to counter their attack, someone pulled me back, a dagger against my throat a second later.

I stilled. The men halted, smirks on their faces.

"Well now," a honeyed voice purred in my ear. "I knew you could fight—I didn't know you could fight this well. I should've warned them."

I swallowed hard. "You're not supposed to be here."

Eamryel laughed. "Oh, father won't be pleased for sure, but there's nothing he can do about it now. He's well on his way to Therondia, and I have to thank you for that, *Tarien.*"

"What do you want?"

He grabbed my shoulder and spun me around, leaning towards me. I gritted my teeth as he dug his fingers painfully into my bruised shoulder. My lips were a thin line as I looked at him, keeping the small knife hidden behind my back. His face was a myriad of colours from the punch Tal had dealt him.

"I told you what I wanted," he whispered, his lips brushing mine, "and now it looks like it's within easy reach."

I refrained from pulling my lips away from his, afraid to agitate him, and there was still the matter of the dagger against my throat. Besides, if I let him know he scared me, he'd win, and

I didn't want to give him that idea. He slipped the shawl from my hair with his dagger, discarding it behind him.

"You're so much prettier without it."

I had one chance, and one chance alone. I slipped the knife between my fingers and brought up my hand in one swift motion like Elara had taught me. He was fast, but not fast enough. I nicked him across the cheekbone just before he grabbed my wrist and pried the knife from my fingers. The dagger was back at my throat as he pushed me against the wall. His eyes were blazing. He drew the dagger along my jawline without pushing it hard. I felt the blade, but it didn't cut.

It made me more determined to get away from him.

He licked his lips, cocking his head to the side. His body was flush against mine, and I felt more than I cared for. Eamryel sighed and tucked a strand of hair behind my ear. The sentiment was so at odds with the situation I actually giggled.

"Listen, *mey shareye*," he said in an undertone. "This can go two ways. You either come with me willingly, and I promise you your stay will be pleasant, or you come unwillingly…"

He let the words linger between us. He didn't need to finish it for me to understand what he meant.

But I would never go willingly.

I pulled up my knee to where it hurt most, and as he doubled over, I twisted his wrist, forcing him to drop the dagger. Without thinking, I ran farther into the alley, his howl following me as I hurtled from one street into the next. The sound of footsteps behind me became louder as they got closer. My heart was racing in my chest, and I ran as fast as I could, but the longer I ran, the more I sank through the still-healing leg.

I cursed my stupidity.

If only Tal were here.

The deeper I ran into the alleys, the more I got lost, and the more frightened I felt. Ironically enough, this was the city I one day had to rule, yet now it may very well be my coup de grâce. I ended up in a dead-end street and turning around, watched my attackers stalk closer, followed by a furious Eamryel.

I watched him advance and backed up against the wall. My breathing came fast and shallow. In. Out. Rapidly. No matter how hard I tried, I couldn't fill my lungs with air. I retreated further, wincing at the pain shooting through my injured leg. Shifting my weight to the other leg, I waited, my eyes never leaving him.

The moment he stepped within reach, Eamryel slapped me across the face, sending me to the ground. The iron taste of blood tinged my mouth. I spit it out, wiped my lips and rose to my feet, lifting my chin and squaring my shoulders.

It was the feral look in his eyes which had me reassess my decisions.

"Too bad," he hissed. "We could have had fun. Now, it'll just be me having the fun."

He brought up his hand and hit me over the head with something hard. I slumped to the ground and was unconscious before I levelled out.

Coming around, I felt my arms were locked above my head, and my ankles were tied together with rope. The strain in my shoulders indicated they were stretched out too far. My vision was blurry, and the pain in my head so fierce my vision swam the moment I moved it the tiniest bit.

Across from me, Eamryel straddled a chair, picking his nails with my little knife. The moment he noticed my eyes were open, he got up and walked over to me in such a predatory way it riled me up. I yanked my restraints angrily, finding they wouldn't budge. He squatted in front of me, a wicked grin playing on his lips as he placed the small knife under my chin. Cold eyes watched me in gleeful anticipation.

"Good morning sunshine. Glad you could join me."

I spat in his face.

He backhanded me across the cheek hard enough I heard my neck crack. The stinging sensation in my cheek wasn't unlike being cut, and it left me dazed. When he placed the knife against the hollow of my throat, I stilled.

"Why do you make me hurt you?" Eamryel sighed, eyeing me like a priced possession. "I don't want to."

I snorted. "You've got your head on backwards."

He pressed the knife lightly into my skin, sending my heart into a frenzy. All it took was one good push. I swallowed hard, refusing to break eye contact.

"There's nothing wrong with me," he said, a smirk on his face.

I looked at him stunned and burst out laughing. His eyes narrowed to thin slits, and when he leaned in closer, I couldn't help but laugh harder. This situation was ridiculous.

"Laugh all you want, *shareye*," he whispered in my ear, his breath hot on my skin, "and we shall see who gets the last one."

It made my skin crawl.

I sobered quickly at the tone of his voice, looking at him. He was close enough. In one swift move I head-butted him, aiming for the bridge of his nose. I heard a sickening crunch, and Eamryel reeled back with a loud howl. He brought his hands to his face, dropping the knife to the ground. I tried to reach it, to no avail—I had no room to move.

Eamryel picked it back up.

Still holding his hand against his bleeding nose, he watched me with a look so dark it promised nothing good. Shivers ran down my spine and I realised I might have gone too far, so I shrank back against the wall, my eyes never leaving him.

"You'll pay for this," he growled.

"This won't go unpunished," I said, swallowing hard. "Once

they find me, you're in more trouble than your ant-sized brain can even begin to imagine."

Curling his lips in a snarl, he wiped the blood from his nose. "*If* they find you."

"They will."

The confidence I heard in my voice was a far cry from what I was feeling. Tal had been right—he was dangerous. It was in the predatory way he walked—in the honeyed tone of his voice —in the calculated moves he made. Everything about him oozed danger, and I didn't doubt for a minute he meant what he said.

I couldn't give in. Every fibre in my body resisted that thought.

"Maybe..." He straddled my legs so I couldn't move them while he picked up the knife. "I should make your predicament a little clearer."

He ran the tip of the knife slowly down my arm like a lover's caress.

"They won't come for you," he murmured, "because they wouldn't even know where to start. Who in their right mind would abduct the *Tarien?*"

"Not someone in their right mind," I said, gritting my teeth.

I half-expected him to slap me again, but instead he nicked my arm with the knife, drawing blood. A hiss escaped my lips.

"You're out of your *nohro* mind," I growled, tugging at my restraints.

It earned me another nick on my arm.

His mouth twitched. "Did you know the body can sustain a lot of small cuts before it succumbs? They even heal rather fast."

I tightened my lips. "You wouldn't."

"Oh, but *shareye,*" he purred, "I will do anything to make you realise who's in control here, for as long as it takes for you to learn."

My skin crawled at his words. I drew up my knees, but he

had my legs pinned down so firmly with his weight, I could barely move. It amused him to no end.

"I love it when you resist me."

Despite my restraints, I tried to fight him. I screamed this time. I bucked, and I cried, but all he did was laugh at me, eyes twinkling in delight.

"You sick and twisted *grissin*! I won't let you get away with this. Ever!"

He smiled. "I don't think you're in the position to make any threats."

I glared at him, feeling spent and out of fight. He raised my chin with his finger and placed a kiss on my lips. I kept my mouth tightly shut. Brushing my cheek with his thumb, he rose to his feet and left me.

The moment he was gone, a stunned daze settled over me as my predicament dawned on me. I was a prisoner. My eyes fell on the single chair Eamryel had previously occupied, and a chamber pot on the other side of the small cell. I slumped back against the wall, pins and needles making their way down to my fingers and arms. Give or take a few hours, and I'd have lost all feeling altogether.

Something told me he was waiting for it to happen.

How much time passed was beyond me. My arms had gone numb a while ago, and the need to use the chamber pot was high, but I refused to soil myself on the off chance he'd get a kick out of that too. With difficulty, I managed to sit up on my toes, taking the strain off of my shoulders. After a little while, feeling started to come back to my fingers, and I cursed my decision as painful tingling snaked down my arms.

"You and your brilliant ideas." I muttered.

Resting my back against the wall so I wouldn't fall over

directly, I closed my eyes, focusing on my breathing. Inhaling through my nose, exhaling through my mouth. And repeat. It helped to calm my fraying nerves, but it didn't help against the unbidden images in my mind. It had been Cerindil who'd taught me the breathing exercise, and thinking of him automatically reminded me of Tal.

I think it's better if you leave. Whatever you were here for, it's better for all involved if we don't get into it now.

I'd sent him off so we wouldn't fight, even though we already had been. I didn't even get a chance to make it up to him.

I was certain they had a search party going on by now, but I didn't question the fact they had no idea where to look. My chest constricted at the thought, and I swallowed the lump in my throat. Nobody knew Eamryel was back in town—he wasn't even supposed to be here, and he wasn't stupid enough to hide me in plain sight. He knew too well what he was doing to leave anything to chance. Maybe he'd had this all planned out before he even came to the engagement ceremony.

The thought alone made me shudder.

It also made him more dangerous than any of us had initially thought. It made him a cold, calculated *grissin* without remorse. There was no doubt in my mind he'd kill me if he got the idea they were getting close. My gut feeling told me if he couldn't have me, nobody could.

Son of a hehzèh.

Footsteps in the hallway alerted me so I quickly sat back on my ass, grunting as the impact jarred my arms and shoulders. Eamryel unlocked the door and walked in, followed by a demure girl.

"Get her ready," he commanded.

"For what?" I croaked.

His lip curled into a half-smile. "Dinner, of course."

If I'd thought things couldn't get any stranger, it had nothing on this statement. I'd expected him to keep me under lock and key for eternity, but he clearly had different plans. The girl stepped inside, her eyes downcast, carrying a bowl with what I assumed to be hot water, judging from the billowing steam. Eamryel tossed several packages on the chair and left us, locking the door behind him.

The girl breathed out deeply, almost as if in relief, and set the bowl aside.

"I'm… I'm sorry," she said, quickly moving over to me.

Up close, I saw a yellow sheen underneath her right eye which was speckled by light blue spots. Someone had hit her not too long ago.

Relief flooded me when she pulled forth a set of keys from her apron and she unlocked my wrists with trembling hands. My arms dropped along my sides, and gritting my teeth, I waited for feeling to come back to them. It was pure agony when it did, and it took me all effort of will not to scream out. When she undid the ties around my ankles, I couldn't help but notice her gaze shifting to the door every other second.

Being able to stretch my legs properly was bliss.

"Thank you," I murmured.

The girl inclined her head and took a few steps backwards, hands folded in front of her, nervously fumbling with her apron. She didn't dare look at me. When I had some feeling back in my arms, I got up and made use of the chamber pot. The thought of even this being in his control turned me cold to the bone.

"I've b-b-brought y-you s-s-some water," the girl stammered. "You c-c-can c-c-clean… can clean yourself… yourself up."

"Why would I go to dinner with that *grissin?*"

She looked at me shocked. "You m-m-must… must go, *Tarien.* If you don't, h-h-he'll s-s-starve you."

"That sounds preferable to the alternative."

"You can't," she whispered, mouth open, eyes wide.

I smirked. "Watch me."

She hung on my arm a second later, eyes widened, trembling all over. I turned to her with a frown.

"Please, *Tarien*," she tried again. "Please g-go. I-I-If I-I don't bring... don't b-b-bring you, h-he will... will punish me."

I narrowed my eyes at her. "He'll do what?"

She just nodded and pulled away, staring at her feet.

"What's your name?"

As she looked up at me from under her lashes, the familiarity in her eyes made my heart skip a beat. Surely...

"Calee... Caleena," she said.

"Nice to meet you," I smiled, walking over to the bowl. "Why are you staying with him if he hurts you?"

She shrugged. "I have... have n-n-nowhere else... e-e-else to go."

I crossed my arms as I stared at her—the pull on my injured shoulder made me wince—trying to figure this girl out. When she looked up at me again, I saw the fading bruise around her throat.

"Did he do that to you?"

Caleena nodded slowly.

"Son of a—" I didn't finish my sentence.

Bile rose in my throat, and it took every ounce of discipline I had not to toss everything out. Dropping my arms alongside my body I gave in and started washing myself, because I couldn't let her get the punishment for my refusal. Caleena looked relieved. She started unwrapping the packages quietly, and as the first one fell open, my breath caught in my throat and I felt like throwing up.

Unsurprisingly, it was a dress—more specifically, it was the dress I'd worn at the engagement ceremony.

Not only had he planned everything out, he had somehow managed to get it. Either he'd been in my room, or someone inside the palace was working with him.

189

"He's insane," I stated, staring at the dress. "Well and truly insane."

She stared at me. "What's w-wrong T-*Tarien?*"

"Everything."

I allowed Caleena to help me into the extravagant dress, closing my eyes at the memories it brought back, dashing away the tears rolling down my cheeks.

"I-I'll do your hair," Caleena spoke quietly. "Eam g-g-gave c-c-clear instructions."

"Eam?"

Caleena blushed, biting her lip. "Eamryel's my brother."

She might as well have punched me in the face for all the good it did me. My breath came in bursts, and I had to grab the chair to stay on my feet. Wide-eyed I looked at her.

"Please be joking?"

Shaking her head, she looked at me, lambent eyes wide. It was only then I could place the resemblance to him—it were the eyes. I turned around just in time to add the contents of my stomach, what little there was of it, to the floor.

"Don't even dare touch my hair," I whispered.

CHAPTER 11

*C*aleena guided me through a damp corridor up a tricky flight of stairs, and through a heavy wooden door. The entire way there I felt like a dead woman walking, my breathing coming short and ragged. Once through the doors, I stood in a sparsely decorated hallway, and breathing became a little easier.

The floors were a stark white marble reminding me of the palace halls—the walls were painted the same white to match the floor. Crimson carpets ran from one end of the hallway to the other, leading to a set of double doors on either side. Aside from a dozen pedestals bearing statues, there was hardly any furniture to speak off,

Getting closer, I realised in stunned surprise the statues depicted the Ilvannian pantheon. I had no idea Eamryel was such a god-loving person. Wrapping my arms around myself, I walked over to the window.The view was of the sea, glittering red and orange in the glow of the setting sun. While I'd seen the sea a dozen times in the distance from my vantage point at the main gate, I'd never seen it this close: Outside the city walls was a stretch of land occupied by enormous mansions, built there centuries ago by wealthy families, and it occurred to me he had to have taken me to one of those, just as it occurred to me I hadn't known the Arolvyen family owned one of them. Hopefully Mother or one of my brothers knew.

"Let's go," Caleena said.

Breathing in deeply and squaring my shoulders, I steeled myself for what was to come next. She guided me through two sets of double doors before we entered the dining room. Eamryel was staring out the window, hands clasped behind his back, looking every bit the *Irìn* in his formal attire. My gaze zeroed in on his eyes the moment he turned to face me.

Fury danced in them when he saw me.

"I thought I told you to do her hair?"

Caleena didn't look at him, so I did instead, chin lifted. "I refused to let her do it."

"You don't make these decisions," he informed me without even looking at me.

He turned back to Caleena. "I told you to do her hair, and when I tell you to do something, you do it. I don't care what she tells you. Understood?"

I glowered at him. "I can make my own decisions perfectly fine."

He stared at me with condescendence, just flat out ignoring my words as if I didn't matter. Caleena took a step back, mumbling an apology to him. With a dismissive wave of his hand and a disgusted look on his face, he sent her out of the room. When he turned back to me, the predatory smile was back, his eyes twinkling.

He quickly licked his lips.

"You look amazing, *shareye*," he said, sauntering over. "Just like you did that night."

I took an involuntary step backwards. He cupped my face in his hand, in the same way Tal had, but there was nothing of the gentleness in it my *Anahràn* had shown. I recoiled at Eamryel's touch.

It was the wrong move.

As he fisted his hand into my hair to pull me close, I stiffened. Unlike before, I resisted the urge to spit him in the face, because if he backhanded me one more time, I wasn't sure what I'd do.

Choose your battles wisely.

When he suddenly kissed me, a ripple of repulsion went through my body, and my stomach churned. I hadn't felt this sick in years.

"Next time," he murmured against my lips, "I won't be so forgiving."

Eamryel let go off me as quick as he'd grabbed me, and pulled his robe straight, watching me with a genuine smile on his face. I was stupefied, my thoughts a jumble as shock mastered me. When he offered his arm I took it out of fear which had settled in my stomach like a restless snake. I was genuinely afraid of what he'd do should I refuse. At the table, he pulled a chair back and invited me to sit down. After he took his seat across from me, he rang a little bell.

"I hope you're hungry," he said. "I've had them make your favourite dish."

"My favour—wait, how do you know what my favourite dish is?"

"I have my ways."

A cold shiver ran down my spine and I rubbed my hands over my thighs, watching him warily. With the scent of fragrant herbs, and roasted venison preceding them, servants bustled in, piling the table with platter upon platter. I didn't take my eyes off of him as he relaxed back in his chair, his lips turned up lightly in one corner. I was afraid the moment I eased, he'd take advantage of the situation. His highly volatile tendencies made him unpredictable at best, and I didn't care to find out what he was like at his worst. He'd already assaulted me more than once —who knew what else he was capable of.

My sheltered life had neither protected nor prepared me for this.

As if we were any normal couple having dinner at our house, he filled my plate with salmon rolls, minnow wrapped in seaweed, venison in gravy, and fruit salad. Everything he put on my plate was something I loved, and the idea he had this extensive knowledge at his beck and call made my stomach convulse. It was when he placed the plate in front of me and held up some salmon to feed me that I pushed my chair back, arms up to show I wasn't looking for a fight.

I was drawing a line.

Eamryel closed his eyes, clenching his jaw. He was trying to calm himself by counting down under his breath, his eyes towards the heavens as if asking the Gods to bear witness to my stupidity.

"Sit down," he ordered, adding 'please' as an afterthought.

I did, but didn't pull the chair closer to the table.

"I won't have you feed me."

In the blink of an eye, his mood darkened like the sky on an Ilvannian summer's day, just before the storms rolled in from the mountains. One moment, he'd been cooing over the delight of fresh salmon—the next thunder struck in the space I was occupying, taking away all air momentarily.

"You'll do as your told," he hissed in a dangerously low voice.

"Or what?" I growled. "You'll send me to bed without food? I don't care. Starve me if you want. I'd rather have that."

Eamryel clenched his hands and closed his eyes, drawing in deep gulps of air. Inwardly, I cursed myself for my words, but I couldn't wouldn't just roll over and let him win. Grabbing the armrests, I watched his every move, ready to jump into action if I had to.

He pinched the bridge of his nose.

"Why are you doing this to me?" he asked in a strained voice. "I'm just being nice."

I harrumphed. "Your version of nice and mine don't see eye to eye."

His chair clattered to the floor when he pushed it back with a strength I hadn't thought he had in him. I jumped out of mine before he could get to me, putting the table between us. What followed was a cat-and-mouse game, which we were both capable of playing incredibly well. Neither of us had the upper-hand, for which I was glad, until my leg started acting up and I noticed I was getting slower.

Slow enough for him to catch me and push me up against the wall. I grunted, feeling more of him than I cared for at any point in my life.

"Are you really this stupid?" he murmured. "Or do you like the pain?"

I smirked. "Let's go for stupid."

A corner of his mouth quirked up as he retreated his hand from my collarbone, tracing a finger along the neckline of my dress, goose bumps following in its wake. I gritted my teeth, looking past him out of the window. It had gone dark by now, so they would have called off any search parties for the night.

His warm breath on my neck made me aware of my plight, and I stilled. It smelled of seafood and *ithri*—which was not altogether unpleasant, but it did nothing to relief my stress. Eamryel dipped his head to my shoulder and sniffed me much like a wolf would, sending a deep shudder through me. I had to do my best not to push him away. He'd explode, I was sure of it.

"You smell so nice," he murmured like a man intoxicated, "of vanilla and oranges and wood."

As one hand rested on my hip, holding me as if I was his already, he ran his knuckles down my cheek with his other hand, his eyes searching mine. They held a glazy haze as if he were drunk. I just stared at him, showing no emotion whatso-ever. I didn't want to set him off.

"We could have something beautiful," he continued his monologue, tucking some hair behind my ear.

It was such a characteristically Talnovar thing to do, I had to turn my head from him, biting back the tears. My chest constricted painfully, my breathing was short and ragged, and my vision started swimming. Maybe, if I could just knock him out, I could escape. It would most likely enrage him and I doubted I'd get far limping as I did, but it would be satisfying—until I got caught, that was. Besides, while I had an inkling of where we were, I had no exact location, so escaping now might very well lead to my death at the bottom of a cliff.

To my astonishment, he wiped the tears I hadn't realised were there from my cheeks.

"If you promise not to run," he murmured, watching me intently. "I'll let you sleep in a room."

When I agreed on not running, I half-expected him to escort me to his chambers, but instead he guided me into a simply decorated bedroom.

There's a surprise if ever I've seen one.

Positioned in the middle stood an enormous canopied bed made of what I could only assume was birch, being as light as it was, adorned with white gauze curtains all around. Identical to the downstairs hallway, the floors and walls matched in pristine appearance. The flowers were the only items adding colour to the room.

By Vehda, no.

My heart sank upon the realisation they were dark-red and yellow carnations, combined with red and purple orchids. I loved those—they were my favourites. As my knees gave way from under me, Eamryel caught me before I hit the floor. He hoisted me in his arms and carried me to the bed, the look on his face stoic.

"You'll find everything you need here. You'll want for nothing."

"Except my freedom," I murmured bitterly.

He tensed. "Goodnight, *Tarien*."

Unsurprisingly, he locked the door behind him when he left. While better than being stuck in a dungeon, it was still a prison, albeit a pretty one with a view. With a deep sigh, I crawled into the bed and under the covers, sitting with my back against the headboard, my knees pulled up. My nerves were taut as a bowstring, ready to snap at even the smallest of sounds, my heart was racing in my chest, and my breathing tried to match it. Getting air into my lungs seemed like the hardest task, so I focused on my breathing exercises.

In through the nose, count to ten, out through the nose, count to ten.

It was a simple trick to kick-start the body into a new way of breathing, but it was easily forgotten under duress. My eyes never left the door, afraid he'd come inside the moment I fell asleep. It didn't bear thinking about what he could do—would do—if he caught me off guard.

AT SOME POINT, I must have fallen asleep from sheer exhaustion. When I woke up, I felt as groggy as I would have after a flask of *ithri*, except I had drunk none. I had the feeling of being watched. Having grown up with guards around me night and day, I had developed a sixth sense for it, and someone was definitely in my room now. I sat up slowly, rubbing my eyes, only to find Eamryel watching me intently, his hand slipping beneath the waistband of his pants.

"Are you serious?!"

I threw a pillow at him, jumped out of bed, and continued with the vases in blind fury. Eamryel bounced to his feet quickly, dodging the vases expertly. One shattered against the wall next to his head, and a shard cut him across the neck as it sailed passed. His eyes flashed furiously when he stormed me, grabbing me around the waist the moment I was out of vases. He tossed me over his shoulder, clamped my legs down to his chest while I pounded away on his back.

It didn't even rattle him.

I knew precisely when he stepped outside. Rain came down by the bucket load, soaking us both within seconds. He dropped me to the ground as if I were a sack of grain, knocking the wind right out of me. Gasping for air, I sat up, but my body refused to cooperate. Next thing I knew, ice-cold water poured over me, adding to the discomfort. While gasping for air, pushing wet hair out of my face, a sudden sharp pain reminding me of a sword-cut seared through my back. It stung so intensely I thought at first he'd carved into me, but when it spread out like fire from the point of impact, I realised it had to be something else.

Screams tore from my lips with every lash.

The pain bloomed across my back first, and spread to my leg, pushing aside all thoughts and fears. When he hit the still healing bruise on my shoulder, my vision went temporarily dark, and I came around to cold stone pressed against my cheek. Pushing myself up, my stomach tightened, and I dry-heaved, then screamed when a new round of pain began. It was so intense my entire body was on fire. No matter how much I begged, he didn't stop, so I curled up into a sobbing ball of sorrow, trying to protect the most vulnerable parts of my body.

Eamryel was panting by now, and the time between the hits lengthened, until they finally stopped. I didn't dare unfurl myself, nor did I dare look up. Receding footsteps told me he was walking away. Hesitantly, I stretched myself, yelping at the throbbing, stabbing pain accompanying the movement. I was shaking like a leaf in a winter storm, threatening to be torn from the branch. I sat up, surprised to find I was gasping for air from exertion.

"Let m-me h-help you," Caleena's voice sounded up.

She was standing a few feet away from me, hands wrung tight into her apron, eyes glistening with unshed tears. Even if I didn't like the fact Eamryel was her brother, I couldn't hold her accountable for his actions.

I just nodded at her.

With a strength beyond her fragile appearance, she helped me to my feet, and supported me all the way to my bedroom. The state it was in made me regret my outburst from that morning, although the reason had fury build up inside me all over again. Hugging myself, I sat down on the edge of the bed, unable to stop trembling.

"You n-n-need to get o-o-out of those... those clothes," Caleena said.

"I need to get out of this house," I said through chattering teeth.

She gave me a wary look. "D-don't let him h-hear that."

I just stared at her. "I refuse to be afraid of him."

Shaking her head slowly, she fumbled with her apron again. "You should be."

"Never."

She tilted her head slightly, her brows furrowed as she watched me. I ran my hand through my hair, grimacing at the pain, and rose to my feet. This dress needed to go. Caleena stepped forward and undid the sashes, helping me shrug out of the wet, heavy garment. Her sharp intake of breath alerted me.

"What's wrong?"

"Your... your s-skin's broken i-in places," she muttered. "I-I need t-to clean it."

I rolled my eyes and sighed. "Your brother's a sick, sadistic *grissin*."

The look she gave me said more than words ever could. After she helped me into the bed, covering me with sheets, she left the room, locking it behind her. At least here it was clear I was a prisoner. I pushed myself up to a sitting position to have a look at my arms and legs. The welts were angry red, double lined marks, and when I ran my hand over them, I could feel the abrasions.

I cursed in the old tongue.

Some welts on my legs sported blood, and I realised what Caleena meant with broken skin. I'd make him pay for this. Someone rummaging at the door alerted me so I quickly pulled up the sheets, fearing it was Eamryel, who definitely didn't need any additions to his perverted ideas. To my relief, it was Caleena, carrying a bowl of water and several vials. When I made to get up, she gave a slight shake of her head, glancing towards the hallway. Seconds later, Eamryel entered the room, turning it several degrees colder in an instant, or so it felt.

I pulled the covers up to my chin, scooting towards the corner of the bed furthest away from him, my eyes following his progress towards the window. The guarded look on his face didn't tell me much, and he avoided looking at me as best as he could.

"How are you feeling?" he asked.

"You've got nerves asking me that."

He wasn't just sick and sadistic—he was at an entirely new level of insane. Clasping his wrist with his other hand, he watched me with furrowed brows, his gaze shifting around the room. His mood darkened instantly. Breathing in deeply, he dropped his arms alongside his body.

"I'll have breakfast sent up," he said through clenched teeth, and turned on his heel, leaving my bedroom.

I shook my head. "I'll never get him."

"He isn't… isn't too bad," Caleena whispered. "If you don't… don't a-a-anger him."

"You know that's wrong for all kinds of reasons, right?" I asked with a frown.

Caleena shrugged. "Father's m-much the same."

"Your father's the epitome of kindness compared to your brother," I snorted. "Admittedly, your father's got a manual of his own."

"How s-so?" Caleena looked at me curiously.

I shrugged. "Because you never know what he'll do in any situation. He's dangerous."

"Father isn't that bad."

I couldn't help but stare. "Your father is the best actor in the whole palace. He's as bad as they come."

With a heavy eye roll she placed everything she needed next to the bed and instructed me to lie down. I surrendered to her administrations only too willingly, and while they were less precise than Mehr's, or knowledgeable like Soren's, she seemed to know enough of cleaning cuts to take away the edge of the pain. It might also have been the cream she used or the sheer exhaustion enabling me to cope with it.

One thing was clear though—I wasn't going anywhere for the next few days.

WHEN EAMRYEL NEXT VISITED ME, three days had passed without him showing his face. Every bit of communication from him had come in through his sister, so when he stepped into my bedroom that morning, surprise washed over me. He watched me from a distance, features as impassive as a statue's.

"You look well," he remarked, emotions ranging from hurt to anger and everything in between passing over his face.

Every fibre of my being went on high alert.

"What do you want, Eamryel?"

His jaw clenched visibly. "I came to ask you for a stroll. I thought you could use some fresh air."

My brows shot up at the second surprise of that morning. So Eamryel did know how to ask for something. I uncurled from my seat in the windowsill, grimacing at the stiffness in my legs as I slid down. Although the welts were healing up well enough, the muscles underneath felt bruised, making it hard to walk properly.

I was about to grab the wall to make my way over when Eamryel took a few strides and showed up at my side, laying a supportive arm around my waist. My initial response was to stiffen, which didn't go down well with him. I felt him tense, and looking up, saw the familiar tic of anger set in his jaw.

"You just hit a sore spot," I said, hoping he'd buy the lie.

He nodded, his jaw working. Neither of us spoke as we left the bedroom, Eamryel holding me up while I hobbled down the hallway to the stairs. I watched it hesitantly. Without as much as a by-your-leave, Eamryel picked me up as if I weighed nothing, and carried me down the steps. I gritted my teeth and closed my eyes, doing my best to not run my mouth at him.

"I knew you could do it." He smirked, placing me back on my feet.

"Don't get your hopes up."

He narrowed his eyes slightly, but instead of flying off the handle, his lip curled into a faint smile. Today was full of surprises. His hand lingered on the small of my back a few seconds before he withdrew and walked some steps away from me. I leaned back against a pillar, forcing my legs to keep me up.

When Eamryel returned, he knelt in front of me, sliding a pair of soft slippers on my feet. I stared at him dumbfounded. Who was this, and what had he done to Eamryel? I wasn't sure what I preferred right about now to be honest. Eamryel being eerily nice, or intensely creepy. Swallowing hard, I made sure I was smiling when he looked at me.

"Thank you."

Remaining silent, he offered me his arm, escorting me to the courtyard where he'd punished me three days prior. My eyes fixed on the spot where he'd beaten me, and goose bumps rose all over my skin. He followed my gaze, and from the way he stilled I could tell he remembered too.

"Come, there's a place I want to show you."

He guided me around a hedge, through a wide corridor lined with columns on either side, and the walls of the house on the other. I realised it was a closed off courtyard, similar to the one at home, just smaller. We continued through an archway lined with rose bushes, entering a garden on par with the palace's.

My heart skipped a beat, my eyes roaming the lush colours, taking in every shade. I inhaled deeply, enjoying the scent of early roses and carnations and lavender and thyme on the air. It came almost as a shock someone so ugly would possess something so beautiful.

"Do you like it?"

My eyes flew open at the hesitation in his voice, and I couldn't help but stare at him. The twitch in his jaw told me he didn't like that.

"It's beautiful," I said hastily. "Thank you for bringing me here."

He stared at me for a moment longer, his eyes searching my face, before he nodded. We walked deeper into the garden, halting at a wooden gazebo erected in its centre. It reminded me of the canopied bed in my bedroom with its white wood and white gauze drapes around it. Two comfortable recliners stood inside, blankets lying folded on top. I assumed they were there in case it got chilly outside, like today. Eamryel helped me onto one of them, picked up a blanket and laid it over my legs.

"Are you comfortable? Not in too much pain?"

Worry was etched on his face, and laced through the tone of his voice, which was at complete odds with the man I knew as a delusional danger. It scared me as much as it annoyed me, and I couldn't keep quiet any longer.

"Why are you doing this?"

He frowned. "Because I care about you."

"You've got a rather poor way of showing it," I muttered, running a hand through my hair. "Do you always hit those you care about?"

Eamryel rose to his feet so quickly I thought he'd hit me, but he turned away instead, hands balled at his side.

"Why can't you just be grateful?" he asked through clenched teeth.

"Grateful?" I stared at him shell-shocked. "Are you joking? There's nothing to be grateful for! You've kidnapped me, hurt me, humiliated me, and you expect me to be grateful?"

Silence stretched out between us, and from the way he moved, or rather, didn't move, I could tell he was trying to keep his anger in check. I couldn't control mine.

"I bet you had this all planned, didn't you? You knew Azra would go to the slums, and you knew I'd follow her! You were waiting to kidnap me!"

I was yelling now, my chest rising and falling rapidly as I fought to keep my emotions in check. If I could have stood up, I would have. Eamryel turned to me, eyes blazing, his voice cold and strained when he spoke.

"That, *shareye*," he began, "was complete and utter luck. I saw an opportunity and grabbed it. It's what you get for going places you shouldn't be."

"You're blaming *me* for this?" I stared at him in disbelief, and ran both hands through my hair, shaking my head as realisation dawned on me. "You're mad. You're completely and utterly mad."

He was on top of me a second later, hands around my throat, legs pinning mine. I clutched at his arms, gasping for air. His voice was barely audible when he spoke.

"Don't ever call me that again," he hissed, "or things won't end well."

With a firm push he let go off me, and stalked off, leaving me behind as a scared, sorry excuse for a being. I knew I'd gone too far the moment I said he was mad, but I hadn't been able to stop myself from saying it, just as I hadn't been able to stop myself from going after Azra.

Maybe he was right. Maybe I did have myself to blame for all of this. I shuddered at the thought, and pulled the blanket around me, inhaling deeply, exhaling slowly. My chest felt tight, too tight for comfort, but the feeling passed, and with it the fear of what had happened. I stared into the direction Eamryel had disappeared in, mouth set in a tight line. As far as I was concerned, I'd stay here until I froze to death, which was a good deal better than being cooped up inside.

SUCH BECAME my life as Eamryel's prisoner. Every morning—like that morning—I awoke to him watching me, one hand beneath his waistband. Swallowing a nasty comment, I slipped out of bed, ignoring the hungry look in his eyes. I'd learned to keep my thoughts and remarks to myself, so I dressed in silence, for once glad of the one layered dresses he'd gifted me. Even though I still preferred trousers and a shirt, telling him that wasn't an option, and I really wanted to go out for a walk today. Although my leg was healing nicely from the looks of it, I woke up stiff every morning, and needed to walk it off.

I could only do this on good days.

On good days, he allowed me to move around, have breakfast or even dinner, but as soon as I did something remotely to his chagrin, he'd punish me for it. These punishments varied from simple threats, to the cane, for which he appeared to have a particular predilection.

With my smartass mouth lacking a filter, the bad days prevailed, and he punished me more than was healthy. Then again, his moods changed faster than the weather on any Ilvannian summer day—one moment, he didn't mind what I said, the next he flew off the handle so quick I dodged him more than once.

By then I'd given up hope of anyone finding me. It had been at least four weeks, and there had been nobody here to check. Loneliness was my constant companion, despite never being alone, and I felt as if all the happiness was being sucked out of me with every breath I exhaled—it was in the heavy feeling on my chest, and the threat of tears behind my eyes every day. They hadn't come, because they had no reason to think Eamryel was behind this. He was supposed to be close to Therondia by now.

I couldn't blame them.

I was sitting in the windowsill of my bedroom, looking out over the scintillating sea in the distance, wondering what it was like to be on it—to be on a ship and sail off to faraway lands—to be free and have my own adventures. I could go everywhere I'd like, with no one telling me what I could, or couldn't do, or holding me prisoner because of who I was. I guessed Eamryel's reasons for holding me had nothing to do with me being *Tarien*, but rather with me.

Being *Tarien* was an added benefit.

A commotion at the door startled me from my reverie. Someone unlocked it and a moment later, a harrowed looking Eamryel stepped in, his eyes zeroing in on me.

"Come here," he ordered.

The look on his face told me not to mess with him this time, so I slid to my feet and walked over. I couldn't help but take my sweet time getting there. He grabbed my arm and hauled me out to the hallway and down the stairs, being everything but gentle.

I hadn't even done anything.

"You're hurting me."

He glared at me. "Then move that sweet ass a little faster, or I'll cane you until you can no longer sit."

He guided me down to the dungeon where he locked the

door behind us. Hugging myself, I regarded him through narrowed eyes as he started pacing up and down the room.

"What's going on?"

He shot me a glance. "They're here."

"Who are?"

"Your brother," he growled. "And that so-called *Anahràn*."

My heart fluttered in my chest as my eyes widened in gleeful anticipation. Maybe, if they'd find me, I could get out of here. Within two strides, Eamryel was in front of me, pushing me back against the wall, body flush with mine.

"Don't even think about it," he said in a dangerously low voice, "or you'll regret it for the rest of your life."

"I'm not afraid of you."

"I don't want you to be afraid of me," he murmured, running a hand across my cheek. "I just want you to love me back."

"You've got a weird way to go about it."

This time, he didn't answer. His eyes roamed my body like a man starving, while his fingers played with a lock of my hair. He licked his lips as his eyes settled back on me, looking torn. His current state of emotions was anyone's guess.

The sound of footsteps was coming in our direction. He clapped a hand over my mouth the moment he heard it and pulled me with him into a corner next to the door where we couldn't be seen. I considered biting his fingers until I felt the edge of a knife just below my ear.

"Don't try anything," he whispered. "Not a sound."

Evan's voice echoed through the hallway, although I couldn't make out the words. Caleena answered in a stammer, but her words were a jumble too. My heart made a leap and was hammering away in my chest when I realised my brother was literally only a few steps away from me—but he could have been at the other end of the world for all the good it did me.

"And your brother hasn't been back?" Tal asked.

My knees went weak at the sound of his voice, my hands

turned clammy, and all I wanted was to run to him. Breathing hard, Eamryel clamped his hand tighter over my mouth, pushing the knife harder against my skin.

I swallowed hard, closing my eyes, willing my racing heart to quiet down.

"I h-h-have n-n-not s-s-seen him in… in weeks." Caleena's stammer was more pronounced than it had been for the past two weeks, but then, they wouldn't know.

"She's got to be somewhere," Tal growled. "She can't have vanished."

There were notes of despair in his voice. I imagined him jerking his hand through his hair now, his jaw set in the typical Talnovar manner when there was something he didn't like to think about.

"We'll find her," Evan said.

My darling Evan, always the diplomat.

"If your idiotic brother had paid attention," Tal hissed, "she wouldn't have gone missing."

"That's not fair," Evan replied in a strangled voice. "Haer's been beating himself up over it. You know that."

"I'll beat him over it if she doesn't turn up soon."

Their voices were moving away from us now, and it didn't take long for them to disappear entirely. A sob left my throat, and all strength left my body, leaving me hanging in Eamryel's arms. He held me, but from the way he stilled, I could tell I was in for it as soon as they had left.

Sure enough, when the danger had passed, he released me, dropping me to my knees. Tears were running down my cheeks freely. Out of nowhere, he pushed me onto my side with his foot, and I fell over, looking into a pair of bewildered eyes.

"You love him," he whispered.

"I don't know what you're talking about," I replied, wiping away the tears on my sleeve.

I pushed myself up to my elbows, but he kicked me down.

He dropped to his knees in front of me like a man defeated, except the look in his eyes was rather of a man coming to an undesirable realisation.

"You love him!" he suddenly yelled. "After all I've done for you, you love *him?*"

I stared at him wide-eyed and slack-jawed. "I don't love him. What are you talking about?"

"Don't lie to me!"

"I'm not!" I growled. "I don't love him, and besides, all you've done for me is hurt me! Why would I ever love you? You're paranoid!"

The moment the words left my mouth, his jaw went tight, and I knew I'd gone too far. Everything happened fast. With a loud roar he kicked me in the side the first time—the second time he tried to kick me, I rolled out of his way and on my back. I caught his foot just before he kicked me a third time and pulled as hard as I could. He fell flat on his back, which gave me time to get to my feet as he pushed himself off the floor, rising to his.

This time, he would not hurt me. This time, I'd fight.

I brought my arms up into a defensive stance, shielding my face, my gaze trained on him. His eyes flashed furiously as he pushed his hair back aggressively. The knife slipped back into his hand, but this time with intent to seriously maim—I could tell by the way he angled it. He mimicked my pose, his eyes never leaving me, and as we circled each other step by careful step, I felt my body didn't like the strain I put it through.

He stepped in and jabbed. I blocked. It was a move to draw me out, but I didn't go for it. The second time he stepped in, he was quicker, and I barely had time to move aside. He nicked me on the shoulder, drawing a hiss from my lips.

I couldn't help but grin at him. "Are you courting me or fighting me?"

He growled low under his breath and lunged at me. I ducked

under his arm, turned and kicked him in the back. While it sent him stumbling forward, he didn't fall. In fact, it only angered him more. He charged at me like a raging bull, pushing me back into a corner until I hardly had room to move. I hit him in his solar plexus, leaving him gasping, but he didn't drop the knife as I'd hoped.

Eamryel proved to be a skilled knife-fighter, and my superior in more than one way. Admittedly, he was uninjured and trained, whereas I had missed at least four weeks or more of mine, and my body was lacerated with injuries. By now, my breath came in ragged gasps and my lungs were burning to where breathing hurt. My arms and legs were heavy and avoiding him became increasingly more difficult.

Cuts criss-crossed my limbs.

After a last attempt of fighting him off, he overpowered me and pushed me into the wall roughly, knife pointed at my chest.

"Kill me then," I breathed. "Rid yourself of me."

He quirked up the corner of his lips.

"Oh no," he whispered, stepping even closer to me. "I'll not kill you, *shareye*, but if I cannot have you, I'll make sure no other man wants you."

While I didn't consider myself exceptionally beautiful like Mother, or even Nathaïr, I prided myself on my looks as they were. All Ilvannians were beautiful in their own way, with our unusual pale skin and various hair colours—a trademark of our people—ranging from stark white to jet black and every monochromatic colour in between. Some people, like Elara and I, added colour to their hair just to stand out. I didn't mind scars or blemishes of any kind, but still I was afraid of what he would do.

He was too unpredictable.

Drawing the dagger past my cheek with its flat side, he tilted it slightly when coming to my jaw and pushed against it, drawing it all the way down to my collarbone. It wasn't a deep cut, barely enough to break the skin, but it was a nasty pain all the same. He cupped my cheek, caressed my lips with his thumb, while his eyes roamed my body freely. Out of nowhere, he pushed himself flush against me, knife all but forgotten between us. His hand slid from my cheek into my hair, and he suddenly yanked my head back. The moment I gasped in surprise, he kissed me, his tongue exploring my mouth eagerly.

He kissed me like a man drowning, which frightened me more than the dagger did.

"If only you could love me," he whispered. "We would have had it all. I'd be good to you, always. I'd adore you, every step of the way. I'd be yours, in every way you desire. If only you could love me."

"Never," I hissed. "The moon and the stars will fall from the sky before that happens."

He rested his forehead against mine, and I felt the cold of the blade trailing my collarbone, down to my breasts, in a lazy pattern.

"You repulse me," I growled.

He stepped away from me, sadness crossing his features. It looked like I'd finally hurt him back, but what he did next was beyond comprehension. Without warning, he pushed the tip of the knife into my flesh where my collarbones met, and dragged it down to below my breasts. The pain it elicited registered as if I'd drunk too much—slowly.

Wide-eyed I looked at the blood staining the dress, and dropped to my knees, hands on my chest. It seeped through my fingers regardless of me trying to stop it. The cut wouldn't kill me if treated, but the question was if he would allow it. Eamryel knelt in front of me, lifting my chin with the tip of the bloodied knife.

"And I've only just begun."

CHAPTER 12

*I*t was still relatively dark when Eamryel dragged me out of my cell and into the courtyard where he dropped me to the ground unceremoniously. The outside world, devoid of sound in this walled confinement, felt as bleak as I did. The only light illuminating us was a small favour from the moon. To add to the growing discomfort, a cold, steady drizzle soaked my simple *Zhirin* silk dress in a matter of seconds. I didn't mind much—I had been drenched in sweat for days which made this situation a somewhat better alternative. At least I didn't smell as bad. I wrapped my arms around myself in an attempt to stop the shivering.

I'd been shivering for a few days now, and I'd been spiking a fever for as long. Most of the time I'd lain on the floor, swimming in and out of consciousness. The cut had begun to fester, and despite trying to clean it with what little water he'd offered me to drink, it had only gotten worse. Although I had no exact idea how long it had been going on, I estimated a day or four, maybe five had passed, based on the meals he'd brought me. I wasn't sure though. After the second day, I'd lost all appetite. Even if I did eat, I could barely keep it in.

My fuzzy sight settled on Eamryel dressed in proper outdoor clothing, looking ready to go out riding. Were we going somewhere? Maybe he'd changed his mind and he would bring me home. The idea sparked hope deep within and I pushed myself to my feet shakily, seeking support against a column. Caleena, who was standing opposite me hugging herself, looked like he had dragged her outside the same as I, wearing nothing but her nightgown.

She looked as scared as I felt.

"What's going on?" I croaked.

Eamryel flashed me a lopsided grin. "Today is your lucky day."

I watched him warily, tucking my hands under my armpits, leaning heavily against the pillar. "I have a hard time believing that."

After he stepped closer to me, he ran his knuckles down my cheek, hand wavering over the scar Amaris had given me. I flinched.

How inconsequential an attack that was compared to... this.

Even though he was smiling, the maniacal expression in his eyes was a clear sign he was up to nothing good.

"You need to work on your trust issues," he said. "Now... there's something else I need to do first. Give me your foot."

"Excuse me?"

He arched a brow. "You want a repetition of earlier this week?"

I lifted my foot as told, and he locked my leg between his knees so I couldn't move. Next I knew, he dragged his knife over it, cutting deep enough to break the skin.

"Son of a *hehzèh*!" I screamed, trying to pull my foot free.

He was stronger.

"No need to insult my mother," he said airily.

My eyes sought Caleena who was watching us wide-eyed, mouth open in shock. *Did I have the same expression?* She shook her head and shrugged. She did not understand what was going on either. When he finished, he let go off my foot. Blood trickled down the sole and in between my toes—it tickled. I clenched my jaw in an attempt to ignore the new flares of pain.

Eamryel sauntered over to Caleena, cupping her face in his hands and stroking her cheek with his thumb, resting his forehead against her like a lover would. For a moment, he had me believe he could be a doting brother, until he slipped a knife into his hand.

"There is a *slight* catch to your release," Eamryel began, his lip quirking up. "You must earn it."

My thoughts came to a screeching halt when it caught onto the word release, and I blinked at him as if I'd suddenly gone stupid. What did he mean by release?

He's joking. He has to be. Only a few days ago he had every intention of keeping me. Why would he let me go now?

Gathering my wits about me, I went over what he had just said, trying to keep my teeth from chattering. "Earn it?"

"All you have to do is stay out of my reach."

The confused look on my face made him laugh, and he added. "Let's see how well you run."

I just stared at him. Every fibre in my being rebelled against the thought of having to run, knowing I wasn't in any shape to do so. The chances of it killing me were rather high, although I felt sure he couldn't care less.

This was all a game to him.

"Now," he continued, "on the off-chance you manage to get home without dying first, let me give you a warning you'd do well to remember. If you tell *anyone* of what happened here, I will start killing people you care about."

"You wouldn't..."

To prove his point, he cut Caleena's throat without even blinking. Her eyes filled with terror the moment she felt the knife. I stood paralysed as she convulsed, gasping for air that would never fill her lungs again, watched as she died a merciless death at the hand of the brother she'd devotedly served. Dispassionately, he dropped her lifeless body to the ground, watching as her blood mingled with the puddles on the cobblestones. I wanted to scream. I wanted to cry. Most of all I wanted to kill him for what he'd just done.

Survival instinct kicked in instead.

"I'll give you a head start," he announced, cleaning the knife on his trousers. "Hunting you won't be any fun if I catch you straight away."

"You're sick," I whispered. "Sick and psychotic, and someone ought to put you out of your misery."

He grimaced. "Don't push your luck, *shareye.*"

Stepping over his sister's dead body as if she were nothing made my blood boil, and had I not been weakened, it would have been enough cause to attack, but I knew better than to give in considering my current state. He stalked over and grabbed my arm, dragging me out of the gate. My chest constricted at the sight of the meadows and the city in the distance. Freedom was so close I could almost taste it. I could feel it on the wind on my feverish skin and smell it in the sea's scent on the air.

All I had to do was run.

Eamryel had tethered his horse to the gate, a bow and arrow slung to its saddle on one side, a sword on the other. My heart sank. He turned to me, cupping my face in both hands, resting his forehead against mine.

"I'll give you till dawn," he murmured. "I'm coming for you then."

Without permission or consent, he kissed me until my lips bled and I was out of breath. Tears brimmed my eyes, and all I noticed was how much I was shivering. I doubted I'd get anywhere—but I had to try. He regarded me with hooded eyes as he stepped back.

"Run *shareye*. Run."

MY FEET PADDED the soft underground as I ran, or rather stumbled, towards the city, the cuts on the sole of my foot a fiery, aching sensation. I was dizzy and weak, but I couldn't stop. I'd be dead if I did. Dawn was almost here, and his horse was a thousand times faster than I was.

I just had to stay out of sight.

My strategy would have been perfect had there been places to hide, but our ancestors had built these houses on the cliffs, leaving the rest open. The plateaus—adding depth to the terrain I wasn't prepared for—were mostly grassy, with the occasional rocks protruding from the ground. I was convinced they were designed to take out toes and feet. By now, my chest was burning, my breathing coming in wheezes, and my vision was swimming.

My head felt as if it was about to explode.

Hoof beats in the distance told me Eamryel was in pursuit, so I pushed myself to go even faster. My eyes focused on the city walls ahead. It couldn't be more than a few miles out, but the closer I got, the farther it seemed to be. If only I could run faster, push through more, but out of sheer exhaustion, I dropped to my knees, hitting a rock as I landed. I cursed inwardly. My body was close to giving up, yet my mind refused. A little more was all I needed, so I scrambled to my feet and continued running, afraid to look over my shoulder.

Out of morbid curiosity, I did anyway.

Eamryel had found me and was aiming an arrow at me. With a renewed burst of energy, I sprinted away. Adrenaline kicked in and I ran as fast as I could, considering the circumstances. The sudden rush made me feel as if I were flying, but it was the feeling of elation which had me believe I could make it. My heart felt fit to burst, unused to the exertion I was putting it through, and my breathing came in ragged gasps. The sheer effort of putting one foot in front of the other was a monumental task—one I wasn't sure I could accomplish.

Up ahead, the city was drawing closer, its walls a promise of safety I'd hated before.

Only a little more.

Something struck me in the shoulder hard enough to send me to the ground, barely giving me time to catch myself, and a howl of anguish escaped my lips on impact. I couldn't stay down, so I tried to push myself up—my shoulder wouldn't cooperate. When I looked, an arrow protruded from it and suddenly, a nauseating feeling of pain threatened to overwhelm me. I had to get up, even if it was the last thing I did—I had to get up and push on. I was almost there. One foot in front of the other. Don't think. Don't look. Push on.

It wasn't far now.

Another arrow barrelled into me—into my calf this time. It sent me to my knees once more, but this time, nothing more than a gasp of surprise left my lips. Looking over my shoulder, I saw Eamryel was close enough that I could see the satisfied smirk on his face. I steeled my resolve and got up. I'd run out of adrenaline, my body felt heavy and my shoulder and leg hurt beyond any imaginable pain. All I wanted was to lie down, close my eyes and sleep it off.

If I lay down, I'd never get up.

Propelling myself forward, I forced myself to not look back. Forward was my goal. The city was getting much closer with each step—I just had to hold on a little longer. Once the city gates came in sight, I started yelling. With a bit of luck, somebody would hear me. With ill luck, Eamryel would finish me before I'd get there.

He was still in pursuit judging by the sound of hooves beating the ground, but it was at a more leisurely pace. I didn't look back. Instead I struggled forward, every step I took slower than the one before until it felt I was wading through quicksand. My arm had gone numb, and I was limping rather than walking, but the road to the city was up ahead.

Almost there.

"I love your fighter spirit," Eamryel's honeyed voice sounded up right next to me.

I was too tired to even look at him.

"Take care, *shareye*," he said. "We'll meet again."

He galloped away, but not in the direction I had expected him to go. Instead of turning back, he went into the city. Slowly, I dragged myself forward, one foot in front of the other. Tears were rolling down my cheeks from sheer exhaustion and I feared I'd never get to the gate, and if I'd never get to the gate, I'd die.

I cursed Eamryel in my head, in the old and the new tongue, in every which way possible, if only because I hoped it would get me home. I had reached the road now, and up ahead the main gate towered high, welcoming everyone inside. I'd never been happier to see it. Few people were around this time of day but those who were turned in shock upon seeing me.

One or two people were talking to me, but their words made no sense. I dropped to my hands and knees, mumbling something about wanting to sleep. Needing to sleep.

"Hey Vixen." A familiar voice drifted into my consciousness. "No sleeping on the job."

There was only one person who called me Vixen.

"Haer?" I croaked.

"I'm here," he murmured. "I'm here."

Next thing I knew, I was floating, yet my body had never felt heavier. I was shivering uncontrollably, and perhaps I was crying. I couldn't be sure. In that moment, I wasn't sure of anything.

I CAME BACK to my senses because of a sharp pain lancing through my shoulder first, and my leg second, drawing out a string of expletives I didn't know I knew. Something snapped, and the moment it slid out of my shoulder, I realised it was the arrow. My head was spinning, so I lay back down, focusing my blurry gaze on the ceiling, trying to get everything straight. I couldn't.

They placed something cool on my forehead, startling me from my thoughts, at the same time as I felt hands moving over my body in rapid succession. A sickening feeling mastered me when I realised it could only be one person. Eamryel. I lashed out with my hands, satisfied when my fist connected, and kicked only to find someone pinning down my legs. I started screaming and thrashing about, crying in pain and frustration.

"Let me go, you sick bastard! Let me go!"

Whoever was holding me, didn't let go. It felt as if somebody was tying me up. Then everything was happening fast. I started shaking uncontrollably, and my head rolled away repeatedly. I couldn't stop it.

"We're losing her," someone muttered.

"Hey Vixen," Haer said from faraway. "You've got to listen to my voice. You're safe now. We're here. Soren's taking care of your injuries. It will hurt, but he will not hurt you. Just stay with us? Stay with me, please? You're all right, nobody can hurt you now."

His voice sounded as if I was submerged—distorted and distant—but it calmed me. Finally, I could get some proper sleep. My body wasn't aching anymore, and the nightmare of what had happened was nothing but a distant memory.

Something was off.

Something was wrong. After what Eamryel had done, there should have been pain. The cuts should have been hurting, as should have been the places where he'd shot an arrow in me. They didn't.

This wasn't right.

It felt like I was drowning again. My lungs were burning, practically screaming for air, but my body wouldn't oblige. My thoughts were drifting too, and I had the faint notion of my body jerking. Still, there was no pain.

I'm dying.

I WOKE UP, gasping for air as if I'd just resurfaced, back arched, eyes wide. Soren's face was inches from mine, looking more than a little worried. I daresay he looked frightened. I was breathing hard, as if I'd just run twenty laps around the training fields. The pain assaulted me from every part of my body a second later.

I cursed and cried at the same time.

"Welcome back, *Tarien*," Soren said. "You had me extremely worried there for a moment."

"The pain," I whispered. "It's too much."

He smiled gently. "I know, we're working on it, but you need to stay with me, all right?"

I nodded slowly.

"Can you tell me what happened?" Soren asked.

I shook my head as Caleena's terrified, sightless eyes came to mind.

"Well," he said unperturbed, "I'm glad you're back."

My voice cracked. "So you can hurt me more?"

"Only if you get into stupid things, *Tarien*," he murmured.

I smiled faintly. No wonder he'd become a healer. His easy words and flashing smile made me feel at ease, even after I'd been dying.

"I need to stitch some injuries," he explained, "and leave some open to wash them regularly. Whatever possessed you to run around like this?"

"I wanted to live."

Soren's lips curled up in a smile. "Good choice. Some here would've torn the world apart had you died."

Someone snorted from behind him.

"Tal?" I whispered.

He was at my side an instant later. The dark circles under his eyes were evidence he had slept little. His hand was jittery while stroking my hair out of my damp face. I ground my teeth at the touch of his hand on my skin and closed my eyes. My stomach fluttered.

"You look terrible," I murmured, looking him over.

Tal sort of laughed, which ended in a strangled sound. "Thank you."

"I'm sorry," I whispered. "Truly I am."

"It wasn't your fault."

In all honesty, I wasn't sure it wasn't, having gone after Azra like I had, and I was more than sure I'd deserved some of the punishments Eamryel had given me. It was definitely my fault, in more than one way, but I was too weak to go into that discussion right now.

"Will you stay with me?"

"I'm never leaving your side again," he murmured, placing a soft kiss on my forehead. "Gods be damned and cursed."

He'd never shown this kind of affection before.

"I'd really like to get some sleep."

"Not yet, *Tarien*," Soren said. "I need you to stay with us a little longer."

"But the pain is gone?"

Tal looked at me with a faint smile. "Soren might have drugged you. Again."

"Oh."

I nodded, resting my head back against the pillow while Soren performed his magic. It was hard staying awake, and try though I might, my eyes closed of their own accord. Sleep was peaceful at first, until my mind replayed the moment Eamryel killed his sister to warn me, and set it on repeat. No matter what I tried, I couldn't save her.

The ease with which he'd killed her shocked me every time.

My terrible flight to the city appeared in this string of nightmares too. I woke up bathing in sweat, my chest constricting painfully as I sat gasping for air.

"Shhh, calm down," Tal said from the darkness. "You're safe."

He lit a candle on the cabinet, its light sparkling in his eyes as it flared to life. The moment he sat down on my bed, I automatically scooted into the corner as far away from him as possible. It wasn't all that far on the small infirmary bed I was in.

I yelped in pain the moment I pulled up my legs.

"Lie still," Tal said in a strained voice. "Soren said you sustained some severe injuries. You're not supposed to get up for a while."

I remembered getting every single injury and was glad my face was mostly hidden in the dark for fear of what he could tell from it. The hurt in his voice screamed at me, and I wished I could do something about it. I wished I could tell him everything, but Eamryel's message couldn't have been more clear. Tell anyone and they'd die. Even with his face barely lit by the candle, I could tell he looked depleted.

"How long has it been since you've slept?"

He ran his hand through his hair and shrugged. "A few days?"

"Really slept. Not caught some soldier's shuteye."

He was quiet for a while, looking away from me. I laid a trembling hand on his—he looked at me, lips set in a thin line.

"I haven't since the day you went missing."

"You need to sleep," I said.

Tal jerked his hand through his hair, shaking his head. "I need to know you're safe."

Almost without thought, I brought my hand to his face, and

cupped his cheek in my hand, stroking my thumb over his jaw. He tensed and swallowed hard, turned his head and placed the gentlest of kisses on my fingers before pulling away. It sent the butterflies in my stomach into a wild flurry. It reminded me of the day things had taken a turn for the worst at Eamryel's—the day Evan and Tal had been so close, and Eamryel had accused me of loving him.

I had denied it, but what I felt now was the same as I had then.

You love him!

Eamryel's screech resounded in my head as if he was standing right next to me. I cringed while my stomach turned itself in a knot. My hands were clammy, my chest tightened as if something heavy was placed upon it, and breathing was hard. What in all the Gods' names was happening?

Tal laid his forehead against mine, and placed my hand over his heart, taking my hand in his. It reminded me only too much of Eamryel, which almost sent me over the edge where breathing was nigh impossible.

"Feel my heartbeat, *shareye*," Tal whispered. "Hear my breathing. Match yours to mine."

I tried, but it was hard.

But the more I tried, the more the panicky feeling subsided. The tightness around my chest loosened, and while my heart was still racing, my breathing returned to a semblance of normalcy. I no longer felt like a fish out of water. This time, Tal took longer to pull away from me, keeping my hand on his heart, his forehead still against mine. He stroked my cheek with his thumb, resting briefly on the scar Amaris had given me, before tucking a strand of hair behind my ear.

I had to remind myself this was Tal.

"Get some sleep," he murmured, suddenly pulling away. "I'll be here."

As he got up, I grabbed his hand. "Stay with me."

"As said, I'll be here."

I shook my head. "*Stay* with me, please?"

Catching on what I was asking him, he ran a hand through his hair.

"It's not appropriate," he murmured.

"Propriety be damned Tal," I whispered. "Please?"

He considered my words before sitting down, kicking off his boots. I wanted to tell him I needed him more than anything but the words got stuck in my throat. Lying down next to me, it soon became clear this bed was definitely not made for more than one person, so Tal pulled me into the crook of his arm, and I rested my head on his chest, inhaling the deep musky scent that was him. He tensed before he relaxed.

This was what safety felt like.

"I'm sorry," I murmured drowsily.

He pulled me close, placing a kiss on the top of my head. "So am I."

"You couldn't even wait a night?" Evan asked.

Upon opening my eyes, I found him standing at the foot of the bed, arms folded in front of him, looking anything but pleased. Tal shot out of bed as if whipped, eyes down as if properly chastised.

"Calm down, Ev," I muttered, rubbing my eyes. "I asked him to."

I propped myself up against the pillows, pulling up the sheets as I watched my brother with irritation. He narrowed his eyes to thin slits.

"Do you invite every man into your bed when life gets rough?"

My ears started buzzing as a haze went over my vision and I

lost it. Lunging at my brother like a tiger going for its prey, I was all claws and teeth as I attacked him. I ignored the stabs and fiery aches my body sent off as a warning as Evan and I went down in a tangle of limbs. His arms wrapped around me like a shield, and instead of landing on the floor, I landed on top of him.

I hit him as soon as I had one arm free.

"You did *not* just say that," I growled, ready to strike again.

He caught both my hands in his, and being stronger than I was, kept me from hitting him again. His eyes were wide and filled with terror as his gaze raked over me. It confused me until Tal helped me to my feet and wrapped a sheet around me in the same motion.

I was naked.

"*Nohro ahrae,*" Evan whispered, still staring at me.

I hissed at the pain in my foot once I put weight on it, remembering with a scowl how Eamryel had marked me. Favouring my other leg wasn't an option either because of the arrow injury. Tal picked me up as if I weighed nothing more than a child and placed me back in bed, tucking me in. The stern look in his eyes told me to back off.

Evan got to his feet, tugging his clothing back in order.

"What happened?"

I hugged myself, looking away.

"She won't talk about it," Tal replied instead. "But whoever got her had it in for her."

Evan pinched the bridge of his nose. "She'll have to talk, eventually."

Tal shrugged at that. "Maybe, but I doubt she'll tell you after your behaviour just now."

My brother glared daggers at him. "I shouldn't have to remind you of your position?"

"Mine's perfectly clear, Ev," he said, sounding tired. "I'd say you seem to have lost sight of yours. She's been missing for five weeks, and the first thing you ask her is if she invites every man to her bed? Harsh."

"You should've known better," Evan growled.

"I did. She wouldn't hear any of it, so I followed up on her request."

"So you'd bed her if she asks you?" he asked through clenched teeth.

For a moment I was afraid Tal would slug him, but he didn't. He just stared him down, shaking his head. Evan put up his hands in defeat, walking backwards.

"Apologies," he muttered. "I went too far."

"Not accepted," I replied. "You're an ass. Leave."

Evan's eyes pleaded with me.

"Shal, please," he began.

"Out!" I roared.

He left with his tail between his legs and I had to do my best not to yell anything profane at his retreating back. The nerve! Tal sat down on the bed next to me as I rubbed my temples, shaking my head. He looked at me with a gentle smile.

"Don't be too harsh on him," he said softly. "None of us have slept much since the day you disappeared."

"His words were uncalled for. They had nothing to do with what happened to me."

Tal smirked. "True, but I have to hand it to him. At least he'll protect your virtue to the end of the world."

I awarded him a flat stare. "He won't live past his own if he makes another comment like that."

Tal snorted, only to look up when the door creaked open, admitting Haerlyon. He looked as awful as Tal did, who rose to his feet the moment he saw who entered, and excused himself with a mumbled apology, telling me he was right outside the door if I needed anything.

It reminded me of what he'd told Evan the day they'd been at Eamryel's.

My heart went out to the both of them.

Neither of them even looked at each other as they passed, but both of them tensed considerably when they did. Haerlyon sat down on my bed and hugged me tight, not letting go until I tapped out.

"Glad you came back," he murmured.

Despite looking ragged and wan, that quick half-smile ghosted on his lips while watching me. I observed him quietly. He'd altered his hair. It was shaved on one side, long on the other, and it looked remarkably well on him. It gave him a bit of an edge I thought he could use. It also revealed a healing bruise around his temple.

"What happened to you?" I brought my hand up to his face, touching the bruise lightly.

He winced. "I disagreed with Tal."

I'd been afraid of that.

Biting my lip, I regarded my brother, tilting my head a little. With a deep sigh, I dropped my hand back into my lap, looking anywhere but at him.

"It's all my fault," I whispered. "I'm sorry he got mad at you."

Haerlyon snorted. "He got mad at everyone."

"I shouldn't have gone away without telling you," I murmured, fumbling with the sheets.

He tilted his head at me. "Why *did* you leave?"

"I saw someone doing business with a Therondian merchant," I replied, trying to decide whether or not I should tell him the truth. "It looked rather shady, so when the person returned to the city, I followed. I couldn't let you know, because it would've drawn attention."

"Did you find out who it was?"

I shook my head.

"No. I tracked him into the slums, but not knowing my way there, I soon lost sight of him."

Haerlyon bit his lip, nodding thoughtfully. "What happened next?"

A deep shudder ran through me as the memory of being cornered and fighting for my life resurfaced. How different it had felt from training. My luck had turned when Eamryel placed a dagger against my throat, but it had been the flight into the dead-end alley which had been my undoing.

Waking up in a cell had only been the beginning. I supposed Eamryel had tried to make my time with him as comfortable as possible, even though our meaning of comfortable were polar opposites. Caleena had warned me, and I'd stupidly gone up against him every time.

It wasn't like me to quiet down and be demure, especially not with injustice being part of the deal.

Caleena.

I shook my head and looked at Haer, eyes brimming with tears. "I cannot tell you."

He was about to say something when the door opened forcefully, and Mother came striding in, Rurin, Tal, and several other council members on her heel.

"Not this again," I groaned, pulling the sheets over my face.

CHAPTER 13

*M*other was a force to be reckoned with, even more so when she swept into the infirmary as if she owned the entire world and could crush it in the palm of her hand. Tal looked everything but pleased, and Soren everything but impressed. With her chin in the air, her shoulders squared, and her noble five-seven, nobody dared tell her off.

Nobody, except Soren.

"*Tari*, as much as I love having you around, please don't bring an entire squadron of squawks down here."

She glared at him. Soren responded by folding his arms and scowling at her.

"I'm not having a repetition of last time she was here," he said, and turned to the rest. "Out, all of you."

They squabbled amongst themselves, protesting loudly as Tal escorted them out of the infirmary with his lips pulled into a wicked half-smile. I watched them leave. One person in the back turned last, and the moment my eyes caught the hardened azure gaze of Eamryel, my heart stopped. He flashed me a smile, drew his finger across his throat and left.

A band pulled tight around my chest at the same time as my

throat squeezed shut. I shot up, gasping for air while clawing at my neck. Someone grabbed my hands. I tried to fight him off.

"Calm down *Tarien*," Soren said somewhere next to me. "Inhale deeply through your nose, count to ten. Exhale slowly, count to ten."

I looked around wide-eyed until my gaze zeroed in on Tal who was watching me through narrowed eyes. He laid his hand on his chest.

Match yours to mine.

His words echoed in my head from the night before, and although I couldn't feel him this time, I tried it by memory, breathing in deeply, exhaling slowly, doing as Soren instructed. The band around my chest loosened, and I gulped in air as if it was water and I was parched.

Everyone was looking at me.

"What was that?" Haerlyon frowned.

"A panic attack," Soren explained, fuzzing over me like a mother hen.

I resisted the urge to swat him away. Mother watched me with a mix of worry and apprehension, her fingers drumming rhythmically on her folded arms.

Had she always looked this pale?

With a desperate groan, I lay back against the pillows, watching her.

"Spare me the lecture Mother." I sighed, rubbing my brow. "I've been punished enough for my mistakes."

"How do you even know I would give you one?"

I waved in her general direction. "All of that."

"You better have a superb explanation," she said, furrowing her brows.

"I do."

She frowned at me. "Go on?"

"I can't," I muttered and turned away from her.

A part of the sheet slid off my shoulders—I was too late

catching it—revealing the myriad of scars on my back. Mother's sharp indrawn breath an indication she'd seen it, I quickly pulled the covers over me, drawing my legs closer until I was more or less comfortable in a foetal position.

"Perhaps it's best if you come back later," Soren said. "She needs her rest."

Haerlyon placed a kiss on my temple and got off the bed. The rustle of Mother's clothing was the only sign she was leaving. Before they did, I overheard them talking with Tal in low voices. For the most part, I couldn't make out their words, except for one: Eamryel. I stiffened at hearing his name.

Only then did I notice Soren watching me, head tilted like a demented owl. I buried my face in the pillow, listening to the rest leaving the room.

"Thank you," I muttered to Soren.

He sat down opposite me. "Politics have no place in this room. How are you feeling?"

"You might want to have a look at her leg and shoulder," Tal said from behind me. "She thought it was a good idea to pounce on her brother."

Soren watched us with an amused expression on his face.

"He was being an arse."

"Haerlyon?" he asked.

Tal snorted. "Evan."

"Who would've thought," he mumbled, motioning me to roll on my back.

He slid the sheet up over my knee and undid the bandage around my calf. His face gave nothing away, but when he started prodding around the stitches and I winced, his lips curled up in a half-smile.

"Sadist."

"Be glad you tore nothing this time," he said. "Your mother's lecture would've been a picnic compared to it."

Tal tried to maintain a straight face, studying his fingernails

231

extensively. Soren bandaged my leg before turning to my shoulder, muttering under his breath.

"Please don't pull such stunts again," Soren said, sitting down on the other bed, wedging his hands between his knees. "You sustained some serious damage this time, worse even than with the wolf bite. If you put *any* strain on your leg in the next three to four weeks, the damage might be permanent."

"What about my shoulder?"

"You were extremely lucky there. The arrow could've shattered your shoulder blade. Instead, it went clean through. Quite some marksmanship." Soren replied. "But only time will tell what the real damage is."

I closed my eyes and rubbed my face. "So basically, I'm stuck here for a while?"

"We can have you moved to your bedroom at some point."

"At least that bed is bigger," I remarked drily.

Tal went straight into a coughing fit at those words. Soren looked quietly amused and rose to his feet.

"Rest *Tarien*."

I SPENT AT LEAST a good week in the infirmary before Soren allowed them to move me to my bedroom. My *Arathrien* were around day and night, always in combination with either Tal, Xaresh or Elara. Even Haerlyon took up some guard duties. It did not surprise me these were either with Elara or Xaresh, yet never with Tal. Evan hadn't come around at all while he was the one person I needed to talk to.

Perhaps I should send him a note of apology.

With Tal preoccupied instructing the guards at the door, I slipped out of bed and skipped to my desk on one leg, grimacing at the uncomfortable feeling on the sole of my foot.

If I ever got the opportunity, I'd return the favour.

I picked up a piece of parchment, dipped my quill in ink and wrote Evan a hasty message saying I wanted to talk to him. Just as I was folding it, two strong arms picked me up from my chair and placed me back in bed.

"Tal!" I growled.

He looked at me forbearingly. "Don't get out of bed."

"It was only a few steps!"

"Don't. Get out. Of bed." He glowered at me.

"I didn't strain my leg," I muttered, and gave him the note. "Here, be a dear and give this to Ev, please?"

Tal's brows shot up in surprise. "Evan's not at the palace."

"What?"

With a deep frown, he sat down on the bed, watching me. He was one of the few who wouldn't beat around the bush when something was going on, and I admired him for that.

"Eamryel came back a day before you returned," he began, "and told your mother they'd been attacked on the road."

I stiffened slightly at the mention of his name, looking anywhere but at Tal in case the look on my face would betray me.

"Evan left the palace a few days ago."

An ominous feeling settled itself in my stomach as I mulled over his words. Worst-case scenarios flew through my mind like a murder of crows on a battlefield as I tried to imagine why Evan would leave. Fear clutched at my heart with claws the size of boulders when my thoughts settled on my brother, or what he could be going through.

If Eamryel had shown up at the palace a day before my appearance, it explained why he'd left me alone. It didn't explain why he'd let me go when he did, why he killed his sister, or even threatened me. Why would he be drawing people out of the palace?

It suddenly struck me.

"It's a trap."

Tal furrowed his brows. "What do you mean it's a trap?"

Here it was, the moment of truth. If I told him what had happened, he'd go mental, but if I didn't tell him, Evan would be in grave danger.

Biting my lip, I pulled up my legs, making myself as small as possible while I looked at him.

"Don't get mad at me?" I whispered.

The pained look he gave me cut like one of Eamryel's knives had. Swallowing hard, I looked away, and told him what had happened the day of my disappearance. The more I told him, the more he stilled, the more his jaw and fists clenched and unclenched. At some point he got up from the bed.

"Eamryel kept you all this time?" Tal asked in a low voice.

"Yes."

He massaged the back of his neck, eyes closed doing his best not to give in to the anger consuming him. Tal raked his fingers through his hair, pacing up and down the room, watching me with an expression I couldn't even begin to place. The colourful array of expressions following next was quite a sight to behold.

"He's the one who—," He swallowed hard to get the words out of his mouth "—who did this to you?"

I nodded.

"He *shot* you?" he asked indignantly.

"Hunted me, actually."

Tal growled like a ferocious beast, the look in his eyes turning to one of pure frustration and fury. When he slammed his fist into my desk, I yelped and scooted to the corner of my bed where I huddled in on myself, protecting my head with my arms, trying not to cry.

Wide-eyed he looked at me, then spun on his heel and left my room. Xaresh came in a second later, his eyes surveying the area until he saw me.

"*Tarien?*"

Silent sobs racked my body as I sat there, my heart racing,

my hands shaking. My body protested heavily against this position, but I didn't want to move. I didn't dare to. This innate fear was ridiculous, and the logical side of me knew this, but the one dealing with the emotions was reigning supreme.

"Everything's all right," Xaresh whispered.

I shook my head. "Everything's not all right. I need to see Mother."

Xaresh shook his head. "You're not going anywhere, Tarien."

"You don't understand," I whispered. "Ev's in danger, I need to tell her."

He placed a gentle on my shoulder. "Tal's gone to warn her."

I looked surprised. "I thought he'd gone to hit something."

He flashed me his easy smile. "Probably that too. Whatever you told him sure pissed him off."

"It'd piss you off too."

"That would be quite an achievement." He whistled through his teeth. "Don't think anyone's ever accomplished that."

I smiled softly. "It's why I like you so much. You don't sweat the small stuff."

"Will you please lie down again?" He sighed. "I don't want to be the one having to tell Talnovar you didn't listen. *Again.*"

"He needs to sort out his priorities," I muttered, lying down.

Xaresh looked amused. "I think he already has."

He rose to his feet and inclined his head, leaving my bedroom to take up guard at the door. I knew I'd be better off sleeping, but Tal's news kept my mind going. There was something not adding up, and it annoyed me I couldn't figure it out. What did Eamryel stand to gain by trapping them?

Sure, he was a man who held grudges like there was no tomorrow, and he enjoyed lashing out punishments a little too much, but aside from his sister being engaged to my brother, there was nothing connecting the two. If it had been Tal who'd ridden out, it would've made sense, but Eamryel had to know he wouldn't leave my side from the moment I returned.

It was something else.

Something I was missing.

A knock on the door startled me out of my reverie, but before I could even call out for the person to enter, Tal stepped back into my room, suited up in his armour, swords on his back. My heart sank at the sight of him, and my head swung left and right in denial. His lips were set in a thin line, and he looked anything but happy.

"You can't go." I swallowed hard. "He'll kill you."

Tal grimaced. "Not if I kill him first."

I slipped out of bed and hobbled over to him, using my bed and whatever furniture was in my path for support. He was with me in three strides, laid an arm around my waist and escorted me back.

"You'll be the death of me first," he muttered, sitting me down. "Stay. In. Bed."

I put my hands between my knees to keep them from shaking, my eyes narrowed. "Why are you going, anyway?"

"*Tari's* orders."

As I narrowed my eyes further, he grumbled low under his breath while running a hand through his hair, watching me with a less than amused expression. I tried to quiet down the butterflies.

"Liar." I muttered.

He relented with a sigh. "Fine. *Tari's* orders *and* I want to kill that son of a *hehzèh* for what he's done to you."

"Wait in line."

"Excuse me?"

"He's mine," I said, regarding him coolly. "Be careful, please? He's deranged and outright insane. Nothing he does makes sense."

Tal nodded, biting his lip. He leaned closer as if to kiss me, only to pull back with a jerk, looking away.

"Promise you'll stay in bed?" he asked, adjusting his armour.

"And listen to advise?"

"If you promise to come back safely."

Neither of us made the promise we knew we couldn't keep. I didn't want to disappoint him any more than I'd done already by making a promise I knew I'd break the moment something had to be done. He wouldn't make the promise, because he had no idea what they were up against.

He inclined his head and moved back to the door.

"Tal."

He turned around, his eyes flashing.

"I promise."

A muscle in his jaw twitched, revealing the ghost of a smile —then he left. Pulling up the sheets, I sat shivering in bed, but it wasn't from cold.

Please keep him safe.

DAYS CREPT by in slow procession with no news of Evan or Tal. It was almost as if time made a mockery of my current state— bedridden and bored out of my mind. I'd read everything Mehr had brought me, including an ancient fairy tale in the old tongue, about a young man getting lost in the woods. Years passed, and by the time he came back, those he'd known and loved had aged and died. In his world, a hundred years had passed, but for him, it had only been a day. Even that wasn't enough to keep me occupied. Not even Soren's visits twice a day could lift my spirits, even though he was one of the few who challenged me enough to keep me entertained for the entire time he spent checking the wounds and cleaning the bandages.

Today was the worst yet.

The weather outside was appalling—thunder rumbled in the distance and it had been pouring since the night. My thoughts went out to my brother and his men, and to Tal and his merry band of *án*. They had to be miserable throughout this weather.

"Your turn," Xaresh said.

I focused on the game of *sihnmihràn* in front of me, my eyes wandering the board for a good move. It was one of the very few strategy games I enjoyed enough to learn, and learn it well, but I had a hard time concentrating on it today. With a faint smile and a trembling hand, I tipped over one of his *inàn* with one of my own, only to have him steal my piece, a wide smile on his lips.

"*Stall.*"

Perhaps if I'd paid more attention, I'd have seen his strategy from miles away, but no matter how hard I tried, I couldn't keep my thoughts on it. The only move left on my end would win me two of his *inàn*, but he'd get all of mine.

One way or the other, the win was his.

"Nice game," I murmured, my gaze drifting back to the window.

Xaresh smiled. "You barely paid attention to it."

"I'm sorry." I ran my fingers through my hair, watching him with a faint smile. "I can't help but wonder how they're doing out there."

"They're fine, *Tarien*," Xaresh said. "They know what they're doing."

But they don't know what they're up against.

I nodded. "You're right, of course."

His words did nothing to settle my fraying nerves, but I had to believe they would be fine. If nothing else, it would keep me from going up against the walls sometime soon. While Xaresh packed up the game, I settled back on the bed, massaging my leg with a grimace. He kept an eye on me while diligently straightening out my room, putting everything back in order. Somehow, he couldn't stand the thought of things not being where they were supposed to be.

"Are you okay?"

"Just a bit sore," I muttered. "It's what you get for lying still for so long."

"You'll be up and about soon enough."

I snorted. "Up, yes. About, not so sure."

"He'll let you train."

"He'd better," I muttered, wrinkling my nose. "I've got the strength of a new-born babe."

Xaresh chuckled softly. "It can't be that bad."

"No training for almost two months! I'm losing my technique, my strength, and I'm sure I've gained a hundred pounds!"

"Don't be daft," Xaresh replied. "You look like you lost a hundred pounds."

"Not helping."

He watched me with a cheeky grin as he placed the chair and table back where they belonged, and I couldn't help but admire him for his everlasting patience. Over the past few days, regardless of my mood, he'd spent time with me, either playing games or just talking, anything to stave off the worst of the tedium. I'd known he was quick-witted, but within the confines of my bedroom, with no one watching him, he was even quicker than usual, throwing back remarks as if he was bantering with a friend.

It was funny when he realised who he was talking to.His face would turn a beet red in a matter of seconds, and he'd stutter up to where he couldn't get any words out. It made me laugh every time, and I always had to assure him everything was fine.

I wasn't like Mother.

A knock on the door alerted both of us, and when Elara opened it to admit Azra, we both looked a little surprised. I hadn't seen her since the day I followed her to the criminal's quarters and got kidnapped.

"Aunt Azra!" I said, forcing a smile to my lips. "I hadn't expected to see you."

She gave me a dazzling smile as she walked in, ignoring Xaresh completely. He raised an eyebrow at her and crossed his arms.

"Be a dear." She turned on him. "Wait outside?"

"I'm not leaving the *Tarien* alone."

Azra pulled herself up to full height, which wasn't much compared to Xaresh' solid build, but it did make him take a step back.

"You'll be just outside her door," she said. "I promise nothing will happen to her."

Xaresh glanced at me, and I nodded, even though my heart was beating frantically inside my chest. I had not forgotten what I'd heard her do—I could only hope she hadn't seen me. With the shortest bow in history, Xaresh left my room, closing the door so hard behind him it rattled in its hinges.

It was unlike him to do so.

Azra turned to me suddenly, a hostile look on her face. I scooted back on my bed against the headboard as she prowled closer. The little voice in the back of my head told me to shout for help, but the look in her eyes kept me from doing so. As soon as she sat down on the bed with her hands folded in her lap, her expression turned softer.

"Why are you here?" I croaked, surprise washing over me at the sound.

"To check up on my favourite niece of course!" she said, looking shocked.

I arched a brow. "Then why did Xaresh have to leave the room if you just came to check on me?"

"Well," she began, looking away for a moment. "I wanted to ask what happened and maybe… well, you know…"

"No," I said. "I don't know. What are you suggesting?"

Azra made a steeple of her fingers as she watched me with concern in her eyes. This whole situation made the hairs on the back of my neck stand on end. What was she playing at?

"Were you hurt?" she asked at length.

I just stared at her. "No, I shot myself for good measure."

Azra sighed in annoyance, shaking her head. "That's not what I meant. Were you hurt… elsewhere?"

An uncomfortable look passed her features, and I suddenly realised what she meant. It also made me wonder why she thought I'd been with anyone who could have taken advantage of me.

What are you up to Aunt?

"He never did," I replied, looking down. "I know he wanted to…"

From under my lashes, I watched Azra's expression turn from concern to fury, her hands balled into fists in her lap.

"Son of a…" she murmured barely loud enough for me to hear.

"What was that?" I asked, looking up, pretending to wipe away tears from my cheeks.

She flashed me a smile. "Nothing, *shareye*. Nothing."

I didn't believe her.

"You know who I'm talking about, don't you?" I asked, watching her.

Azra looked up with a shocked expression on her face which was completely at odds with the shrewd look in her eyes.

"I have no idea what you're talking ab—," she began.

"Don't lie," I interjected. "I can see it in your eyes, and I know where you were the day I disappeared. You have known it all along…"

The atmosphere in the room shifted from false cordiality to malevolence in the blink of an eye, and Azra was on me just as fast.

"Who have you told?" she hissed, eyes flashing with rage.

"No one," I replied, back firm against the headboard.

"Don't lie," she growled. "I know you've been talking."

"I've not told anyone it was you I followed," I said, trying to steady my voice. "How stupid do you think I am?"

"Stupid enough to tell the *Imradien boy* who's done this to you."

I narrowed my eyes. "You knew?"

"I had my suspicions," Azra replied, "but I wasn't sure until you returned all beaten up."

I didn't know how long I'd been staring at her before I found my voice. "You *knew* he would do this?"

"You never do with Eamryel," Azra said. "That man's a loose arrow not even his father can control. He nearly blew it all."

"Excuse me?"

"Nothing for you to worry about." She suddenly smiled, fixing me with her gimlet eye. "But you should worry about that man of yours."

For the life of me, I couldn't imagine what she was talking about.

"You make no sense."

Without warning, she grabbed my ankle and pulled me towards her with a strength belying her looks. My scream was cut off by her hand clasping over my mouth, her face inches from mine.

"Listen carefully dear niece," she hissed in my ear. "You don't tell *anyone* what you saw that day, or what you think you may have heard today. Do not talk of what Eamryel has done to you, or I promise those closest to you *will* pay the price."

I glared at her, refraining from biting her finger, and managed to get free of her grip.

"I'm tired of your threats," I growled. "Yours. Eamryel's. Whatever you think you'll accomplish, I promise I'll be there every step of the way to stop you."

Azra's lips curled up in a wicked smile. "Oh, I expect you to be, *shareye*, and I can't wait to see the look on your face when this is all over."

My lips curled up in a wolfish snarl. "Get out of my room."

She obliged with a sneer on her face, looking down at me as if I were prey and she the predator. Tugging her attire back into something that resembled she hadn't just been in a brawl, she turned on her heel and left my room. Pure frustration at being unable to do anything, and complete indignation at the gall Aunt Azra had, I picked up the candle from my nightstand and threw it across the room with a loud scream.

Xaresh caught it against the shoulder with a grunt.

"I thought you had no strength," he muttered, rubbing his shoulder as he returned the candle to its proper place.

I glowered at him, folding my arms in front of me.

"Easy tiger. I'm not the enemy."

"You'd be better off if you were," I muttered softly.

He looked up at me. "Come again?"

I waved my hand dismissively, stretching out my legs, scowling at the pain.

"Let it go," I said, "if you know what's good for you."

"Are you threatening me?"

I smirked. "I would if I knew it'd help."

Xaresh shook his head with a deep sigh and sat down on the bed, a worried look etched on his fine features.

"Something big is going on, isn't there?"

"I'm not sure if it's big." I sighed, rubbing my temples. "But something's definitely going on."

His brow furrowed into a deep V-shape, and his hands lay entwined in his lap. I watched as several emotions crossed his face, as if he was trying to come to some kind of conclusion.

"Is your aunt behind it?"

"Why would you think that?"

He smirked. "Because you threw a candle at my head."

"I missed."

"I'm glad your aim was off." He snorted, rubbing his shoulder in memory.

I doubted it still hurt him. "Xaresh?"

"Yes?"

"Don't look into it, please?" I sighed. "Promise me?"

He gave me a wry smile. "You know I cannot, *Tarien*."

"What's with us not being able to make any promises?" I said in a half-laughed, half-choked up voice.

Xaresh ruffled my hair and got up with a grin. I wrinkled my nose at him as he walked over to the door.

"Elara will watch over you," he said.

My heart went out to him the moment he stepped out of my room, and Elara stepped in. Whatever he was about to do would get him into trouble, without me having said anything. He couldn't become a casualty.

CHAPTER 14

For almost four weeks, the weather was a mixture of heavy rain, windstorms, and a deluge which sent the city into a right fit of fear. Parts of the slums and the third circle had washed away during it, so they had turned the training fields into a refugee camp for those without homes. The palace had never been busier, and for once I was glad I was still confined to my bedroom.

There was still no news from Evan or Tal.

The only good news was Soren allowing me short walks in my room for a brief period of time. It usually turned into me pacing up and down with a distinct limp, grumpy and annoyed at there being no news. Soren was watching me with one elbow resting in his hand, his other hand tapping against pursed lips.

"Try not to limp," he said.

"Try not to breathe," I retorted, gritting my teeth. "You ever been shot by an arrow?"

Soren smirked. "I try to avoid that."

"One of these days," I threatened, glaring at him.

"Not likely."

A part of me wanted to wipe that smirk off his face—the

other part loved the easy banter too much to stop it. It reminded me of Haerlyon, or even Tal on a good day. Thinking of him instantly soured my mood, causing me to shift focus. I immediately sank to my knee.

"All right, that's enough," Soren announced, directing me back to the bed.

I sat down with a sigh of relief, glad to be off my legs. Kneeling in front of me, he slid my nightgown over my knees to inspect the arrow wound. The stitches had come out slightly over a week ago, but while the skin was healing nicely, it was still painful to walk on it for an extended period of time.

Soren massaged the skin around the injury with his thumbs.

I flopped back on the bed with a loud groan, biting my pillow to keep the screams from leaving my bedroom in case people started wondering.

"When did you turn into such a softy?" Soren asked.

I gently kicked him in the chest by way of an answer, and it satisfied me to hear him grunt. Just as I pulled away the pillow to reply, he started massaging my calf, drawing out a yelp.

"*Grissin!*"

He laughed.

Elara opened the door to see what we were up to, arching a brow. I waved her away, but judging by the look on her face, I knew she wouldn't go.

"The two of you enjoy this entirely too much," I muttered, pushing myself up on my elbows. "Sadists."

"It's not every day I get to make you scream, *Tarien.*"

I stared at him. "It's a good thing Tal and Xaresh aren't here."

"Or Evanyan for that matter," Soren replied matter-of-factly, finishing up the massage.

"I still wonder how you ever got hired with a mouth like that."

He laughed again, looking amused. "Good thing I wasn't hired for my mouth."

"Good thing indeed."

Soren made to reply when Xaresh roared his name through the hallways. We looked at each other bewildered before both of us turned to get ready. He packed his bag and left my room at a dead run—I started looking around for the easiest outfit in my wardrobe.

"Help me dress," I ordered Elara. "I'm not staying here."

She knew better than to argue with me right now. We both knew there could be only one reason Xaresh would be roaring like that.

They'd returned, and if they called for Soren, it couldn't be any good. I had to see for myself. Elara helped me wriggle into a heavy overdress, tied it with an easy sash, and helped me into a pair of slippers before we stepped out of my bedroom.

The change of scenery was welcome, although the reason for it less so. People gaped when they saw me limp passed and bowed as an afterthought.

Upon arriving in the courtyard, an upset anthill came to mind—people were *everywhere*. My eyes darted around, looking for Evan's tell-tale white ponytail, Tal's impressive height on a horse, or even Haerlyon's shorn hair.

I saw none of them.

My breathing came in ragged gasps as I rubbed my hands on my thighs, a habit I'd taken on whenever anxiety threatened to overwhelm me. Feeling how wet my dress was, I realised it was drizzling steadily. My eyes darted over men leaning against the walls, looking exhausted, haggard and injured. The stench of blood and rot was everywhere, so I quickly covered my nose with my sleeve. Within no time, the courtyard had been turned into a makeshift infirmary.

I walked amongst them as if in a nightmare, my head swivelling left and right to take it all in.

An *àn* had a nasty gash across his face, and his eye was shut. A second look revealed it was missing. A deep shudder ran through me, chilling me to the bone. Another man had an arrow protruding from his chest. His eyes were closed, his face set in a painful grimace as he gulped in shallow, laborious breaths. Even from here I could hear the wheezing every time he exhaled. What struck me the most was red, bubbly liquid coating his lips. Blood. I didn't need to be a healer to know it wouldn't be long before he passed away.

Up ahead a tarpaulin appeared to be the hub of it all. Dread suffused my body, turning my limbs to lead, stealing all thoughts from my mind like a thief. My eyes settled on a mop of white, blood-clotted hair when someone moved, stopping my heart dead in its tracks.

By Vehda, no! Don't let him... he can't... he has to... I've not... he hasn't... we haven't.

My feet started moving of their own accord, and next thing I knew, I was running.

Evan and Tal were lying on makeshift bearers, covered in blood and grime, neither of them awake. In fact, both looked as if they were dead. My eyes darted around, and settled on Haerlyon, who looked hurt and was leaning on Tiroy, and then to Rurin towering behind him, murmuring something to Mother, a dark look in his eyes. The right side of his face was covered in bruises, and he had a bandage around his head, but he looked the most alive of all.

As my eyes locked on Tal, a sudden convulsion went through my body as if I was about to vomit. As quick as my limping gait would take me, I made my way over to him, and was stopped short by someone grabbing me around my shoulders and pulling me back.

My initial response was to turn and hit—my fist stopped inches from Xaresh's face.

"Don't look," he murmured.

"Are they—," I gulped, looking at him.

He shook his head. "Not yet."

Moments later, gloomy looking *àn* carried them inside. I stepped out of Xaresh's arms and followed them to the infirmary where Soren was preparing himself, casting me a sombre look as I slipped inside. He shook his head slightly, but I couldn't tell if it was because I shouldn't be there, or if it was because I'd walked there. Either way, I didn't care.

I found myself a place in a corner and out of the way.

I wrapped my arms around myself to keep away the cold, even though it had settled in my bones, while looking at my brother. Evan's hair was clotted with blood on one side, setting of his pallid complexion even more. It reminded me of the night I saved him from the wolf, and he'd barely survived. He looked even worse now. Soren cut open his shirt, barking orders to the other healers to wash and prepare him.

My gaze travelled to Tal, who was being helped by one of the other healers I knew by face but not by name. While I didn't doubt his skills, it irked me Soren couldn't help both of them. I trusted him more than the rest put together. I wanted to take a step forward, but decided against it, and instead blended back into the shadows while watching them work.

At some point, Soren cursed.

Soren never cursed.

"*Tarien?* Could you come here, please?"

I frowned, but walked over, hands trembling lightly. Soren looked at me.

"Show me your hands."

"What an odd thing to—," I began.

"Please," he interjected, watching me warily.

After I showed him my hands, he nodded to a flask next to him.

"Clean them with that. I need your help."

"What?" The healer assisting him echoed my question.

He watched me stone-faced. "Now."

Deciding this was a discussion I'd lose, I rinsed my hands

with the strong smelling liquid from the flask and turned back to him, regarding him wide-eyed.

"What do you need me to do?"

"Stitch him," he replied. "On the inside."

I shook my head. "Whatever gave you the idea I can stitch?"

"It's either that, or he dies."

That decision was easy. With a quick nod to him, I listened to his explanation of what I had to do. Apparently, a small blood vessel needed stitching, and Soren was working on another serious injury.

Now it was up to me to try. No pressure. No pressure at all.

I had barely begun, forcing my hands not to tremble, when someone barrelled into the infirmary, screeching loud enough to awaken the dead. From the corner of my eyes, I saw Soren hand over his work to the second healer before stepping aside, laying a gentle hand on my shoulder. He squeezed it, most likely to encourage me, and walked over to Nathaïr.

I felt anything but courageous.

"I demand to see my fiancé!" Her shrill voice echoed through the infirmary.

Evan winced slightly in his unconscious state. I snorted.

"Please, leave the infirmary, *Irà* Arolvyen. There's nothing you can do, and we're doing the best we can," Soren said in a voice as cold as ice. "If you don't comply, I'm afraid I have to see you removed."

"Not before I've seen Evan," she hissed. "Where is he?!"

"I'm asking you one more time."

Nathaïr cursed him in the old tongue. I winced at her words, hoping he didn't understand.

"Why is *she* here?!" she shrieked suddenly. "If I can't be here, she can't either!"

"I can let her go, but your soon-to-be husband will die. Your choice."

She squealed. "She's not even a healer."

250

"And you're not helping. Guards, escort the lady out. Now."

Her cries, pleas and demands echoed through the infirmary first and the corridor later, carrying through the palace like a banshee's wail. I felt sorry for her, but I understood Soren. It had surprised me he had allowed me to stay.

"How's it going?"

"Nearly done I think," I said, fighting to keep my lunch in, "but how would I know?"

Soren had a look, and when he was satisfied with the result and certain I'd done a proper job, he told me to wash my hands thoroughly. As I did, I noticed one of the other healers starting to clean Evan's hair from the blood. A sudden sense of guilt overtook me and I looked at Soren.

"Can I?"

He nodded, leaving the other healer looking stunned first, and happy second when he realised he didn't have to do it, eagerly returning to assisting Soren. The pain in my leg was almost unbearable, but I would not complain while Tal and Ev were fighting for their lives. I poured some water over my brother's head and gently massaged the blood clots out of his hair. He winced the moment water slid down his temples, but it didn't wake him up.

The more I washed his hair, the more blood seeped into it. Judging from the amount, there had to be an injury underneath.

"Soren," I said, "this can't be good, right?"

He ran his hands over Evan's scalp, a thoughtful expression on his face. "It appears to be a cut, but we'll have to shave his hair to be sure."

"Poor Ev," I mumbled and stepped back to let Soren do his work.

"He'll live, *Tarien*," Soren said. "Your brother's strong."

I just nodded by way of reply before limping over to where they were working on Tal. He sported an ugly slash from his shoulder, across his chest, down to his hip, but I could tell it wasn't too deep. Despite this, it needed to be stitched and bandaged. I swallowed hard when I saw his face. It looked like someone had stomped on it. His nose was broken, the right side of his face a galaxy of bruises, and a cut similar to mine ran across his left cheek.

It made me smile faintly.

Whoever had gotten to him had made it personal—I didn't have to guess who it had been. If I'd ever catch him, I'd gut him. Like a fish.

The healers shooed me out of the way so I sat down on a bed, deciding my leg needed a rest.

SOMEWHERE DURING THE WHOLE ORDEAL, I must have fallen asleep. When I woke up, the infirmary was quiet except for deep breaths on either side of me. I sat up rubbing my face, wincing at the stiffness in my leg.

"You'll be feeling that for a while," Soren said from across the room, "but your leg's fine otherwise."

I stifled a yelp the moment he spoke and stared in his general direction.

"You might want to give people a heads up before you become a disembodied voice," I muttered, swinging my legs over the bed. "You scared me."

"Guilty conscience?" he chuckled, stepping into the light.

He looked as tired as I felt with dark circles under his eyes, and jittery moves as if he hadn't slept in weeks.

"You look terrible."

Soren snorted. "Have you looked into a mirror lately?"

I laughed softly and shook my head. "I'm avoiding it."

"Thank you for helping," he said at length, parking himself in a chair at the end of the bed. "I'm not sure I'd have succeeded."

"I'm surprised I did."

His lips curled at the corners. "You really need to start appreciating your own skills."

"She needs to start appreciating herself," Tal croaked, followed by a deep cough.

I nearly jumped from the bed upon hearing his voice, and slowly turned to look at him, calming my frantic heart. I sat down next to him while my gaze swept over him in scrutiny. His mouth lifted at the corners as a grimace stole over his handsome face.

"*Nohro ahrae*," he muttered. "That hurts."

"It'll hurt for a while, I'm afraid," Soren said. "Your eye socket and nose are broken."

Tal groaned. "Estimated recovery time?"

"Your guess is as good as mine."

"What use are you again?"

Soren smirked. "I'll remember next time I have to patch you up."

He rose to his feet and stepped away. Tal was looking at me with wonder in his eyes.

"You're a good sight to wake up to," he murmured softly.

I caught the sob in my throat and laid my hand inconspicuously in his. He rubbed my finger with his thumb.

"You're a horrible sight to look at though," I replied, trying to smile. "I'd be scared to death if I'd awoken and everyone is happy."

The rumble in his chest was meant to be a laugh, but the contorted look on his face told me it hurt him.

"Don't make me laugh," he gasped. "That damn well hurts."

"What did you think it'd feel like? Someone tried to gut you."

He scowled. "I told you not to make me laugh."

"Sorry."

He brought up his hand and ran his thumb over the scar on my cheek, resting it on my lip. Soren cleared his throat, so Tal dropped his hand, and I scooted out of the way.

"Let him drink this," Soren said, handing me the cup. "It'll take the edge off the pain."

While Soren helped him sit up, I put the cup to his lips so he could drink. After only a few drops, his eyes rolled back into his head and he fell back to sleep.

"You drugged him, didn't you?" I asked.

"He needs rest."

I smiled faintly. "We all do. Go get some sleep, I'll stay here and yell if something goes wrong, provided you lay off the manhandling me for a few days."

Soren rubbed his face, smiling impishly. "You drive a hard bargain, but I'm willing to accept the deal. I really do need some sleep."

"Goodnight, Soren."

"Goodnight, *Tarien*."

I watched him disappear into the antechamber before I got up and sat down next to my brother. His chest rose and fell rapidly, his eyes moving fast behind his eyelids as if he was watching something.

He was dreaming.

Pushing the hair—or what was left of it—out of his face, I gently placed my hand on his cheek, singing the lullaby Mother always sang for us when we were children. His breathing slowly deepened and his eyelids fluttered less.

"I'm sorry Ev," I murmured, my eyes darting over him.

The part where his hair had been shaved off sported a cut the size of my hand, one of his eyes was black and blue, and his lip was split, but other than that, he looked all right. However, his upper-body was wrapped in so many bandages, he wouldn't need a shirt for the next few weeks.

I couldn't help but wonder what had happened to them, or why it had taken them so long to get back. I assumed the weather was a massive player in that game, but even then, over four weeks was a long time.

"You'd better live through this," I murmured. "I still need to accept your *nohro* apologies for that stupid remark and probably apologise for having jumped you."

He remained silent. A part of me had hoped he'd wake up like Tal had, but where his injuries looked bad, Evan's looked more severe. Placing a kiss on his forehead, I tucked him back in and sat down on the bed between them, keeping a silent vigil.

SOMEONE SHAKING my shoulder woke me up, and when I opened one eye to a slit, I found Haerlyon sitting on the edge of my bed, a playful half-smile on his lips. It didn't reach his eyes like it usually did though.

"Thought I'd find you here," he whispered.

I rubbed my eyes, pushed myself up, and launched myself at him, barely giving him time to catch me in his embrace.

"Thank the Gods you're safe."

"Thanks to Tal," he murmured in my hair. "He took that blow to the chest for me."

"Isn't he the hero then?"

Haerlyon let go of me again, looking me all over. "You look well."

"You've been gone for over four weeks," I muttered, running a hand through my hair. "What did you expect?"

"Honestly? For the palace to be levelled to the ground."

I stared at him. "What. Why?"

"You were right in thinking it was a trap," he said, shaking his head, "but it was worse than we expected. Half an army was waiting for us."

I shook my head. "That makes no sense. Therondians?"

"No," Haerlyon replied. "Ilvannian men. Sell-swords."

"That makes even less sense," I sputtered. "Who was leading them?"

He shook his head. "No idea. Some random guy I never caught the name of. We didn't stick around to chat."

"Not funny."

"Either way," Haerlyon continued as if I had said nothing at all, "it turned out we were only about a day's ride behind Evan. His men were already engaged in the fight, half of them were dead, and those still left were injured. Ev had sustained quite a few injuries as well, but didn't collapse until we arrived. Rurin took over control, and we fought."

"How come you stayed away so long?"

Haerlyon pinched the bridge of his nose. "I think the fight lasted about three days before the sell-swords gave up. After that, it took a while to take care of the injured and the dead. Almost everyone in Evan's squadron was killed."

"That's horrible," I gasped.

"Taking all the injured home in the terrible weather we had was even worse. We had to leave the dead behind."

I shuddered at the thought and was suddenly reminded of Azra's threats. I wondered if this had been part of her plan, or part of Eamryel's plan.

"You're home now though," I said, hugging him again. "Safe and sound."

Haerlyon just nodded, but I could tell something was bothering him.

"What's wrong?"

"There was just something off," he replied, a frown on his face. "Not only did they know Evan was coming, which makes sense if it was a trap, but it was almost as if they expected us as well. I mean Tal, Rurin and myself."

A shiver ran down my spine. "That's odd indeed."

It also meant whoever was on their payroll was still in the palace, relaying messages to either Azra, Eamryel, or one of their underlings. The thought alone made my skin crawl.

Whoever it was, I had to find him.

"Anyway," Haer said, "I just wanted to check in on you and them. How are they?"

I smiled faintly. "Soren drugged Tal. He woke up a few hours ago, and he'll probably be fine again at some point. Ev hasn't woken up yet, but he's alive."

"Thanks to you, I heard. Though granted, if you were to believe Nathaïr, you were killing him."

I snorted. "I was afraid I would."

"He's breathing." Haer grinned impishly. "You've done something right."

"It's on Soren's account, not mine."

He stroked my cheek. "Don't sell yourself short."

"Why is everyone being such wise-asses these past hours?"

"Because we've stared death in the face and laughed at it?"

I smirked. "You should've been a poet."

"It *would* keep me alive," he murmured.

"Your writing's terrible!"

He looked at me affronted. "It's not!"

"You cannot call your scrawling writing," Mother's voice sounded up behind us.

We turned to look at her. Her unbound hair hung in dishevelled ringlets over her shoulders and back, dark circles under her eyes a clear sign of the little sleep we'd all been subjected to. It warmed me to find her barefoot under her nightgown and dressing robe.

For once, she didn't look like the stern *Tari* at all.

She looked like our mother.

"How's Rurin?" Haerlyon asked.

She shrugged, sitting down on the side of Evan's bed. "Not as bad as these two, but definitely in pain. The healer has given him something to sleep, but he tosses and turns like a madman."

"Ev was like that too earlier," I said, watching her in awe. "Singing helped."

Mother looked at me amused from under her lashes, then turned to Ev, running a hand over the shaven side of his head.

"He'll not like this," she murmured. "Proud as he was of his hair."

I chuckled. "I don't know. It gives him somewhat of an edge."

"Now we still look alike," Haerlyon muttered with a lopsided-grin, running his hand over the shaved side of his head.

It needed a new shave.

"You'll never look alike." I chuckled. "He's more handsome."

Mother snorted at that. Haerlyon glared at me and nearly toppled me off the bed as he pushed me playfully. I grinned at him. From the corner of my eyes I saw Mother smiling at us with a sadness in her eyes which hadn't been there before.

"Everything all right, mom?"

I hadn't called her that in forever.

She nodded slowly. "I'm fine, *shareye*. Just tired."

"That makes two of us."

"Three," Haerlyon chimed in. "Haven't slept in days."

Mother smiled gently as she stroked Evan's good cheek, and I couldn't help but feeling jealous. She hadn't done this with me at all—not once since I got injured. Biting my lip, I settled my back against the headboard of the bed, pulling my knees up a little.

"If only we'd realised sooner," Mother murmured. "I should've known it was a trap."

"It's not your fault," I said, looking at her warily. "Whoever's behind this has it in for us."

Mother glanced up at me. "Why do you think that?"

"I think they're picking us off one by one," I said, looking at her. "First the poisoning, where I was the only one not targeted. Next we know, I get abducted, for whatever reason is beyond me. They set a trap for Evan, who in turn is a trap for Haerlyon? These are no longer coincidences Mother."

By my deduction, I realised she had to be next, and I shuddered at how that could possibly play out. Exhaling, I ran my hands through my hair.

Gods, I needed a bath.

Mother placed a kiss on Evan's forehead, then on Haer's, and mine, a gentle smile on her lips.

"Look after each other. I've got a country to run."

We watched her leave, arms wrapped around herself as if to ward off everything. I'd have loved to hug her, but Mother wasn't the affectionate type—not with me at least.

"You know more, don't you?" Haer asked me once she was gone.

I shrugged. "Maybe I do, maybe I don't."

"You've got that look on your face."

"Trust me when I tell you it's better if you don't know."

Haerlyon sighed softly. "I wonder if it matters much if I do or not. At this point we're fighting an unknown enemy who seems to know our moves before even we do. It feels unfair."

"Life's rarely fair."

"Now who's wise?" he muttered.

I grimaced. "The one who doesn't make me talk."

With a nod he rose to his feet, pecking me on the cheek. "I'll go see if I can sleep some. I'm dead on my feet."

"Sweet dreams."

He left me with a dismissive wave of his hand. Looking to my side, I found Tal watching me, a worried look in his eyes.

"Do you really think they're going after you one by one?" he rasped and coughed.

I swung my legs over the side and helped him sit up, placing the cup of herbal water against his lips.

"You're drugging me, aren't you?"

I smiled softly. "All is fair in love and war. You need rest. We'll talk when you feel better."

With a quiet nod, he downed the cup in one go and settled

himself back into the pillow. With a groan, he turned himself on his side, and while drifting off, wrapped an arm around my waist as if I was a pillow to be hugged.

I smiled softly, brushing the hair out of his face.

Despite the bruises and broken bones, he was still a handsome man to look at. I was sure he'd make some woman happy one day. To my surprise, the thought not only made me cringe, but it made me think up ways to get rid of her.

Maybe Eamryel was right.

Shaking my head, I tried not to dwell on that thought, dispelling the memories of the day I'd fought him—the day Tal and Ev had been so close, yet so far. Tal was now snoring lightly behind me, but the moment I tried to get out of his embrace, he pulled me back instinctively.

This would be a long day.

CHAPTER 15

After their return, life gradually eased into a semblance of order. The refugee camp spread out on the training fields emptied as people went back to their homes, and most of the men who'd gotten injured during the battle pulled through. Only two of them had died. I spent my days in the infirmary helping Soren tend to Tal and Evan, both of whom were more than a little irritable and snappy at the best of times. An added bonus was Soren monitoring me without having to put me through the strenuous torture of walking so he could see how I was doing.

After almost seven weeks, I was still limping.

"Better than having no leg at all," Soren commented drily after hearing my endless complaints during his massage.

"I know," I muttered. "Patience just isn't my forte."

He smirked. "Really? I had no idea."

I rewarded him with a blank stare.

"I'm surprised she's let you keep that tongue," Tal said from where he sat nestled against a pile of pillows.

"Or that she still allows you to massage that leg," Evan added. "Without kicking you."

"Oh, she's kicked me all right. More than once."

Both of them sounded as if they were choking.

I rolled my eyes. "I wish the two of you were still out cold."

In all truth, I was glad they were being cheeky. It was better than having to deal with their chagrined faces and moans of imminent death.

A commotion at the door had us all look up. A trio of *àn* bustled in, the middle one looking rather sick, incessant wails escaping his lips while he was being dragged inside by his comrades. Soren shot to his feet. I followed more elegantly.

"What happened?" Soren asked.

"His horse spooked, throwing him off. He hit his head on the cobblestones," one of them said.

"And the horse stepped on his leg," the other supplied. "Doesn't look pretty."

I moved out of the way as Soren guided them over to one of the treatment tables, a serene calm stealing over him as he prepared to get to work. It amazed me every time to see him go from saucy to composed in a mere matter of seconds. Mother had the same quality. Somehow, I never had been able to school my expressions that well.

"*Tarien*, would you be so kind?" Soren asked.

Lately, to my surprise, he had involved me in treating minor injuries, explaining what he was doing, and why. Both *àn* looked surprised when I stepped forward, the indecisive look on their faces showing they weren't sure how to behave.

I just smiled at them and stepped up.

While I did nothing more than clean wounds and apply bandages to the less severe cases, it gave Soren and his crew time to deal with the more serious injuries. It also taught me many things about the anatomy of our kind, which in turn led me to the realisation Eamryel had known perfectly well where to hit or cut to make it hurt without it being fatal.

The thought alone made me shiver.

Soren flitted around the *àn* like a busy bee, but the grave look on his face told me whatever needed to happen would not be nice.

"The damage to his leg is too severe," he said, shaking his head. "It'll kill him unless I take it off."

Both *àn* stared at him wild-eyed.

"But that'll cost him his job!" one cried.

The other huffed. "Or it's his life. I'd much rather lose my job."

"We'll find him something to do," I said, glancing at Soren.

Soren nodded solemnly. The look in his eyes told me more than he cared to let on.

"I will need you two to hold him down," he told the guards. "If you can't stand blood, don't look at it."

I snorted and bit my lip.

"If you want to leave, *Tarien*," he continued. "You don't have to be here."

"I'll stay. I don't know where everyone has gone and you can't do this alone."

He smiled faintly and nodded.

"Who'd have thought," Evan said. "Something other than fighting that could occupy you."

"There's still blood involved," Tal remarked.

I turned on them. "Will you two shut it?! You're the worst crowd ever."

Soren let out a short breathy laugh and shook his head. The two men, completely baffled by what was going on, stared from my brother, at me, and at each other.

"Surprise." I flashed them a wry smile. "We're just like you lot, and we bleed just the same."

"Are you ready?" Soren asked.

"No."

What followed was even worse than what I'd endured at Eamryel's hands. While Soren had drugged the man to the best

263

of his abilities without it killing him, it wasn't enough to keep the pain at bay while he took the man's leg off. He screamed and tossed in the restraints that were his comrades' arms and bodies.

I felt sorry for him and felt suddenly very selfish when I realised I'd be happy if I limped the rest of my life.

By the time Soren ended, a heap of blood-soaked rags covered my feet—my dress and arms didn't look much better. Thankfully, the guard was still out cold, but his comrades looked like they would be sick. In all truth, I wasn't feeling too well myself.

"I'll go out for a bit of fresh air," I murmured, and turned on my heel.

Once out of the infirmary, I hurried to get outside, footsteps behind me indicating one of my guards was following me. As soon as the fresh air hit me, I turned to a flower bed and added the contents of my stomach.

"I don't think I want to know what happened," Elara said.

I shook my head, wiping my mouth on my sleeve. This dress was ruined anyway.

"No, you don't," I replied.

Elara arched a brow when I turned to her. "You look like you rolled through someone."

"It feels like I did."

She shuddered. "I'll have someone draw you up a bath, and I'll send Queran down here."

With a nod I watched her leave, and hobbled over to the fountain, sitting down on the edge. The haggard reflection of a pale, drawn face with wide, shocked eyes covered in blood spatters from forehead to neck stared back at me accusingly. I scowled at myself and cupped my hands in the water, distorting the image. The water was fresh and ice cold on my heated cheeks, and a whole deal more welcome than the sticky blood.

"I sure hope that's not yours."

I looked up with a start to find Grayden standing at the other side of the fountain, thumbs hooked in his belt as he watched me. My lips curved into a smile.

"Just a man I killed for being too frank with me."

He blanched for a moment. "Point well made, *Tarien*."

"When did you get back?"

"Not too long ago," he replied. "Came to check on the poor sod who fell off his horse."

I smiled faintly. "Lost his leg, but he'll be fine otherwise."

"I had no idea you were a healer?" he asked, sounding surprised.

"I'm not," I replied with a shrug, "but it's his blood coating me."

Grayden frowned. "I won't ask."

"He's in the infirmary."

Inclining his head, he sauntered around the fountain and disappeared inside the palace. The man's screams before he passed out were still reverberating inside my skull, raising the hairs on my neck and arms. While splashing more water in my face, I heard someone walk up to me.

Everything happened fast from the moment they laid a hand on my shoulder, to where he landed in the fountain. Haerlyon spluttered and gasped as he resurfaced, watching me wide-eyed while water dripped down his face.

"*Nohro ahrae!* Seriously?!"

Doing my best to keep a straight face, I hid the smile behind my hand, watching my brother slosh out of the fountain.

"Don't laugh," he warned me.

I bit my lip hard, only to burst out laughing seconds later. Hiccoughing with glee I backed away from him as he stalked closer, his intent written all over his face, and when he pounced, I was too slow. Before I knew it, he had dumped me into the fountain. I spluttered to the surface, dashing water out of my eyes.

"*Grissin!*"

Haerlyon was howling with laughter, slapping his thighs, madly dashing away the tears rolling down his cheeks. When he looked again, he went into another fit of giggles until he could barely breathe. By then, we'd gathered quite an audience.

"Here," he said, "let me help you."

I trusted Haerlyon as far as I could throw him, but I did allow him to give me a hand. Instead of him helping me out, however, I helped him back in. What followed was a water-fight between the two of us leaving us soaking wet and breathless.

Mother's delicate cough stopped us mid-move, and Haerlyon looked at me as if he got caught doing something naughty. I could only imagine the look on my face mirrored his.

"Reception chambers," Mother said. "Now."

DRIPPING water on Mother's fine carpets, we stood with heads bowed and shoulders hunched. Haerlyon's fingers laced into mine, like they always did when we were in trouble. Mother just stood there, the simmering look she gave us scorching me to my soul.

She was all kinds of unhappy.

"*What* were you thinking?" She used the tone of voice usually reserved for those she was about to send to prison. "*Were* you even thinking?! Do you have *any* idea how much of a spectacle you made of yourselves?"

We both shrugged. I knew Haerlyon cared as much about appearances as I did, and probably even less.

"If only you had an ounce of Evan's decorum," she muttered.

"If only Ev had been born a woman," I retorted. "Life would've been much easier for all of us."

Haerlyon squeezed my hand in warning as Mother fixed me with a furious look.

"Maybe it would have been, but here we are and I got landed with a daughter like you," she snarled, turning away with a disgusted look. "Nothing to be done about that."

Every muscle in my body tensed at that comment. My jaw set and I gritted my teeth while Haerlyon nearly broke my hand by squeezing it so tight. I knew he was trying to keep me from making a remark I'd regret for the rest of my life.

Mother paced up and down in front of us, one hand resting on her forehead, the other on the small of her back. She looked troubled.

"Never mind," she muttered. "We have more pressing matters than your reputation."

My brows shot up in surprise. Did she really just disregard that comment as if it was nothing? I clenched my fists behind my back, watching her stoically.

"Yllinar's returned," she continued. "With good news, I might add."

I snorted derisively. "Nothing that man ever comes back with is good."

Mother glared at me.

"The Therondians are willing to negotiate with Ilvanna to come to an agreement," she said. "He hasn't worked out the details yet, but for as long as we have conducted no meeting, he's negotiated a truce."

"So they can stab us in the back during the meeting?" I asked.

"How can you be so distrusting?" She asked.

I shrugged. "Call it gut-feeling, Mother."

"Regardless," she said, looking at us. "There will be a party in two days' time to welcome him back, celebrate his success, and generally to put people at ease again. They need to believe everything's gone back to normal."

I had to hand it to her—although the party itself sounded like a disaster, she was right in saying people needed to feel things were as they should be. It would make it easier to find out who was behaving suspiciously.

"Can we go now?" Haerlyon asked, his arms wrapped around himself, teeth chattering.

I could feel him shiver beside me, and I had to admit I wasn't feeling all that warm either. Mother gave us a once-over with a disdainful look, only to frown when her gaze settled on me.

"Why are you covered in blood, daughter?"

"I thought I'd go and murder my reputation."

The warning look she shot me didn't need any words, and she dismissed us with a wave of her hand. Haerlyon and I fled her room as if we were little kids.

"I swear she was about to roast you on the spot," Haer murmured as we made our ways to our rooms.

"Roast me *and* eat me."

He chuckled. "You do need a bath though."

"You could've fooled me."

Laughing, he pulled me into a tight embrace, and placed a kiss on my forehead.

"Don't let Mother rile you up, all right?" he murmured. "It's not worth it."

"Do you think she meant what she said?"

Tears rolled down my cheeks unbidden, and I dashed them away, feeling more than a little annoyed with myself.

He shook his head, wiping a single tear away. "No, I don't. Now go change. You smell awful."

"You don't exactly smell nice either."

With a quick kiss on my temple, he let go off me and waved as he strolled off. Nothing ever really seemed to get to him, and I couldn't help but feel slightly jealous of that. It made me wonder what it was like not having a care in the world.

THE DAYS LEADING up to the party were a frantic mishap of everything that could go wrong, going wrong, and I tried to spend as much time out of Mother's line of sight as I could. Today it meant I skulked around the infirmary, helping both Evan and Tal look anywhere near presentable.

Soren was leaning against the wall, arms folded in front of him, fixing me with a sour look. "When are any of you going to listen to me?"

"When the stars fall from the sky and the moon turns into the sun," I replied with an easy grin.

He rolled his eyes and pushed himself off the wall, shaking his head with a mumble as he made his way into the antechamber.

"Have you been working on your retorts?" Evan raised an eyebrow.

"I wouldn't dare."

"You're incorrigible," he murmured, carefully swinging his legs over the bed, just as I helped Tal sit up.

"It's why you like me."

He flashed me a smile, shaking his head softly. Tal brushed his hand past mine, a habit he'd taken up doing whenever other people were around. I grinned at him, lacing my fingers with his behind my back, until the door swung open and Nathaïr marched in, followed by two servants.

Tal pretended to be busy getting up, eyes firmly fixed on the floor in front of him. Cheeky bastard. Soren peered out of the antechamber, saw who it was, and disappeared again with a shake of his head.

I'd have done exactly the same.

Ever since Evan's return three weeks ago, she'd come in every day to demand an update, even when everything was the same. For once, I couldn't fault her. Ev had been out of it for a few days before he started showing any signs of waking up. It

269

was just the manner in which she dampened the atmosphere in a room which annoyed me.

She looked me up and down. "I can't imagine sticking around here's so much fun."

"It's quite educational," I replied. "You should try it on for size."

If looks could kill, I'd have died on the spot. Deciding I wasn't worth her time, she swept over to Evan, getting into an animated debate with him. Why did she always sound like an entire flock of birds twittering? I tuned her out to the best of my abilities, focusing instead on getting Tal to his feet.

It was hard for him to do so with the healing cut on his chest, and the moment he used his abs to get up, he grimaced and sunk back.

"Let me help you," I murmured.

He glared at me. "I'm no use to you if I can't get up by myself."

"You probably won't be much use anyway," I replied with a faint smile. "Aside from looking handsome."

His brows shot up in surprise at those words, and I felt my cheeks flush. Why was it so hot in this room all of a sudden? I had not meant to say that out loud. Fanning myself, I looked anywhere but at him, busying myself with straightening the shirt I'd brought for him. Tal laid a hand on mine, and raised my chin with his other hand, his emerald eyes blazing, and a roguish smile on his lips.

I swallowed hard, ignoring the frantic butterflies.

"Help me up." His breath tickled my skin. "I'll be damned if I let you go to that party alone."

"Glad you're not stubborn."

He smirked. "It's one of the quintessential traits of an *Arathrien*. You won't get hired without it."

"Whatever could be the reason?" I rolled my eyes.

Even Ev and Nathaïr snorted at that. Tal laughed.

With a shake of my head, I sat down next to him, wrapped an arm around his waist as he circled his arm around my shoulders. We got up together after three tries, but it was clear Tal was shaky on his feet.

"Just give me a second," he breathed out, a grimace on his face.

Keeping my arm around him, I found Evan watching us with his head slightly tilted, a faint smile on his lips. He averted his eyes the moment he saw me looking. My gaze drifted over to Nathaïr who was flitting around him like a busy bee straightening him out, and the helpless look on Evan's face.

My heart went out to him.

Beside me, Tal grunted and dropped back on the bed, clutching his chest, breathing hard.

"You should stay here." I sighed, sitting down next to him. "Xaresh and the others will be there."

Tal scowled. "I have to be there."

"You *want* to be there. There's a difference."

His scowl deepened, but he didn't argue.

"I promise I'll be careful," I murmured for his ears only. "No crazy things."

"You're a walking disaster," he growled softly under his breath. "Freak accidents seem to happen around you more than around anyone else."

"Thanks for the vote of confidence."

He gave me a faint smile. "You know I'm right."

"Even so," I said with a deep sigh, "you should get some rest. The party won't be for another few hours."

Grumbling incomprehensibly, I gave him room to lie down again. Evan and Nathaïr quietly made their way out of the infirmary, and it surprised me to find she was supporting him.

Perhaps she wasn't as bad as I thought.

Tal brushed his fingers over the scar on my cheek, forcing me to look back at him.

"You've got that look on your face."

I raised an eyebrow. "What look?"

"The one where you try to solve the world's problems."

I tucked some hair behind my ear and folded my hands in my lap, looking at him with a frown.

"Answer me honestly."

"Always."

I bit my lip and swallowed hard. "Am I hard to love?"

"Whatever makes you say that?" he asked softly.

"Answer me, please?"

He traced a finger passed my jawline, following the healing cut running down to my collarbone, leaving goose bumps in its wake.

"You're asking the wrong person," he murmured, looking up with that pained expression. "But no, you're not hard to love once you get beyond the rough exterior."

I harrumphed, rubbing my cheeks, considering his words quietly.

"All right, I've got to get ready for this stupid feast," I said at length, rising to my feet. "This had better be the last one."

Tal looked slightly amused. "It won't be, and you know it."

I scowled at him, although he wasn't the reason for it by far. While he was wrestling the sheets from under him, I watched him from under my lashes, wondering what about him kept drawing me back. The moment he fixed his gaze on mine, I looked away.

"Help would be appreciated."

"Right," I murmured. "Sorry."

He shook with silent laughter as I fumbled around to get the sheet from under his shoulder. When I shot him a warning glance, he just chuckled. As I was tucking him in, I noticed bloodstains on the bandages.

"I'll ask Soren to have a look," I said, peeking under them to see what had caused it.

Although no healer, I could tell the angry red splotches of skin around the edges of the stitches didn't look good. In fact, it looked a lot like my leg had after the wolf bite, except the smell wasn't so bad.

"You might just have overdone it getting up." I meant my words to soothe him, but I wished they'd soothe me too. "Rest. I'll have to lock you up if I see you tonight."

He pressed his lips together, narrowing his eyes.

I gave him an impish grin, ruffled his hair and rose to my feet. He grabbed my hand and placed a kiss on it. With a faint smile, I left the infirmary after having informed Soren.

To my surprise, Queran, the youngest of my *Arathrien* was waiting for me, a light blush on his cheeks as if he'd come running here. I noticed for the first time he was barely older than a boy—he didn't even have an *araith* yet. Tal rarely left him alone with me, and if he did, usually one of the others was close by.

I observed how his breathing quickened upon seeing me, eyes widening slightly. He'd never looked so intimidated by me before. Or was it fear?

"Queran, are you all right?"

He nodded. "I am fine, *Tarien*."

His voice was strained when he answered. Deciding I had no time to deal with whatever was going on with him, I picked up the pace to my room. My breath caught in my throat when I opened the door and my gaze settled on crimson and yellow carnations, and red and purple orchids lining the walls and covering the floors. It was as if someone punched me in the stomach and covered my mouth, taking away my breath.

Staggering back, I clutched my chest while trying to suck in air. A wheezing sound as if someone was choking me sounded in the back of my mind until I realised I was making it. Wide-eyed I looked at Queran, who stood to the side, a bewildered look on his face, not making any move to help me. The world tilted just before my vision went dark.

Everything was on its side when I opened my eyes.

Mehrean's face was inches from mine, looking more than a little worried.

Rubbing my head, I pushed myself up with a groan, wincing at the sharp pain in my shoulder, and feeling as if the world was swinging the other way.

"What happened?"

Mehrean looked somewhat amused. "I was going to ask you the same thing. Queran said you fainted."

"I must have." I frowned, rubbing my face.

I knew I hadn't just fainted. It had been a full-out panic attack, and I hadn't been able to stop it. The flowers in my room were a message, and it was one I didn't particularly care for.

He was watching me.

"Time to get you dressed." Mehr smiled, helping me to my feet.

She frowned upon entering my room, seeing the multitude of flowers.

"Someone's outdone himself." She whistled.

I wished he hadn't. Sighing deeply, I followed her into the other room where a bath had already been drawn up, and everything I needed was laid out.

"I'll be happy when this has blown over." Quickly I undressed and stepped into the tub. "I can't imagine anyone enjoying these lavish parties."

"As long as it's not their wine and food," Mehr said, "people will enjoy anything."

"I suppose."

While she set to her usual routine, I stretched my legs in the tub, wincing at the sharp pain shooting through my calf, bringing my thoughts back to the soldier who'd lost his leg two days prior. His healing process would take much longer, and he had to learn to live with just one leg. I didn't envy him, but I did feel sorry for him, and all because of a freak accident.

I'd been incredibly lucky.

With a light shake of my head, I surrendered to Mehr's care, finding her slender hands massaging my scalp took away the edge of the worries.

If it could only take away the sinister feeling in my stomach.

CHAPTER 16

*O*nce Mother had gotten around all the formalities, the musicians struck up their tunes, and people started celebrating in earnest. If there was one thing Ilvannian nobility excelled at, it was enjoying a party. I appeared to be an exception to that rule. Standing to the side, one arm wrapped around myself, and the other resting on top of it, I raised a glass of *ithri* to my lips. It tasted of summer with its honeyed sweetness, and of winter, with its variety of added spices. It tasted of good times to be had when drunk enough.

If everyone was having a good night, I would do my best to have one as well.

Off to my left side, Evan and Nathaïr were in a deep discussion with another couple their age, and I was glad to see a smile on Evan's lips, even though it was at odds with the strained expression on his face. He was in pain. Haerlyon was off on the dancefloor, keeping up appearances with a comely girl. Even from this distance, I could see it was awkward.

"I feel for your brother," Xaresh murmured from my side.

"Which one of the two exactly?"

He smirked. "Both."

"Why doesn't anyone ever feel for me?" I pouted, turning to him with a grin.

"Because nobody would survive the sentiment."

I huffed. "Harsh."

A second later, Haerlyon picked my glass out of my hand, gave it to Xaresh, and pulled me out onto the dancefloor. The grin on his face nearly split it in half as he spun me around once, placing a hand on the low of my back while taking my other hand in his. Before I knew, we were sailing over the dancefloor, my brother smiling like a madman. People cleared the floor to watch us, clapping and laughing as we passed them.

He was having a good time, and if I was being honest with myself, so was I.

His happiness was infectious, and I noticed I was grinning as stupidly by the end of the dance as he was, until my eyes settled on a pair of blazing, predatory ones I knew only too well.

Their current weather prediction was a storm.

Swallowing hard, I looked away from Eamryel, my heart beating frantically in my chest as Haerlyon spun me out of his sight.

"Is everything all right?" he asked, following my gaze.

I nodded. "Yes. Fine."

I dreaded the moment the music changed. When it did, Eamryel was there, bowing deeply. Although I could see the suspicion on Haerlyon's face, my brother did not know what had passed between the two of us, and I had no reasonable explanation to turn him down without drawing attention.

When he settled his hand on the small of my back, and took my hand in his other, he pulled me close against him. I tensed. As the musicians struck up a slow tune, he put us into motion, and I followed automatically, my eyes fixed on his as his were on mine.

"You look absolutely breath-taking tonight," he murmured. "So perfect."

My skin crawled at his tone of voice and I looked away, my eyes searching the room for Xaresh or Elara—preferably both. Still holding my hand, he trailed a finger over the cut in my neck, goose bumps following in the wake of his touch. He licked his lips.

"You enjoy what I do to you," he murmured.

"Not even a little."

His eyes turned steely, and as he guided us into a spin, he pulled me even closer so I could feel *all* of him. I shuddered.

"This is what you to do to me," he growled into my ear, breathing in deeply. "You're all I ever think about."

His breath tickled my skin, but it didn't elicit the same response as when Tal had done it. A shiver scurried down my back and from the look on his face, I could tell he enjoyed the effect he had on me. I wondered why nobody was paying attention to us. Surely the look of horror on my face had to show how much I didn't like what he was doing.

"Let me go," I said in a small voice. "You've had your fun."

"I love it when you beg."

The hot look in his eyes did nothing to quench my fear. My gaze darted across the room hoping to find Elara, or Xaresh, even Evan or Haerlyon. Heck, at this point even Nathaïr would be better than him.

Why couldn't I find them?

The music stopped, and Eamryel let go of me except for my hand. He placed a kiss on it and bowed befitting my status, an alluring smile on his lips.

"Thank you for this dance."

I inclined my head and hurried away from him as quickly as I could. Xaresh was where I'd left him, laughing and talking to Talnovar. Surprise washed over me, before I narrowed my eyes and stared at him.

"I thought I told you not to come?"

"I thought I told you I had to go," he replied.

There was something off about him, but I wasn't sure what. Placing my hands on my hips, I looked him over, lips pressed together. His mouth turned into a cavalier grin lighting up his entire face, sending my stomach into cartwheels.

He caressed my cheek with his thumb.

"You're so beautiful when you're mad," he said for my ears only.

I clapped my hands over my mouth to stifle a laugh. "You're drunk!"

Tal raised one eyebrow, giving me a closed-lipped smile.

"What if I am?"

Shaking my head at him, I shook with silent laughter. "You never get drunk on the job."

"Good thing he isn't on the job then." Xaresh scowled. "Not sure what Soren gave him, but he's been as giddy as a girl ever since he arrived."

"Not drunk then, but drugged," I said.

Tal leaned forward to me and nodded. "A bit of both, but the pain is gone at least."

"I've told you to let your hair down," I said with a frown, "but this might be a bit too much."

I wasn't sure what to make of it. On one side, it was good to see Tal eased up for a change, but on the other I was afraid it would befuddle his senses should worse come to worst. Even injured, Tal was a force to be reckoned with, but like this, he'd not even be able to stomp a dent into a sack of grain.

Poor Tal.

"I'm going to get some fresh air," I announced. "Someone please stay with him?"

I jerked my thumb in Tal's general direction.

Xaresh sighed. "I'll stay with him. Promised Soren to look after him should he collapse. None of you could carry him back."

"I'd leave him there." I snorted. "For good measure."

"That hurt, *Tarien*." The roguish grin was back on Tal's face.

I rolled my eyes. "Let me talk to you again tomorrow and see what you prefer. Me hurting you or the embarrassment of remembering this."

"Take Elara or Caerleyan with you," Xaresh said. "Don't go out alone."

Elara was standing near the entrance to the terrace and followed me outside the moment I passed her. The night-air held a tinge of warmth, carrying the intoxicating scent of blooming flowers, but despite the promise of summer, it was still crisp. Hugging myself, I hobbled through the garden with Elara just one step behind.

I was about to round a corner when angry voices drifted our way.

Elara flattened me against a wall, a finger against her lips to keep me quiet, as we both strained to listen. Not that it was necessary—their voices carried.

"Your son nearly screwed up the entire mission," Azra hissed. "If he hadn't let her go, all of our plans would have gone to waste. You need to restrain him."

I didn't need to hear the second voice to know who she was talking about.

"Eamryel does as he damn well pleases," Yllinar sneered. "I brought him to stay out of trouble after he got his ass handed to him by that *Anahràn*. He snuck away the moment he saw his chance. You think I have any influence over him?"

"Try harder," Azra growled, "or I will. If he so much as lays a hand on her, I will kill him myself. If he endangers this mission one more time..."

"I know. I know," Yllinar muttered. "I'll send him off somewhere."

Azra fell silent.

"How are the preparations going?" she asked at length.

"Better than expected," Yllinar replied, sounding rather

pleased. "More and more people are willing to join our cause. The negotiations with the Therondian king went better than expected. They're waiting for your signal."

"Good," Azra said, sounding thoughtful. "Good."

"Are you sure you want to do this?"

Azra sighed. "She's taken everything from me."

They were getting closer, so Elara grabbed me by the arm and propelled me forward, away from them, and back to the party. I limped as fast as I could, grimacing at the pain. Once back in the courtyard, I sat down on a bench, gasping for air. Elara leaned back against the wall, lips set in a thin line.

Yllinar was the first to pass us, forcing a smile on his face and hoisting his glass while he walked back inside. He didn't look happy. Azra didn't follow at all.

"Eamryel did that to you?" Elara asked, encompassing all of me with a wave of her hand.

I knuckled my temples where a headache was forming. "He made sure I wouldn't tell. People will die if I do."

"We're not easily killed," Elara huffed, sounding offended. "You should've told us."

"Tal knows," I murmured softly. "I had to tell him, for Evan's sake."

Elara exhaled slowly and plopped down next to me on the bench, legs stretched out in front of her, rubbing her thighs.

"You should've trusted us," she said, hurt clear in her voice. "At least Xaresh and me."

"I trust you. It's why I didn't want to tell you, because I don't want you to be on his next-to-kill list."

"Next to kill?" she asked with a frown.

I nodded slowly. There was no sense in keeping it from her. "The day he released me, he killed his sister in front of my eyes, just to show what he'd do to everyone I loved should I talk."

Elara paled.

"He's mad," she muttered.

"He's beyond mad," I replied, placing my hands between my knees to keep them from shaking. "You cannot tell anyone Elara. You must keep quiet. To everyone. Not even Tal can know. In fact, I order you to remain silent on the subject."

She glared at me, a baleful look her face. "I hate it when you do that."

"I know."

We sat in silence for a while until the temperature had dropped to uncomfortable lows, forcing us back inside. My teeth were chattering, and I felt convinced not even a warm bath could thaw me. Elara kept her distance, widening the gap between us. She was hurt, and I couldn't blame her for feeling that way, but it was hard. I could only hope she understood why I hadn't told her and that she'd forgive me one day.

My eyes darted around the hall to find Xaresh and Tal. Their impressive height usually made them stand out in a crowd, but no matter where I looked, I couldn't find them. Elara, still following me at a slight distance, surveyed the room with a light frown creasing her brow. My heart was racing in my chest.

"There you are!" Haerlyon hissed from right next to me. "You've got to come."

"Why?"

He stared at me flatly. "Tal and Eamryel are fighting."

"Oh dear Gods."

Haerlyon guided us at a dead-run to a part of the less frequented areas of the garden. The sound of metal clashing with metal rung through the silent night, urging us on. By the time we arrived, Tal and Eamryel had their weapons locked and were staring each other down.

"Where's Xaresh?"

"In the infirmary," Haerlyon muttered. "Someone hit him over the head. He was bleeding to death."

I gave him a droll stare.

He shrugged. "What? It looked that way."

"What do you expect me to do?"

Haer rubbed the back of his neck, flashing me an impish grin. "No idea, but they're fighting over you, so I thought you were the best one to make them stop."

"Fighting over me?"

"According to Xaresh, he was bringing Tal back to the infirmary when they encountered Eamryel and his friends," Haer explained. "He said something about you."

"So Tal decided it was a good decision to fight him?"

Haerlyon shook his head. "Actually, Tal kept his cool. It was Eamryel who challenged him."

"Of course he did," I growled.

It was clear Eamryel was having the upper-hand. Despite his skill, Tal was too injured and too inebriated to keep this going for long. The impact on his sword had to jar him to his very core, pulling at the stitches and the injuries, and Eamryel kept battering into him.

"I need to stop this," I muttered.

Elara handed me her sword. In the moonlight I could tell she still wasn't pleased with me, but she wouldn't interfere in this one. I turned back at the same time as Tal stumbled and fell, and Eamryel sought to strike.

My sword met his as I parried his blade.

"Stay out of this," Tal grumbled behind me. "It's not your fight."

"It's every bit my fight," I spat back.

Between the two of them, Elara and Haerlyon pulled Tal, who protested every step of the way, out of there. Eamryel curled his lips into a half-smile, lowering his sword.

"I'm not fighting you," he said. "I wouldn't want to hurt you."

I smirked. "You're under the assumption you would."

He took a step closer to me, leaning in. "You surely have a high opinion of yourself, *Tarien*."

"It could never match yours."

He huffed, running his knuckles down my cheek. Somewhere off to the side I heard a deep, wolf-like growl.

"You should really leash your dog," he whispered, "before he takes a bite out of the wrong person."

"Challenge my *Arathrien* again, and you'll wish you'd won this fight."

The familiar tic of anger was back in his jaw. "I'll have you on your knees begging me to stop before long."

"If wishes were fishes."

"*Don't* get me started," he said in a low growl.

Perhaps I was feeling too secure knowing I had Elara and Haerlyon at my back, but I didn't want him to see how much he frightened me. If he did, he knew he had won, and I'd be damned if I gave him that satisfaction.

"I suggest you leave now," I said, staring at him, "before I call the guards."

He pressed his lips together. "Have you forgotten my threats?"

"No," I said, "but I know you'll be in grave trouble if you follow up on them."

Eamryel blanched at my words, looking suspicious. He rested his sword against his shoulder, regarding me with icy eyes.

"This is far from over." He turned on his heel, but before he walked away, I stopped him.

"Eamryel?"

The moment he turned to look at me, I punched him in the jaw, sending him stumbling backwards. I grunted and shook my hand, not sure I hadn't broken any fingers. Eamryel looked at me with a dazed expression on his face, rubbing the spot I'd hit him. Fury flashed in his eyes momentarily, before he pivoted and stalked off. Grinding my teeth, trying to keep myself from shaking, I walked over to the others.

"Nice punch." Haerlyon whistled.

I scowled. "It should've hurt him more than me."

"I'll teach you how to punch properly," Tal said, leaning heavily against Elara.

"You," I began, clenching my fist at my side, jaw set, "won't be teaching another thing in your life if you ever pull a stunt like this again."

He snapped his mouth shut, staring at me.

"Let's go," I muttered.

Soren was hardly surprised to find us entering the infirmary. If anything, he looked amused by it. Xaresh was sitting in a chair looking rather gloomy as Soren finished up bandaging his head. The scowl on his face deepened as he looked at Tal, his expression turning into one of passionate murder. He even appeared to be contemplating the how.

Tal's nose was bleeding, his lip was split and blood trickled from a gash on his forehead. Folding my arms in front of my chest, I looked at both of them.

"And you're supposed to protect me?"

They both had the decency to look at their feet. Elara and Haerlyon excused themselves and hightailed out of the infirmary. Soren snorted.

"Maybe I should find a new *Anahràn* and *Sveràn* who'll take their job seriously," I muttered, "because the two of you sure made a mess of things tonight."

Xaresh opened his mouth, and closed it again, shaking his head. Tal hissed as Soren cleaned out the injuries on his head.

I rubbed my temples. "When did everything become so complicated?"

"It didn't," Soren commented as he stuck the needle into Tal's forehead.

I winced on his behalf. Tal was already halfway asleep, most likely exhausted from being drugged, drunk and beaten.

"Complicated is what you make of it," Soren continued. "It can be as simple as you want it to be."

I sighed, running a hand through my hair. "You don't understand."

"Maybe not," he replied, "but I've seen you change over the course of weeks, and I'm not sure if it's for the better."

I tilted my head at him. "Change isn't always bad."

"True."

He remained quiet, leaving me mulling over his words. I thought I was doing rather well all things considered, unless anything reminded me of Eamryel, but maybe after what had happened tonight, things would get better.

Maybe.

"Let me get you to your room, *Tarien*," Xaresh said, rising. "You look dead on your feet."

"Look who's talking."

He smirked, thanked Soren for the help and guided me out of the infirmary with his hand between my shoulder blades. I couldn't help but notice the tremor running through him. He instructed Elara to stay with Tal to keep him from doing more stupid things.

"I doubt he'll be able to get up anytime soon," I said. "What got into him?"

Xaresh merely smiled.

Only when we were back in my room, and he was sure we were alone, did he drop the facade, a tormented look on his face.

"Sit down," he said, taking a seat in one of the chairs.

With his hands folded in front of him, he leaned forward, looking at me as I sat down opposite him, a frown on his face.

"I know you told me not to look into it," he began.

My heart sank. "Oh Xaresh—"

"I think something bad is about to happen," he interjected, shaking his head. "I don't know much, and I only overheard bits and pieces, but I talked to some people, and it's a feeling—I can't shake it off."

"I know what you mean," I replied, resting my head in my hands. "Too many accidents are happening for them to be coincidental."

Not to mention the threats at my address, and the conversation we overheard, but I didn't want to tell him about it. If Azra found out we knew, we were dead.

"Eamryel's the one who kidnapped you, isn't he?" Xaresh looked at me, his head slightly tilted.

"You guys are too perceptive for your own good," I growled.

Angrily, I pushed myself to my feet, pacing up and down the room. Everything was going downhill fast and nothing I did was making it any better. Elara was mad at me for not trusting her, Talnovar behaved like a complete and utter fool, and Xaresh was looking into things he should leave well enough alone. Then there was Eamryel with his high creep-levels, and Azra with a hidden agenda. I needed to find out who the 'she' she'd mentioned to Yllinar was, though a gut-feeling told me I already knew.

"What did he threaten you with?" Xaresh's question startled me from my reverie.

"He'd kill you if I talk," I replied, avoiding his gaze. "To make sure I'd understand the ramifications, he killed his sister."

I drew a shaky hand through my hair, flashing him a wry smile.

"Guess she died for nothing."

"If he didn't want people to know," Xaresh said, "he shouldn't have been so obvious about it."

Looking at him, I raised an eyebrow. "What do you mean?"

Xaresh's jaw tensed, and he clenched his hands so hard his knuckles turned whiter than usual. I'd never seen him like that.

"When I was taking Tal to the infirmary," he began, "Eamryel was boasting to his friends. About you."

"About me?"

Xaresh looked away. "Yeah. About how he'd make you his, mark his words."

It stunned me until it didn't and I burst out laughing, shaking my head.

"By *Vehda*." I snorted. "He's more delusional than I thought."

"I may have slugged him."

I stared at Xaresh. He rubbed his jaw, looking mildly apologetic.

"Is that how you got that cut?"

He just nodded.

"I thought Haerlyon was vague about the details." I shook my head, stifling a laugh. "But seriously, don't punch anyone on my account. It's not worth the trouble."

"It felt good though."

With a faint smile, I sat down on my bed, rubbing the hand I'd punched Eamryel with. Something definitely wasn't right.

"Please, be careful?"

"I'm always careful," he replied with an impish grin. "I might have to give Tal another warning though."

I huffed. "He's been behaving like an ass."

"He's been beating himself up over the fact he can't protect you, *Tarien*," he said. "And Eamryel challenged him, not the other way around. What did you expect him to do? Bow down and decline?"

I smiled wryly. "If he'd been smart, yes, but I understand why he did it."

Biting my lip, I looked away from Xaresh, feeling the heat rise to my cheeks.

"I just don't like seeing him hurt," I murmured.

Xaresh chuckled softly. "You two should talk to each other sometime."

"Our conversations always seem to end in fights."

"That's what I said, you need to *talk* to each other."

I harrumphed, folding my arms in front of me. "You should've been a priest."

"I considered it."

Despite my annoyance and rising fear, my brows shot up in surprise, and I laughed.

"I really cannot imagine you as one," I mused, watching him with a slightly tilted head. "I rather like you as you are now."

He smiled softly. "I'm not going anywhere."

"Promised?"

"Promised."

While I wriggled out of my dress and into something more comfortable, Xaresh kept his gaze fixed on the door. He was a sweetheart and if anything were to befall him, I wasn't sure what I'd do.

"I'll stand guard at your door," Xaresh said. "You know where to find me."

"Take some rest Xaresh. I need you with Tal out of order."

Looking back, he flashed me a smile. "Stop worrying *Tarien*. You cannot save the entire world."

"I know," I murmured, "but I can at least try."

CHAPTER 17

A loud crash startled me awake, and it took a few seconds for my eyes to adjust and realise light was pouring into the room from the hallway. In the opening of the door, two people were grappling with each other, doling out punches and drawing out grunts. I jumped out of bed, grabbed my long dagger and stalked closer in the hopes they hadn't noticed me.

Xaresh had his back towards me, but I could tell he was struggling against the hold around his throat. He went for a short uppercut, but failed. Although a trained fighter, from the way he was moving I could tell he was getting anxious.

Come on Xaresh, you know how to do this.

All his attacker had to do was keep the strong hold around Xaresh's throat until he would slip into unconsciousness. Xaresh wasn't giving up that easily—from the way his muscles tensed, I figured he was gathering all his strength. He hit his opponent in the solar plexus full force.

It wasn't enough.

In my desperation to get to Xaresh quickly, I knocked my foot against an overturned chair and cursed.

The sudden disruption startled them both, and as Xaresh turned, the attacker seized his opportunity—a metal blade gleamed in the corridor lighting seconds before the assailant plunged it into Xaresh's unguarded side. I screamed. His eyes widened in shock. The assailant pulled out the knife, allowing blood to spurt from the wound. Xaresh dropped to his knees, his expression one of confusion as he brought a trembling hand to his side, bringing it back up bloodied. I could see him swallow and blink.

Paralysed by what just happened, I stared at the hooded attacker, eyes wide.

"They warned you," he said in an undertone. "He should've kept his nose out. He's the first, but he won't be the last."

Slipping out of my room like a thief in the night, the assassin disappeared from sight. Xaresh fell over at my feet, and I dropped to my knees, my hands feeling around for the wound, finding it just below his right rib. Dark blood trickled alongside his body, and I could hear he was having a hard time breathing. Swallowing hard, I cradled him in my arms, trying to keep the tears from streaming down my face.

I tried not to break down.

"You promised," I whispered, gulping away the lump in my throat. "You promised."

He laid his hand on my arm as I hugged him, rocking him like a baby.

"I'm sorry," he said, a grimace of pain crossing his face as dark blood spilled from his mouth, coating his lips. "I have to admit *Tarien*, it hurts. A lot."

I nodded softly. "I know."

"Will… will you do me a favour?" he wheezed.

"Anything."

"Take my body home?"

I swallowed the lump in my throat, my voice thin when I spoke. "I'll do you one better. I'll bring your family here."

He smiled at that.

"Tell the others I had an amazing time?"

I half-laughed, half-sobbed at that. "You can't go."

"I'm sorry Shalitha," he whispered. "Sorry I have to break my promise."

He'd never called me by name before.

Shaking my head hard, I placed a kiss on his forehead, wiping away some blood. "You didn't. You couldn't."

"Promise me one thing?" His breathing was laborious, his voice pained.

I nodded again.

"Talk to Tal? Really talk, I mean," he said.

"I will."

With every breath he took, dark blood pumped out of the wound, and I knew the moment he passed away. His head rolled to one side and his body went limp in my arms. I wailed—loud, ragged sobs tore from my chest until my throat was raw from it.

Someone pulled me away from Xaresh, and I screamed, fighting whoever had a hold of me, drawing out grunts and hisses. They were stronger though and wrapped me in a tight embrace. Tears rolled down like an endless river, and when they took Xaresh's body away, more came.

Whoever was holding me stroked my hair, shushing me, placing kisses on the top of my head, rocking me, and at some point I realised it had to be Tal. I turned in his embrace and clung to him as if my life depended on it, my sobs growing in intensity, racking my body until I was sore all over. When I'd spent all my tears, all I could do was sniffle and stare.

Still Tal rocked and held me.

"He's gone," I whispered in disbelief. "He's gone."

"I know," he murmured into my hair.

Placing his hand on my head, he pulled me against his shoulder. The bandages on his chest chafed my cheek, but I didn't care. His heart was beating steadily under my ear, a reassuring *thump-thump-thump* telling me Tal was alive and well. He tried to steady his breathing, but I could tell he was having a hard time too.

I looked up at him. He was looking at me.

In fact, he was staring at my lips, a look of sadness mixed with something else in his eyes. I felt his hand slide into my hair slowly, and before I knew, his lips were on mine, kissing me as if he was afraid to ever let me go. My whole body froze for a second, before melting entirely into his, answering the kiss as if he were my life raft. He pulled back as quickly as he'd kissed me, eyes wide.

"Sorry, we shouldn't," he whispered.

"No, we should." My voice was hoarse when I spoke.

With uncertainty dancing in his eyes, he cupped my face in his hands, kissed the tears from my cheeks, and placed his forehead against mine.

"It's not appropriate," he murmured against my lips.

"Propriety be damned."

His eyes searched mine in wonder before he leaned in, his lips brushing mine. His body tensed when he kissed me again. It was sweet, and tender, and everything it hadn't been with Eamryel. For a few moments after the kiss, I didn't want to open my eyes, afraid this was just a dream, until Tal ran his thumb over my lips.

He watched me in pure wonder.

Every kind of known and unknown feelings raced through me, yet I couldn't pick a single one of them to describe my current state of emotions. I felt bereft and empty on one side, yet at the same time, I felt happy and elated, and for the first time in weeks, safe. Melancholy overtook me so suddenly I didn't know what to make of it. I felt confused, guilty even for sitting here with Tal as if nothing had ever happened.

Yet a lot had happened.

In the space of a few minutes, I'd lost my *Sveràn*, a dear

friend, and one of the very few people who'd never tried to change me. The realisation brought on a new onslaught of tears. Tal wrapped his arms around me, but I pushed him away this time, stumbling out of his embrace. Blinded by grief, I knocked into a table and a chair, before I found my way to the garden door.

I fumbled with the lock until I heard it click open and staggered outside, gulping in waves of fresh air. It was pouring, as if the Gods themselves were weeping over the loss of such a gentle soul. I turned my head up, letting the rain soak me while washing away the tears. Footsteps sounded up behind me, and I guessed it to be Tal. Although we didn't look at each other, his hand sought mine, fingers lacing together as a silent promise to each other. Salt tears mingled with rain until I was no longer sure which was what. The pain in my chest had to be my heart dying and shrivelling up, and it would be a matter of minutes before I'd drop to the ground and die. But those minutes passed and nothing happened. I wiped my eyes and stared absently at Tal.

His expression mirrored my feelings.

We'd both lost someone dear to us.

He squeezed my hand and turned to face me, his lips quirking up in a roguish half-smile which never quite reached his eyes. I wished he'd kiss me again. Saying nothing, he pulled me back inside my room. Candles had been lit, and servants were scurrying around to scrub the floor and get everything in order.

Elara stood at the door with Queran, both looking pale and wide-eyed, but where Queran looked a little squeamish, Elara looked as if she was about to tear someone's head off. The minute she saw us, she stepped inside, worry etched on her fine features.

"Are you all right?" she asked me, eyes darting over me. "He didn't hurt you?"

I shook my head, wrapping my arms around myself. "No. He didn't get the chance. If anything, I caused him to kill Xaresh sooner."

"What happened?"

It was Tal who asked this time, sounding every bit the *Anahràn* he was supposed to be right now. Gritting my teeth, I tried to keep them from chattering before I related what I'd seen.

"If I hadn't made a sound," I whispered, "he might not have..."

I swallowed hard. Tal took my face in his hands, forcing me to look at him.

"*Tarien*, nothing of this is your fault," he said firmly. "You cannot blame yourself for his death."

But I did, just as I blamed myself for Caleena's death. Just as I would no doubt blame myself for their deaths one day.

"*Tarien?*"

We all looked up to find Rurin standing at the door, a grave look on his face.

"Your mother wants to see you and Talnovar," he said before turning on his heel and disappearing from sight.

"Terrific," I murmured.

Elara handed me my dressing robe. Tal's jaw was clenched, but I wasn't sure if it was because of what happened, or the pain in his body. A thought suddenly struck me.

"How did you know to be here, Tal?"

"I think everyone in the palace heard your scream," he said. "But it was Haer who came to fetch me."

I frowned. "He was here?"

"He helped take Xaresh away."

"Oh..."

Tightening the sash around my waist, I started out of my room, trying not to look at the spot on the floor where Xaresh's blood had stained it.

"It should've been me," I murmured.

"He knew the dangers, *Tarien*." Elara spoke from my left. "He knew this could happen. We all do."

I sighed. "Doesn't make it fair though."

"Life's rarely fair," Tal replied from my right.

They were the same words I'd spoken to Haerlyon the night of their return. Had he somehow heard them?

Mother was waiting for us in her reception chamber, dressed in her night attire like me, but looking a lot worse. There were bags under her eyes as if she hadn't slept in weeks, and her skin was pallid, almost as if she were ill. To my surprise, she hugged me tight, stroking my hair.

"Thank the Gods you are safe," she whispered. "Why are you so wet?"

"I've been outside."

She put me at arm's length, frowning. "Why would you do that?"

I shrugged. It had felt like the right thing to do, even though I was regretting my decision now. Both my nightgown and dressing robe were soaked. Mother looked over my shoulder, raising an eyebrow.

"Why's Elara here?"

"Because she's my *Sveràn* now, *Tari*," Tal replied. "Considering what happened tonight, I want two guards on your daughter at the very least. Night and day."

Mother narrowed her eyes for a moment, sighed and shook her head, indicating for all of us to have a seat. I was the only one who did. Elara and Tal took up position behind me. I rubbed my forehead, and curled up in the chair, trying to regain some warmth.

"Xaresh's murder will be public knowledge within a few hours," Mother said. "People at the palace will fear the notion that an assassin made it inside and got out unchallenged. We need to tell a different story."

"What do you suggest?" I croaked.

While I didn't like the idea, simply because Xaresh deserved so much better, it made sense. People would start demanding having their own guards, and more such nonsense.

"We'll tell them he got previously injured during training," she replied. "He didn't notice it was that bad until it was too late."

"That makes no sense, Tari." Tal frowned. "He'd have felt an injury like that."

"Not if it's internal."

Everybody stared at me—Mother surprised, Elara with a frown and Rurin even somewhat impressed. The only one who remained stoic was Tal.

I shrugged. "What? I've spent enough time in the infirmary to know an internal injury can cause death. Soren told me."

"I'm not sure what I like least," Mother said, "you training with weapons or spending time at the infirmary learning the healer's trade."

"At least both things are useful."

Mother closed her eyes and rubbed her temples. Tal laid a hand on my shoulder, giving a light shake of his head when I looked at him. The warning in his eyes made me roll mine.

"It's not a bad idea," Rurin offered. "I've heard stories of men dying who looked perfectly healthy the day before."

"They call that war," Tal scoffed.

Rurin merely stared at him. "You know what I mean."

"It's so unfair to Xaresh." I sighed. "All for the sake of the fragile nobility. Honestly, they should grow a pair."

"Shalitha!" Mother gasped in shock, her eyes widening.

"What? It's true. Maybe if they stop their dainty behaviour, pretending to be delicate flowers ready to wilt at the bare touch of sunlight, Ilvanna would be worth something, and nobody would have to die at the hands of an assassin."

Mother groaned audibly, passing a hand over her face. "One

day, you'll be a fine *Tari* I'm sure, but I will pray to the Gods you'll have learned some manners by then."

"I'm not in the baker's trade, Mother. I don't sugar coat things."

Tal went into a coughing fit behind me, mumbling an excuse as he turned away. Elara looked at him worriedly. No doubt he'd feel that for the next few hours.

"I've noticed." Mother's lips curled into a half-smile, "and I appreciate it, but now is not the time to argue about Ilvannian aristocracy."

I smirked.

"Xaresh's family needs to be informed," Mother continued, "and his burial prepared."

"Actually, Mother," I said, uncurling myself from the chair, "I'd like to ask for a favour?"

She tilted her head slightly. "What is it?"

"Bring his family here, and offer them a job," I said.

"Why?"

I bit my lip, fumbling with the knot on my robe. "He's been providing for his family since his father's death two years ago. With him gone, they have nothing."

"That's only fair," Mother said before turning to Tal. "As *Anahràn*, it's your task to notify his family. Please put together a small party and leave at dawn."

He crossed his arms, pressing his lips together. Casting him a furtive glance, I saw his jaw tic, his body tense. He didn't like having to go, but he could hardly disobey the *Tari's* orders. Not even he was that brave.

"As you wish, *Tari*," he said curtly, and bowed.

Between the nightly ordeals crashing down on me, and my chattering teeth, I had trouble focusing as the conversation continued. Tal's hand on my shoulder startled me back to awareness and with a nod of his head, we left the room. My feet were pins and needles during our walk back, and nobody spoke. Not until we were back in my room.

"I can go," Elara offered as she closed the door behind her.

Tal shook his head. "No, the *Tari's* right. It's my job."

"But you're her best defence," Elara objected.

"I'm still injured," Tal said. "I won't be any good to her."

Elara folded her arms, narrowing her eyes. Shaking my head, I grabbed a pair of wide trousers and a blouse from my cabinet, disappearing into the next room to redress. I wasn't sure they'd seen me leave, but it wasn't even a minute later when they both called my name in fear. Towelling my hair dry, I stuck my head around the corner.

"Keep your pants on, I'm right here."

Tal glared at me.

After I was sufficiently dry, I put on my clean clothes and got back into the room. Elara was leaning against the wall, rubbing her temples.

"Tal's gone to gather his troops," she said as I opened my mouth to ask. "He said he'd see you before he'd go."

I snapped my mouth shut and nodded, hunting around my room for my boots. Elara watched me warily, her lips turned up in the corners.

"Elara?"

"Hm."

"Thank you."

She frowned at me. "What for?"

"Guarding my stupid ass."

"We all have our weak spots."

I chuckled softly at that, only to sober up quickly. Slipping my boots on, I grabbed a cloak and turned to her.

"Shall we go for a walk?"

THE NIGHT-SKY WAS a dark blanket with tiny holes allowing light to sparkle like a thousand little diamonds, giving us a glimpse of what the world beyond would look like. Drawing my cloak tighter about me, I leaned back against the bench, staring up. Elara was sitting next to me, long legs stretched out, eyes heavenwards, elbows leaning on the bench.

Her eyes filled with tears.

"Do you think he'll keep watch over us from up there?" she asked softly.

"I do."

If only because the alternative didn't bear thinking about. Whether or not he was a star amongst many, he was gone from our lives, leaving only memories. My chest tightened at the thought and wayward tears trickled down my cheeks.

"I'll miss his calm presence," Elara said in a tight voice.

Tears were rolling down her cheeks now, yet she made no move to wipe them away.

"I won't miss him pulling me out of bed before the crack of dawn for training," I said, letting out a short laugh.

Elara snorted. "Don't worry, we'll help you remember him that way."

I groaned.

"Remember when Tal had given him some *ithri* at *Wanenyah*?" Elara grinned. "He didn't realise until after he'd finished it."

I laughed at that. "He had no idea what left or right was."

"Or up and down for that matter."

"I mostly remember the payback he gave Tal." I giggled. "Wasn't it ground biscuits in his cup after training?"

She nodded excitedly. "Xaresh had never run as fast in his life."

"Nobody outruns Tal though."

"We would now."

I snorted. "Don't let him hear you say that."

WHILE WE SAT REMINISCING about the past, the sky gradually turned lilac set off with dark purples and bright pinks, heralding a new day, and with it Tal's departure. Elara escorted me to the courtyard where a small group of sullen men were checking their gear and getting ready to ride. I noticed Haerlyon and Tiroy were among them.

Tal strode over to me while wriggling one hand into a leather glove, his eyes fixed on mine. He cupped my cheek in his gloveless hand, stroking the scar like he was wont to do whenever I was close. I could see the hesitation in his eyes to kiss me, and although I wanted nothing more than that, there were too many witnesses.

We had no way of knowing who'd seen us before.

I laid my hand on his, swallowing hard. "I wish you didn't have to go."

"I wish I didn't have to leave you," he echoed me in a low voice, "but here we are. Don't do anything stupid, please? I couldn't bear the thought of losing you."

I nodded, my throat tightening. "Come back to me."

"I'll always come back to you."

Standing on tiptoe, I placed a chaste kiss on his cheek while resting my hand against his heart.

"If you don't come back," I said in a hoarse voice, "I'll find you and kill you."

He smirked. "Is that a promise or a threat?"

Tears were brimming my eyes, but I refused to let them fall. He took my hand in his and placed a kiss on my knuckles as he bowed. Before either of us could do anything we might come to regret, he turned on his heel, mounted his horse, and urged it onwards.

"We'll look after him," Haer said, flashing me his impish grin. "I promise."

"You'd better keep it."

He waved as he nudged his horse to a trot to follow the others. Elara laid her hand on my shoulder, squeezing it lightly.

"He knows how to look after himself."

"That's what I'm afraid of."

Elara gently turned me around and walked me inside, even though that was the last place I wanted to be right now. The palace was slowly awakening, including the aristocracy. News of Xaresh's death was spreading like wildfire, so when I passed, people stopped and stared. Keeping my lips pressed together, my hands balled at my sides, it was all I could do to keep it together and not yell at them.

"We should clear out Xaresh's room," Elara said, "before servants start pawing through it."

I nodded and followed her. To our surprise, the door to his room was slightly ajar, and candlelight flickered through the crack. Elara grabbed a dagger from her belt and gave me the one she kept in her boot.

"A girl can never be too precautious," she murmured as she handed it over.

She tiptoed over to the other side of the door, motioning me to stay where I was. While she counted down on her fingers, I pushed the door open—slowly. She slipped inside quietly, and when I followed, I dropped the dagger in surprise. Elara had Queran pinned with his arms behind his back, dagger at his throat.

The room was in complete disarray, and knowing Xaresh, this wasn't how he'd left it. Books and papers were scattered through the room as if they'd been thrown carelessly over someone's shoulder. Every piece of his wardrobe lay criss-cross on the floor, and his mattress was barely on the bed.

Everything was a complete chaos, except for his desk.

"What are you doing here?" I asked through gritted teeth.

Queran paled, whimpering as Elara tightened her grip. "I... I was trying to find something. F... for Tal."

Elara inched the dagger further towards his throat as I took a step closer. I narrowed my eyes at him, my brow creased.

"Don't lie."

"H... honestly!" he whimpered. "Talnovar asked me to look for his diary!"

"And when did he ask you that?" I asked, trying to keep my cool.

"Just a moment ago!" he squeaked.

I raised an eyebrow, giving a light shake of my head. "Tal just left. Take him to the cells. He's lying through his teeth."

Elara looked troubled.

"I'll be fine," I said. "I'll stay here."

She nodded, propelling Queran out of the room. My heart sank the moment they left, and I noticed I was trembling. Why had Queran been going through Xaresh's room, especially so shortly after his death? Had he known? The thought alone made me sick, and it took me all my self-restraint not to throw up right there.

I closed the door and started straightening out his room, annoyed at Queran for defiling it by making such a mess. Xaresh had been one of the cleanliest and organised people I'd ever known. Even in my room he kept straightening things if he thought they were off. If he'd see this, he'd have a heart attack. I swallowed away the lump in my throat and set myself to the task at hand.

I placed the valuable things aside for his family, together with other memorabilia he collected over the years here. Several small wooden animals stood in the windowsill. He had whittled all of them with great love and care—Xaresh had loved doing it. I picked up a small owl, its eyes carved as if they held the wisdom of ages, the small lines of feathers on its body detailed to the touch.

This was exquisitely made.

"Oh Gods," I breathed, and sank to my knees, clutching the owl to my chest. "Why did it have to be you?"

Dashing the tears away from my cheeks, I put the owl back and continued arranging Xaresh's room. In the future, it would house another *Arathrien*.

Stop thinking, I told myself angrily.

Having something to do took my mind off the worst of things. When I picked up a book to place it back on the shelf, a piece of paper fell out. I nearly dropped it when I saw what it was—a clear overview of names with suspicions scribbled below them. Xaresh had found out much more than he'd led me to believe.

"Fool," I murmured. "You stupid, wonderful fool."

A knock on the door alarmed me and I spun around to see Evan sticking his head around the corner, a smile on his face. I folded the piece of paper behind my back and tucked it deep inside my boot.

"Is everything all right?" he asked with a frown as he saw me hopping around on one leg. "Eh, Elara said you'd be here."

"I'm fine. Got something in my shoe."

At least I wasn't lying about that. Ev nodded.

"How are you holding up?"

Without prior warning my eyes teared up, and he was with me in a few strides, collecting me in his embrace. Wrapping my arms around his waist, I allowed the tears to come, wondering if it would ever stop. He never said a word until I started sniffling. I wiped my nose with the sleeve of my shirt and dabbed my eyes, looking up at him.

"Sorry," I murmured. "I'm a mess."

Evan smiled. "I'd have been surprised if you weren't. A good man has been killed."

"It was cold-blooded murder."

"We'll get whoever is responsible," he said, tucking a lock of hair behind my ear. "I came to fetch you. Mother's going to make an official announcement and she wants us there."

Before Evan guided me out of Xaresh's room, I grabbed the owl from the windowsill, hugging it to my chest. My brother's brows rose briefly, but he made no comment.

THE THRONE ROOM was a giant beehive. People's murmured voices created a continuous buzz until Mother silenced them by raising her hand. Sitting to her right side, my eyes darted over the assembled crowd. There were nobles, guards, *àn*, servants, even citizens had found their way here. Everyone was looking at Mother, all except for one. Azra. Her eyes were fixed on me, and the moment I looked at her, she flashed me a wolfish smirk. She pointed at me for my eyes only, shook her head, and drew a finger across her throat.

I stilled.

"It is with sadness in my heart I have to inform you of Xaresh Nehmrean's untimely death due to a tragic accident."

Mother's voice brought me back to the here and now. When I looked back, Azra was gone.

"The upcoming week will be one of mourning," Mother continued. "At the end, we shall say our farewells during the burial rites. Pay your respects while you can and be respectful to those around you."

Tired of having to keep up appearances, I excused myself the moment Mother finished and fled the throne room, Elara in tow.

"We need to talk," I murmured.

CHAPTER 18

*E*lara stared at the piece of paper as if it was written in a foreign language she'd never heard of before. She sat gawping at me for a long time before she finally found her tongue.

"Where did you find this?"

"Xaresh's room," I said, one hand on my head, the other on my hip, while pacing up and down my bedroom.

"The night before he… before he was killed, he told me he feared something big was going on, but he promised me he didn't know much, just bits and pieces. But this…"

Elara nodded slowly. "It's more than bits and pieces."

"I expected Queran," I murmured. "But Rurin. Mother will be devastated."

"You cannot tell her Shal. Ever."

I swallowed hard and nodded. "I know. We cannot tell anyone, really. You've seen what they did to Xaresh. If they find out what we know…"

"And after what we've heard…" Elara said, shaking her head slowly. "We can't take any chances. How good is your memory?"

I snorted. "Better than people give me credit for."

She handed me the note. "Memorise it and burn it."

"Why me?"

Looking away briefly, she rolled her fingers into fists and back again, cracking her knuckles. I shuddered at the sound. When she looked up, I saw the determination on her face.

"It won't end with Xaresh," she said. "You know it as well as I do. I might be next, or maybe Tal, but not you. Never you, if we're to believe that."

Shaking my head to dispel the sickening feeling in my gut, I looked down at the paper, breathing out sharply. I was glad his handwriting were neat fluid lines, or I wouldn't have been able to commit any of it to memory.

"Should we tell Tal?" I asked.

Elara wrinkled her nose. "How much does he know already?"

"He's got a target painted on his back."

"Then yes."

I nodded slowly, rubbing my cheek. "I was afraid you'd say that."

Peering at the paper again, I growled and threw it away. Elara snatched it out of the air, looking anything but impressed.

"I can't remember it," I sighed. "Not now anyway."

"Put it somewhere safe and we'll get back to it later," Elara said, stretching.

Folding it, I tucked it back in my boot, figuring on me would be the safest of places. Elara had the tell-tale V-frown on her face.

"What's wrong?"

She shrugged. "I think we need to question Queran."

"I'm afraid I'll punch him if I come too close."

Elara's lip curled up in a wry smile. "You and me both, but I have the feeling we might get something out of him, before someone else does."

"I hate your reasoning."

SOMEONE HAD GOTTEN to Queran before us. His sightless eyes were staring up at the ceiling, his throat cut from ear to ear much like Caleena's had been. I turned away with one hand over my mouth, the other on my stomach as it twisted itself into an uncomfortable knot, fighting to keep everything inside. Elara stood motionless at the open cell door, eyes hard.

"*Ruesta mey mahnèh.*" She murmured.

I turned to see her walk inside and squat down next to him, closing his eyes. Leaning against the wall, I wrapped my arms around me, shaking my head.

"Elara?"

"Yeah, I won't go out on my own again either," she muttered. "Although I think they killed him for other reasons."

I nodded. "Even then."

When we heard voices coming towards us, Elara stepped out of the cell and in front of me, ready for whatever would come. It was the jailor with Evan and several guards in tow. My brother frowned deeply when he saw me there.

"What are you doing here?"

"I wanted to talk to my guard," I replied, "but I guess I'm too late."

Evan looked into the cell, jerking his hand through his hair, or where it used to be. The confused look on his face told me he still hadn't gotten used to it.

"I'll deal with this. Elara, please take the *Tarien* somewhere safe?"

"There are no uninhabited islands anywhere close, Sir."

He stared at her flatly. With a smirk on her face, Elara guided me away from the cells, out to the garden, and the training fields.

"Where are we going?"

"I need to blow off some steam," she said. "I'm guessing you could do with the same."

I flashed her an impish grin.

TRAINING WAS GOOD, although strange with just the two of us. No matter how much we needed to calm down, neither of us was really into it. Our attacks were weak, our balance was nowhere to be found, and defence had called it a day. Deciding it would not work, we lay down on the grass instead, watching the clouds pass without a care in the world.

"I wish I was one of them," I sighed.

"One of what?"

"The clouds." I turned my head to look at her. "I could move on merrily without having the weight of the world on my shoulders."

She smirked. "You'd get bored within minutes."

"True."

Folding my arms under my head, my thoughts went out to Tal and my brother now well on their way to deliver bad news to an unsuspecting family. I definitely wouldn't want to be in their shoes.

"I need to do something," I muttered as I sat up. "I'll go see if Soren needs any help."

"You like it, don't you?" Elara asked, getting to her feet.

I shrugged. "I guess."

THREE DAYS PASSED with nothing significant happening. If anything, the days were positively boring, and despite the horrific murders, life at the palace wasn't any different in the following days than it had been the weeks or even months before. Everything progressed naturally, people went about their business as if it was any other day, pursuing the same routines they always did, meeting the same people, and complaining about the same problems.

Elara and I felt the loss of Xaresh greatly, especially with Tal gone too.

We'd spent most of our time either holed up in my bedroom, or with Soren, keeping ourselves busy. Although Elara didn't much like the infirmary, she agreed cutting and rolling bandages was a good deal better than nothing, and Soren seemed to appreciate our help, although the other healers scoffed at our presence.

It was a good thing they weren't in charge.

"How did you come to be in charge?" I asked one day.

He looked at me, eyes twinkling. "Good references."

"They must like you."

"Hardly." He chuckled. "Most give me the cold shoulder, but they listen to reason."

I looked positively shocked. "You do reason?"

Elara snorted. "One day *Tarien*, that tongue of yours will get you into trouble."

"Who says it hasn't already?"

The unspoken truth hung between us, but the furtive look she cast my way told me she'd understood.

"We all have the same goal here." Soren turned to me while grinding down herbs in the mortar with a pestle. "It doesn't matter who's in charge as long as everyone does their job."

"The council could learn something from you," I said, rolling up another bandage.

"Speaking of which." Soren nodded in the direction of the door.

Evan had just entered, his eyes guarded, shoulders hunched ever so slightly. Something was wrong. I jumped to my feet, disregarding the bandages that had been in my lap. Behind me

Soren muttered something foul, but I was too focused on my brother to pay attention.

"What's wrong?"

Evan looked up somewhat startled, giving me a one-shouldered shrug. "Nothing's wrong. Mother wants to see you though."

I raised an eyebrow. "I don't believe you, but fine."

"She's in her own chambers."

Tugging my sleeves down, I stepped passed him with a massive eye-roll. He looked away and down, fidgeting with the cuffs of his sleeves. Elara followed hurriedly, and from Soren's cursing I figured she'd dropped the bandages in much the same way I had.

"What was that all about?" Elara asked when she was at my side.

"No idea."

It became clear the moment we stepped into Mother's chambers and got knocked back by a wall of heat. She was sitting in front of the fire, a blanket drawn over her lap, despite it being a warm day. Her lacklustre features and sunken cheeks setting off the high cheekbones and pointy chin shocked me to my core. The colour of her skin was at least three shades lighter than normal, and her eyes lacked the life usually present.

She hadn't looked like this three days ago.

"Mother?"

I knelt down in front of her, laying my hands in her lap while my eyes scoured her face. She smiled at me, placing a trembling hand against my cheek.

"What's happening? What's wrong?"

"It's time we start making preparations for your *Araithin,* daughter." Her voice was feebler than I remembered it to be. "For the next full moon."

I froze and stared at her, trying to comprehend what she was saying.

"But it's just been a full moon," I mumbled, blinking stupidly. "I don't understand."

At that moment, Rurin stepped into her room. Elara's head snapped up, her eyes narrowing slightly as he approached. I forced myself to stay on my knees—if I didn't I knew I'd attack him, and he wasn't worth it right now. Swallowing hard, I turned back to Mother, taking her hands in mine.

"There's no rush getting my *Araith,* Mother," I said. "You'll be *Tari* for at least a hundred more years. You have to be."

She shook her head slowly. "I don't think I'll be able to."

I swallowed hard. "What needs to happen?"

Mother smiled gently. "You must go to *Hanyarah* after the burial. Mehrean will take you, and Elara should go too. They don't allow men there. Everything you need to know will be explained there."

"How long will I be gone for?"

"For as long as is necessary to place most of your *Araith.*"

Wrinkling my nose, I looked at her. "As long as it's before the next full moon."

"Yes."

Under any other circumstances I'd be thrilled to leave the palace, going on my own adventure, but with the latest incidents, it was an accident waiting to happen. My stomach clenched itself in a knot, and I rubbed my hands on my thighs, my mouth going dry. I rose to my feet slowly and placed a gentle kiss on Mother's forehead.

"You've got to stay alive though," I murmured. "I don't care what's wrong, you have to live."

Mother laughed, but it was raspy and ended in a coughing fit so bad there was blood on her hands when she pulled them back. Rurin was at her side almost immediately, handing her a kerchief. When our eyes met, he shook his head. Frowning, I left them, my thoughts going into overdrive. The tight knot in my stomach did nothing to ease the fear.

"She's dying." My voice was hoarse when I spoke. "No wonder Ev looked so upset."

Elara rested a hand on my shoulder, saying nothing as we made our way back to my room. Once inside, I flopped down in a chair, shaking all over.

"This can't be happening. Something's off. This can't be happening."

Elara sat across from me, a deep frown on her face. "She looked terrible. Do you think Soren knows?"

I shrugged, running a shaky hand through my hair. "Could be. If he does, he might know why."

Suddenly, comprehension dawned on me, and I shook my head. Getting to my feet, I started pacing up and down, rubbing my eyes and blowing out my cheeks. There had to be a reason Azra had gone to such extreme lengths to cover up getting herbs, if that was indeed what she'd gotten. Rubbing my temples, I tried to recall what she had ordered, but I couldn't for the life of me remember what it was.

With a loud growl, I turned and wiped everything from my desk, watching as it clattered to the floor. The carved owl rolled against my foot, and as I picked it up, tears stung behind my eyes. Swallowing them away, I traced my finger over its head, following the delicate texture handcrafted into it with love and patience.

"What are you trying to tell us?" I murmured.

The owl just stared at me with those wide, wise eyes, gazing into a faraway distance. What had Xaresh been thinking of when he whittled this piece?

Why can't I remember?

"You've got that look on your face again," Elara said, curling her lips up.

I sighed while I placed the owl back, and turned to her, leaning against the desk.

"Have you ever had that feeling where you are positive you know something, but you cannot exactly grasp what it is?"

She nodded. "I'd say that's me most of the time."

I pushed myself off of the desk and started pacing again.

"Eamryel could kidnap me," I began, "because I followed my aunt into the criminal's quarters. I overheard her ordering herbs."

Elara arched a brow. "Herbs?"

"Yes, but I can't remember which ones." I ran my hands through my hair. "And I have this feeling, knowing what they are might get us further."

"What if we try to look it up?"

I stared at her for a moment, feeling a grin spread over my face. "Of course!"

As if it were a mascot, I grabbed the owl from its perch and tucked it away safely. Carrying it felt as if Xaresh was still close. He'd have solved this puzzle in a matter of hours.

FEW PEOPLE WERE present at the library this time of day—most were out in the gardens, enjoying the first warm day of the year. Others were most likely preparing themselves for dinner. Elara and I made our way over to the section on herbs, plants and gardening, one of the few areas I'd never been interested in. We both grabbed some books and scrolls, dumped them on a table and started perusing the pages. It was admirable for Elara to help considering the fact I couldn't even remember the names.

She had no clue what she was looking for.

My heart expanded just a little when I looked at her, brows furrowed in deep concentration. Closing my eyes, and massaging my temples, I thought back to the day Eamryel had kidnapped me. My heart started racing almost immediately, and my chest tightened, heralding another panic attack. I pictured

Tal that one night in the infirmary, laying my hand against his chest, telling me to match his breathing to slow my heartbeat.

It had worked then. It worked now.

My thoughts wandered back to the shadier parts of town, the combined scent of herbs invading my senses just as it had that day. Azra was inside, greeting the salesman. It struck me as strange I couldn't remember much of my surroundings at all, while I remembered the frantic beating of my heart and the confusion.

"Do you have any fa—, perhaps some...?"

I growled under my breath, squeezing my eyes shut to focus even harder, yet after several tries, I still came up empty. I was ready to abandon this whole quest, when this nagging feeling started. Elara watched me with an amused expression playing on her face.

"Well?" she asked.

I sighed. "Nothing. I can't remember, but I have a feeling I know it?"

"All right," she said, looking thoughtful for a moment. "Close your eyes and talk me through it. Tell me what you hear, see and smell."

Although it felt stupid, I did what she asked—I closed my eyes again and tried to remember that day. I started at the gates, explaining what I was doing, what I was seeing, and where I was going. I halted in front of the shop, pressing myself against the wall, listening carefully.

Do you happen to have any fair lady? Perhaps some Narcissus?

"I remember!" My eyes flew open, and I looked at Elara.

She regarded me with brows raised. "Share?"

"Fair lady and Narcissus."

"Why do I get the feeling it will still take forever to find out what they are?"

I shot her an impish half-smile. "Beggars can't be choosers."

A soft growl escaped her throat as she settled back to poring over the books. I scanned line for line, but after two books and a dozen scrolls, we still weren't any further than when we'd started. Elara's slamming a book shut was testimony of her failure as well. She rose to her feet to stretch, a look of profound displeasure in her eyes. Looking around, I realised we were alone, and the light was slowly receding from the windows.

"Maybe we should call it a night," Elara suggested, rubbing her eyes. "We won't find anything."

I pressed my lips together, stifling a yawn. "You're probably right."

We gathered the books and scrolls, returning them to their places in companionable silence. Elara suddenly stilled, and tilted her head, brows knitting together. I wondered why until I heard the sound too—soft, measured steps on the tiled floor. We stuffed the books back hurriedly, but one of them landed on my foot. Clapping a hand over my mouth, I refrained from cursing out loud, but the sound of the book thudding on the floor was like an echo in the deafening silence of the library.

We tiptoed away from this aisle, remaining silent and inconspicuous. Elara drew a dagger and gave me her extra. I couldn't help but notice a pattern in this, and I reminded myself to start moving around with a weapon strapped to my body too, for good measure.

Since torches and oil lamps were detrimental to the library's contents none of them were allowed inside. The only light source we had was the pale light of the waning moon casting its eerie glow inside, stretching the shadows to preposterous lengths. I was trembling slightly, but wasn't sure if it was from fear or cold.

The sound of something crashing to the floor from our right startled us.

I bit back a yelp of fear, willing my frantic heart to calm down lest it'd go into overdrive. I focused on Elara's calm breathing in front of me, wishing I didn't spook as easily. I wouldn't have before Eamryel—now I saw ghosts at every turn. Something else clamoured to the floor, but this time from behind us.

Elara grabbed me, pivoted a hundred and eighty degrees around me and pushed me away. As I stumbled back, crashing into a cabinet, the sound of metal on metal echoed through the empty library like a gong, reverberating in my bones. Elara grunted, and I saw her shape go down on one knee, clutching her side.

I shot forward, catching her assailant around the waist, crashing into another row of cabinets. Next thing I knew, Elara pulled me away from him, and the brief moment of respite was window enough for him to disappear into the shadows.

"You need to get out of here," she hissed.

"Not alone," I muttered. "You're coming with me."

She was silent, cocking her head to the side. I mirrored her. There was no sound in the library whatsoever. We decided to risk it and dashed for the door as straight as we could. Once I got there safely, I realised Elara wasn't with me. My breath caught high in my throat as I looked around.

A loud grunt not far behind me drew my attention, so I spun on my heel, and stared wide-eyed at Elara grappling with our assailant, trying to wrestle a dagger from his hands.

At first they were evenly matched. Elara doled out punches and nicks as often as the attacker did, but I noticed her movements were getting slower after a while. So did he. In one swift motion, he twisted the weapon out of her hand, and hit her in the stomach.

Elara doubled over with a loud groan, gasping for air as she dropped to her knees. It was all he needed to grab her by her hair and place a dagger against her throat. Both were breathing laboriously, I could hear it from this distance, and suddenly, comprehension dawned on me. She had gotten injured during their first fight, and she'd never meant to get out of here. I took a few steps forward, but stopped as Elara shook her head, face contorted in pain.

"Always the saviour," the assailant scoffed. "Saving no one."

"Shal, run," Elara hissed. "Run while you still can."

I stood frozen on the spot, watching her with clenched fists, trembling all over. This wasn't happening. This couldn't be happening. My *Arathrien* were amongst the most skilled fighters in Ilvanna, and now they were being overpowered this easily. How? I knew the answer as soon as the question had formed in my mind.

The element of surprise. None of us had any idea what we were up against.

"You've got to fight," I begged her, forcing away the lump in my throat. "They can't win."

Elara smiled at me, albeit sadly. "My fight's over, *Tarien*. Yours has only just begun. Make us proud."

My breathing came in shallow, rapid gasps as I realised what she was saying. Behind his mask, the assailant raised an eyebrow, a smile reaching his eyes.

"You should listen to her," he said. "You'd best start running."

Everything happened in a matter of seconds. Before he'd even finished his sentence, he slit Elara's throat and let go off her hair. She dropped to her knees, blood gushing from her neck. It were only seconds, but it felt like a lifetime before she fell dead to the floor. I should have run like she had told me, but instead I charged right at him, lashing out with the dagger as soon I was close. It cut his skin, and he hissed, pulling back his hand. Rather than fleeing, he returned the favour and inched closer to me.

I fended off his first thrust as I stepped over Elara's body. Glancing down, her sightless eyes peered up at me reproachfully. In that one second, he shot forward, overwhelmed me with relative ease, and we went down to the ground. I grunted at the impact jarring every bone in my body the moment he landed on top of me, and used the momentary confusion to push him off of me and scramble away. He was quicker though, and grabbed the hem of my dress, yanking me back. I fell against him, and as he caught me, he pressed cold metal against the skin below my left ear, right in that soft spot where it was easy to push through and stab. Warm blood trickled down his hand, onto my shoulder.

I stilled.

"You should've run," he hissed in my ear. "You're lucky though. You're the one person I'm not allowed to kill. Yet."

Something about his voice was familiar, but I couldn't place it. My heart was racing in my chest, both from fighting and from fear, and I could feel my palms turn sweaty and my throat tighten.

I could not have a panic attack right now.

"They must've something planned for me," I said, doing my best to sound confident.

"If only you knew."

I clenched my jaw.

"Now," he continued, "do you need more reasons to cease your activities?"

"I never will."

He chuckled at that. "Are you sure? Because from the way I see it, there are at least six more reasons, although one's already well on her way. Maybe seven if we count the priestess along, eight with the healer?"

His threats riled me up enough to be stupid and risk it all. In one swift motion I grabbed his wrist and twisted it. The dagger clattered harmlessly to the floor, and in that brief respite, I staggered to my feet and started running without looking back. I hated leaving Elara behind, but she'd have died for nothing if I didn't. Although they didn't allow him to kill me, I had the feeling they had no scruples in severely harming me.

I BARRELLED into the infirmary without a moment's hesitation, not knowing where else to go at this time of night without drawing too much suspicion to my headlong flight and dishevelled appearance. While I doubled over, gasping for air, Soren stormed out of the adjoining room, looking rather tousled himself.

"Tarien? What are you doing here?" He looked around, frowning. "At this time of night?"

"Elara's dead."

He stared at me, collected himself, and placed his arm around my shoulders, guiding me to the room he'd just come from. It turned out to be his living quarters. Wrapping my arms around myself, my gaze darted around the place, not really registering anything. Soren sat me down on a chair, and as he placed a blanket over my shoulders, touched the cut on my neck.

"What is it with you and sharp objects?" he murmured.

I heard him rummage around in his cabinets. My thoughts went over what had happened in the library, but where I'd expected to cry, there was nothing. A numb feeling settled over me like a heavy blanket, leaving me feeling empty on the inside. I felt detached, as if what had happened had nothing to do with me and everything with what I'd read in a book. The accidents were sad for the character, but that was it. I was in the infirmary because I'd done something stupid, and Elara would walk in any moment to berate me.

A cold, wet cloth scraped my skin. I registered the motions as a fact—Soren was cleaning the cut, assessed it for depth, then decided it wasn't enough to stitch. Instead, he bandaged my neck as if wrapping a scarf around my throat against the cold.

I just sat there, staring into nothing. Feeling nothing.

Soren placed something warm in my hands, wrapped the

blanket around me and sat across from me. My eyes steadily zeroed in on him.

"Should we tell someone?"

I just nodded, and Soren rose to his feet.

"I'll be right back," he said, and turned to look at me. "Where?"

"Library."

He left in silence. My hands were trembling so heavily I placed the cup of tea on the table, jerking them shakily through my hair before grabbing the blanket tight. Looking around skittishly, I kept glancing over my shoulder at the door until I could take it no longer and rose to my feet, settling myself in the corner of Soren's bed from where I could see everything. I huddled in on myself while wrapping the blanket tighter around me.

My thoughts circled back to everything that had happened. Xaresh killed, Mother ill, Elara dead. All of it was my fault. If I hadn't followed Azra into the city and got abducted by Eamryel, Xaresh would never have had a reason to look into it, and none of them would've been pulled into this mess. Absently I searched for the whittled owl, only to find it missing.

I dropped my hand to my sides in defeat, letting the tears run rampant down my cheeks.

It was too much.

CHAPTER 19

*H*ushed voices—sounding rushed and worried—drifted in from the infirmary, but they always did around here so I didn't pay much attention to it, despite the familiar ring they had. I crawled back into bed, pulling the covers up over my ears to drown out the sound.

"She's been like that for the past three days." Soren's voice sounded up from the doorway. "She's not spoken a word since."

"What happened?" It was Haerlyon.

I perked up at his voice. If Haerlyon was back, it meant Tal was, but it didn't explain why Haerlyon was at the infirmary unless something had happened. I slipped out of bed and passed a startled Soren, making my way inside.

Tal lay on a table, Tiroy and Evan at his side. His eyes were closed, and although he was breathing, it didn't sound good—it sounded heavy and rattling. Dazed, I walked over, my eyes darting over him as I approached. At first sight, nothing appeared to be out of the ordinary, until I saw the bloodstains on the shirt peeking out from underneath his leather coat.

My hands trembled when I undid the clasps, sliding my hands under his shirt to pull it up. An involuntary moan escaped his lips and his eyes fluttered. My cheeks heated instantly. His shirt stuck to his chest in places, and he grimaced when I pulled it loose.

"We need to soak it off," Soren said from slightly behind me.

I nodded.

"Do you want to help me?"

He knew I wanted to. I knew he was coaxing me into speaking, but I didn't feel like it, afraid that once I started, I'd never stop.

"She still hasn't spoken then?" Evan commented.

I gave him a droll stare before turning to get a bowl, pitcher and enough cloths to wash the shirt off. Soren smiled wryly.

"She'll speak when she feels like it, I'm sure."

Evan ran a hand over the shaved side of his head, looking troubled. "We need to know what happened. You said Elara was dead in the library, but—"

He broke off his sentence so suddenly, my head snapped up, my eyes narrowing to thin slits.

"But what?" I asked in a hoarse voice.

They all gaped at me.

"But what, Ev?"

Evan closed his eyes briefly, rubbing the back of his neck while avoiding my gaze. "There was no body."

I shook my head, sure I hadn't heard him correctly.

"Come again?"

"There wasn't a body," he repeated, shaking his head. "The tiles looked like they had been scrubbed clean recently, but Elara wasn't there."

If he'd stabbed me right there and then, it would have had the same effect, barring the bleeding. I stared at him in disbelief, dropping the pitcher to the floor as my legs gave way under me. Evan circled his arm around me to keep me from falling down and guided me over to a chair. Clutching the cloth in my hand, I started trembling, swallowing back the lump in my throat. I'd

much rather curl back up on myself, but Elara deserved more
—better.

"He must've dropped her body somewhere." Fumbling with
the cloth, I mulled over Evan's words. "It's the only explanation."

My voice creaked and sounded tremulous to my own ears,
but at least I wasn't crying. Yet. Evan squatted in front of me,
riveting arctic eyes solemn as he looked at me. He took my
hands in his. Despite his size, Evan was always gentle, in every
possible way.

"I'm sorry I have to ask you this," he said, looking contrite,
"but what happened?"

My face contorted as a sharp pain lanced through my chest.
To keep from falling apart altogether, I focused on our
conjoined hands while relating what had happened without
letting on to the reason we were at the library. Glancing up, I
noticed everyone was listening with rapt attention, except for
Soren who had mercifully set to tending Tal.

"But why were you in the library?" Haerlyon asked once I
finished.

I shook my head. "Best if you don't know."

"You keep saying that," said Evan frowning, "but you can't
keep shutting us out."

I rose to my feet, looking down at him. "Try me."

My jaw set, I went to help Soren, sponging the places where
Tal's shirt still stuck to his injuries. Evan laid a gentle hand on
my shoulder and squeezed it lightly.

"We'll find her."

Tears welled up, so I just nodded, dashing them away madly
once my brothers had left. Soren was watching me from under
his lashes, but refrained from making any comments. My gaze
swept over Tal, lying there motionless except for the rise and
fall of his chest. Every time I touched him he stirred, sending
my stomach into a fluttering frenzy. Whenever Soren stuck a
needle into him though, he winced, and it surprised me he

hadn't screamed out yet. Then again, it wasn't like him to do so. He'd grunt or curse, but he would never scream.

"Can you help bandage him?" Soren asked once he finished. "He's a bit too heavy to do it on my own."

"Who're you calling heavy?" Tal asked gruffly.

Soren smiled. "Welcome to the land of the living *Anahràn*."

He grunted and rubbed his face, his gaze zeroing in on me a second later, flashing me that roguish grin I loved so much.

"You're a sight for sore eyes," he said, lifting his hand to touch my cheek.

I burst out in tears.

"You're not supposed to cry over that." His brows shot up in surprise.

"Elara's dead," I sobbed, burying my face in my hands.

It was silent for a moment. In the next he sat up, pulled me into his arms, and held me tight as grief crashed into me like a tidal wave. Tal nuzzled my hair, murmuring incomprehensible words, his tone soft and soothing. We stood like that until Soren cleared his throat. Tal cupped my face in his hands and placed a kiss on my forehead.

I swallowed hard.

"What happened to you?" I asked hoarsely.

In the meantime, Soren helped him shrug out of his coat and blouse so we could bandage his chest. Old wounds had opened up, and there were some new ones, which neither of us asked about as we bandaged him up.

"No more riding in the next few days," Soren warned him. "Else it'll never heal properly."

"Yes, sir."

Soren left us the moment Tal was properly bandaged. As I placed my hands on his chest, he shivered noticeably and closed his eyes, steadying his breathing. For me it was a way to calm down, feeling his steady heartbeat under my fingers. He brushed my cheek with the back of his hand, tucking my hair behind my ear. When he leaned in, I thought he'd kiss me, but instead he whispered.

"You need a bath, and a clean set of clothes."

Folding my arms in front of me, I stared at him, undecided if I should feel offended or complimented.

"Pot and kettle."

He smirked, and pulled me into his embrace, vibrant emerald eyes boring straight through me.

Cue the butterflies.

"Is Xaresh's family here?"

"I assume so." He rubbed the nape of his neck, looking bashful. "I was out cold when we arrived."

Rubbing my hands together, I stepped back, looking at him. "I guess I'd best go make myself presentable."

Tal slipped to his feet, grunting as the impact jarred him. Grabbing the leather jacket from a chair, he shrugged it onto him, grimacing at the pain.

I frowned. "Where do you think you're going?"

"With you." He gave me a deadpan stare. "Surely you didn't think I was leaving you alone?"

"It'd be better," I muttered, wrapping my arms around myself. "Everyone close to me dies."

He snorted. "Let them try."

ONCE I LOOKED REMOTELY DECENT, Tal escorted me to Mother's reception chambers. She was looking better than last time I'd seen her, although she was still ghastly pale. From the corner of my eyes, I saw Tal halt upon seeing her, eyes widened. I brushed my hand past his by way of reassurance, even though I felt none of it myself.

Three women were standing off to the side—two clearly younger than the third, whom I assumed to be Xaresh's mother.

She, and one of her daughters, kept her eyes downcast. It was the other daughter who was bolder, piercing violet eyes following my every move as I walked over to them.

She reminded me of Xaresh so much it hurt.

"What's your name?"

She looked up at me, eyes defiant. "Samehya."

"Nice to meet you Samehya," I said. "I am sorry for your loss."

She inclined her head stiffly, lips set in a thin line, shoulders squared. Her mother pulled her back, but she wouldn't budge, and instead kept looking at me, head tilted.

"He was very fond of you," Samehya said. "And now he's dead because of you."

I winced at her words, if only because they were true.

"I know."

"Did you mourn him?"

Narrowing my eyes ever so slightly, I nodded. "Of course."

"Good. He was a good man."

Samehya's hands were clenched at her sides, and her eyes misted over when she said this. She looked down, angrily wiping the tears away. I wished I knew what to say to comfort her, but I didn't know this girl at all. Instead, I turned to her mother and sister, greeting them and giving my condolences. They were more demur than Samehya by far.

"I promised Xaresh to give you jobs here at the palace," I told them, my hands clasped tightly behind my back. "You are free to take me up on this offer."

"I want his job," Samehya said without a moment's hesitation, eyes on me. "I want to be an *Arathrien.*"

I glanced at Tal.

"How far are you willing to go?" Tal asked, fixing her with a stern gaze.

"To the end of the world if I have to."

He raised an eyebrow in amusement. "Training starts before

dawn every morning for a few hours. You'll be pushed to your limits and beyond, every day."

"I don't mind."

"You might get killed on the job."

Samehya stilled for a moment and inclined her head. "I know, but if this job was good enough for my brother, it's good enough for me."

She looked at me, those wide violet eyes filled with determination.

"I want to know why she's so special," she said inclining her head at me, "for Xaresh to have given his life for her."

Tal smirked. "You don't just get to step away from being *Arathrien.* It's a position for life, and you have to earn it."

"I told you. Whatever it takes."

Tal whistled under his breath and nodded, looking at her. "The day after tomorrow at dawn. I'll see you on the fields."

Samehya inclined her head, her lips curling up in a smile as excitement washed over her features. The tough exterior hid a much more complex interior. I turned to her mother and sister.

"And you?"

"We'd be happy enough in the kitchens, *Tarien*," Kalyani said, still not meeting my eyes, "or as servants. We can do that."

I nodded. "Very well. I'll see that arrangements are made. Your quarters have been prepared already. I'll have El— one of the guards, escort you to your room."

Tal went to instruct the guards at the door before guiding the three women out of the reception chambers. I rubbed my face as I turned to Mother, a heavy weight settling on my shoulders.

"I assume you've heard of Elara?"

She nodded. "I have. I have made preparations for a double burial."

"Thank you."

I pivoted on my heel and made to leave the room when she

called me back. Turning around, I found her standing right behind me. She placed her hands on my shoulders and a kiss on my cheek.

"Be careful daughter," she whispered. "Now that Elara's gone too, you are too exposed. Please make sure you are with someone every minute of the day?"

"Apparently it doesn't matter if I'm with someone, Mother." I sighed, jerking my hand through my hair. "They've neutralised two of my best guards with little trouble. Whoever is targeting us, knows their strengths and weaknesses. They know our strengths and weaknesses. Maybe being alone will save people's lives."

Mother's lips twisted up in a half-smile. "I'm not sure it works that way, but I have faith in you, daughter. Your *Araithîn* will still be held during the next full moon. You will still leave tomorrow. I've asked Haerlyon to bring you to *Hanyarah*."

Behind me, Tal stiffened. Mother noticed it too.

"I've been informed you are not allowed to ride, *Anahràn* Imradien," she said, "and as much as I'd love to entrust my daughter into your hands, she needs you far longer than one day. Besides, I believe you have a job to do here while she's gone."

He arched his brows.

"She needs new *Arathrien*."

Talnovar rubbed his face as a soft groan escaped his lips. He pressed them in a thin line while he watched her, eyes expressionless.

"As you wish, *Tari*."

Although Mother smiled, it never reached her eyes. She dropped her arms to her sides, stifling a yawn.

"If you'll excuse me," she murmured.

I placed a chaste kiss on her cheek and left the room, Tal on my heels. Once we were well out of earshot, he took my hand to stop me.

"What's wrong with her?" he murmured, glancing around to make sure nobody overheard us.

"Not here."

INSTEAD OF FINDING AN INDOOR REFUGE, we opted for an outdoor one we hadn't visited in ages. The last time had been with Haerlyon and Evan when we were still considered children, and life didn't demand our complete and utter devotion. Before we ducked inside the cave entrance, Tal lit an oil lamp to light our way through the damp, dark corridor, but once through, sunlight nearly blinded us.

Tal blew out the oil lamp and set it aside.

Up ahead, bright blue water sparkled in the sunlight. The cavern wall ran up high enough to be safe from any kind of weather, or assassins, unless the latter came in through the entrance. I carefully navigated the steps and stones to the small patch of levelled ground at the edge of the pool. Tal followed more nimbly.

I sat down at the water's edge, pulling up my knees, wrapping my arms around them. Tal sat down beside me, leaning back on his elbows.

"I forgot how beautiful it is here," he said, looking around.

"And quiet."

He quirked up one side of his lips. We just sat there in silence, listening to the birds chirping overhead as they flew to and from their nests in the cavern wall. From the corner of my eyes, I noticed Tal watching me, his expression shifting the longer he looked.

"What happened?" he asked at length.

"We got attacked in the library," I said, looking away from him. "We were trying to find something when we heard a sound and realised we weren't alone. Elara got hurt during the first brawl, but she didn't tell me. Instead of making it to the exit with me, she went after the attacker on her own. She got in some punches and kicks, but the injury slowed her down, giving him the upper-hand. He cut her throat."

I was surprised at the ease with which I told him.

"Why were you there?"

This was the moment. Did I want to draw Tal in further and risk his life, or would I tell him a lie that would undoubtedly piss him off should he ever find out the truth? Running a hand through my hair, I turned to look at him.

"You've seen Mother," I said. "She's getting sicker by the minute, although I have to admit she looked rather well today, but it's happened so fast."

"You think there's foul play involved?"

I nodded. "I remembered what Azra had ordered in that herbal shop the day Eamryel kidnapped me. I wanted to see if I could find what it was, and what it was used for. If I can figure that out, maybe I can help her."

Tal sat up and took my hands in his, gaze fixed on mine. I had expected him to be angry, but instead I saw sorrow, and something elsesomething I couldn't quite put my finger on.

"We'll figure this out."

To my surprise, he settled himself behind me and pulled me against him, wrapping his arms around me while resting his chin on my shoulder.

"There's more, isn't there?"

"Yes."

"Are you going to tell me?"

I shrugged. "Maybe."

He suddenly tensed behind me, his arms tightening around me just a little, so I lay my hand on the arm around my shoulder hoping to ease him up.

"I don't like you're going away without me," he murmured in my ear. "The road's dangerous."

"But Mother's right, you shouldn't strain yourself more than you absolutely have to. You need to take your rest, or you won't be of any use to me in the future."

He snorted and nuzzled my neck. "I wouldn't be so sure about that."

Goose bumps chased each other across my arms.

"I had no idea you could be this cliché," I said, rolling my eyes.

Tal laughed at that, his voice echoing against the cavern walls. He was trembling a little.

"For once, I'll listen to advice," he said, "but it doesn't mean I have to like it. Haerlyon can protect you just as well."

"He'll be saddle-sore by the end of this."

"Haer doesn't mind being out of the palace," Tal replied. "He prefers it over being cooped up with the insanity."

I snorted. "Can't blame him."

Tal turned my head with a gentle push of his finger, and before I knew it, his lips were on mine, the taste of him invading my senses, blocking out every thought or feeling unrelated to him. Underneath the scent of horse and blood was his own unique musky scent, and combined with the smell of fresh air, crisp water and earthy rock, it made for a heady combination.

The butterflies went into a frenzy.

All too soon, he ended the kiss, his hand lingering around my jaw, his eyes remaining closed for a second longer. When he opened them, he looked almost sad.

"What's wrong?"

"A lot of things," he said, "but nothing to add to your worries. Come on, we'd best get back before they think we've run."

I gave him a wry smile. "Doesn't sound like a bad idea."

"Yes. Yes, it does," he said with a laugh.

"Why?"

He grinned as he rose to his feet, helping me up. "Because they might hunt me down for kidnapping the future *Tari*."

"It's not kidnapping if I go voluntarily."

"Still a bad idea." He chuckled, moving back to the entrance where he lit the oil lamp.

THE PALACE WAS in a complete uproar by the time we returned. A crowd of people had gathered in the hallway, trying to look over each other's shoulders, pointing and whispering. Tal and I frowned at each other and pushed our way through the congregation. Some glanced at me angrily, blanching when they realised who it was, and made room.

The moment I stepped into the clearing I stopped dead in my tracks.

Elara's corpse, or rather what was left of it, was lying on the floor, her body mutilated beyond recognition—except for her face. Sightless eyes stared at the ceiling, mouth set in the grim line I remembered it being in when the assailant killed her. Tal placed a hand on my upper arm before stepping past me, and knelt next to her body, covering his nose and mouth.

Guards were trying to disperse the crowd, so nobody left. Evan and Haerlyon stood on the other side of the clearing— Haerlyon looked the way I felt, ready to toss whatever was inside. Evan looked rather white around the nose, but kept a composed face. The moment Tal stepped out of the crowd, he joined him, hiding his nose in the crook of his arm. They started conversing in low tones.

"Poor thing," someone said off to my left.

"Wasn't she one of the *Arathrien*?" another one added.

"Must've been a tough job," a third commented. "I'd kill myself too."

A loud buzzing in my ears drowned out the rest of the words. Clenching my fists, I stepped into the clearing, straightening my shoulders.

"Everyone who doesn't have any business being here, please leave," I said, "or I must ask the guards to do it bodily."

Most seemed to decide it wasn't worth the trouble. Only those who thrived on sensation and gossip stuck around at first, withdrawing the moment the guards made to arrest them. Once the corridor was cleared, I turned to the rest, swallowing away the bile in my throat.

"We have to get her out of here."

"I'm open for suggestions," Tal said, rising to his feet.

He appeared ready to vomit.

Tal and Evan carried her towards the infirmary where Soren almost immediately shooed us out, instead guiding us to another room adjoining the infirmary where the scent of death washed over us the minute we stepped in. Haerlyon turned tail immediately. I covered my nose and mouth with my arm, wishing I'd followed my brother after only a few seconds inside. Tal and Evan looked grim but soldiered on, placing Elara on a stretcher next to Xaresh.

Even Queran was here, although they'd placed him off to the side. It was still a mystery why he'd been killed, but his name on the list was enough admission to know his slate wasn't clean.

"Sorry for the smell." Soren offered all of us cloths to hold against our faces.

The scent of lavender and rosemary chased off the ugly smell of corpse and death, so I inhaled deeply, glad for the reprieve it gave.

"Where did you find her?" I asked, looking at Evan.

"In the hallway."

My brow furrowed in a thoughtful V-shape. "Why would anyone do that?"

"To cause a spectacle, I guess." The cloth he was practically inhaling muffled Tal's voice. "They got exactly what they wanted."

"Yes, but why?"

"Power," Soren said. "To show off they have power."

Heat rose through my body, spreading to my chest, my arms, and my neck, almost as if someone was trying to roast me, while at the same time the sick feeling increased. Staggering back against the wall, I rubbed my eyes, finding my vision blurry first, and darkening seconds later. This wasn't good. I slid down the wall and noticed the floor rising to meet me.

I CAME AROUND to a fierce throbbing in my head, and four faces peering at me with wide eyes and frowns.

"Personal space, ever heard of it?" I muttered, trying to sit up.

A strong pair of hands pushed me down.

"Lie down," Soren instructed. "Unless you want to hit your head a second time."

"Can we at least move her to a decent room," Haerlyon whimpered. "I can't stand the stench much longer, and there isn't much we can do for them."

Tal began picking me up, but Haer stopped him. "Let me, you need to take it easy."

"And you promised to heed the advice," I added.

He scowled at both of us.

HAERLYON BROUGHT me to my room as promised, Evan and Tal in tow. My bed felt incredibly soft compared to Soren's as Haerlyon placed me in it. I wanted to sit up, but he pushed me back, a stern look on his face

"Will you listen to advice for once too?" he grumbled.

I sighed and slumped down, rubbing my head. "You guys have to stay out of this."

335

"Too little too late," Evan said. "I don't think we have a choice."

"You do. Step away from me," I said. "Turn your back, don't ask questions."

Haerlyon looked at me. "How much exactly *do* you know?"

"Enough to get people killed."

"Let me guess," he said with a sigh, rolling back and forth on his feet, "our journey tomorrow will be dangerous?"

I shrugged. "Most likely."

"Good," he grinned suddenly. "I can do with some action."

"You're out of your *nohro* mind," I muttered.

A fierce, throbbing pain settled behind my eyes, making the world swim whenever I focused on something.

"I don't know what you guys are up to," I murmured, "but I will close my eyes for a bit. Tomorrow's important, and I have to do... to do... stuff."

Their voices swam in and out of consciousness as I drifted off to sleep, and someone pulled the blankets on top of me just as I slid into that state where sleep is within grasp, but you can still notice what's happening. Somewhere someone settled on my bed—I could feel it dip, but I was too out of it to protest. If they came to kill me, they could have me. I was tired of running and skulking about like a thief in the night, but instead of killing me, someone placed a kiss on my temple, tucking my hair behind my ear.

"Sleep, *shareye*. You're safe."

CHAPTER 20

I awoke to the sound of light snoring close by, and when I turned on my other side, I found Tal's face inches from mine, looking deeply relaxed in the throes of sleep. His white hair spread on the pillow like a halo, except for a few strands covering the bruises and cuts on his temple and cheek. Free from worry and responsibility, he looked years younger. The moment I stroked some hair out of his face to get a better look, he shot up, ready to fight.

I scooted back on the bed, watching him warily.

"*Tarien?* What are you do—." He stopped midway his sentence, rubbing his face as he looked around the room.

When comprehension dawned on him, he jumped out of bed, clutching his chest as he landed on the floor, a grunt escaping his lips.

"I must've fallen asleep."

"It's fine."

I pulled up my knees and wrapped my arms around them, eyes trained on him. He looked so desperately out of sorts standing there, unsure what to make of the situation, it was almost laughable. Running a jerky hand through his hair, he watched me from under his lashes.

"It's not appropriate."

"You know my thoughts on that," I replied, stifling a yawn.

The throbbing sensation behind my eyes had lessened, but it was still there, and my stomach lurched whenever I moved too much.

"How are you feeling?" he asked, arching a brow.

I shrugged and winced. "Terrible, but I suppose that's normal considering what day it is."

"You hit your head hard last night," Tal offered. "You should take it easy today."

"Would if I could, but I'm expected to do the spee—" I cursed under my breath when I realised I hadn't prepared the speeches at all. I had no idea what I would say at the burial.

I slipped out of bed and swayed over to my desk. A sudden scream startled me until I realised I was the one producing the sound. I stared at the wooden owl sitting on my desk, casting me an accusatory glare, but it wasn't until I picked it up with trembling hands that I realised it was coated in dry blood.

I dropped it immediately, staring at it wide-eyed.

"Hey, calm down," Tal said from behind me, laying a hand on my shoulder. "What's wrong?"

I pointed at the owl. He picked it up with a frown, a confused look on his face as he regarded me.

"What about it?"

He didn't know. Of course he didn't. How could he? He was gone when I found it—gone when I needed him the most. I swallowed hard and collapsed into the chair, placing my hands between my knees to keep them from trembling.

"I got it from Xaresh's room the day he was killed," I whispered. "He's been making them. There were several more of those whittled creatures, but the owl reminded me of him. I just couldn't leave it there. The night they killed Elara, I had it on me, but I lost it."

Tal's knuckles went white around it.

"You're saying someone placed it here?"

I offered him a half-shrug. "I have no other explanation."

Tal shook his head, his voice strained. "They're playing games."

"I hate this game," I muttered, running a hand through my hair. "It scares me, and I don't like being scared."

Tal smiled. "Being scared is good though."

"How do you reckon?"

"Because it tells you when to run or when to fight."

I huffed. "It rather makes me want to curl up in a corner and never come out."

"Yet here you are, out of bed," he said. "Looking rather bedraggled, admittedly, but you're out of bed."

"Because I need to write my speeches for today," I sighed, looking down at my feet. "Although nothing I'll write will ever do them justice."

Tal knelt in front of me so I had to look at him, wrapping my hand around the owl. "Then write nothing."

"I must say something."

"And you will," he said. "Just speak from the heart. There won't ever be truer words."

I stared at him for a while longer, my gaze sliding from those vibrant eyes to those inviting lips as they turned into the smile I loved. Tal snaked his hand into my hair, but just as he pulled me in for a kiss, a knock sounded on the door. He growled low under his breath, let go rather reluctantly while getting to his feet and stepped out of reach before the door opened, arms clasped behind his straightened back.

My *Anahràn* had returned.

Mehrean walked inside, followed by several servants

carrying buckets and other equipment to draw up a bath. Tal bowed stiffly, lips set in a thin line.

"I'll be at the door, *Tarien*."

He left before I could say anything. With a deep sigh, I turned to Mehrean, who was watching me with curiosity.

"What's that?" I asked, nodding at the box.

"A gift from your brother."

I rose to my feet, focusing on where the box was on my bed, taking deliberate steps as not to show how wobbly I really was. When I lifted the lid, I stared at the contents slack-jawed. I picked the fabric out of the box, revealing an off-shoulder sapphire dress with moderate sleeves, and a decent neckline.

"Which brother?"

Mehrean chuckled under her breath. "Haerlyon."

"Remind me to thank him later."

WHEN I SUBMERGED myself in the hot, steaming water, warmth suffused my body to where even the stiffest muscles started to relax, and although going over a ritual so inane on a day like this felt wrong, it felt necessary at the same time. A soft purr escaped my lips when Mehr set to washing my hair, massaging my scalp along the way.

It felt so normal I didn't want it to end.

"I'm sorry for what happened to them," Mehrean mumbled. "They were good people."

"I wish it'd been me."

Mehrean's hands stilled for a moment. "Be careful what you wish for."

In that moment, I wanted nothing more than to tell her everything like I once had. I wished I could confide in her, in my brothers and Tal, and solve this problem together, but while

I'd promised the assassin I wouldn't stop, I also wasn't sure I was ready to continue. He'd mentioned eight more reasons I should cease my activities, yet there were thousands why I shouldn't. I couldn't leave my people to these monsters, whatever they had planned. As much as I didn't enjoy the thought of becoming Tari much sooner than intended, it was my prerogative to protect them.

At all costs.

Swallowing hard, I shifted my focus back to Mehr's administrations, trying to enjoy this little bit of respite for as long as it lasted. Knowing my luck, it wouldn't be all that long. All too soon Mehr finished, and it was time to get out of the tub. Instead of taking the offered towel from her, I walked over to the mirror which I'd avoided looking into for far too long.

The reflection staring back at me differed from what I remembered—drawn, haggard, and thinner. Much thinner. I'd definitely lost most of my physique, and I knew it would take months to get back in shape. My skin was a myriad of red scars and still healing injuries, but it wasn't until I turned to look at the ones on my shoulder and leg, right where Eamryel had shot arrows into me as if I were a boar, that I realised the full extent of what had happened.

While the injuries had closed, they were still very much visible, and I knew it would take months for these scars to heal up nicely, if they did at all. Mehrean draped a towel over my shoulders, looking at me via the mirror.

"You know what they say," she said smiling. "What doesn't kill you, strengthens you."

My lips curved into a smile. "Perhaps, but it sure as hell doesn't improve the view."

"Better be ugly on the outside than the inside," she replied. "But it's time to get dressed. Your mother will be waiting for you."

Just as Mehrean finished doing my hair, there was a knock on the door, and Tal allowed himself inside, looking splendid in his formal attire. Rising to my feet slowly, I stared at him. He returned the favour, and I could see that knee-weakening grin spread across his features, until he seemed to realise we weren't alone. The impassive look returned, and he inclined his head.

"Ready when you are, *Tarien*."

I bit my lip, running my hands over my sides. "I doubt I'll ever be."

"You've got this," Mehrean said. "It'll be hard, but you can do this."

Not trusting my voice, I just nodded, and followed Tal out of my room. Although I breathed in deeply, it came out ragged regardless. The corridors were remarkably empty at this time of day, which surprised me until I realised everybody had to be outside already.

"Are we late?"

Tal shook his head. "No, we're on time. Your mother must have planned it this way."

"Lovely."

Once outside, a mass of people greeted us with deafening silence, lined up on either side of the garden to create a path towards the stairs leading down to the training fields. Even from this distance I could see the two pyres with two white shapes on top. My chest constricted at the sight of them, and a part of me felt as if I was walking to my own funeral.

The thought it should have been mine persisted throughout the long walk to Mother standing near the top of the stairs, flanked on either side by my brothers. They had both donned their army regalia. To my surprise, Azra stood to Haerlyon's side, her face serene and composed. Xaresh's family stood next to Evan, all dressed in the finest clothes I'm sure were arranged especially for today.

Elara had no family who could say goodbye.

Both her parents died a long time ago, and she'd been an only child. Mother had taken her in as a reward for their years of service to the throne, unwilling to let a young child grow up in the streets, but I didn't meet her until much later, when the both of us started training under Cerindil.

We'd not been friends.

I pecked Mother on the cheek when I reached her, shocked at how frail she felt under my hands on her shoulders. Tal bowed from a safe distance. Breathing in deeply, eyes focused on the pyres, I calmed myself, even though I had to force back the tears. In my mind I imagined Elara telling me to get on with it, there being no point in delaying the inevitable. It would only make it worse. I imagined Xaresh telling me to just breathe and keep doing that. What was the worst that could happen?

I turned around, and as I did, Tal slipped something into my hand. It was the whittled owl. Tears brimmed my eyes, and when I looked up at him, I saw he was having a hard time as well. With a slight nod in my direction, he took up position next to Xaresh's mother.

It was time.

"*Mey Irìn. Mey Irà.*" My voice rang out strong and clear. "I'm sorry to have to welcome you to such a sad and grave gathering, but I am grateful for your presence."

I proceeded with some official announcements, giving thanks to those who helped with the preparations, welcoming everyone officially and all other kinds of nonsense I'd much rather skip in lieu of what should be said, although as much as I wanted to, I couldn't tell the truth. I couldn't tell anyone they'd been killed in pursuit of uncovering a conspiracy going on right here at the palace. Not only because I'd put my loved ones in danger, but because it would create panic on such scale, the results might overshadow the outcome of when the enemy would win.

I shuddered at the thought.

"Xaresh was a paragon of perfect manners," I said, "and a well-respected member of the community, always ready to help where necessary, always a friendly smile."

I swallowed hard. "There were times I hated that friendly smile. Especially when it woke me up too cheerfully before the crack of dawn, telling me it was time to train."

Some people chuckled. Others just smiled. Xaresh had been one of those people you couldn't hate.

"I remember one morning when I refused to get up. He—" I swallowed again, squeezing the owl in my hand for reassurance"He rolled me into my blankets, hoisted me onto his shoulder and carried me down to the training fields. I thought *Anahràn* Imradien would die laughing."

People chuckled.

"He didn't mind the same routine day in, day out. In fact, I daresay he thrived on it, and he made damn sure the rest of us did too. He was a kind, gentle soul with an infinite amount of patience—and trust me when I tell you there have been times I expected him to run out of it—but he only got mad at me once, and that was for good reason."

When next I spoke, my voice was softer.

"How I wish he could be here to yell at me now."

The audience was as quiet as a mouse. I heard sniffles here and there and saw some people dabbing away tears. My eyes settled on a pair of grey ones I hadn't seen in a while. Grayden was watching me intently with a tight-lipped smile on his face, but the moment he noticed I was watching him, he turned away and left. Were that bruises on his face?

"Xaresh was a good man," I continued. "I thank him for his time as *Arathrien*. For being my friend and confidant, I thank him. For giving his life in my service, I owe him a debt I can never repay."

Tears were rolling down my cheeks now. A pair of arms wrapped around me, and when I looked, I found it was Samehya

344

holding me, her face buried into my shoulder. I wrapped an arm around her, holding her close while she sobbed. Recovering myself, I lifted my chin, focusing once more on the people assembled.

Elara deserved the same amount of attention.

"As you may have seen," I said, dabbing the tears away. "There isn't just one, but two pyres."

People fell silent again, their eyes settling back on me. I had a momentary feeling of being out of place—detached from myself and my surroundings, almost as if I was watching myself from a different angle. With a shake of my head, I dispelled the feeling, and stared back at the crowd.

"Elara," I began, a half-laugh escaping my lips. "She was the complete opposite of Xaresh in every possible way. She was loud, present, and as chaotic as they come. But she was also strong, resilient, and one of the best fighters we had."

Tears continued trailing down my cheeks, and I had to do my best to not start blubbering and turn into a complete mess. My throat was tight, and it was hard to keep my anger in check.

"But as good as she was, she encountered someone who was better. Whoever got to her, tried to make a point by mutilating her to where she was barely recognisable. We should allow no one capable of doing this to wander freely, so trust me when I tell you I will find who did this, and bring them to justice."

People nodded and voiced their consent. Not too loud, but loud enough for me to hear. I didn't dare glance at Azra.

"For her time in my service as *Arathrien*, for becoming a friend in the strangest of times, and for laying down her life, I'll be forever in her debt."

There were no more words I could speak without breaking down or telling people more than they should know. I let go of Samehya and turned to the stairs. Since they'd died in my service, it was up to me to send them on their way.

"I'm here," Tal whispered from behind me.

345

Grateful for his presence, I picked up the hem of my skirt and started down the stairs with my head held high, tears still flowing. I had to concentrate on finding secure footing. Down on the fields, guards handed us torches. The pyres up ahead were impressive structures, dwarfing the two bodies lying on top. My chest constricted at the sight of them, my vision going blurry as new tears mastered my emotions. I made my way over to the pyre pure on memory.

Tal took my hand in his, squeezing it tight.

"I can't believe this is it," I whispered. "I cannot do it."

"Yes you can," Tal laid his hand over mine. "Together."

Together we placed a torch inside Xaresh's pyre, and several guards around it followed our lead. We repeated the procedure with Elara's pyre, and walked back to the foot of the stairs, watching them go up in flames from a distance. Without even thinking about it, I buried my face against Tal's chest, sobbing uncontrollably. He wrapped his arms around me and just held me, his body tensed as if he was ready to hit something.

Knowing Tal, he probably was.

IF LIFE WERE a fleeting memory gone by in the blink of an eye, their loss would have been bearable to a certain extent, because I'd know I would die shortly after. I could live for a hundred more years now with the memory of their burning imprinted on my mind, and I was afraid that with time, it would push away the memories of how they had been alive.

"We should go back," Tal murmured into my hair. "You need to get ready."

"I don't want to."

Laughter rumbled in his chest. "I swear *Tarien*, if I got a silver piece for every time you say you don't want to, I'd be a rich man right now."

"I thought you already were."

He smirked, let go of me, and led me back up the stairs. Mother, my brothers, and Xaresh's family were still there—the crowd had dispersed, scattering throughout the garden and palace in small groups. I wiped my nose on the back of my hand, drying my tears with the underside of my sleeve.

"That was a beautiful speech *Tarien.*" Kalyani stepped forward, took my hand, and placed a kiss on it. "You really did know my son."

I smiled softly. "Of course. We all did."

"Did he really roll you into your blanket?" Samehya asked with a grin.

Looking slightly amused, I nodded. "He did. Tal couldn't stop laughing."

"You should've seen the look on your face," Tal snorted. "Priceless."

Samehya giggled. "I never thought he'd do something like that. He was always so proper."

"Oh, he had a wicked streak all right," I said. "It just didn't show often."

Even though it was good reminiscing about the past, Tal was right, I had to go get ready. Glancing at Mother, I saw her conversing with Rurin, and I couldn't help but notice the severe tremor in her body which hadn't been there before. My jaw clenched at seeing Rurin standing so close to her, knowing he was part of the conspiracy. Excusing myself, I walked over to them, stepping in range just enough to possibly overhear what they were talking about.

They fell quiet the moment I came close though, and Mother beckoned me forward.

"I came to say goodbye for now," I said, placing a kiss on her cheek, "and to tell you to get some rest. You look horrible."

She smiled faintly. "I feel horrible."

Resting her hand on my cheek, she smiled at me. "You did really well today. I'm proud of you."

For a long time, I'd been waiting to hear those words, but now that she finally said them, they didn't hold as much meaning to me as I'd hoped they would.

"Be careful on the road," she whispered. "I don't think you're out of the woods yet."

I gave her a wry smile. "Let them come Mother. I'm tired of playing their games. I'll be prepared this time."

"Good."

I placed another kiss on her cheek and turned on my heel, pinching the bridge of my nose as I made my way inside. Footsteps alerted me of someone following me, but I didn't have to look to know it was Tal.

BACK IN MY bedroom I noticed someone had already packed my saddlebags, but only with the bare necessities. Stuffing the owl at the bottom, I made sure I couldn't accidentally lose it, and added a few others items I wanted with me, along with my sword and long dagger. I'd be damned if I went on my way without them. Grabbing trousers and a blouse from my wardrobe, I turned to Tal.

"No peeking."

He wrinkled his nose. "Spoil sport."

"Have to keep the mystery alive."

Tal rolled his eyes at me, but the roguish grin on his face told me he didn't mind one bit. I slipped into the adjoined chamber and wriggled myself out of the dress, letting it slide through my hands before placing it over the chair. Deep down I wondered if I'd ever see it again. A knock on the door had me shoot into my clothes hastily, but when I peeked around the corner, I saw Tal was already on it. Undoing my hair from its elaborate form, I walked over to him, brows shooting up when I saw he was holding something.

"What's that?"

Tal swallowed hard as he turned around. My heart skipped a beat when I saw it was Elara's armour.

"She should've been wearing that today," I said.

He nodded. "I know, but I figured she'd forgive me if you'd wear it on your journey to *Hanyarah*. It's not as if—"

He left the obvious hanging in mid-air.

I brushed his cheek. "Thank you."

The armour was nothing more than a chainmail vest and a leather jacket—regular attire for the army—but it looked nothing remotely close to their official regalia, because it had to be functional rather than pretty. I ran my hand over the chainmail, looking wistful.

"If only she'd worn it…"

"It wouldn't have covered her throat," Tal reminded me.

I nodded softly. "But it would've protected her the first time. It could've saved her life."

Placing the armour aside, Tal pulled me close, enveloping me in a tight embrace, and nuzzled my hair.

"You don't know what could've happened," he murmured. "And there's no point in wondering about the ifs."

"I know, but it's hard not to think about it. She had to have known she wouldn't make it, so when I sprinted to the exit, she stayed behind to ambush him. How can I ever repay her?"

Tal shrugged, flashing me an impish smile. "By not dying?"

"Sounds fair."

He released me from his embrace and stepped back. "Let's get you into that armour and see you off."

I scowled at him. His lips quirked up as he boosted the chainmail onto his arms, turning to me.

"Put your hair back up."

I stared at him, but did as he told me. I'd seen Elara struggle with it once when her hair came undone while putting the chain vest over her head—it hadn't been pretty.

"Give me your hands," Tal instructed.

He had his arms through the sleeves of the armour, and when I gave him my hands, he shrugged the chainmail onto mine. I grunted.

"*Nohro ahrae!* This is heavy!"

Tal smirked. "You thought it'd be light?"

"I'd hoped so."

He laughed, shaking his head. "Stick your head in, and shrug it over. Once your head's through, you can stand up."

Getting my head through wasn't the biggest problem, getting it over my head was. Every time I tried, my injured shoulder locked itself, refusing to go further up. On the fourth try, the chainmail landed on my head painfully, and hiccoughing with laughter, Tal helped me out getting it in place.

I yelped in pain as it landed on my shoulder.

Tal winced. "Sorry. I forgot."

"It's all right." I grimaced. "How do you guys put up with this?"

"Practise."

I glared at him. "You're joking, right?"

"I wouldn't dare."

Grumbling, I allowed Tal to put a belt around my waist, tugging the chainmail up so it'd be supported. The leather jerkin followed, and as Tal closed it, it was clear Elara had been less busty than I was.

"All right, well, this just has to do," Tal observed, taking a step back to regard his handiwork. "It's better than nothing."

Testing out my movements, I realised it was hampered by the jerkin just a little, but not enough to pose a problem, or so I hoped. Never before had I fought with armour on, and I could only hope today wouldn't be the first time.

"When I come back." I muttered, "you'll have to train me in this."

Tal nodded. "Deal."

We stood staring at each other for a long time until he jerked a hand through his hair and looked away. I plucked at the leather jerkin and the chainmail, feeling rather odd to be wearing something of Elara's, yet at the same time, it comforted me. Between Xaresh's owl and Elara's armour, they were still protecting me.

Tal slung my saddlebags over his shoulder and handed me my sword and long-dagger.

"Let's see you on your way."

I STARED down at Tal as he strapped my dagger to the saddle and checked the bridle and stirrups for the hundredth time. His hand brushed my ankle, my leg, and even my hand as he moved around Orion to double, and probably even triple check. Anything to stall my departure. Once he had nothing left to do, he held my stirrup, refusing to look up.

I desperately wanted to touch his face, lift his chin and kiss him, but with the entire palace staring at us, it was better not to.

"Be safe." The strain in his voice was audible only for me.

He wrapped his hand so tight around the reins his knuckles were white, and the familiar tic in his jaw was back.

"I will be," I murmured.

He flashed me a quick roguish smile. "If you don't come back, I'll find you and kill you."

It were the same words I'd spoken to him when he'd gone to get Xaresh's mother and sisters and hearing them returned both constricted my chest and made the butterflies in my stomach soar.

"I know."

Taking the reins in my hand, I inclined my head. Tal stepped back and bowed, his eyes never leaving me. It was the hardest thing to urge Orion on and leave him behind without looking back. What if something happened, and I'd never see him again?

CHAPTER 21

The procession going through the streets of Ilvanna was much bigger than I'd expected. Aside from Haerlyon, Mehrean and myself, at least two dozen guards accompanied us, amongst whom I'd spotted Tiroy. I couldn't say it surprised me. Haerlyon was making a habit out of bringing him along whenever he had to go out, and I couldn't blame him.

I'd have taken Tal if I could have.

Once free of the city, I gazed over the plateaus to the coast where mansions rose from the earth like a gap-toothed grin. A shudder ran through me and I quickly looked away, feeling my skin crawl underneath the layers of armour at the memory of what had happened there. The thought of Eamryel hunting me like prey squeezed the air from my lungs and made my hands go clammy.

Match your breathing and your heartbeat to mine.

Tal's words had become a mantra for whenever a panic attack threatened to overwhelm me, and even though it had only a fifty-fifty chance of helping, I kept trying. I hated the feeling, and I hated the fact Eamryel still had this effect on me, but if I were to believe Soren, trauma like this would stay with me for a while. I'd come to live with it, accept what happened, but it would never go away.

For that alone I'd make him pay one day.

"You're looking dangerous, sis." Haerlyon had ridden up beside me and was giving me the up-and-down glance, looking fiendish.

"Can't be too careful these days," I replied with an eye-roll.

He flashed me a half-smile. "True that, but I didn't even know you had an armour."

"I don't."

"Whose are you wea—" His eyes widened when he came up with the answer himself. "Oh. Well, not a bad idea actually. Whoever came up with it is brilliant."

I snorted. "Don't tell him that or his ego will get the best of him."

"It already did."

I stared at him for a long time, only to burst out laughing which caused me to yank Orion's reins, spooking him badly enough to send him rearing. My saving grace was my quick decision to hold on to the saddle before he could throw me off, yet instead of continuing forward calmly, Orion shot off in a frenzy, leaving me clinging to him as he went into a mad dash. I prayed to all the Gods he wouldn't throw me off. The land sped by below him as he continued his headlong flight, and at some point I just closed my eyes, hoping he would stop before long.

Orion continued, and from the sound of crushed leaves underfoot I gathered we'd entered the forest. When I opened my eyes, I found us barrelling straight off the beaten path, through the undergrowth, and passed low-hanging branches. I flattened myself against his neck, but I got nicked and scratched all the same. Gradually he slowed down to a trot, and then to a halt in the middle of absolutely nowhere.

Pushing myself back up, I turned in the saddle. There was no sight of the others. They had to have lost me when Orion went off-track.

"Oh great job Orion," I muttered. "You figured you could get me killed out here?"

Orion whinnied, and pulled his head down, nearly yanking my arm out of its socket. Cursing Tal's protectiveness under my breath, I slid out of the saddle, landing on ground which was softer than expected. My knees buckled, sending me face first into the moss-covered forest floor.

"Beast," I muttered as I pushed myself to my feet.

Orion snorted this time, turned slowly, and bumped me out of the way with his rump. I just glared at him, taking the reins leisurely in my hand. The last thing I wanted was for him to take off again, stranding me here. In the distance, I could hear my companions' shouts, and while I stood yelling an answer, realised the echo would carry my voice—everyone could hear me, and I had no mind to get attacked by wolves again. Turning back to Orion, I put my hands on my hips, huffing.

"You really had to get me lost, didn't you? You unbelievable beast of a horse! Why did you have to go and get us here!"

I realised I was stomping my feet like a tantrum-riddled toddler while Orion quite simply ignored me.

Dropping my hands by my sides, I sighed, shaking my head. Gathering the reins in one hand, I tried to turn Orion about with my other on his flank so we could walk into the general direction of the shouting. No matter what I tried though, Orion wouldn't budge.

"You're joking, right?"

With an eye-roll worthy of my sister-in-law, I tried to push him into motion, but he still couldn't be bothered.

"Maybe I should leave you here for the wolves," I muttered. "Serves you right."

His ears pricked up, and he turned his head, watching me with big, baleful eyes. He snorted straight in my face.

"Oh, gross!"

Swinging his head back, he yanked the reins, and almost pulled me off of my feet. If I didn't know any better, I'd swear he was doing this on purpose. The next moment, he sidestepped in my direction, but I was quicker and able to avoid him crushing my toes.

"No," I said, pushing him away. "Monster. Not on my foot. I saw what you guys can do with legs. Wasn't pretty."

Orion whinnied and nuzzled me, nipping at my coat.

I stared at him. "No."

"I'm glad to find you're as spiteful to your horse as you are to everyone else."

I stiffened at the sound of the voice coming from behind Orion. As I ducked under his neck, resting my hand on his flank, my gaze settled on Eamryel a few feet away, sitting leisurely on his white gelding. Blood rushed to my cheeks, while my hands tightened around the reins.

"What are you doing here?" I hissed.

"Let me rephrase that for you," he quipped, sarcasm lacing his every word. "Eamryel, it's so good to see you. How have you been?"

"I don't care."

I ducked back under Orion, gathered the reins, grabbed the pommel and placed my foot in the stirrup. All I needed was a good momentum to get into the saddle, and with Eamryel watching I was more determined than ever to do this right. I couldn't. Between my resisting shoulder, the heavy chainmail and the stiff leather jerkin, there was no way I'd be able to mount without help. Resting my head against Orion's flank, it took everything I had not to let hot tears of frustration run down my cheeks.

Eamryel would never see me cry again.

"Let me help you."

He had dismounted and was now watching me, arms folded,

his face expressionless. At least he wasn't laughing.

"Don't touch me," I hissed. "You've helped me enough."

Eamryel looked away, and glancing at him from under my lashes, I found him biting his lip, keeping his temper in check.

"What are you doing here, anyway?" I muttered, turning to look at him.

"Hunting."

I arched my brow. "Convenient."

"For you," he said. "Yes. The forest can be a dangerous place if you don't know your way off the beaten tracks."

"And I suppose you do?"

He smiled at that, inclining his head. "I do."

In the distance, I could still hear my entourage calling for me. Gathering Orion's reins, I tried to get him to move again, but aside from taking a few steps towards me, he still wouldn't listen. My knuckles were white from how tight I held onto him.

Eamryel sighed, running a hand through his hair. "Let me help you up, and I'll bring you back to your company. No matter what you think of me, I'm not here to hurt you."

"You had a change of soul?"

"Do you want my help or not?"

I scowled. "No, but I don't see how I have a choice."

True to his words, Eamryel boosted me into the saddle without ever laying a finger anywhere in the wrong place. He mounted his own gelding and cajoled Orion into following him in the direction we'd come from. My gaze swept over him, and I saw the quiver of arrows and bow hanging from his saddle.

Perhaps he had told me the truth, yet last time he went hunting, it had been me who was prey.

"Why are you even helping me?"

His eyes turned dark when he looked at me. "Believe it or not, *Tarien*, I do not wish to see you dead."

"So the beast does have a heart," I murmured.

Although his lips lifted at the corners, I wasn't sure he'd

actually heard me. By now the shouting was coming from a closer proximity, so Eamryel pulled up short.

"Be careful where you're going *Tarien*," Eamryel said as I stopped next to him. "Not everything is what it seems to be, and not everyone is loyal to you."

I frowned. "How do you know?"

He merely smiled at me. "The less you know the better. Your party is up ahead. Safe travels."

With those words, he turned and left, disappearing into the thicket without so much as looking back. This had been by far the weirdest encounter between us, and it almost made me wish he'd been his explosive self, if only because a righteous Eamryel just didn't seem—right. I nudged Orion on and just as Eamryel had said, my brother and the rest were in the clearing up ahead.

Haerlyon was the first to see me.

"You took your sweet time," he growled.

I patted Orion's neck. "Sir kiss-my-ass here decided it wasn't in his best interest to go back just yet. Took me forever before he'd listen."

"We've lost precious time as it is," Mehrean said. "We can make it before nightfall, but we need to push."

"Let's push it then." Haerlyon nudged his horse back to the road, followed by the rest of us. My thoughts went back to Eamryel and his selfless act of helping me. It was too much of a coincidence he'd been there at that moment, and I was certain he knew more than he'd let on to.

"You should have your face looked at," Haerlyon commented from my side. "Looks like some nasty cuts."

I shrugged. "I'll live."

"I should hope so."

THE JOURNEY TOOK LONGER than expected, and after hours on

horseback, I couldn't be sure which part of my body was still functioning according to design. During the afternoon, a steady wind had picked up, and the loud drumming of rain on the canopy had battered my ears incessantly, adding a headache to the building discomfort. While it prevented us from getting soaked through completely, heavy drops assaulted us regardless. My legs were aching fiercely from clamping on to Orion, my hands were numb from the watery cold, and my cheeks were one fierce stingy sensation.

Journeying wasn't all it was cracked up to be—it was a good deal more miserable.

Everyone huddled in their cloaks, thoughts turned inwards. If they were anything like mine, they wished for warm food, a roof over their heads and something hot to drink. Mehrean was the only one who didn't seem bothered by the weather at all, sitting straight-backed and confident on her horse.

Sometimes I wondered if she was from another planet.

Nudging Orion on, I went to ride beside her, surprised at seeing a big smile on her face. How could anyone be happy in this weather?

"How come you're not as wretched as the rest of us?"

"Because there's nothing to be wretched about," she said, looking at me. "We could have been out of the forest and drenched in seconds. As it is, we're relatively dry."

"Relatively indeed."

She arched a brow, looking amused. "Don't tell me the woman always having dreamt of going on adventures is regretting it now?"

"I'm not exactly enjoying it either."

Mehrean laughed softly. "You'd make quite the adventurer."

"Shush."

"We're almost there anyway," she said at length. "I can imagine you'll be sore."

I snorted. "You don't know the half of it."

JUST BEFORE NIGHTFALL, we arrived at a mountain ridge on the outskirts of the forest. In the fading light, everyone was a mere shade against the darker shadow of the cavern wall. When I dismounted, my knees buckled, and I had to hang onto my saddle to stay on my feet. If I ever got back to the palace, I'd add an extensive riding routine to my training. Haerlyon and the *àn* walked around a little stiffly, but no more than that.

I felt as if my legs would never obey me again.

"Now what?" Haerlyon asked, hands on his hips. "There's nothing here."

Mehrean merely smiled. "Don't judge everything by first impressions. Grab the reins and follow me. *Tarien*, you first."

I was glad my face didn't show in the growing darkness, because the scowl there would definitely have been amongst the ugliest of looks. Taking Orion's reins in my hand, I took a step towards her, and realised the throbbing pain in my leg was the old injury playing up. My day was getting better and better I decided while limping after her.

Up ahead, Mehrean suddenly disappeared inside the wall, stopping me short. Around me, startled gasps told me I wasn't the only one who had seen it happen. Good, I wasn't going insane just yet. Grabbing the reins tight, I followed her, and just when I thought I'd walk straight into the wall, I found myself in a narrow passageway instead. Up ahead were lights, but they were dim.

"Let Orion pick his way. He'll know where to go."

Mehrean's detached voice coming from the darkness did nothing for my frazzled nerves and the dread settling in the pit of my stomach. Orion picked his way through the tunnel at a leisurely pace, not at all bothered by the complete darkness. Behind me, the echo of footfalls and hoof beats reassured me the others were following.

What I encountered when I stepped out of the tunnel was beyond my wildest imagination.

It opened into a wide clearing beyond, revealing torches lit all around, their dancing light a welcoming sight. Up ahead, it looked as if the night sky had fallen down, took its stars, and settled itself in this strange, tranquil place. Somewhere in the dark, the song of a lone bird echoed against the walls. My eyes tried to fix on everything as I looked around in astonishment, and although the night was hiding most of this place, I figured daylight would reveal an immensely beautiful area.

"What is this place?" Haerlyon asked in awe.

"Welcome to *Hanyarah*," Mehrean said. "More commonly known as the Sisterhood."

From the darkness, robed women appeared, some of whom took the reins from the men and guided the horses away. One woman diverted from the group and walked straight up to me, her pure white hair a beacon in the darkness. Up close, she looked vibrant and alluring. No wonder most men were staring at her.

"*Tarien*," she said in the same mellifluous voice Mehrean mastered, "welcome to *Hanyarah*. My name is Laelle."

Laelle placed both hands on my upper arms and kissed each cheek lightly before stepping aside, putting her hand between my shoulder blades to guide me along. I limped forward and stopped, turning back to Haerlyon. *Haniya* were guiding the men away into another direction.

"Where are they going?"

"Men aren't allowed to go beyond the clearing," Laelle explained. "They'll be housed elsewhere."

My brows knitted together. "Will I be able to see them?"

"Not until you return to the palace.

Laelle escorted me into the direction she'd come from, not amused by my questions.

"They'll be well taken care of," Mehrean murmured to my other side. "Promised."

I nodded, deciding the retort on my lips wasn't worth the trouble it would cause. Surely they'd take care of them to the best of their abilities—I just hoped they'd do the same with me. As we stepped beyond the circle of torches, my eyes needed to adjust to the surrounding darkness, hiding the path before us. The clopping sound underneath my feet indicated a wooden pathway, and as Laelle took us over a bridge, I could hear water stream below.

It was beyond the bridge that dark shapes began looming up on either side of us, and the stars I'd seen before turned to light inside of wooden huts, and to torches outside. Laelle finally removed her hand from me, so I turned around and around, taking in my surroundings in wonder.

"It looks even better in daylight," Mehrean whispered.

"I bet."

Laelle and Mehrean walked me further into their sanctuary, and as we passed, women appeared in doorways or out of nowhere. They bowed when I came close.

"That's really unnecessary," I murmured.

"It's not," Laelle answered. "It's time you came into your own, *Tarien*."

I wrinkled my nose, looking down and away from her. If it were up to me, I'd change the law on female inheritance and let Evan rule the *nohro* country. We halted in the middle of another clearing where a large wooden building loomed like a giant, dwarfing all surrounding structures. From all around this clearing, robed and hooded figures dressed in the same garments streamed in, forming a circle around us. A shiver ran down my spine as the solemnity of it all came crashing down on me.

It had all begun the moment I stepped out of the tunnel.

A soft hum began on my right and soon picked up around us as every woman in the circle added her voice. All hairs on my body stood on end, and I took an involuntary step backwards, hugging myself.

"Don't be afraid," Mehrean murmured in my ear. "Nothing will happen."

"Mind if I don't believe you?"

Swallowing hard, my gaze zeroed in on Laelle now standing in front of me. Eamryel's words came to mind unbidden, establishing a dreadful feeling deep inside of me.

What if they meant me harm?

Laelle's clear voice startled me when she spoke.

"Sisters, behold your *Tarien*! In our presence, she shall be stripped of everything, so that the burden of her past shall be shed, and the path to her future opened. I ask you to witness her transformation from cygnet to pen. Let tonight be in celebration, so that tomorrow her transformation may begin."

"What does she mean, stripped of everything?" I asked Mehrean under my breath.

Mehrean laughed silently beside me. "Exactly that."

The second Laelle touched the leather jerkin to undo the clasps, I slapped her hands away in sheer fright, looking at her wide-eyed. She narrowed her eyes at me, an unamused expression crossing her face.

"It's part of the ritual, *Tarien*," she hissed with a frown. "Let me unclasp it."

I clenched my jaw, staring her down. "I can do it myself."

"It's not how this goes."

"Let her do it Shal," Mehrean mumbled. "If the ritual isn't performed properly..."

She left the words unspoken between us.

I grumbled, but nodded. "All right then."

When Laelle went for the clasps again, I tensed, but instead of swatting her hands away, I clenched my fists to my sides and allowed her to do what she needed to do. The leather jerkin came off easily enough, but she needed Mehrean's help to get the chainmail off. It felt like I was doing an awkward dance shrugging it over my head, but once it was, it slipped to the ground in a soft jingle of metal on metal.

I felt naked.

My boots were next, followed in rapid succession by my trousers and my shirt until I was standing buck-naked in front of a group of women I didn't know, sharing intimacies I hadn't even shared with Tal. While I'd never really been shy of my body, this public display was more uncomfortable than I cared for, so I wrapped my hands around strategic places instead, glad for the night covering up the scars.

"Take your arms away, *Tarien*," Laelle whispered, "and turn around."

"You must be joking..."

She shook her head. Glaring daggers at her, I did as she instructed, but when I tried to turn around fast, she made me go slower by laying a hand on my shoulder. An image of Mother having to do the same flashed through my mind, and I shook my head. Those weren't thoughts I cared to dwell on right now.

To my surprise, once I'd gone full-circle, Laelle and Mehrean stepped away, and three other women walked up. Two of them carried pitchers, one of them a towel. It didn't take any stretch of the imagination to guess what they would do. Brazing myself by closing my eyes, I waited for the worst—the worst being ice cold water poured over my head, drawing out a high-pitched shriek fit to rival the birds I'd heard. My eyes flew open while my body froze on the spot. With chattering teeth, I waited until the third woman towelled me down, but she took a long time starting.

I stared at her in surprise. She stared back unflinchingly.

"This water cleanses you from your past troubles. While not gone, may they guide you on your future path. This towel represents those around you, those who shall help you, and those who shall be close. They'll be your comfort even when you think you're alone."

Finally, she started rubbing me dry, but she was nowhere near considerate about it. In fact, by the time she finished, my skin felt as if it was on fire and chafed in uncomfortable places. If I didn't know any better, I could've sworn she'd sanded off the scars in the process. The three women bowed, almost as an afterthought, and stepped back into the circle.

Next up was Mehrean, and when she came close, the scent of vanilla, oranges and wood enveloped my senses. I bit back tears, eyes on hers.

"I'm sorry if this weirds you out," she murmured, "but I wasn't allowed to tell you."

I gave her a wry smile. "Something tells me it's hardly begun."

"You're not wrong there," Mehr replied.

She rubbed the oil into my skin quietly, which became awkward the moment she had to involve my breasts in the bargain. I was glad that was all she had to involve, because I was sure the rest would've gone even beyond our friendship. The oil gave me a false sense of warmth until a sudden gust of wind swept through the valley.

"Dear Gods," I hissed, gritting my teeth. "Cold."

"Almost there," Mehrean whispered, only to continue in a louder voice so everyone could hear. "This oil functions as protection in every sense of the word. May you be guarded at all times, the good, and the bad, mentally and physically, so you may perform your duties as *Tari* to the best of your abilities."

We shared a look, and I felt my chest constrict.

"Last part," Mehrean whispered before she moved back to her place in the circle.

Two women walked up and once in front of me, bowed deeply, offering a package which turned out to be a heavy long-sleeved robe which I could tie in the front. In the darkness, it was hard to make out what it looked like exactly, but I smiled at the prospect of not having to walk around entirely naked. One of them took the garment from me, and together they helped me shrug it on.

"This robe is your shield in the outside world. May it protect you and serve you on your path."

Half of their words made no sense, but I felt certain there was rhyme and reason to it. Laelle stepped into the middle of the circle, turning slowly so she had looked at all women present.

"You have all been witness to the first initiation. For your presence, I thank you! For your time, I thank you! Now, I would like to invite you all inside for refreshments."

I thanked the Gods and Goddesses quietly for the chance of food. My eating habits were nowhere near healthy, but after having been on a horse for most of the day and having been put through this ordeal, my stomach was growling and snapping at me like a hungry beast. My dreams of delicious food were interrupted when someone hooked their arm through mine. Mehr flashed me an open smile as she briefly rested her cheek against my arm.

Gods, she was small.

The inside of the large building marked it as their kitchen, dining and assembly hall, and my eyes immediately zoomed in on tables laden with all kinds of foods reminding me of a banquet at the palace.

"I don't think we ever have this much up," I murmured. "This isn't all for me, is it?"

Mehrean shook with silent laughter. "They don't get to prepare an *Araîthin* like yours every year."

"I suppose not."

Laelle invited me to sit with her at the head table on the dais, reminding me of what it was like at home. It surprised me in a setting like this because I hadn't expected a hierarchy amongst the *Haniya*. Somehow, I'd always imagined them as loving, peaceful women who went about their business on their own terms, instead of being told what to do by a leader.

I reminded myself to ask Mehr about this later.

Much to my chagrin, Laelle offered an unofficial word of welcome to me before we could dig in, expressing her hopes and wishes I'd find my stay to my liking. So far, I wasn't much impressed, but it had more to do with the fact they'd made me undress before every single one of them, rather than their hospitality.

When we could finally tuck in, I made sure I didn't stack every bit of appetising food on my plate and wolf it down. The smell of venison and gravy was good enough to make my mouth water, so I started off with that, adding some mashed potatoes. The food at the palace was always much more luxurious when something official was going on, and also much smaller.

Bite-sized, they liked to call it.

Hunger on a plate as far as I was concerned. No matter how much I ate, it never sustained me, and even if it did, it usually lasted no longer than the walk to my bedroom to feel hungry again. This was proper food. Home-cooked, proper, filling food, and exactly what I needed right now.

"Remind me to tell Mother to put this up next time," I told Mehrean. "This is so much better than our party-food."

Mehrean chuckled. "Agreed."

I wasn't sure how much I ate, but by the time I finished, several women had put the middle tables aside and had joined in music, singing, dancing, or all three. Everyone was smiling, others were outright laughing, and some sat in a corner, watching the festivities with an amused look on their face.

One thing was sure though—they were all enjoying themselves.

It was unlike anything I'd ever seen at the palace, where even parties were political gatherings and the scene of many a drama acted out. Here, none of that happened. The *Haniya* appeared happy to just celebrate, rejoice and live. Today was today, and tomorrow would be different.

No wonder Mehrean had such a positive outlook on life.

By the time night was well on its way, I suppressed yawns more often than I cared to count, and failed miserably at the attempt of stifling them more than half of these times. I was sure my head would topple backwards if I kept yawning like that.

"Let me show you your hut," Mehrean said at some point. "You look dead on your feet."

"I'm dead on my ass," I murmured. "Not even sure I'll be able to get there."

"It's not far."

Mehrean helped me to my feet, and after wishing Laelle and the others at our table a good night, we left the dining hall. The air outside was refreshing, crisp, and I inhaled deeply, feeling the fresh air burn in my lungs.

"It's a nice place."

"Don't let the exterior deceive you," Mehrean said solemnly. "There's a reason I do not want to live here."

I glanced at her. "Let me guess, you won't share the reason?"

"No," she said.

"I figured as much."

She guided me to a cottage on a road just off the dining hall, and it surprised me it was the only one there. The door opened into a one-room hut with a built-in bed to the left, a fireplace in the middle, and a table and chair off to the right. My saddlebags hung over the chairs, my clothing lay folded on the table, and the fireplace had already been lit. Candles threw dancing shadows across the wall of the hut, adding to the comfortable warmth.

Despite it being sparsely furnished, it was welcoming.

"Everything you need is here," Mehrean said, sweeping her

arm across the room. "If you need anything, I'll be three huts over."

She turned to leave, and as I watched her step out of the door, I realised I didn't want to be alone.

"Mehr!"

"Yes?" She turned back to look at me.

I stared at the wooden floor planks, swallowing hard. "Stay with me?"

"I thought you'd never ask."

CHAPTER 22

That night, dreams plagued my sleep, leaving me bathing in sweat and gasping for air. After the third time, I stayed awake, slipped out of bed, and placed the covers back over Mehrean who was still sound asleep. She looked so young and innocent with her lilac-tinged hair spread out over the pillow, features at ease, it tugged at my heartstrings to know she could die too.

The fire had died down to embers, and most of the candles had been blown out, creating an uncomfortable chill in the hut. Wrapping the robe tighter around me, I knelt in front of the fire and set to building it up, welcoming the warmth as it roared back to life. From the table, I picked up one of my boots and withdrew the piece of parchment from the toe. Xaresh's handwriting was fading—it wouldn't be long before it became unintelligible, and there were still a few names I had to memorise.

Sitting down cross-legged in front of the fire, I set myself to the task Elara had given me, determined to see it through. Having this information was enough to get me into trouble, but if any of the others found it, they'd pay the price. I needed to get rid of it as soon as possible. As my eyes went over the parchment, my heart suddenly lurched at one name.

Laelle.

I'd read it at least a hundred times before, but until now the name had held no meaning. It also made Eamryel's warning valid. I ran a trembling hand through my hair, staring at the paper, hoping the letters would rearrange themselves into different names.

Oh, dear Gods.

All of a sudden, everything became even more messed up when I realised the one person who had the power to elevate my status was in cahoots with the one threatening my life for a reason unknown to me. It didn't take a mastermind to figure out Azra was up to something big, especially if this many people were involved. Mother falling ill was beneficial to her, although I doubted I could attribute it to convenience. Whatever she'd gotten the day of my kidnapping had to have something to do with Mother's sickness.

I just didn't know what.

If Mother were to die, I was her successor and would be appointed *Tari* before her body had gone cold, unless something were to happen to me. If I could not claim the throne, it would fall to Azra, but then it made no sense why she didn't just kill me right off the bat, and the assassin had been rather clear—no harm was to befall me.

Azra needed me for something else, that much was clear, although I couldn't for the life of me imagine what it was. If Laelle was working with her, the only thing she could accomplish was me not getting my *Araith*, but that would be too suspicious, and somehow I doubted every Sister here knew their leader was up to no good. She undoubtedly had her own reasons for being involved, but it made no sense.

None of it.

Resting my face in my hands, I stared at the paper in my lap, wondering what to do with this newfound knowledge. It didn't bring me any closer to a solution. Rather, the opposite—it took me miles away from it and it frustrated me beyond belief. It was as if all I could do was wait for events to unfold and hope things would somehow turn out for the better, because if it didn't, the consequences would be too severe.

Not everything is what it seems to be.

Eamryel's words echoed through my mind. After what had passed between us, I'd never guessed I'd place any merit in his words, but it looked like I had no choice. The irony wasn't lost on me. Not even he was who he had appeared to be—I'd long since learned everyone had ulterior motives, I just needed to figure out what his were.

My safest bet was that he still wanted me.

I realised I was still staring at the paper, yet none of the names stuck. Folding it, I placed it back where it came from, and resorted to staring out the window, arms wrapped around myself.

Dawn arrived in an intertwining colour scheme of pinks and purples, creating a masterpiece of aerial art. I loved these kinds of morning skies, different from all the others, if only because they reminded me of myself. Watching the sky change, I decided it was time to get back to my training, and there was no better place for it than here, but when I went to get my equipment, I found none of my weapons had been brought to the cottage. I considered getting them until I decided I'd be better off with physical exercise, anyway.

I slipped into my trousers, blouse and boots, and was out of the cottage before Mehrean woke up. She'd have an opinion on me going out training, and I didn't much care to hear it right now. I'd respect the rules, as long as they didn't impede my freedom any more than they did at home.

Experience taught me it didn't end well for anyone involved.

At this time of day, few women were out and about. Those

who appeared to have a duty to attend to paid me no more heed than a greeting in passing. I meandered through several streets until I came upon a clearing at the water's edge which was big and quiet enough to do some training.

I started off with a warm-up and soon immersed into a tranquil flow I hadn't felt for a very long time as I went through the motions fully aware of what I was doing—focused and determined to get every step right. For the first time in months I felt close to being myself again.

The physical training was harder than I'd hoped, but not as I'd expected, and I was determined to get it right. The moment I started on my push-ups, I realised the mistake I'd made. My shoulder locked up painfully as soon as I tried to push myself up, preventing me from even finishing the movement, sending me back to the ground instead. I'd have to let Soren have a look at it once I returned home. It was my sword arm and not being able to lift it could mean the difference between life and death. Right now, I couldn't defend myself, and I hated the idea. All my training had been for nothing.

I cursed loudly.

"I'll make him pay for this," I muttered, turning on my back for sit-ups.

Just as I was about to continue, someone cleared her throat, and tilting my head backwards, I found Laelle standing over me with her arms folded, looking everything but amused. I rolled my eyes when I sat up and turned to her.

"Walk with me," Laelle said through clenched teeth.

Rising to my feet, I noticed women standing off to the side, eagerness and curiosity plastered to their features. Nothing must ever happen here if something like this caused them to look like that.

"While you are here," Laelle began, guiding me back into the general direction of my cottage, "you cannot just go out and do whatever you like. We have rules here."

"I don't see how anything's wrong with training," I said, looking honestly confused.

"There's nothing wrong with training," Laelle said. "There *is* something wrong with your attire, however."

"What? My clothing?"

She flashed me a half-smile as understanding hit me.

"I'm supposed to wear that robe the entire time I'm here?!"

She nodded. "Or at least until we give you something else to wear."

I wrinkled my nose.

"How is that in any way related to getting my *araîth*?"

Laelle stiffened beside me and stopped walking. I turned to face her.

"Getting your *araîth* is a sacred affair entrusted to the Sisterhood. It means you must go through several rituals before the first line is etched into your skin. Until that point, you are subject to our rules."

"Well," I said with a shrug, "you could've just told me that last night. If I'd known, I'd not have taken it off."

She stared at me as if I'd grown two heads. "Are you serious?"

"Absolutely."

She shook her head. "No *Tarien ever* needed to be told to keep it on. They just did."

"Yeah, well, I'm not your average *Tarien*." I smirked and continued my way back, "but I'll keep it in mind for the future."

I left Laelle standing where she was, shocked and confused while I strode back to my appointed cottage. Did she really expect me to walk around mostly naked until she deemed it fit to give me something else to wear?

Not in a lifetime.

I slammed the door shut when I walked in. Mehrean sat upright in bed, looking wide-eyed and flustered. Bless her, she'd still been asleep. Her gaze zeroed in on me, and her brows crinkled into a thoughtful V-shape.

"What's wrong? And what in all the Goddesses' names are you wearing?"

"Your rules are what's wrong, and I'm wearing clothing, like any sane, normal being would."

Mehrean stared at me. "From your words I take it Laelle found out?"

"She has, and she wasn't pleased. At all."

"No doubt."

With a disgusted sigh, I took off my clothing and wrapped myself in the robe, a shiver running up and down my spine at the cold touch of the fabric. Laelle had better make sure that wherever she'd take me for her rituals was warm.

"Why had you gone out anyway?" Mehrean asked, sitting up cross-legged in the bed, dragging her fingers through her dishevelled hair.

"I went for some training," I said, pulling up a chair in front of the small fire.

With a frown, I added some logs to it so it could get back to life, and sat down in the chair, rolling my head from side to side.

"How did it go?"

"Not well," I said, looking at her. "There seems to be a blockage in my shoulder. No doubt Eamryel destroyed more than I thought he did."

Mehrean nodded softly and slipped out of bed, wrapping the blanket around herself. She grabbed a teapot and cups, added water to a kettle and hung it over the fire. With a content smile, she settled cross-legged at my feet, reminding me of a cat.

How could she be so calm?

"What's up next on the madhouse agenda?" I asked with a sigh, rubbing my face.

Mehrean smiled. "I'm not sure you want to know, but think of something you could offer."

"Offer?" I asked, frowning. "Whatever for?"

"Will you question everything?"

I shrugged. "Most likely."

She chuckled softly as she leaned forward to pour boiling water into the cups. A fragrant, herbal scent filled the hut almost immediately.

"Try not to make them regret their decision of letting you come here," she said at length, watching me.

I snorted. "Trust me, I'd much rather be at home too. This place is even more of a prison."

"It's not as bad as one," she said, handing me the cup.

I scowled. "It is."

"Why are you so against this?"

While watching the fire, holding the warm cup in my hands, I mulled over her question. It wasn't me being against all of this, it was Laelle's part in this story not sitting well with me, but I could hardly tell Mehr without having to divulge all the details.

I shrugged.

"You know I hate being the centre of attention."

Mehr shook her head as she rose to her feet. "You'll be the *Tari* one day Shal, you'll have to get used to it."

"I know," I said, diverting my eyes as she set to dress herself. "But if I allow myself to get used to it now, I have to admit Mother is dying, and I'm not ready for that."

She shot me an apologetic look and placed a kiss on the top of my head.

"She's not gone yet," she whispered. "Your mother won't just give up."

With a heavy heart, I nodded. Her words made sense, and I knew Mother would fight with everything she was worth, but the matter of the fact at hand was she was dying, and I'd become *Tari*.

Unless Azra got her way.

THAT AFTERNOON, I stood in front of a cave entrance surrounded by all the *Haniya* once more, clutching the wooden owl tight in my hands. If my assumptions were correct, the offering would be to appease the Gods and Goddesses, although the reason behind it was beyond me. Then again, I didn't quite believe in their existence so it sounded like a waste of time to begin with, but I'd promised Mehr to keep an open mind.

Laelle stood at my side, her lips a thin line as she looked at me.

"Once you go in there, it's between you and the Gods," she said for my ears alone. "There is no clear-cut way to go about it. Do what feels right for you, just don't forget to make an offering. They get testy when you don't."

My brows shot up in surprise. "You talk about them as if you chat to them daily."

"Someone should teach you restraint," Laelle muttered.

My look went dark. "They tried and failed."

She rubbed her temples and shook her head lightly.

"Just make sure you do as I instructed, *Tarien*?" She pinched the bridge of her nose. "Don't make a mockery of this."

I nodded at her. "I won't."

My eyes picked out Mehrean between the *Haniya*, and the encouraging smile she gave me was enough to settle my nerves. A low hum started up behind me, and looking around, I realised it were the women making the sound. It almost sent me running into the cave, wanting to get away from the general idiosyncrasy as soon as I could.

I didn't begrudge them their beliefs and rituals—I just didn't want to partake anymore.

Strategically placed oil-lamps along the walls lit the tunnel, reminding me of the spring back at the palace I'd visited with Tal only two days before. A sudden pang of longing threatened to overwhelm me, and my throat tightened. Following the lights deeper into the cave, I pushed the feelings away while wiping beads of sweat from my brow with the back of my hand.

After two turns, I stepped through a set of heavy curtains into a dimly lit humid cavern. For the first time I was glad for wearing just the robe. As my eyes adjusted to the light cast by hundreds of candles arranged haphazardly around the room, my gaze settled on a shrine in the middle. Twelve bowls sat around it, and upon closer inspection, I saw they were filled with tokens representing the Gods.

I recognised the bow for Vehda, Goddess of the hunt, and the dagger for Esahbyen, God of war and violence. Walking around, I realised I recognised the tokens for Xiomara, Goddess of women, and Navah, Goddess of love, but the rest of them were either too weathered or too abstract.

Growing up, I'd never really put much stock in the Pantheon.

Yet here I was, standing at one of their shrines, clutching a wooden owl to my chest as if it was the last thing on this world keeping me sane. I wasn't sure how to proceed. Laelle had told me to follow my intuition, but right now it left me hanging. Sitting down cross-legged in front of the shrine, I wiped the sweat from my brow, and placed the owl in front of me.

"Well then," I said, resting my hands on my knees. "Now what?"

There was no answer, obviously, and while I sat there contemplating what to do the temperature kept rising, but although it was hot, it wasn't at all uncomfortable. The heat settled deep into my bones, driving away aches and stiffness I thought I'd never get rid of—it made me drowsy.

Make your offering and decide what it is you want to ask from the Gods.

As if I'd want to ask them for anything. If there really was something they could do from up above, they could start by keeping my loved ones safe in the upcoming battle, no questions asked. Taking the owl in my hand, I lay back, folding one arm under my head while holding it up, looking at it.

"What would you ask for?"

The longer I stared at the owl, the heavier my eyelids became, and it didn't take long before I drifted off to sleep.

"Now we decide what it is you truly desire," a smoky voice said.

It belonged to a statuesque male, sharp, electric blue eyes sparkling as he watched me, thumbs hooked in his belt. There was a certain mischief in those eyes as he sauntered closer, and it was then I realised I was on my feet, rather than lying down, clutching the owl.

"And you are?" I arched a brow.

A corner of his mouth lifted. "Someone ought to teach you your pantheon."

"I've never been good in trusting people I cannot see." I offered a half-shrug, watching him wearily. "Besides, it's just a dream anyway, and my desires don't exactly matter."

"Interesting dreams you have." He grinned, stepping even closer. "But truly, what is your deepest wish?"

I rolled my eyes. "For people to leave me alone and stop playing their stupid games?"

He ran his knuckles over my scarred cheek, tutting at me. "That's not it."

I harrumphed, folding my arms in front of me. "Well, if you know what it is, why bother asking me in the first place?"

"Because it's the first step on your new path, *shareye*." He leaned in and breathed in sharply, sending shivers down my spine.

I took an involuntary step backwards.

"Enough with the high creep factor," I muttered, wrapping my arms around me. "Who are you?"

379

"Some call me Laros, others prefer the name Arenos, but out here, you people have adopted Esahbyen for me."

I pressed my lips together, a slight frown on my face. "You're telling me you're a God? A real, living and breathing entity who lives up in the sky and does nothing at all for any of us?"

He crinkled his nose, lips curling in a sneer. "We do things for you."

"Such as?"

"Well, you're still alive," Esahbyen said with an exasperated sigh and an eye-roll that could've popped his eyes out. "I count that as doing something for you."

I huffed. "Last time I checked, you weren't there."

"Well, you didn't die that night, did you?"

I opened my mouth to retort something, until I remembered what night he was talking about, and shut it again.

"Fine, you win."

He smirked. "Good. Can we go back to the matter at hand?"

"My deepest wish?"

"Exactly."

I glared at him. "You're a pain in the ass."

"You're no picnic either." He sounded a little peeved, electric blue eyes flashing in annoyance. "But there's a reason the rest sent me here, I'm sure."

"They hate you as much as the rest hates me?"

Esahbyen threw his head back, roaring with laughter and slapping his thighs. Shaking my head, I ran a jerky hand through my hair, trying to figure out what my deepest, darkest wish was.

"I really have no idea," I said at length, annoyed with myself. "There's enough I want, but I'd call none of them a desire."

"What about your guard?"

I flashed him a wry smile. "Yeah, if you could get Xaresh and Elara back, that would be great."

"Not them," he said a little vexed, inspecting his fingernails. "Despite popular belief, we cannot bring back the dead."

"What about him?" I asked, watching him.

Esahbyen grinned. "Do you not desire him?"

"Why ask me if you already know the answer? Besides, it's a different kind of desire."

"What about your Mother? I could keep her from dying," he said, tilting his head as a look of curiosity stole over his otherwise immaculate features. "Wouldn't you want that?"

I swallowed hard, looking down at my feet and away. "It wouldn't solve the problems. They'd find other ways to get what they want."

He folded his arms, regarding me levelly. "Now we're getting somewhere."

I cast him a deadpan stare.

"Would you want them stopped?"

I shrugged. "I suppose, but even then, just stopping them won't be the answer. Whatever their plan, it's nothing in the grand scheme of things. For all I know, they might just be a small part of something much larger, and stopping them would only escalate things. I'd not want to plunge my country into a war without knowing the stakes."

Esahbyen remained silent this time. The only thing he did was tilt his head slightly, reminding me of an owl. Oh, the irony.

"I just wish that as *Tari*, I'll know what to do," I replied, biting my lip, "because right now, I've no clue what left or right is, and this whole situation makes me testy. I'm sure Mother knows what to do."

"So it's wisdom you seek?"

I shrugged, rubbing my shoulder. "Maybe. I don't know. Some things just can't be changed, and most of it depends entirely on action and reaction."

"Let me know when you've figured it out," Esahbyen said, taking a step backwards. "I'm afraid our time is up."

Biting my lip, I looked down at the owl in my hand, took a step forward and held it up.

"They told me to offer you something, to get help in return."

His lips curled up in a smile, an amused look flashing in those mesmerising eyes. It surprised me the moment he stepped back and shook his head.

"You need it more than I do. I've no use for trinkets."

My eyes narrowed. He laughed, and as he did, both he and the surroundings disappeared.

When past and future come together and love and hatred silently gather. When darkness your only companion at night, only then shall be your return to the light.

The words of the damned prophecy spoken in his voice echoed through my mind when I awoke with a fierce throb behind my eyes, along with a parched throat, and a body slick with sweat. His voice, those words, they tugged at a memory long forgotten. I knew I'd heard it before, speaking those exact same words, but I couldn't for the life of me remember when. My vision was lapsing in and out of focus, my breathing came ragged, as if I'd run too fast, too hard, and I knew I needed to get out of there.

I pressed the heel of my hands against my eyes, but it brought no relief, so half-blind, and half-panicky, I stumbled out of the cavern and into the tunnel. A sudden gust of wind whipped up my robe, connecting with my hot skin, sending shivers running up and down my body until I was trembling all over.

Once outside, I dropped to my knees, gulping in lungs full of fresh air. I registered someone placing a blanket around my shoulders, and from the murmurs around I gathered I wasn't alone, but I wasn't capable of any response as the realisation of what just happened settled in.

Had I really been talking to a God?

I couldn't have been. It had to have been some kind of dream infused by the heat and herbs. Hallucinations. A figment of my imagination. Yet it had all felt so real, and there was no chance I could've made up that conversation on my own. Then again, it wouldn't have been the first time I'd been stuck in some weird fever dream, so I shrugged it off as that and pulled the blanket tighter around me in desperate need of comfort.

"Shal?" Mehrean murmured to my side. "Are you there?"

"No."

She chuckled softly. "Glad to have you back. Come, it's time for the second part of the ritual."

"There's more?" I groaned, rubbing my face. "I'm quite done with it."

"Just this one left. After that, Ione will start on your *araith*."

Although I didn't relish the thought of being a pincushion for an extended period, getting my *araith* was something I'd been looking forward to for years. When Evan and Haerlyon had gotten theirs, they'd been ever so excited and full of stories, boasting of how long they'd managed to sit through one session. It had taken them both somewhat over a month to see it finished.

I had less than three weeks, and mine was twice the size of theirs.

As Mehrean guided me along, I realised we weren't going to the hut. Instead, she escorted me to a large, natural pool off to the side of the cave where steam billowed up in tendrils of mist, and the scent of fresh rain and warm wood wafted my way.

"You guys really are a decadent bunch, aren't you?"

"We don't even come close to you people at the palace."

I snorted. "We don't have a hot spring."

"Not at the palace," Mehrean replied, violet eyes twinkling mischievously, "but there's one in the city."

"Why didn't I know this?"

She laughed. "Because you're not meant to know everything."

"On the contrary," I began, shrugging off the blanket, "I am supposed to know everything. Well. Soon."

Mehrean took off the robe and instructed me to get into the water. It was scalding hot the moment I stuck my foot in, but it was preferable over the incessant trembling. Wading deeper, I let out a sigh of relief, and when I turned back to Mehr, I saw she'd gotten in behind me, pushing a floating bucket in my direction.

"What's this?"

"You really can't do anything without questioning it, can you?" she asked, head slightly tilted. "Just enjoy it. This isn't unfamiliar to you."

I stared at her a moment longer, until I saw the contents of the bucket and realised this would be exactly like home, except for the tub being a good deal bigger. A lazy grin spread across my features.

"All right. I'll try."

Truth be told, having something this mundane went a long way towards feeling normal, and even somewhat safe. I trusted Mehrean with my life, whereas I had no reason to trust Laelle. Every time the woman spoke, she set my teeth on edge, triggering a fight-or-flight response like nobody's business.

Up till now, she'd hadn't even done anything which left me to wonder what she was up to, but her name was on that list for a reason, just like Rurin's, yet that reason was beyond me. I had the sinking feeling things would unfold sooner than I'd like, and I felt nowhere near ready. In fact, I didn't even feel like I was close to knowing what was going on, and the guilty feeling of indulging in all kinds of niceties here while Mother and the others were off fighting said battle didn't help either.

Xaresh and Elara were already dead, and soon others would join them. I just knew. A deep shudder ran through me as if in warning. Hugging myself to fight it off, it occurred to me I shouldn't be enjoying anything, whether or not it was part of the ritual. Considering the circumstances, they should've started on my *araith* the moment I'd arrived, rituals be damned. My family and my country were in a time of need, and I couldn't waste any of it.

I stiffened beneath Mehrean's administrations. "When will this Ione place the *Araith*?"

Mehrean's hands stilled. "As soon as we're done here."

"Then let's get this over with."

CHAPTER 23

*I*n the middle of the square where I'd been stripped off my clothing the day before stood a high structure. Up close it appeared to be a combination between a bed and a table, and to its side stood a young woman, whom I guessed was Ione, with wavy hair the colour of periwinkle, and comforting, upturned eyes which gave her an altogether friendly look.

She looked frail next to Laelle's impressive stature though.

Everyone had gathered around us, looking like a multi-coloured array of exotic birds. They'd dressed up for the occasion. It was normal for everyone to be present during the first few hours of Ione placing the *Araîth*, but the rest of the sessions would be in her hut until she finished. The last lines would be inked during the *Araîthin* under the scrutiny of every aristocrat in the realm. It was also the moment where the *Arathrien* would be officially linked to me through their *Araîth*.

It saddened me to know Xaresh and Elara would never have theirs finished.

Laelle welcomed me with two chaste kisses on the cheek, a false smile plastered to her face. The reserved look she gave me could mean anything. The young woman at her side introduced herself as Ione, confirming my suspicions.

"A pleasure to meet you, *Tarien*," she said in a distinguished singsong voice holding more strength than she looked like she had. "Have a seat."

While I sat down, Laelle welcomed everyone to the final part of the ritual, telling us something about all the *Tarien* before me, and how they'd prided themselves in tradition. The furtive glance Ione gave me along with the lift of her lips and a slightly mischievous look left me wondering. Mehrean wore the same expression, but when I looked at her questioningly, she just shrugged.

"As such," Laelle said loud enough for everyone to hear, "I ask you to bear witness to this event, so that everyone knows *Tarien* Shalitha an Ilvan received her *araîth* according to protocol and tradition."

Murmurs rose around us, and as Laelle looked at me, the hard line of her lips was a clear sign she was far from happy. This time, I hadn't even said or done anything.

"Good luck, *Tarien*," she said, scorn in her voice. "When it's too much to endure, let Ione know."

I nodded, refraining from a smirk. Laelle straightened her shoulders, lifted her chin and took up her place amongst the rest of the *haniya*, as did Mehrean. It left Ione and me in the middle, regarding each other with curiosity.

"Mehrean told me you're not one for tradition." Ione looked at me from under her lashes, giving me a slight, close-lipped smile. "Care to shake things up a bit?"

"I'm not sure I follow."

Ione turned to me. "Up till now, every *araîth* ever placed was black. I'm thinking of using blue ink for yours."

"Blue?"

"Several shades of blue, in fact."

A slow grin spread across my face, the mischievous look in both her eyes and Mehrean's suddenly making sense.

They were helping me go against tradition.

"Let's do this."

A little voice in the back of my head told me Mother would be furious, and I knew Laelle wouldn't take kindly to the insubordination either, but in all truth, I was tired of abiding by the rules, and walking on eggshells to ensure I didn't offend anyone. In my case, I probably offended people simply by existing if my aunt was any indication, so I might as well give them a reason.

"Lie down on your stomach, please."

Although the excitement about going against the grain made it impossible to lie still, as soon as Ione tapped the first ink into my skin I stiffened. As a fiery pain spread through my foot, it took me every ounce of will I possessed not to pull back the first few times. Thankfully, after a while, the pain became a dull throb which I could mostly ignore.

My eyes drifted over to the women in my line of sight, some of them solemn and quiet, others looking outright bored. I could hardly blame them. This had to be by far the most tedious part of the ritual. My gaze zeroed in on Laelle, whose brows knitted together in pure consternation as if she realised something wasn't going the way it should.

The smug look on Mehrean's face, who was standing next to her, might have had something to do with it.

Out of the blue, the pain increased a hundredfold from one minute to the next, reminding me of what Mother had said about how much I'd be able to take, and how it differed from person to person. I'd reached my limit for the day. Ione had stopped and was wiping away some blood. My jaw went slack when I saw the result.

Starting at the back of my foot, just underneath the sole, a sophisticated web of fine lines moved up to halfway my calf. A straight line in the middle was the base from which an intricate pattern of fluid lines branched up the side of my calf, forming leaves and flowers interjected with geometrical designs. It was unlike anything I'd ever seen. It was bold and daring, yet feminine and gentle. The blue colours she'd used made it extra special, and I couldn't stop staring at it.

"This is stunning," I exhaled.

Ione's cheeks turned red. "Do you like it, Tarien?"

"I love it."

In my peripherals, I saw Laelle walking up, Mehrean only a few steps behind. For the first time, I noticed they carried themselves similarly, and I realised Mehrean had been at every part of the official rituals, like Laelle, and not just at the side-lines. The only thing which was different, was that Laelle did the talking. Ione straightened her back, clasping her hands in front of her.

This was the moment.

Laelle shrieked the moment she laid eyes on the *Araith*, what little colour she possessed draining from her face. For the first time since I'd met her, she was speechless. Satisfaction washed over me at her response. Mehrean took a long look at it, whistling under her breath.

"I'd say that's your best piece yet, Ione," she said, a slow grin spreading across her lips.

"This is unheard of," Laelle hissed, turning on Ione. "What were you thinking?"

Ione lifted her chin. "That black doesn't suit the *Tarien*. That's what I'm thinking."

Laelle backhanded her hard, but when she went for a second strike, I caught her wrist, holding it firmly.

"Don't do that again," I warned. "She's done this with my permission."

Laelle glared at me. "Your permission doesn't matter here, *Tarien*. It's outside protocol. Ione knows this."

"As a matter of fact," Mehrean interjected, "it's not. No

protocol states an *araith* should be black. It's just what everyone has been going with."

Laelle narrowed her eyes at Mehrean while attempting to free her wrist from my grasp—I held on for good measure. Ione cupped her cheek with one hand, staring wide-eyed at her leader. Around us, murmurs rose from the other *Haniya* who didn't know what we were discussing.

"It should be clear by now I care little about your precious protocol," I said. "It's my body. I decide what is done to it."

Technically, that wasn't entirely true, the scars Eamryel left on me testimony of that fact, but in this case, I had a choice. Besides, it wasn't as if I could change it now. Laelle turned a dark shade of red before exhaling deeply and regaining her composure.

"Very well," she said through clenched teeth. "It is what it is. Your mother might have a thing or two to say about it though."

I shrugged. "Not your problem, is it?"

The moment I let go of her wrist, she pulled it back angrily and turned to the crowd, a fake smile on her lips. She thanked every single one of them by name for being here and witnessing the event before sending them on their way. When she turned to us, I was sure she'd fly off the handle again, but instead she stalked off, shoulders straight, chin lifted, lips pressed together.

"That went better than expected," Mehrean said, her eyes still on Laelle.

I laughed under my breath. "You enjoy antagonising her, don't you?"

"I see you didn't object to the idea either."

"Fair point," I grinned before looking at Ione. "Are you all right?"

Ione nodded. "I'm fine. I expected her to do something like this."

"Does she always do this when things don't go her way?"

Neither of the women spoke, but the looks on their faces told me more than words could have expressed.

Shaking my head, I slipped to my feet, grimacing at the sharp pain shooting through my foot.

"Tomorrow will be in my hut, *Tarien*. Right after breakfast." Ione was gathering her supplies. "I'm sure Mehrean can show you where it is. We'll go for as long as you can handle it."

"I'll be there."

EVERY DAY SINCE THAT DAY, I spent my time with Ione to get my *araîth* finished, lying on my side or stomach for hours on end trying not to move a muscle as she tapped away steadily. My stamina was still enough to go on for several hours, unless she was working on a particularly nasty spot like my hip. During these days, we barely saw anyone, which worked well for the both of us.

From time to time, Mehrean came by to see how things were going, and even Laelle made appearances to check on Ione's progress. She never stayed longer than a few minutes and never spoke a word to either of us. The only way we knew if something was wrong or not was when she either grunted—or didn't.

The woman had issues.

One day when she came by, and Ione was working on my ribs, Laelle seemed to be in an even fouler mood than usual, and she made sure we knew.

"If I *ever* catch you doing something like this again," she hissed to Ione, "I'll throw you out."

Ione had merely nodded, staring at her feet. The frailty I'd seen in her the first day we met was back, and I realised it wasn't frailty exactly, but self-preservation. Laelle didn't do much more than glower at her, pulling herself up to her full height, and I couldn't help but wonder why she lashed out like this. If Mother would abuse her power like that, she'd be dethroned within a matter of hours.

Over the course of the next few days, during times like breakfast and dinner when we were cooped up in the dining hall with everyone else, I made a habit out of studying Laelle and her interactions with others. On the surface, she appeared nice, greeting everyone and talking to them briefly, but the tiniest details of her body language and facial expressions betrayed when she was at odds with someone. Her smile would never reach her eyes and her entire posture was rigid. It was usually the much younger women she did this with.

As for the *Haniya* around her own age, I guessed the ones she grew up with, she was more agreeable. Whenever she touched them on the arm or shoulder, it was genuine, and I could tell most of these women responded to her in kind. Only a few of them gave her the cold shoulder in much the same fashion she did to almost everyone else.

Mehrean was the only person she seemed to love and hate simultaneously. Whenever she entered the room, Laelle scowled, even if it was for just a few seconds, but the look in her eyes was one of love and pride. No matter where Mehr went, her eyes always followed her—not outright, but clear enough for someone sitting right next to her.

There was something going on between them I couldn't put my finger on, but when I asked Mehrean about it one night, she just shrugged it off.

"Laelle is a special kind of person. She isn't too bad once you get to know her though."

I huffed. "I've decided not to give it a try."

Mehrean smiled, turning back to hanging laundry to dry. It looked so mundane it was weird watching her do it. I knew for a fact she never did this at the palace. Then again, neither did I.

"I just don't get why she's so upset over the colour," I said, pulling up my knees.

"Probably because nobody asked her permission," Mehr said, turning to me with an impish grin. "But she's forgetting an *araîth* is created and formed by someone like Ione, and not her. Ione has the artistic freedom to create whatever she wants in whichever colour she sees fit—I just made sure Laelle remembered."

My lips lifted in a half-smile. "You're a nasty piece of work when you choose to be."

"I'm just pragmatic."

"Sure, let's call it that."

She stuck out her tongue and turned back to what she was doing. I carefully ran my hand over the side of my leg where the *araîth* was, tracing the abrasions on my still healing skin. Even a blind person could feel what my *araîth* looked like. A part of me desperately wanted to show it to my brother, knowing he wasn't far away, but as much as I hated the rules and traditions, I didn't want to stir the beehive any more than I already had. I doubted Mehrean would forgive me for it.

"Do you think it will upset Mother?" I asked at length.

"No."

I frowned at her. "That came out quickly."

"Because I know your mother will love it."

"Again with the certainty," I said, wrinkling my nose. "What are you, a seer?"

Mehrean snorted. "Hardly, but anyone with a pair of eyes can see she's proud of you no matter how much you rebel against her."

"I must be blind then."

She smiled "Must be."

With a shake of my head, I untangled myself from the bed and added more wood to the fire, watching the flames leap to life and settle for dancing rhythmically to an unheard tune. While staring at their dance, my thoughts drifted off to Tal, guilt flooding me for not having thought of him as much over the past few days. I missed him. I missed his riveting laugh and the twinkle in his eyes when he flashed me his roguish grin, exciting the butterflies in my stomach to a wild flurry every single time.

I missed how he stood behind me, arms folded, features impassive, ready to pounce on anyone who came too close, and I missed our training sessions where he harped on me, pushing me to get better—to be better. Above all, I missed our arguing and the smartass remarks passing between us as if we'd been married for hundreds of years.

"Gods, keep him safe," I murmured under my breath, swallowing the lump in my throat.

The fire roared to life and I couldn't shake the feeling I was being watched. Aside from Mehrean, however, who was now poring over a piece of parchment, there was nobody in the hut. My skin crawled at the thought *they* might have heard and taken note. I snorted at my imagination when I realised I was starting to believe my own hallucinations.

"You're delusional," I muttered to myself, rising to my feet hugging myself.

"What was that?" Mehrean asked, looking up at me.

I shook my head. "It's nothing."

Rolling into bed, I pulled the blankets tight around me and curled up into a foetal position, suddenly too exhausted. According to Ione, she needed two, maybe three days to finish up till where she was allowed. Then, we'd return to the palace where the last lines would be inked onto my face during my *Araithîn*.

Another party I could do without.

ON THE THIRD day after my chat with Mehrean, Ione announced it would be the last part she'd have to do. I could sit down, as she'd be working on my neck up till my jaw. I didn't relish the thought, especially not after she'd warned this would be painful, but at least it was the last part for a while.

"You remind me of Soren," I said as she started.

"Soren?"

I gave her an impish smile. "The palace healer. He's a sadist too."

"I'm not sure that's a compliment."

"It is." I chuckled.

Ione looked amused while she continued tapping the ink into my neck. No matter how hard I tried to block it, the pain was intense, and there were times I had to ask her to stop. It was a back-and-forth game which seemed to last forever, and at some point I was sure she was getting annoyed with me.

"What do you do at the palace all day?" she asked at length.

I wrinkled my nose. "Getting bored if I'm not careful, so I do combat training, physical exercise, attend mandatory classes, or explore the city, much to everyone's annoyance."

"Why combat training?"

"Because the idea of a woman not being able to fight is outdated and stupid," I replied. "We're just as good as men are, and should be allowed to defend ourselves."

Ione smiled softly. "Aren't you ever afraid of getting hurt?"

"I wasn't," I replied.

But I'm not so sure now.

The thought scared me more than I liked, and swallowing hard, I pushed it to the back of my mind. Fear was what would get me killed if I wasn't careful.

"What kind of combat?"

I glanced at her from the corner of my eyes. "Anything they're willing to teach me."

"They?"

She sounded genuinely interested, which rather surprised me. We'd had a lot of conversations over the past three weeks, but never any as personal as the one we were having now. Most of the times, both of us had been quiet and focused.

It occurred to me she was doing it on purpose.

"My brothers, Evan and Haerlyon," I replied. "And my *Arathrien*... or, who's left of it."

She nodded softly. "I heard what befell two of them. I'm very sorry for your loss."

"So am I."

We fell silent, and as if on cue, the pain intensified. A loud growl escaped my lips as she tapped into a particularly painful spot an inch from my ear. She didn't apologise. Ione never did, and I admired her for it.

"Mehrean told me you are good at fighting," Ione said after a while, trying to divert my thoughts from what was happening.

"Not as good as Tal or my brothers though."

"Who's Tal?"

I was silent for a while, wondering how to explain Talnovar to her. Not only was he a childhood friend, and *Anahràn* of my guard, he was so much more than that. And yet, there were no real words to describe the bond between us—lover or partner didn't even begin to define him.

"He's my *Anahràn*."

It would have to do.

"Who was the handsome man you said goodbye to when you came here?"

I chuckled softly. "That would be Haerlyon, my brother."

"You don't look alike."

"He takes after father," I replied. "Just like Evan. I take after Mother, or so I've been told."

Ione looked amused. "She's a rebel too?"

"Oh, no." I chuckled softly. "In that regard, I take after my father. He was a bit of a free spirit."

"You must feel penned up inside the palace."

"You have no idea."

Ione was silent for a moment before she spoke, her voice barely audible when she did. "I used to be like you until I lost everything I had. My only choice was to come back here."

"What happened?"

She stopped, and looking at her, I realised she was trembling. Collecting herself with a deep sigh, she tilted my head and continued.

"My husband was killed in a raid a few years ago," she said, "along with our infant daughter. Before I could properly track the bastards down and kill them, Mehrean had gathered me and took me here."

I swallowed hard. "That's… I'm sorry."

"It's okay," she whispered.

From the corner of my eye I saw her dashing away the tears, before she continued her merciless tapping. She was rougher this time, but I bit through it. This pain was nothing compared to what she had to be feeling.

"What was her name?" I asked carefully.

Ione stopped again, a ghost of a smile on her lips. "Avyanna."

"That's a beautiful name."

"She was a beautiful girl," she said, smiling at the memory, "with hair the colour of liquid silver, and wide, adoring eyes the colour of heather in summer. She used to have a smile for everyone, no matter who it was."

The love in her voice nestled so deep within me, I felt tears rolling down my cheeks. Since Ione was still happily tapping under my jaw, I couldn't wipe them away.

"I wish I could've met her."

"So do I."

The rest of the session went by in silence, the only sound in the entire hut us breathing and the tapping of Ione's instruments.

As Ione finished up, shouting reached our hut. Ione froze immediately, eyes going wide. I shot up fully alert, instinctively placing Ione behind me, listening where the noise was coming from. It was hard to tell as the sounds seemed to come from all around us, echoing off the walls, which could only mean one thing—it came from everywhere.

"I need to go," I said, looking around the hut for something that could function as a weapon.

"Please stay," Ione whispered in a strangled voice. "Don't go. You don't know what's out there."

"Which is exactly why I have to go."

Her eyes were as wide as saucers, and I assumed an old fear was resurfacing. Was this what had happened to her husband?

"I'll be back, I promise."

"So did he," she said in a tremulous voice. "Don't make promises you can't keep, *Tarien*."

I gave her a wry smile. "What else will you have me say? It's my duty to go."

As she seemed to make up her mind, face going blank, she turned away from me and walked over to her bed. She pulled up the mattress, leaned over to reach inside the bedstead, and pulled out a sword, looking at it longingly.

"At least go out armed."

I took the sword from her, weighing it in my hand. It was heavier than I was used to, but it had to do.

"Hide somewhere they cannot find you. Don't come out until you are absolutely sure they're gone. Whatever happens, don't come out before. If…"—I swallowed hard—"If anything happens to me, go to Mehrean, or if she… if she didn't make it either, find Haerlyon, or any of my men. Tell them to bring you to the palace. Once there, tell Talnovar what happened, or find Evanyan. They'll help you. Just tell them I sent you."

Ione wrapped her arms tight around herself, the frail

appearance back once more. Perhaps it wasn't even self-preservation, but just plain, old fear.

I felt for her.

"*Tarien?*" she whispered as I made my way to the door.

I turned back to her.

"Be safe."

"I'll try," I replied grimly.

CHAPTER 24

*D*usk was already setting on the valley, turning the sky a beautiful gold set off with scarlet streaks like a fire at night. Shouting assaulted me from all directions the moment I stepped outside, and in the distance smoke was billowing—something was on fire. Out here, on the outskirts of the village, nothing was happening at all, but as I approached the road towards the dining hall, the realisation of what was happening dawned on me.

Hanyarah was under attack.

Shouting and the sound of fighting grew in intensity the closer I moved to the square—the clang of metal on metal echoing off the cavern walls adding their dissonance, sounding as if an army of thousands had arrived while in reality it may be only dozens. As I rounded a corner, a pair of feet with one slipper on and the other lying forgotten to the side caught my attention. Dull eyes stared up at the night sky, a dark substance staining the *Haniya's* otherwise immaculate white robe. I'd seen her around, but never caught her name.

I knelt next to her, and closed her eyes, trying not to gag at the invasive scent surrounding her. Fury rose inside of me at the thought of people intruding this sacred place, desecrating it, and killing its inhabitants. And for what? Rising to my feet, I settled the sword firmly in my hand and stalked closer to the sounds.

I wasn't prepared for what I saw.

Bodies littered the ground and were trampled by a tangle of legs as if they were no more than the dirt beneath the soles of their boots. The horizon was ablaze, casting eerie shadows on the valley walls. My gaze swept over the scene in frantic confusion, unable to settle on anything for long.

A splash of purple amidst the pale, broken limbs ahead of me caught my attention, sending my heart into a frenzy, pumping adrenaline through my body. Focused on what lay ahead, I made my way through the battlefield where I registered men fighting, some of whom looked familiar, while others did not.

Why were they fighting each other?

I was barely in time to parry a sword blow. The sudden impact registered as it sang throughout my body, eliciting a howl of pain as my shoulder locked in the progress of blocking it. My eyes settled on a young man, who I realised couldn't be more than a teen. Although I had deflected his strike and ripped the sword out of his hand with a well-aimed hit, I realised I couldn't fight—I couldn't defend myself. Wide, doe-like eyes regarded me in increasing fear, waiting for an attack I knew wouldn't come.

"Run, before I change my mind," I hissed, eyes focused on the next.

The splash of purple turned out to be Laelle. Someone had cut her throat professionally, starting at one ear, and over to the other in one fluid motion, reminding me of how Elara had died. Her violet eyes had lost all emotion, staring dully up at a sky she'd never see again. A part of me felt sorry for her, but I wasn't sad to see a traitor go. If I were to believe Xaresh's notes, she'd played a part in her own demise, but while she'd had it coming, none of these women did.

In the corner of my eyes I caught another man charging me with his sword raised above his head. What a stupid thing to do —everyone knew it'd leave you exposed. Keeping my sword low, I sidestepped, ducked, and ran my sword through his midriff. The smell of blood permeated my senses as I pulled back my blade and a deep shudder went through me—nobody had ever told me it would feel so soft and squishy. I wiped the sword on my trousers while watching the body crumple to the ground dispassionately.

He deserved it.

It scared me how little I'd felt taking his life. A shout from my left startled me in time to dodge a well-directed blow at my head. I avoided a few more before I got a stab in, grimacing as pain lanced through my arm. The man grunted and fell over, but I wasn't sure I'd killed him. My eyes settled on a mop of white hair and an impish grin seconds before he collected me into a bear hug.

"Haer!"

He nuzzled my hair, placing a kiss on the top of my head. "I was afraid they'd already gotten to you."

"I just entered this hellhole," I replied. "What's going on?"

"No idea. They arrived with the setting of the sun and went on a full rampage. Huts from here to the entrance have been set ablaze, and they had killed women at every turn before we got here. They were tearing the place down. We need to get out of here Shal, there are too many of them."

I shook my head. "We can't abandon them."

"We might have to."

"No."

Haerlyon growled under his breath, staring at me thin-lipped while running both hands through his hair. "Now is not the time to exercise your stubbornness."

"I'm not," I said, "but think about it. There's only one way in, so only one way out, and you can bet your ass they'll have the entrance covered. We wouldn't even get anywhere."

Haerlyon was about to say something when he suddenly pushed me behind him, deflecting a strike aimed for my back. Several seconds later, a small group of enemies surrounded us. I gritted my teeth and adopted a fighting stance, biting away the fierce pain in my shoulder. It wouldn't be pretty, but I had to try. Once the mayhem started, we were parrying strikes from every direction, and more than once Haer covered my back. Between him and Tal's excessive training habits, I remained alive.

For now.

"We can't win this," Haerlyon breathed out heavily. "We have to find a way out."

"We need to get word to the palace," I said.

Haerlyon frowned, gasping for air. "How?"

"I don't know."

More men were coming our way, so we stood back to back, swords at the ready. Not in my wildest dreams had I ever imagined I'd be fighting alongside my brother, nor had I thought it would be this exhausting. Every part of my body was trembling —the sword in my hands grew heavier by the minute, and each parry, each strike jarred me until I felt certain all my bones had turned liquid.

It would be a matter of minutes before someone got me.

Somewhere during the fight, Haerlyon and I had split up. I could see white hair in the onslaught, meaning he was still standing, still fighting, but he was too far for me to reach him, and there were still more charging me. Pushing all thoughts aside, I prepared myself for a final stand-off. This was all or nothing.

I took down four of them on sheer will before a fifth ran his blade across my ribcage. Time slowed down as pain bloomed from my side into my chest and back—a fiery, stinging sensation taking control of my entire being. My sword slipped from my numb fingers and clattered to the ground which was rising to meet me. I dropped to my knees, gasping for air. When I looked up, a man—an Ilvannian no less—pointed his weapon at my throat, ready to run me through. My eyes settled on a pair of sketchy marigold ones, watching me unblinking like an owl. My hand found its way to my side, and upon bringing it back, I noticed it was covered in blood.

Glad it's not the side of my Araith.

I chuckled at the thought, surprised at the notion I could worry about something so trivial while my life hung in the balance. As my opponent pulled his arm back to strike, somebody else did the courtesy of adding a sword to his chest. My eyes widened when he crumpled into a heap at my feet as the weapon was pulled back, revealing a blood-covered, grim-looking Tal.

I could only stare, believing him to be a hallucination—a mirage my mind conjured up as I lay dying.

Dark, stormy eyes changed to warm and caring the moment his gaze fell on me. My expression must have alerted him, because he dropped to his knees in front of me, concern written all over his face.

"What's wrong?"

"How are you here?" I whispered in disbelief.

His eyes ran over me to assess the damage and settled on my side, turning the look on his face dark. Before I knew, he'd picked me up in his arms and carried me away.

"Where are you taking me?"

"Soren," he replied, looking at me.

The look in his eyes harboured guilt above all, but there was more, although I couldn't place my finger on it.

"How did you know to be here?"

Tal's jaw clenched as if remembering something unpleasant. "Rurin told me there would be an attack on this place."

"But he's the enemy," I blurted, confusion settling in. "What are you talking about?"

Whether or not I liked it, I had to come clean, so I told him about the piece of paper I'd found in Xaresh's room and the names on there, including Rurin's. Tal's mood darkened the more I told him, and at some point I was sure he'd drop me. Instead, he hoisted me up further, his muscles bunching and tensing beneath me.

Why was I paying attention to this now?

"Why haven't you told me before?"

I gave him a deadpan stare. "Between Xaresh's and Elara's death, your injuries, their burial and my leaving, we haven't exactly had much time to talk, did we?"

He scowled. "I suppose. It explains why Rurin knew."

"It doesn't explain why he's on the list though," I muttered.

Nohro, the pain was getting worse by the minute.

"How much longer?" I murmured, trying hard to ignore the severe itch.

"We're here," Tal said, jaw tight, the look on his face one of murder.

I was about to ask what was wrong when an all too familiar voice sounded up.

"How kind of you to bring her, *Anahràn*," Yllinar said. "Now, if you could please hand her over?"

Tal tensed beneath me. "Over my dead body."

He placed me on my feet and stepped in front of me— shielding me. I wrapped my good arm around him, resting my head against his back to keep from falling over.

"I was afraid that would be the case," Yllinar said, "so I came prepared."

My eyes narrowed, and I perked up, taking a careful step around Tal who placed his hand on the dagger on his back, ready to pounce. With a wave of his hand, Yllinar summoned a group of men, and my heart sank when I saw they were holding both my brothers and Soren captive.

"Son of a—," I muttered. "What do you want, Yllinar?"

His lip twitched up. "You."

"And if you get me, will you let them go?"

"You have my word."

Haerlyon jumped at those words with a howl and was pulled back immediately. He fell to the ground with a grunt and was forced back on his knees by the man behind him holding a dagger to his throat. Evan's gaze fixed onto mine, stoic as ever, a faint smile on his lips as he inclined his head—he understood what I had to do.

It's our duty.

I swallowed hard and nodded, my eyes drifting over to Soren, who looked the most impassive of all. In fact, I could swear he looked a little annoyed. Tal faced me, eyes wide, and for the first time in my life I saw fear in them.

"You cannot do this," he whispered for my ears alone. "You don't know if he'll keep his promise."

I bit my lip. "I don't see how I have a choice. If I don't do this, he'll kill all of you."

"And who's to say he won't do that anyway after you're gone?"

"I don't know," I whispered, looking down. "But I have to risk it."

Tal cupped my face in his hands, his eyes searching mine. My chest constricted, and my breath hitched as my eyes searched his face, taking all of him in. We had no way of knowing if Yllinar would keep his word, but I had to do this to give them a chance. Any chance. Tal swallowed hard, fisted his hand into my hair and kissed me hard. My body melted into his as he pulled me closer and for a moment the world ceased to exist.

Pulling back was the hardest thing either of us had ever had to do.

I stepped around him while clutching my side, trying to keep to my feet. Risking a glance down, I realised my shirt had turned a deep, rusty red, and it was sticking to the injury.

"I'll come," I said, squaring my shoulders. Gods, that hurt, "if you let them go first."

With a simple nod from Yllinar, they released my brothers and Soren, who dashed over, and carefully lifted my shirt to see the damage. The curse under his breath told me it wasn't good.

"She needs help."

Yllinar regarded Soren levelly. "All right. You'll come too."

"Fine."

Soren turned back and started fussing over me, muttering something about me and sharp objects. It made me chuckle and wince at the same time as he pulled some fabric away from the injury.

"That hurts," I muttered under my breath.

"That's what weapons do."

I glared at him. Yllinar coughed.

"If the two of you are quite done. It's time for us to leave."

Everything happened fast from the moment he spoke those words. At the same time as he grabbed my arm and pulled me along, two men grabbed Tal, pinning his arms behind his back. I screamed. He yelled and cursed, trying to fight them off—they were stronger. Yllinar pulled me back against him as I tried to break free, hauling me away bodily. Both my brothers and Soren had weapons drawn against them to keep them from helping Tal.

A third man stepped forward, and without even stopping, plunged a sword into Tal's abdomen.

A banshee wail tore from my lips, and I jerked even harder at my restraints, but an uninjured Yllinar was stronger. Surprise washed over Tal's features, followed by a painful grimace, and when the men released him, he fell to his knees, breathing hard.

"Eamryel told me to give you his regards," Yllinar said, watching Tal with contempt.

Without sparing him another glance, Yllinar propelled me forward while I kicked and screamed for him to let me go. He ordered his men to bring Soren, but to free my brothers. I kept my eyes trained on them for as long as I could, and saw them run over to Tal, trying to staunch the wound. I knew from Soren's teachings he'd die if he didn't get any help soon."Stop squirming," Yllinar growled, "or I'll send my men back to kill your brothers too."

My heart sank. "You promised. You promised you wouldn't hurt them!"

"I promised not to hurt your brothers," he said. "I never mentioned the Imradien boy."

"Let Soren go," I whispered. "Let Soren tend to him, please? I'll come with you willingly, causing no trouble. I'll behave."

Yllinar smirked. "As tempting as that may sound, *Tarien*, your healer is right. You need help."

"So does he!"

"I'm afraid those in charge have a different opinion."

I started struggling again to get free, kicking and screaming for Yllinar to let go of me, but the more I did so, the weaker I became, and I wasn't sure whether it was from exhaustion, loss of blood or grief. Tal and my brothers were out of sight by now, and the Gods only knew what happened next. Tears rolled down my cheeks at the realisation I might never learn what befell them—him.

For all I knew, he was dead already.

Yllinar halted at the clearing, barking orders to his men while dropping me unceremoniously to the ground. The sudden impact blew stars into my vision and had me gasping for air.

Soren was at my side a second later, rolling me carefully on my back.

"One day your stubbornness will kill you," he muttered.

"I wish it killed me now."

He gave me a sympathetic glare before turning to the injury. It hadn't looked good the first time judging by how he'd responded, but the way he went completely quiet now told me it was even worse.

"I'll need my equipment if I want to have any chance of saving her," he said.

Yllinar looked down at us with a frown. "I'll have someone go get it."

Soren gave instructions and true to his word, Yllinar sent a man running to fetch. In the meantime, Soren set to pulling the fabric of my shirt from the wound which was nowhere near comfortable.

"Can you get onto your side?"

I nodded softly, and with a bit of help, managed to do so.

"How bad is it?" I asked softly.

"Bad."

"On a scale of one to ten?"

He grimaced. "At least a twelve."

"Your counting is off," I muttered and coughed. "Will you be able to heal it?"

"If that *khirr* hurries up."

We shared a smile, but the worried look in his eyes told me he had no way of knowing if he could fix this. In all truth, I wasn't sure if I wanted him to. Whatever Yllinar and Azra were up to, going through it dead sounded much more preferable right now. They could have the throne and Ilvanna for all I cared—it wasn't worth the trouble it was causing.

I never pegged you as a quitter.

Tears welled up in my eyes at the memory of Tal's words during one of our training sessions. It felt like a lifetime ago

409

when he had said them, and I had scoffed at him then, but now, they were all that kept me from just lying down and giving in.

The moment someone gives up is the moment I cannot save them anymore.

Soren had told me one day, when I was helping him out in the infirmary after Evan and Tal had been brought in, that they'd survived mostly on willpower. Both of their injuries had been severe enough to kill them, but neither had given in. They'd fought with everything they had to come back.

I had to believe Tal was doing the same thing right now.

I had to do it too.

"Get her up." Yllinar's voice cut through my reverie. "Our departure is long overdue."

Soren rose to his feet. "We cannot move her. It'll kill her."

Yllinar turned on him so fast I was sure he'd hit him. He didn't, and I realised he had a better check on his temper than his son did.

"Get her to her feet," he hissed. "Now."

Soren folded his arms in front of him, jaw set firmly.

"Get me to my feet," I whispered, focusing on Soren. "I'll not be at his mercy on my back."

He looked down at me and shook his head. "Moving you might kill you."

"They'll not get me that easily," I replied, attempting a reassuring smile. "I refuse to bow down to them."

Soren looked at me with pity a moment longer, relented with a deep sigh and helped me to my feet. I could barely stand on my own, but I had to try. For my family. For my people.

I couldn't die.

Not yet.

"At least let me ride with her." Soren turned back to Yllinar. "If you are keen on keeping her alive that is. I can at least check her vitals while we're on the road."

From the look on Yllinar's face, I could tell he wasn't amused with the idea, but at least he was smart enough to understand the merit in Soren's argument.

"Ride off, and I'll make sure you regret that decision."

We both nodded.

THE PARTY LEAVING Hanyarah was small—smaller than the one I had entered with, and with a pang of guilt, I realised I had no idea what had happened to any of them during the fight. In fact, I hardly knew anything of what had happened if I was being honest. Not that it mattered. All I had to focus on was staying in the saddle, and staying alive, but both those challenges were harder than I had expected when I decided not to give up.

"Where are you taking us?"

My voice was feeble, lacking strength and confidence, and I hated hearing it, let alone feeling like it. Yllinar looked at me, his expression unreadable.

"You'll see."

"At least let us know how far the ride will be," Soren said. "She won't survive more than a few hours without rest, if that."

Yllinar smirked. "Well, do the best you can, *healer.*"

"I don't perform miracles."

"Looks like now is as good a time as any to get started on that," he replied with a smirk. "If she dies, you die."

Soren tensed behind me, but said no more. He tightened an arm around me to make sure I remained seated.

"All right, you heard the man," he murmured for my ears alone. "So you've got to help me out here a bit, *Tarien.*"

"How?"

"Don't die on me."

I let out a short bark of a laugh which turned into a coughing fit and a yelp of pain.

He snorted behind me. "That's not the way to go about it."

411

"Then don't make me laugh."

We fell silent. I was getting more tired by the minute, and as much as I loved to oblige Soren and not die, I wasn't entirely sure I could keep that promise. More and more I caught myself nodding off, waking up only because Soren either poked or pinched me, followed by a mutter to stay awake. Whatever I would do, falling asleep wasn't allowed, so I tried to focus on the terrain around us changing slowly.

The rolling hills of Ilvanna made way for flat land and pastures as far as the eye could see. Cottages, black against the fading golden sunset dotted the sky line haphazardly. The road we were on was well-tended, better than the ones we had in Ilvanna, and I realised we'd left our country.

This had to be Therondia.

With the light fading, it was easy to spot the bright-lit encampment in the distance, and I realised Yllinar had to be taking us there. Soren sighed in relief.

"Almost there," he murmured. "Do you think you can hold on?"

"I'll try."

Night had fallen when we arrived at the encampment, and by then I was barely hanging on. The moment Soren dismounted, I felt myself slip off the saddle, but where I had expected to fall to the ground, someone caught me. I opened my eyes to a crack, and when I did, my heart stopped as a pair of steely grey eyes fixed on mine. My mind caught up too late to the implications of what I'd seen as my body gave in to its injuries.

It was too much.

EPILOGUE

*W*hen I regained consciousness, the pain in my ribs had subsided to a dull ache, but moving was painful. My throat was parched and my stomach was protesting loudly. Although I remembered everything that happened at *Hanyarah*, everything after was a blur, except the eyes staring back at me after I slid from Orion's back.

I was certain about one thing though—I was a prisoner, and my future had become a possibility rather than an inevitability. As I tried to sit up, my head reeled, sending me back to the straw mattress I was on. The impact on my back and ribs drew out a grunt.

"Stay down for a bit longer."

Soren's voice drew my attention to the corner of the tent where he was sitting, arms wrapped around his knees, chin resting on them while looking quite miserable. It was hard to distinguish in the pale light filtering through the tent, but the shadows under his right eye looked more than just lack of sleep.

"What happened?" I croaked.

"Do you want the long or the short version?"

"Any version," I muttered, scowling at him.

"After you blacked out, they gave me the time and tools to patch you up." He slurred a little and spoke as if it hurt him. "After I finished, Yllinar had a go at me for taking so long. I think he broke a rib, and my eye socket, and I can't feel my lips."

"I'll kill him," I growled. "Mark my words."

"Don't, *Tarien*." He sounded tired, no exhausted. "We're in no position to make any demands, and don't forget your brothers, or your mother. None of them are safe either."

"How do you know?"

"Because I told him, with the instruction to make your predicament very clear to you."

The voice belonged to the assassin, but the person stepping inside couldn't be him—the same one who caught me as I fell off my horse. With my mouth hanging open, I stared as Grayden ducked into the tent, dressed in dark armour bearing the royal insignia of Therondia.

"You?!"

"It's a pleasure to meet you officially, *Tarien*," Grayden said, bowing deeply. "I'm afraid I have to apologise for misleading you."

I sprang to my feet and charged him, negligent of the injury on my ribs or the searing pain lancing through my side. My sudden speed surprised Grayden enough to take him down to the ground, but he was stronger than I was and had me pinned underneath him in a matter of seconds.

"As much as I love to throw down with a woman," he grunted, wiping blood from his lip, "now is not the best time. If you behave, I promise it won't be all bad. If you don't behave…"

His eyes swept over Soren in such a tell-tale way I knew exactly what he meant. Sitting back on his heels, he let go off my wrists, allowing me to return to the bed of straw.

"Your threats are getting old."

"So is your erratic behaviour," he replied. "You should learn some restraint."

I folded my arms, ignoring the fiery ache in my side.

"Did you enjoy killing them?"

He tilted his head, a slight frown creasing his brow. "No."

"Why did you do it?"

"I have my reasons."

Grayden turned away and touched his lip, scowling as his fingers came back bloodied. I was glad to know I had hurt him enough for it to be an inconvenience.

"Who are you really?" I asked, my head slightly tilted.

"Why does it sound like you're interrogating me?"

I shrugged. "Because you owe me some answers at least."

"Someone ought to leash that tongue of yours," he said with a charming smile, "although I have to say, I kind of like your wit."

"Don't get used to it."

Grayden turned back to me, hooking his hands in the collar of his armour—to take the strain from his shoulders, I knew. The look on his face was one of quiet contemplation as he regarded me, but instead of replying, he turned away, shaking his head.

"Food and drink will be brought soon. Take it. We will leave first thing tomorrow."

"Where are you taking me?"

He turned back with a faint smile. "Somewhere they won't be able to find you."

"Thanks for the specifics."

The moment he left the tent, I lay back with a loud grunt, pulling up my shirt. Soren was at my side almost immediately, checking the injury.

"He's not wrong in you having to learn restraint," he muttered. "You keep undoing my work."

"He killed Xaresh and Elara."

Soren glanced up at me. "I gathered as much. Why did you attack him?"

"Because it felt like the right thing to do."

"I swear, you should have been born a man." He sighed, rubbing his cheek. "It would've suited your personality better."

I smirked. "Perhaps, though I really see no problem with it. I can be ladylike, in lady-like circumstances."

"No, you can't."

"Thanks for the vote of confidence."

His lip quirked up in a half-smile, but he didn't reply. Instead, he examined the stitches on my ribs. None of them had torn, but he did tell me to rest while I still could. While I hated lying down and being vulnerable, I realised he was right. If Grayden intended on taking me on another journey, I'd need all the strength I could get.

"You need to escape," I said at length. "He knows you might warn the others if he sets you free."

"If I stay, I might learn where exactly he's taking you. Once I know that, I can try to escape."

I stared at him. "You're a fool."

"Just taking a page from your book. Besides, from the looks of it, they can do with a healer."

"So can our men and women."

Soren's lips curled up in a gentle smile. "They have healers, *Tarien*. And I know how to hold my own."

I just glared at him instead. There was a rustle at the entrance of the tent, and a second later, a scruffy-looking soldier stepped in, carrying a tray with two bowls and two tankards. He dropped it unceremoniously to the ground, spilling half the contents of all containers.

"Thanks for nothing," I muttered once he had left, picking up a bowl smelling vaguely of broth.

Soren sniffed at it, pulling a face. "Well, I guess it's better than nothing."

"Bottoms up."

When we finished, we put the plate aside and sat down with

our backs against the straw mattress, legs pulled up. Despite us being prisoners, it felt good having someone with me I trusted.

"Whatever you do, please get word back to my brothers."

Soren nodded. "I will."

Realising something, I yanked my boot off and pulled the piece of parchment from it, handing it over to him.

"It's barely readable by now, but keep it safe, and give it to Evan or Tal should you ever come back. If not, burn it."

"What is it?"

I bit my lip as I looked at him. Even now I wanted to protect everyone, but I realised I was in no position to do so and Soren was the only one I had. I leaned in and whispered in his ear, not trusting my voice to not carry out of the tent. He paled significantly at my words.

"Are you sure?" he whispered.

I merely nodded. "Hide it well."

EARLY NEXT MORNING, Grayden entered the tent with no announcement, tossing a leather coat and a woollen jacket in my general direction. Soren was still asleep next to me, looking peaceful. I couldn't bear waking him up. Picking up the materials, I followed Grayden outside with a limp—the cold of the night had seeped into my leg, triggering the old injury.

I sure hoped he wouldn't bring me somewhere it was always cold.

Shrugging into the coat and cloak, I tried to keep up, glancing at my surroundings from under my lashes. Fog hung over the damp fields like a winter cloak, the scent of rain heavy in the air, although I couldn't remember it raining last night.

"It'll be a stiff ride," Grayden said as we arrived at the pasture where the horses were hobbling quietly. "Tell me when you need a rest."

"Since when do you care?"

He didn't respond to that as he helped me mount Orion. In the dark of night, it was hard to make out my surroundings, but I remembered the terrain being flat—flatter than what I was used to. There had been no hills, no plateaus, just endless stretches of land as far as the eye could see. This was Therondia, and it hadn't impressed me—nor had their leader.

Once we cleared the encampment, Grayden set off into a gallop, looking back to see if I followed. With Soren still his prisoner, and me not wanting to risk his life on a whim, hoping to find my way home, I decided showing restraint was in my best interest. Besides, I could hear hoof beats following us at a distance, which had me wondering.

I urged Orion on so I'd be riding side by side to Grayden, waiting until we went back to a trot to speak.

"Why didn't you just kill me? You've had several chances already. Why risk being discovered?"

Grayden glanced at me, voice strained when he spoke. "Despite popular belief, *Tarien*, I do not enjoy killing people."

"Tell Xaresh and Elara that."

He looked away, but not before I saw the pain in his eyes. When next he spoke, his voice was filled with anger.

"It's easy for you to talk, isn't it? Growing up in a safe sheltered life where everybody dances to your tunes, doing your every bidding at every whim at every moment of the day."

"You're welcome to trade."

He glared at me. "Have you ever known any hardship in your life?"

I remained silent, my thoughts drifting back to the day they had found father in the stables, choked on his own blood. Although I hadn't seen it, I had heard people talk about it often enough to have made a mental picture, and it wasn't pretty.

"You look like you're rather well off too," I replied. "Pot and kettle anyone?"

Grayden's lips thinned. "Stop talking as if you know anything about me."

"Then don't assume you know anything about me," I retorted. "It's easy to judge a book by its cover, so if you don't, I won't."

As of that moment, neither of us spoke again, at least not until I needed a rest. Even though it was brief, it was enough for the pain in my side to settle a bit. Mounting was still a challenge, but Grayden helped me out without comment, and despite the fact he could have been rough about it, he wasn't.

He was an enigma.

On the one hand, he was a cold-blooded killer with enough blood on his hands to haunt him three lifetimes, on the other hand, he was the kind and gentle person I'd met at the gates so long ago. At times, the man I'd spoken for surfaced, but was quickly buried again. It was easy to judge a book by its cover indeed, and maybe I was judging him too harshly. Then again, he had admitted to killing Elara and Xaresh, and he had been remorseless about it while doing it—not even when we talked about it had he shown any form of guilt. For someone telling me he didn't relish killing, he was calm about it.

WE ARRIVED at the coast after nightfall and fear clutched at my heart. Grayden had said he'd take me somewhere they couldn't find me, but surely he wouldn't take me overseas. The moment I dismounted, he roped my wrists together none too gently, and the cold, calculated look was back on his face.

"Let's go."

Without waiting for me, he pulled me along. I stumbled forward, barely able to catch myself, grimacing at the painful stitch in my side. I had always prided myself on not being afraid easily, but I feared what was coming next. If Grayden planned on doing what could be the only logical conclusion, my chances of ever getting home dwindled to non-existent in a matter of seconds.

Don't fear the unknown.

Sure. Don't fear what you didn't know. That was the best advice my shell-shocked brain could come up with right now? Shaking my head, I took step by careful step as not to trip over the uneven terrain. The farther we went, the worse it got. It was the moment we stepped into loose sand that I tripped and Grayden pulled me back up by my wrists.

"You'd better find your sea-legs *Tarien*," Grayden said, looking at me. "You will need them."

My heart dropped at his words.

"You can't do this," I whispered, convinced this was all a bad nightmare.

He looked at me, and for a moment I could see the same pain as the night before. It made little sense though.

"I can, and I will."

His voice sounded detached and from far-away, while my brain mulled over what he'd just said. This couldn't be happening—it just couldn't be.

"That's her?" A gruff voice startled me from my thoughts.

As Grayden pulled me up short, I stumbled and fell to my knees, too shocked to be embarrassed about the situation. Looking up, I saw an outline of a man in the moonlight, but I couldn't make out anything else.

"Ten gold," Grayden said, "as was the deal."

The other man huffed. "She'd better be worth it, or I'll come back and skin that pretty face of yours."

"Trust me, she'll sell for much more on the Khyrinthan market."

BOOK TWO EXCERPT

DANCE OF DESPAIR
Chapter One
Talnovar

Accompanied by a thousand voices raised in an eerie lament, flames danced against the dark backdrop of the night, licking up the pyre in their hungry conquest for more. As the haunting melody reached a crescendo, goose bumps rippled across my arms and slithered down my back, leaving in its wake a feeling of awe first and desolation second. My thoughts were a whirl of whys and ifs chasing each other in an endless loop of despair.

The hollowness established at the top of my head as blood slowly drained from it. A slow buzzing began in my ears, turning into a deep ringing that reverberated inside my skull. A sharp pain pierced my eyes at the same time as a strangling sensation wrapped around my throat. My mouth ran dry, halting a wail of pain on the tip of my tongue. The ache in my chest was to such an extent that it made me want to carve it outwith a blunt knife if I had to. No amount of pain would ever come close to what I was feeling now. Every fibre of my being fought the gut reaction my body had to the undeniable truth in front of my eyes.

No matter how hard I tried, there was no denying the slim chance of survival.

It had been non-existent.

My gaze swept up the burning pyre as it succumbed to the unrelenting craving the flames awarded it. An otherworldly howl pierced the silent night as my mind fought the fire for its ferocity. I was unable to hold it back any longer. The part of me that still struggled against this new reality was at war with the side that wanted to give in to the grief and deal with it on its own terms.

I didn't care much for those terms.

Despite knowing the body on the pyre wasn't Shal's, considering where it had to be instead, was a thought I didn't want to entertain at all. For all we knew, it was at the bottom of the sea —irretrievable—or worse. My legs were no longer capable of holding my weight and they gave way from under me. The grass underneath my hands and knees was wet and instantly returned my thoughts to Shal's demise.

I could only hope she had slipped into death unconsciously.

A hand on my shoulder returned my attention to the present and looking up, I found the *Tari* looking down on me, hard eyes hiding a deeper sadness. Rurin hovered just behind, his gaze never leaving her. Ever since she'd fallen ill months ago, before they had taken Shal, he'd been her silent shadow.

"Rise, *Anahràn*," she said, not unkindly. "Your knees are no place to be on in front of Ilvanna."

I swallowed hard and gritted my teeth.

Ilvanna be damned.

Even so, I rose to my feet, recollecting my emotions till none of them were neither visible nor tangible. Within seconds I returned to the husk of a person I'd become since hearing the news of Shal's death. The *Tari* watched me, her eyes dulled by pain now twinkling with curiousity. They were so much like *hers* my chest constricted painfully, and I looked away. It was a hand on my cheek that returned my gaze to my *Tari*, only to find her standing close and on tiptoe.

She was so much smaller than her daughter. How had I never noticed?

"Your grief for her is admirable, Talnovar," she said, "but don't let it consume you. She wouldn't want that."

"Yeah well," I muttered, tugging at my bracers. "I doubt she wanted to die, yet here we are."

Something flickered in the *Tari's* eyes—something akin to anger, but not quite. Her jaw set in the typical *an Ilvan* manner and pulling back her hand, she straightened herself to her full height. Even though the top of her head barely reached my shoulders, I would never mistake her lack of height for lack of authority.

She had plenty of that.

"Talnovar Imradien." The tone of her voice brooked no argument, which was emphasised by the hands on her hips.

I folded my arms, looking down at her, my anger matching hers. In my peripheral vision, I noticed movement behind me and realised Evanyan had come closer. Between Rurin and him, they could easily wrestle me to the ground if they thought I was a danger to her, but, not in a million years would I consider attacking my *Tari*.

We both exhaled at the same time.

"My apologies," I mumbled, jerking a hand through my hair. "It's just... hard."

"I know."

We needed no more words. Looking up at the pyre revealed it had crumbled entirely. The body had been burnt to ashes. Whoever it had been, their family had been well-compensated by a rite most could only dream of. It sickened me to my core that this was what had to be done to close off a life I couldn't let go off.

"Arayda," Rurin murmured to her, fondness in his voice. "You should get inside. It's getting too cold."

Without waiting for permission, he draped his cloak around her frail shoulders, drowning her in the sheer size of it. Like myself, Rurin was a tall man, although his build was lean rather than muscular. He dwarfed the *Tari* without even trying. A gentle smile ghosted around her lips when she upturned her face to watch him.

"Please excuse me," I said in a strained voice, stepping back for a bow.

Without waiting for her approval, I hightailed it away from the field and back up to the palace, taking the stairs two steps at a time. People jumped aside as I paid no heed to my destination.

I knew exactly where I was going.

The tightness in my chest returned as I ran my fingers across the silk of the last dress she'd ever worn. In the twelve moons since she had been gone, nobody had really bothered tidying up her room. Everyone at the palace had treated her disappearance as a minor nuisance, expecting her to return all backtalk and sarcasm within a matter of weeks. Yet as time passed and there was no sign of her return, rumours had begun to spread—rumours I'd done my best to ignore.

Imagine the shock when Soren returned a little over a moon ago with the news the *Tarien* had perished at sea. At first, I had denied all plausibility of her death, claiming she could've somehow gotten out on a rowboat. Surely, whoever had paid good money for her would have been careful with a prize like that.

That was until stories returned of the terrible storm that had raged the Kyrinthan Gulf and had even made landfall on the Therondian shores. Villages had vanished without a trace people had had no time to escape. Eyewitnesses claimed the wind had blown so hard it had been visible, spinning and churning in an awful maw of destruction, tearing apart everything it came into contact with.

If the news hadn't come from reliable sources in the form of spies, I would not have believed it. As it was, all that was left of her was in this room, scattered about like cheap items, while they'd become priceless antiquities. Without conscious thought, I picked up the dress and brought it to my face, inhaling the faint scent of oranges, vanilla, and wood—her scent.

Even now it stirred emotions I should have kept buried. Father had been right all along—falling in love with her had gotten her killed, while I was supposed to have protected her.

She had died because of me.

A sob caught in the back of my throat in an inarticulate growl. My hands fisted the fabric in an attempt to hold on to what little I had left of her.

It was all I had.

"Hey lover boy. Mother wants to see you."

Haerlyon stood lounging against the doorpost, looking his usual smooth self while chewing on something. To anyone who knew him, it was clear he was anything but himself. His eyes, usually full of mischief, were hard and cold, and the everlasting smile on his face never quite reached them. Upon hearing the news of his sister's death, he hadn't even flinched. In fact, he had looked relieved. Even at her burial today he hadn't bothered showing up.

All that time, he had blamed her for Tiroy's death at *Hanyarah* and now she'd received due payment in his eyes.

I wanted to punch him.

"Coming," I muttered, draping the dress over the back of the chair where I'd found it.

With a last look at her room, I followed Haerlyon into the corridors, keeping a safe distance from him so I wouldn't be tempted to make him trip or walk into a column by accident.

"Why does the *Tari* want to see me at this ungodly hour?" I asked.

Haerlyon shrugged. "Beats me. Ask her. I'm just your average errand boy."

Average my ass.

I decided it was in my best interest not to speak my mind and huffed instead, regarding him quietly.

Not only Tiroy had died that night.

Tari Arayda sat in front of the fire, a cup of tea in her hands, a blanket folded around her small shoulders. She looked up the moment I entered. A smile was on her lips, although that might very well have been the shadows of the fire playing across her features.

"Come." Her voice was soft, feeble. "Sit with me."

It was as much a request as it was a command, so I took the chair next to her, stretching my legs.

"There's tea if you want any," she said at length. "Forgive me for not pouring it for you."

"Nor should you, *Tari*," I replied, my lips quirking up at the corners. "After all, I'm but a servant in your army. A *Tari* has no business waiting upon the likes of me."

She snorted. "You're too much like your father at times."

My brows shot up in surprise until I remembered they were of the same age and had most likely grown up knowing each other.

"Mother used to wish I was more like him," I replied with a shrug, settling back in the chair.

Tari Arayda smiled kindly, a hint of a remembrance in those light mysterious eyes. She'd known my mother too, but where it brought a smile to her face, it only brought misery to mine, adding to the guilt I'd felt since the news of Shalitha's death.

"She was a remarkable woman indeed," the *Tari* murmured.

Pinching the bridge of my nose, I closed my eyes, suddenly exhausted with the world and everyone in it.

"Why did you want to see me, *Tari*?"

She stared at the fire, mysterious eyes suddenly hard, the set of her jaw promising determination if nothing else.

"Tell me truthfully, Talnovar," she began, turning to face me. "Do you believe my daughter is dead?"

I arched a brow. "You've heard the news, *Tari*. She has to be."

"Don't be coy with me, *Anahràn*," she almost growled. "Answer my question."

It required me to dig deeper into my feelings than I honestly cared for right now, but one didn't deny the *Tari* a request unless it was at one's own peril. I was of half a mind to say I thought she was, but deep down inside, in that part where emotions and beliefs are stashed for safekeeping against a cruel world, I knew I didn't quite believe it.

Not until somebody presented me with her body.

"I don't think so," I replied at length.

"Think so," she began, "or know so?"

Rubbing my jaw, I regarded her quietly. Despite her illness, she looked as strong as ever, but I knew it was a lie. Underneath the blanket, she was trembling, and it could hardly be from cold. The room was so stifling hot I regretted not having taken off my leather armour.

"We can't know for sure," I answered with a shrug. "Unless someone goes looking for her."

A smile instantly pulled her lips at the corners, lighting up her entire face, mischievous look included.

"Good, you're catching on."

I stared at her. "I'm not su—"

"I need you to go find my daughter, Tal." *Tari* Arayda spoke softly, glancing around the room as if she were afraid to be overheard.

"Excuse me?"

She rolled her eyes. If it hadn't been for the situation, the gesture would have been comical, knocking several years off of her age.

"I don't believe my daughter perished at sea," Arayda said, her eyes boring into mine. "Call it a gut feeling, or wishful thinking, I don't care. Whatever happened out on sea, Shalitha survived, I just know it, and I need you to find her."

My jaw dropped.

"And how do you propose I do that, *Tari*? We just sent her off with a grand ceremony. If I leave now, people will think I've gone insane."

"Good."

If at all possible, my jaw would have dropped even further. As it was, I could do no more than stare at her and wonder if she'd gone entirely mad. Something on my face made hers relax, and she smiled.

"You're not an idiot, Tal," she said, her voice hoarse. "The madder they think you are, the better."

"Why, *Tari*? Why now?"

The look of compassion and anguish on her face nearly undid me.

"I'm dying, Tal," she whispered, shaking her head softly. "When I do, if Shal has not been reinstated, my sister can lay claim to the throne, and trust me when I tell you that she will."

My blood ran cold at the mention of Azra. There was something about that woman that set my teeth on edge and made me wish I was anywhere but near her.

"Judging by the look on your face, I trust that's a bad idea."

She merely nodded, pressing a kerchief against her face. When she started coughing, I could see blood staining the fabric

428

in her hand, and with each cough it became worse until she was doubled over and wheezing. It shocked me to see her like this.

"*Tari?*"

Gently I helped her sit up to return air to her lungs. Her features were suddenly wan and haggard, and blood stained the corners of her lips.

"You should rest," I murmured, looking at her.

Without preamble, I lifted her in my arms, receiving the second shock in a matter of minutes at how little she weighed. My *Tari* snorted at my insolence but didn't argue the matter.

"Tal," she murmured as I laid her in bed, drawing the sheets over her. "Promise me you'll find her."

I ran a hand through my hair, looking troubled. "How, *Tari?* With Shal gone, and you soon, I am but an army *Anahràn.* Leaving will be seen as deserting."

"Make it look like a desperate man's attempt."

CHARACTERS

House an Ilvan

Arayda	Tari
Azra	Sister to the Tari/disowned *Tarien*
Gaervin	*Husband to Arayda. Deceased*
Shalitha	*Tarien*, daughter of Arayda
Evanyan	Zheràn, first born son of Arayda
Haerlyon	Zheràn, second son of Arayda

House Imradien

Cerindil	Ohzheràn. Father of Talnovar
Talnovar	Son of Cerindil
Leyandra	*Wife to Cerindil. Mother of Talnovar and Varayna*
Varayna	*Daughter of Cerindil; sister of Talnovar. Deceased*

House Arolvyen

Yllinar	Noble. Father of Eamryel, Nathaïr and Caleena
Eamryel	Son of Yllinar
Nathaïr	Daughter of Yllinar
Caleena	Daughter of Yllinar. Half-sister to Nathaïr and Eamryel.

House Lahryen

Fehrean	*Anahràn* in the army. Father to Amaris and Allithaer
Syllahryn	Wife of Fehrean. Mother to Amaris and Allithaer
Amaris	Son of Fehrean

Allithaer   Son of Fehrean

Council
Chazelle   Leader of the Council
Nya   Chazelle's right hand.

Hanyarah (sisterhood)
Laelle   *Anhanyah*
Mehrean   *Haniya* residing at the palace. Friend to
                       Shalitha
Ione   *Araîtiste*. Designs and places *Araîth*.

Denahryn (brotherhood)
Soren   Master healer
Dahryen   Master healer (retired)

Nobles
Elara   Noble. Arathrien
Queran   Noble. Arathrien
Caeleyan   Noble. Arathrien

Commoners
Kalyani Nemhrean   Commoner. Mother of Xaresh
Xaresh Nemhrean   Commoner. *Sveràn*. Arathrien
Samehya Nemhrean   Commoner. Sister of Xaresh
Tynserah Nemhrean   Commoner. Sister of Xaresh
Grayden Verithrien   Commoner

Pantheon

Aeson	God of music, arts, and medicine
Arran	God of fire, inventions and crafts
Esahbyen	God of war, violence and bloodshed
Eslandah	Goddess of wisdom, knowledge and reason
Nava	Goddess of love and passion, pleasure and beauty
Rawend	God of travel, communication and diplomacy
Savea	Goddess of harvest, nature and seasons
Seydeh	God of water and seas
Vehda	Goddess of hunt, protection, and the moon
Xanthier	God of law, order, and justice
Xiomara	Goddess of life, marriage, women, and childbirth
Zoray	Goddess of hearth and home, and family

GLOSSARY

Royal terms:

Tari	Queen
Tarien	Princess
Arathri	Queen's guard
Arathrien	Princess' guard

Military terms:

Ohzheràn	General of the army
Zheràn	General
Inzheràn	Lieutenant-general
Imhràn	Colonel
Inimhràn	Lieutenant-colonel
Mahràn	Major
Anahràn	Captain
Sveràn	Lieutenant
Àn	Men-at-arms

Sisterhood:

Hanyarah	Sisterhood
Anhanya	Leader of the sisterhood
Haniya	Sister

General:

Araîth	Tattoo; the size depends on what class someone is born into
Araîthin	Feast held in honour of the one receiving their full araîth
Araîtiste	The artist placing the Araîth
Inàn	a pawn in Sihnmihràn
Irìn	lord(s)
Irà	lady(ies)

Ithri	an alcoholic beverage of vanilla, often drunk with oranges and ice
Khirr	idiot (m)
Lyadrin	beggar
Mahnèh	my friend
Qira	idiot (f)
Shareye	my dear/my love
Sihnmihràn	a strategic board game similar to chess
Sihra	miss
Wanenyah	Winter Solstice

Expletives:

Grissin	Bastard
Hehzèh	Bitch
Nohro Ahrae	Damnit!

HIERARCHY

	Tari	
Ohzheràn	Tarien	Council
Zheràn	Royalty	
Inzhèran	Nobility	
Imhràn	Merchants	
Inimhràn	Commoners	
Mahràn		
Anahràn		
Sveràn		
Àn		

A MESSAGE FROM KARA

Dear Reader,

First of all, I want to thank you for taking time to read Crown of Conspiracy. I truly hope you enjoyed reading it as much as I enjoyed writing it. The story has been sitting on a shelf for fifteen years, and I am glad I finally plucked up the courage to share it with the outside world.

I am happy to announce that book 2 in the Ilvannian Chronicles, Dance of Despair, is in the making, although I do not have a publication date yet. You can follow me on Instagram and Facebook for extra information.

If you want to be kept up to date on my progress, upcoming events and other news, feel free to sign up for my monthly newsletter at www.karasweaver.com. When you sign up, you can download the free eBook Song of Shadows, the prequel to Crown of Conspiracy.

One more thing before you go. I'd be much obliged if you could leave me a review on amazon or Goodreads, so that people may find it. As an Indie Author, I have to make a name for myself, and I hope you want to help me out! Thank you so much in advance. It's highly appreciated.

Until next time. Happy reading.
Love,
Kara

ACKNOWLEDGMENTS

First and foremost, my gratitude goes out to my husband who has put up with months of me spending behind the computer, while he took care of the children, and supplying me with an almost endless stream of coffee and chocolate. Thank you for sharing your logic when I needed it most.

Without the challenge Luc and Soma set me, Crown of Conspiracy would never have been written. Without their continuous support, I would have stopped. I'll be forever in your debt for giving me that last push.

Many thanks to Jeroen, Candyce, and André for reading the first version of the second draft, Michelle for being my beta reader, and Becka for being my wonderful editor. Without any of you, this book would still have been at second draft stage.

Last but not least, Natalie, thank you for everything else, from the new cover, to formatting to my website, you've done so much for me, I'm not even sure how to express my gratitude.

ABOUT THE AUTHOR

Kara S. Weaver currently lives in the Netherlands with her husband, two children, and Kita the cat. English teacher by day, and aspiring author by night, Kara has always loved creating fantasy worlds and characters. Not all of them have found their way on paper yet.

When not teaching or writing, Kara is well versed in the mysterious ways of binge-watching Netflix, and speed-reading books. Occasionally, she whips out her DSLR camera to take pictures, but those days are far and few between.

If you would like to share your thoughts, ideas, or comments on Crown of Conspiracy or Song of Shadows feel free to contact Kara S. Weaver at: weaver.kara.s@gmail.com .

f facebook.com/authorkarasweaver

instagram.com/kara_s_weaver

Printed in Poland
by Amazon Fulfillment
Poland Sp. z o.o., Wrocław